DAMAGED GOODS

The way the guy looked at Vic sent waves of horror coursing through her body. If he tried to lay a hand on her then she'd fight to the death if need be. The veins in his neck bulged with tension and he kept clenching his teeth. He was definitely a steroid freak; no one's face looked naturally that mean. His limbs were huge – long and thick – and his hands were the size of small dinner plates. He was a brutal-looking, cretinous, mad-dog son of a bitch and she was trapped in his car with him. Then he produced the gun.

A MOMENT OF MADNESS
A TANGLED WEB
Fairfax and Vallance mysteries

DEADLY AFFAIRS
INTIMATE ENEMIES
A WAITING GAME
TO DIE FOR
TIME TO KILL
John Anderson mysteries

DAMAGED GOODS
A Victoria Donovan mystery

DAMAGED GOODS

by
Georgina Franks
A Victoria Donovan mystery

CRIME & PASSION

First published in Great Britain in 1997 by
Crime & Passion
an imprint of Virgin Publishing Ltd
332 Ladbroke Grove
London W10 5AH

Crime & Passion series editor: Pan Pantziarka

ISBN 0 7535 0124 4

Typeset by Avon Dataset Ltd, Bidford on Avon, B50 4JH
Printed and bound in Great Britain by
Mackays of Chatham PLC, Chatham, Kent

Acknowledgements

Thanks to Peter Darvill-Evans and Pan Pantziarka, for the enthusiasm, Bill Davies, for the technical information, Matthew Collin and his top book, *Altered States*, and numerous chums for their patience and help especially Mike, Maz, Emerald, Duncan, Charles and Colette.

Contents

ONE
An Obligatory Broken Nose

Wednesday

Nick Swift felt chipper. Everything was going smoothly and he was ahead of schedule. A test drive was booked in for twelve o'clock, and the afternoon was set aside for closing the company's new sponsorship deal and notching up a few moe points on his profit-share bonus. Money in the bank. It gave him a smug warm feeling to know he was financially better off than he'd ever been. Even the monthly maintenance payments to his ex-wife, Mady, were not burning the hole in his wallet they used to. He finished off some paperwork then snapped the top back on his gold fountain pen and placed it on the desk in front of him. He moved it back and forth a few millimetres until it rested perfectly parallel to the crisp laser-printed documents next to it, then he checked his fingernails for any traces of grime. Satisfied there were none, he propelled his swivel-action leather chair back from his desk and cast a glance through the Landor Motors' showroom window. As yet there was no sign of Adrian Boxall.

Outside on the forecourt, a canary-yellow fuel-injected sixteen-valve coupe sat waiting to be thrust into life. Swift knew the deal was as good as done; come noon tomorrow, the lease papers should be signed and the Liguri 700 would be earning the business revenue by the hour. It all added up to Landor Motors being one of the most successful car showrooms in the South-east. Contract leasing was easy money – and on cars like the Liguri the income contributed nicely to the annual turnover. He checked the time: seven minutes to noon. Seven minutes to make sure his assistant salesman, Craig Johnstone, was looking presentable. He had sent him to the washrooms for a final spruce up before meeting their blue-chip client.

Swift got up from his executive chair and marched across the showroom. Time was getting on. He opened the door of the washroom and watched Johnstone checking himself for those small but potentially damaging imperfections that could cost him the deal. Swift had told Johnstone about the time he had been within a whisker of securing a sale on a Mercedes SL but the client had backed out at the last moment. Later, and to his horror, he had caught sight of himself in a rear-view mirror and with sick realisation noticed a stray ball of mucus that must have been perched on the rim of his nostril all morning. Johnstone had laughed but Swift was sure it had cost him the deal. He was keen to see no one else ever made a similar mistake, and he now maintained a fastidious control over his – and his staff's – appearance.

'Tie,' he shouted, walking over to where Craig was standing at the wash-basins. 'Straighten your tie,' he went on, grabbing hold of the brightly-coloured tongue that refused to lie symmetrically between the pointed collar flaps of his assistant's shirt. 'That's why button-down shirts were invented: to keep your tie in place.'

'Christ, you're as bad as my mother,' joked Craig, allowing the older man to take control of the final touches. 'Did you do national service or something? I'm meeting a client, not going on an army parade.'

'No lip, you,' Swift replied, pointing a finger a centimetre from the young man's nose. 'You'll thank me when you get a little something for sorting out this account, won't you?'

2

'Yeah, cheers, Nick. Only joking,' said Johnstone, lowering his eyes and smiling.

'Look, Adrian Boxall's your fifteenth test-drive punter since you joined,' Swift went on. 'Hopefully he'll be your easiest and most lucrative. I don't want to see you fuck it up 'cos you're looking like something the cat dragged in.'

Johnstone screwed his face up in protest. It was obvious that he thought he'd made an effort, but Swift wasn't going to lavish him with praise; he didn't want the ginger-haired young upstart getting above his station. Swift knew that Johnstone was looking forward to bumping up his meagre salary by securing a renewal on the account with Boxall's employers.

'Derek Landor likes consistency,' said Swift. 'He doesn't want to lose his oldest customer just because he isn't able to be here himself to go through the procedures. What did he say to you yesterday?'

'He said "Boxall's a young man and you're a young man." He also reckons that I know more about the car than he does in terms of performance. Apparently he's already agreed the terms of contract with Edwin Charlwood; all we have to do is let his favourite boy enjoy himself for the afternoon.'

'That's it,' said Swift. 'Now, you finish off in here and I'll see you back in my office. And Johnstone . . .'

'What?'

'Don't overdo the aftershave.'

Johnstone ran slightly shaky fingers through his close-cropped ginger hair and then exhaled sharply into his palm to check for any hint of bad breath. He was pleased to find there was none. He exited the bathroom and walked back to join his senior manager, whose immaculately tidy showroom office was the headquarters and engine room of the entire Landor Motors operation. Derek Landor's office was more plush – there was more leather upholstery and the seat behind his desk was a little more accommodating of its owner's ample bulk – but Johnstone had noticed that very little of the nuts and bolts of running the business happened in there. He noticed that Swift had already prepared the papers for another year's extension to the Charlwood lease. 'You don't think it's jumping the gun a little bit, do you?' he asked cautiously, 'seeing as I haven't even met Adrian Boxall yet.'

Swift looked up from the paperwork and crooked his mouth into a cynical smile. 'What, the Charlwood lease?' he said, sounding startled. 'You kidding? It's a yearly ritual. They're not going anywhere else. Why do you think they come to us and not some flash joint in London, where their offices are?'

Johnstone concentrated on looking as if he was thinking hard about what Swift was saying, but he didn't really have a clue.

'I'll tell you why,' Swift went on. ''Cos old man Charlwood and our man Landor went to the same bloody grammar school down the road in High Wycombe. It's the old boy network. It was Landor Motors' first contract back in the sixties: the days of Jaguar E-types and Jensen Interceptors. The cars have changed but the management's the same.'

Swift locked the prepared lease forms in the drawer of his desk and leant over to speak more closely to his assistant. 'Don't worry. I met Boxall at the annual Charlwood's banquet so there should be no problems at all. Just get in there and give him all the old chat.' Swift's dark brown eyes sparkled with vitality and confidence. 'You know the drill,' he said. 'Take the car around the block a few times with Boxall as a passenger; give him the spiel about the features, specs, performance, etcetera, then let him at the wheel for a bit before offering him the chance to take it home for the night.'

Johnstone knew this wasn't standard procedure for regular punters, but companies with accounts at the showroom were entitled to a few preferential perks. He carried on listening to Swift.

'If you let the potential buyer take the thing overnight,' he explained, 'you've already got the advantage. If they wake up and see it sitting in their driveway the next morning, it's as good as getting six months' non-returnable deposit cheque over the counter. It's basic psychology,' he said, tapping the side of his head with his finger. 'You've got to convince your man he can't afford *not* to have one of our cars.'

Swift seemed to excel in all areas of the business, thought Johnstone, whether it was financial or retail. He knew he had a lot to learn before he could be like him. Customer relations seemed to be Swift's speciality, though. He maintained an air of mature confidence with every deal he undertook and Johnstone felt envious of his irreverent humour and gung-ho approach to tense situations. It seemed to go against all he'd been told by his tutors on the retail management course he'd attended.

'Anyway, I've got to make myself scarce by about three this afternoon,' Swift continued. 'In case you've forgotten, it's the Motor Show next week and I'm due to meet the new promotion geezers to firm up the deal on the Chalfont & Buckingham sponsorship. Christ, it's all go. And make sure this stays as I leave it while I'm away,' he warned, wagging a finger at the neatly arranged surface of his desk.

Although the two salesmen worked from the same room, Craig Johnstone knew he was the guest, the new boy, who had been permitted to share a small corner of his superior's tidy domain. He wanted to be Nick Swift one day. And he definitely wanted a sharp suit like the one which was currently setting off his boss's rangy frame to perfection.

Johnstone had just finished dealing with a customer's telephone enquiry when a fair-haired man in his mid-twenties strode through the main entrance to the showroom dressed in casual but expensive clothes.

'There's your man,' Swift said. 'Mister Racing Green. Right. Come with me. I'll introduce you.'

Johnstone followed his manager out of the office and into the reception area to greet Adrian Boxall. 'Mr Boxall, nice to see you again,' said Swift, oozing insincere charm. 'You know, Derek Landor was going to be driving the Liguri himself today, then you booked in for the test drive a couple of days ago. He's quite miffed about it. Gave us a bit of a laugh didn't it, Craig?' he went on.

Johnstone grinned and made a noise of agreement. He closely observed Boxall's features. He had the freshly scrubbed skin and tousled hair of so many of his peers. He probably even used men's designer skin care products – something his father's generation would be highly suspicious of. He looked every inch a member of the young privileged class who did the Season: Henley; a May ball or two; Ascot; the occasional game of polo. Johnstone realised that the young man who stood before him had known greater luxury and riches than he ever would – bar a lottery win or an unlikely marriage to an heiress.

After a brief chat, where Boxall had sounded off in a plummy voice how his promotion had been 'a complete surprise' and how his Lotus now seemed 'a little past it even though it had been a twenty-first birthday present', Swift led the way outside to where the Liguri sat gleaming on its starting block. He held open the passenger door for Boxall and handed the keys to Johnstone. 'See you in an hour or so,' he said. As Johnstone turned the key and allowed the machine to roar into powerful life, he turned his head to see Swift making a rude gesture out of Boxall's line of vision. Craig liked Nick Swift. He was a bit of a lad, his boss.

Derek Landor spread an ample amount of goose liver and port paté on a wafer-thin triangle of toasted bread and salivated; as a starter it was his favourite. He mentally cursed how successfully vegetarianism seemed to have taken a hold of the minds of his children's generation. Had he indulged in this luxury at home his daughter would have admonished him for it in an over-emotional whine. It seemed that the politics of the soap-dodging hordes had found their way into even his household. Even in his own home he wasn't safe from the relentless barrage of political correctness that seemed to dog his life. Road protesters, animal liberation nutcases, a vegetarian for a daughter. Where was the promised backlash? he wondered.

Still, a sumptuous, guilt-free lunch with his seventy-six-year-old mother was no time to upset himself about the state of the nation's youth. He contented himself with the prediction that he was in for an afternoon of uninterrupted indulgence, and lunged at the rich morsel. Across the table, his mother smiled and signalled for the servant to pour the wine: a 1988 Pouilly Fumé.

'And where do you say Veronica has applied for work after she leaves university?' asked Gayle Landor.

'Well, that's the problem, mother. Her latest plan is to take a year out to travel before settling down to work,' he replied, his jowls wobbling as he shook his head in disbelief. 'Got her heart set on visiting some disease-infested part of Southeast Asia. Do you know,' he said, pointing animatedly with his paté knife, 'I found a copy of that Revolutionary Social Worker's rag or whatever it's called in the lounge the other day. Deborah lined the parrot's cage with it. Still, she's not a bad kid, really, considering everything. You're very fond of her aren't you?'

'You know, sometimes I fancy I see something of the young me in her. She'll buck her ideas up once she's left college and has to find her way in the world.'

'All the same, we did spoil her just a little when she was very young, didn't we?' said Derek. 'We had to – to make up for Sally going.' He smothered the last of the triangles of bread with the remaining paté, absorbed them in his cavernous mouth then washed them down with a large draft of vintage wine. He swallowed contentedly, anticipating the main course. There was silence for a moment while Mrs Landor imbibed minute sips from her glass and stared into the middle distance, her gaze drifting across the table, over the head of her son, and out through the tall windows of the vast dining room. Her pale, podgy skin hung from her face like a rubber mask which, covered as it often was with an excess of foundation and powder, resembled something worn by players in some bizarre theatre of the grotesque. Toast crumbs speckled her upper lip and remained there, held fast by a thick application of rose-coloured lipstick.

Derek Landor shifted his chair to the side and gazed out of the window at the driveway where his purple MGF 1.8 injection sat neatly on the gravel looking as if it would leap up and bite any stranger who approached it. He had every reason to feel as content as a pampered pet. Things seemed to have settled down again since the upsets of the past year.

7

Overstuffed, overpaid, and without the stress of an unsteady income or a boss who might grow weary of him one day, Derek Paul Landor could lunch in comfort, secure in the knowledge that his salesmen were about to earn him more cash by securing an extension to the Charlwood lease. Derek was glad some things remained consistent.

Comfort was all around him, in fact; his mother's palatial estate radiated wealth from every corner. The dining room boasted a collection of Queen Anne furniture, a genuine Daubigny landscape was hanging over the Adams fireplace and gold leaf decorated the walls of the drawing room, the reception areas and the bedrooms.

'You'll have to take me for a spin in the Liguri another time, then,' said Gayle Landor, closely watching the servant who was clearing away the settings of the first course.

'If there is a next time. Couldn't really turn down the chance of leasing the thing out. Stand to make thousands on it. Some whizz kid type, Charlwood's latest protégé, taking it for a test drive this afternoon. Should be getting an earful of chat from Johnstone right about now,' he said checking his watch.

Gayle smoothed her woollen dress to make a comfortable settle for one of her Yorkshire Terriers as another servant carried the creature to her on a cushion and placed it on her lap. 'I'm glad I've been able to see you before you whizz off to the Motor Show,' she said. 'It'll be the first one I haven't attended since you've had the business. I really don't think I can face it this time. Despite all my wealth there is nothing to rid me of the pain of this damned arthritis. No amount of money will provide a permanent relief. Anyway, you don't want to hear about my troubles. I need to discuss business matters of some delicacy with you. It's about Alan,' she went on, as two silent and efficient waiting staff brought a haunch of venison and richly basted vegetables to the table. 'I've been thinking of including him back in the will. I know the trouble he caused but it's all a long time ago now and he is, after all, a Landor: our flesh and blood.' She wagged a gnarly bejewelled finger at her corpulent son.

Derek blanched. Alan was a problem he'd rather forget.

How could a child of his be such a tearaway? The Landor name was synonymous with class, style and success – all the things Alan had rejected. Derek had realised a long time ago that Alan had inherited more from his deceased wife than her blonde good looks. Even before she died it had become obvious he was not a happy child. Those temper tantrums had been intolerable. As he caught his first glimpse of the ample lunch coming toward him, however, he instantly banished the difficult recollections to the attic of his memory. The hunk of meat dripped succulent juices on to a silver plate and the aroma of well-roasted flesh set his mouth watering. He could feel his jaws beginning to ache with longing.

'What do you think?' she continued. 'As you know, I'm not apt to behave rashly; I've seen the mistakes and upsets that result from too hurried a decision when one is blinded by emotion and one's own desires.' She adjusted the cushion slightly and stilled a bony hand upon the head of the dog, which whimpered in response.

The comment was not lost on Derek but his attention was diverted: he was watching the servant carve the slices of venison and anticipating the moment he would seize upon it as his own. 'To what extent were you thinking of bringing him back into the fold?' he enquired, his eyes lighting up as the first cuts of meat appeared on his plate.

'Nothing too generous of course; a token, really. Twenty-five thousand – something like that. Deborah told me he'd called round a couple of weeks ago and seemed to be working hard these days. Still has that garage, doesn't he?'

Derek nodded. 'Not the sort of garage you may be thinking of, mother. It's in a very run-down part of south London. Still, if he won't do anything about his appearance, what can we do? I could hardly find him a position at Langley Grove. It was bad enough when we took on that mechanic friend of his, that Bruton boy we had to sack. Look at the trouble that caused us.'

'Oh, I suppose you're right,' she sighed. 'I just don't like to think there's a member of my family who's incapable of bettering himself. He does seem to be making more of an effort these days, though. Deborah thought so anyway. He's not as sullen and difficult as he was.'

'He is twenty-seven, mother. He should have grown out of being sullen, as you call it, ten years ago. I was running a successful business by the time I was his age. And married. Alan's never brought a girlfriend to meet us and he can barely manage to pay his rent on time from what I've seen of the way he lives.'

'Seems to be getting on quite well with Richard, though. Veronica, of course, still loathes him – she told me so last week.'

Secretly, Veronica was Derek's favourite child, in spite of her sympathies with road protestors and unwashed hippies. 'Alan ignores Veronica. That's why she dislikes him,' said Derek. 'He takes time to show Richard some new computer games but he won't pass the time of day with Veronica. Probably envious of her education, but he blew his chances in that department.'

'Richard's such a sweet boy,' Gayle went on. 'He's Deborah's child all right, like Alan is Sally's. Deborah's done a marvellous job with Veronica. It's such a shame that Alan couldn't find it in himself to see her as his new mother. Still, we can't go on punishing him forever.' She paused while the serving staff deposited a small amount of food on her plate. 'Veronica may as well be Deborah's real daughter. They're such good friends. If only things had been different, Derek. I can't help wondering how different they would have been if you hadn't married Sally. You were so headstrong back then. God knows the amount of times we tried to warn you Sally was unstable. And I still say she sent your father to an early grave. When Alan turned out the way he did, I thought I would join him. None of this would have happened if it hadn't been for Sally's problems.'

Derek wished she'd shut up. They'd been through this a thousand times. Yes, it was probably true he married too young. And yes he had probably ignored the warning signs of his first wife's mental instability – but she had been so attractive. He was a young man then, trying to build a dynamic career in the most exciting decade of the century and it had done no harm to have Haver Dean's most beautiful daughter hanging on his arm.

He reflected on how his share of the inheritance on his father's death had been a not unwelcome cushion to his difficult personal circumstances at the time. It had meant he could afford to send his increasingly highly-strung wife to a psychotherapist. And, as if by a miracle, his business projects could be funded; the family trust fund hadn't nearly covered the capital investment required to set up his first car showroom. It all seemed such a long while ago, Derek thought, but it seemed he was never going to be allowed to forget his mistakes. Being his mother's only child, however, had its benefits, and it wouldn't do to upset her. He had witnessed her rages from as early as he was able to recognise his own reflection and, now that she was old, he would not like to cause an attack of high blood pressure when she was in a mind to change her will at the slightest misunderstanding.

Every time she summoned him to one of her lunches he knew he would have to endure a matriarchal diatribe of the wisdom-of-age variety. The lunch was always worth it, though, and he felt himself able to put up with the inconvenience of her chatter if he was able to satisfy his gastronomic interests. He continued to listen to her histrionics, nodding his head at the right moment, looking remorseful when necessary, and conceding deference when it was required.

This minor irritation was nothing, however, compared with the harsh shrill of his pager, which rang out around the dining room, waking the sleeping dog into a fit of barking, and silencing Gayle Landor. Derek fumbled under the flap of his jacket and unhooked the pager from his belt. The machine felt warm in his hand, kept snug by the promontory of excess flesh which hung over his trousers. The message which flashed before him brought on an immediate case of indigestion: RETURN TO HAVER DEAN IMMEDIATELY. LIGURI IN TEST-DRIVE COLLISION. DAMAGE EXTENSIVE. DRIVER INJURED. He felt the blood drain from his bloated face. This was worse than the robbery. And casualties? Seventy-five thousand pounds' worth of car possibly beyond repair. God knows what had gone wrong.

The food in front of him suddenly looked unpalatable. A trickle of blood seeped from the chunk of venison where his fork had been primed to steady the meat; it now took the pressure of him leaning on it for support. It was a good thing he was sitting down otherwise he might have keeled over. He knew immediately that he shouldn't betray the truth to his mother; it wouldn't do him any favours if she thought that he was slack in keeping control of things while he was away from the showroom. He hooked the contraption back on to his belt and continued carving at his lunch although his heart was racing and he felt weak.

'What is it they want now?' she fussed. 'Never give you a moment's peace it seems. What do they do when you go on holiday?'

'I rarely do, mother,' answered Derek, then shovelled a huge slice of meat into his mouth. He chewed determinedly. There was no point rushing off and upsetting his digestion. He was feeling faint and lunch would see him fuelled to cope with whatever crisis awaited him. It wouldn't do to face the situation with an empty stomach. He would leave after this course.

'Well. Who is it? What do they want?' Gayle persisted, fixing her watery blue eyes on her son's face. There was no privacy for Derek when in the company of his mother. It seemed that because some half a century ago she had performed the duties of motherhood with vigorous enthusiasm she was still allowed unrestricted access to his thoughts, movements and personal life. One only had to look at the way she fussed over the dogs to know that, even in her twilight years, she needed to interfere with and maintain control over what she saw as the subordinate members of her family and household.

'It's Nick,' said Derek, concentrating on remaining calm and taking the knife and fork to his lunch. 'Wants me to pop back and check his schedule for Friday. I was going to meet him later; I didn't have time to brief him this morning, but he's closing an advertising deal this afternoon and has to leave early.'

Gayle pursed her lips in a gesture of annoyance but Derek

felt relieved that he had managed to come up with something to keep her questioning at bay. The slight respite he felt at successfully deceiving his mother was quashed by thoughts of the disaster that awaited him. His stomach lurched as it received another layer of food and he realised he had a sudden rare loss of appetite. Telling the truth would be a mistake right now. Whatever had happened, Gayle would somehow trace the fault back to him and spend the next ten years going on about it. 'I'm going to have to leave now, I'm afraid,' he said as apologetically as he could.

Gayle looked offended and alarmed. 'Why can't you phone him? Rushing your food like that. You'll give yourself another ulcer.'

'Because we have to go through a number of things before Birmingham,' he explained again patiently. 'He's going to be top dog in action, picking up the scent of future favourites and getting the tip-off from the press boys as to what's hot and what's not in next month's trade report and the glossies. I would look pretty daft if I'd not gone through details properly because I was lunching with you, wouldn't I?' he went on, all the time wishing it were true. He even managed a smile. 'These things happen . . .'

His voice trailed off as he vacantly watched another of the dogs contentedly chewing a piece of the rug which covered the carpet in front of the expansive fireplace. 'I have to be going, mother,' said Derek in the knowledge he was facing an uncertain afternoon and wishing he was going to be spending it in the luxury of the Landor estate. Gayle usually took a nap until about 5 p.m. which meant that Derek could relax and take advantage of the drinks cabinet while the servants kept him supplied with whatever took his fancy. He had been hoping to get a bit of shooting practice in – Ballard could have operated the clay-pigeon gadget – and he'd fancied checking up on Veronica's pony. She'd been a bit lax recently in keeping up her visits and the poor thing needed to know it was still cared for. Still, all that would have to wait. He dropped his napkin over the remains of his lunch and gulped down the last of his Pouilly Fumé. Damn it that he'd only been allowed two glasses of the stuff! The rest would be down the throats of the kitchen staff within the hour, he suspected.

His jacket on and his keys in hand, he walked over to kiss his mother goodbye. He usually planned his departure so that if he said he had to leave at seven o' clock, he'd be gathering himself together by half six. Actually getting out of the front door was a lengthier process than in most households. Gayle made a habit of dropping some bombshell of guilt or piece of information with far-reaching ramifications just as he was saying goodbye. That way, she knew she would keep her hold over her only child long after he had left her house.

She was particularly likely to pull this kind of stunt if she'd not been given her preferred eight hours of attention. Today's short-lived visit was primed for such a move. Through urgency, Derek somehow managed to fast-talk his way out before she had time to collect her ammunition. With a glass of wine and a more than adequate lunch inside her, she was a little slow off the mark. At her age, she wasn't too good at thinking on her feet and she preferred having the tranquillity of a restful afternoon to hatch a drama. She had time only to mutter something about having to discuss the Alan business again soon and he was out of the house before she could do anything about it.

Derek manoeuvred his ample bulk into the accommodating cream leather seats of the MGF and turned the ignition. Even in this moment of crisis the luxury interior of his latest acquisition subconsciously pleased him; the white dials and the ovoid features were characteristic of the best of British car manufacturing quality. He paused for a few seconds then shoved the gear stick into first and made for the gates, leaving a spray of gravel in his wake. Once on the road he called Nick on the mobile. Please God, don't let this be as bad as he feared.

'Thank Christ you're on the way,' said Swift. 'We couldn't get through on the mobile. I'm at the Netcalfe Hotel. Boxall went straight into it. We don't know what happened yet but there's an unholy mess here. It's no use explaining the damage. I think you'd better come and see for yourself. What's your ETA, Derek?'

'I'm about seven miles away. I'll be with you in no time. The Netcalfe, you say. Didn't they just have a huge extension built on to the restaurant? Big ad in the local paper and all?'

'Yeah, that's them. Although I don't think they planned on it being a drive-in.'

Feeling queasy and with a desperate need for coffee, Derek turned the MGF on to the Haver Road. He could see the flashing blue lights from the top of the hill and there appeared to be a crowd of rubber-necks gathered around the Netcalfe Hotel, not to mention a stream of cars inching their way past the scene of the accident and slowing up the flow of traffic. With a car like the Liguri involved, he suspected a good number of them had come to gloat. That was typical of scum like that. So quick to jeer at someone who had built himself up to a certain position. Jealousy at hard-earned success. He'd seen it any number of times. The way other drivers cut him up or shouted abuse at him because he drove a car which said wealth, success, power.

There had been no reason for him to feel unsure about Boxall taking the car out. Top brokers needed to be seen in an impressive vehicle. Charlwood & Co boasted a team of at least ten of the finest investment dealers in the country. Old man Charlwood wouldn't have sent a fool out to handle a car with this kind of power. Something really unfortunate must have happened. He was about to find out what it was.

As Landor pulled up to the hotel, about five police cars and a horde of onlookers obstructed his vision. Nick Swift's large frame was the first thing that made any sense to him. Swift raised a hand of recognition and shouted to one of the duty officers that this was his boss. A beat constable cleared a path and allowed Landor to swing the MGF into the short driveway of the hotel. As Derek stilled the engine, the full horror of the damage confronted him. The conservatory extension, which had been advertised as Haver Dean's soon-to-be-number-one dining spot, was reduced to a pile of glass and twisted metal. The contents of hanging flower baskets had been catapulted far and wide around the unwelcome guest and some of the restaurant furniture had been mangled beyond recognition, squashed into abstract shapes by the force of a V8 engine stopped in its tracks.

For a moment, Derek couldn't move or think of anything useful to say. For all his skill in the world of business, he wasn't much good in a crisis which demanded a demonstration of communication skills and quick thinking. His physical appearance undermined what self-confidence he had. This was made worse by the feeling of all eyes upon him as he propelled himself out of a car which he now felt looked conspicuously small for his overweight frame. It took a couple of attempts before his body cleared the door frame. Nick Swift, self-assured and fast-talking, took the situation in hand. He rested a hand in the middle of Derek's back and spoke quietly to him before they engaged with the officer in charge at the scene.

'You've just missed Boxall being taken to the A&E. That's why this bloody lot are still gawping. He was conscious throughout. Until the paramedic gave him a shot, the guy was screaming in agony. It was terrible. They had to take an oxyacetylene cutter to the steering column to get him out.'

'What's his condition? I mean, he'll survive won't he?' asked Derek realising a maximum third party insurance payout wasn't good for business, regardless of what happened. It would up the insurance premiums by an astronomical amount. And then there was public liability to think about. He looked down at the deformed mass of plastic and metal that had been the snout of the car and sighed heavily.

'Thank God, yes. The accident wasn't fatal but they're not sure about his legs until they get him into the hospital. They were in a bad way. Multiple compound fractures at least. And of course his nose was broken by the airbag. And he's got chest injuries. He wasn't a pretty sight when they carted him off.'

From the back of the collision, the car looked as pristine as when it had left the showroom. Still gleaming, the flared, chromium-plated wheel arches were as sleek and gently undulating as the hips of a reclining woman. The buttery yellow paint of the car's body was unflaked and smooth until, that is, you reached the middle of the car. From there forward, the best of Anglo–Italian road car design was reduced to a concertinaed collision of glass and bodywork. The windscreen had fractured into a mosaic of colourless opaque particles but hadn't shattered, and it looked as if it could still cave in if anyone so much as blew on it. Contrasted with this was the shower of glass which had fallen on to the roof and bonnet of the car from the restaurant windows when the 350 bhp machine had reached its reckless destination. A surreal thought passed through Derek's mind: if only he could saw the car in half and join its unscathed rear to the front of one which had suffered a reverse fortune.

Nick Swift continued. 'The guy talking to the officer in charge is Bob Waterhouse, the owner of the Netcalfe Hotel. I don't have to tell you how unhappy he is.'

Landor looked over to where a balding man of roughly his own age was standing hands on hips while the officer nodded in an understanding fashion. 'What about Johnstone?' asked Landor. 'Was anyone else injured?'

'Luckily no. Some painters and decorators were putting the final touches to the restaurant extension but had gone to lunch. It's unlikely they would have been injured, though. The car was stopped by the upright supports of the entranceway. Still, it's a miracle there was no one in the path of the vehicle. Johnstone was at Langley Grove when it happened. He'd already taken him through the preliminaries and had been out in the car with Boxall for about forty-five minutes. Standard procedure. The bloke seemed confident at the wheel; there were no worries, Derek. Of course, Johnstone's in a right state. He looked really worried, poor kid. Thinks it's his fault. I had him stay there while I came to handle the situation – do the PR bit if you like. All kinds of accusations were flying around.'

'Like what?' asked Landor.

'Like Boxall couldn't see a bloody thing, apparently,' he answered. There were so many questions Derek wanted to ask, beginning with why the driver had careered out of control in the first place. This had never happened on a Landor Motors test drive before. They'd had a car stolen but never written off. It wasn't good. The officer in charge at the scene calmed the agitated Bob Waterhouse for a moment and came over to where Nick and Derek were standing by the MGF. They shook hands and the officer introduced himself as Sergeant Grant.

'Mr Landor, your senior salesman, Mr Swift, has filled me in on most of the details but I need to go over a few things with you for the accident report. It's better we do this back at your showroom – Langley Grove isn't it? As you can imagine, this is more complex than a run-of-the-mill RTA involving only one vehicle. For a start, there's the extensive property damage and the implications of Boxall's complaint that the airbag inflated before the car crashed. It was, according to him –' he consulted his notes '– what caused him to lose control of the steering and take a sharp left into the Netcalfe Hotel.'

'He told you this?' asked Derek, flabbergasted and staring into the beady blue eyes of the officer.

'No, sir. By the time we arrived, he wasn't making any sense at all. He was in such pain by then it wouldn't have been appropriate to pursue such enquiries. The first witness on the scene, Mr Waterhouse, got the story about the airbag. Of course, the car was still moving after it had deflated, and when Boxall really did make contact with the conservatory, the thing was useless. Got the obligatory broken nose for nothing. The injuries sustained would seem to confirm this was the case but as yet we can't be sure. We have to wait until the hospital can give us an update on his condition.'

Derek was shocked – possibly more so than when he'd originally been paged. 'That's nonsense. It can't have happened,' he said. 'Not with a car like the 700; not with any of our cars. These vehicles are thoroughly safety-tested before they come anywhere near us. It's not possible. It only had 500 miles on the clock.'

'I'm just filling you in on what's been said, sir. All I know is we have an incident involving one injured party and thousands of pounds of damage to private property. At the moment, it's not a question of blame from our point of view; it's a matter of piecing together what went wrong and taking a load of statements for insurance purposes.'

Waterhouse marched over at the mention of insurance. 'We were due to open next week,' he whined in a distinct Midlands accent. 'My wife's in London shopping for new accoutrements. She could be back any time this afternoon. What am I supposed to tell her?' he shouted, becoming suddenly more angry as he seemed to take an instant dislike to Derek. 'What the bloody hell are you doing letting kids like him use this road like bloody Brands Hatch?'

Derek felt invaded and vulnerable. He was glad when Nick Swift stepped forward slightly to come between him and the aggressive Mr Waterhouse, who looked as if he was about to take a swing at Derek. It did not look as if the presence of a police officer would stop him venting his frustration on the man he seemed to hold directly responsible for the destruction of his planned business expansion. Nick Swift's calm, professional presence did, however, and Landor wasn't the only man to look relieved that Swift was there to make Waterhouse think twice about the consequences of his actions. Grant didn't look as if he'd welcome any complications. To have to make another report from the scene – this time, one of assault – would have been an irritating inconvenience. Landor looked at Grant expectantly. He felt like a small boy wanting his dad to protect him from the nasty bully in the playground.

Grant took it upon himself to diffuse the situation. 'Look, Mr Waterhouse. I can understand how you feel but a man's been seriously injured here. It's unfortunate your property was damaged but you and your family are safe and well. You can rebuild your restaurant extension in a couple of weeks. I hope the same thing can be said about Mr Boxall's legs.' This seemed to calm the aggrieved hotel owner for a moment and he looked quite shamefaced at his previous outburst.

Swift looked at his boss, widening his eyes and exhaling sharply in a gesture of relief. The rubber-necking audience had failed to budge and Grant ordered one of the uniforms on traffic duty to clear them from the area.

'You did right, Nick, leaving Johnstone at the showroom,' Derek said quietly. 'Don't know how he would have handled our friend here.'

'You can imagine how he feels, though,' said Nick. 'He's cursing himself for letting Boxall go alone but he's also relieved he wasn't in the car at the time, of course. He said he had no qualms about the bloke being able to handle it. He currently drives a Lotus Esprit.'

'Lots of trouble, usually serious.'

'What?' asked Swift.

'Oh, it's what the acronym LOTUS is supposed to stand for,' said Landor, 'according to Jeremy bloody Clarkson. Christ I need a drink. This has not been a good day.'

'You can bloody say that again,' whined Waterhouse. 'It shouldn't be allowed, letting people drive cars like that in a residential area. Supposing my missus had been walking along that pavement, or anyone's missus come to that?'

Landor could see Bob Waterhouse wasn't going to take the incident philosophically. He ignored the rhetorical question and turned to Grant. 'What happens now?' he asked.

'We get a truck to pull the damaged vehicle out from where it crashed and take it to the police station where it will remain until you or the manufacturers collect it. I'm advised to warn you there is a charge for this, sir,' Grant said as if the cost was a matter of utmost gravity.

'Alternatively, you can provide one of your own vehicles to tow the wreck away. It's up to you. I've taken statements from Mr Waterhouse and a couple of other witnesses. I'll accompany you two gentlemen back to your showroom, now, if you don't mind, and go through your procedure for test-drives and take a statement before we call it a day. Then we'll have to wait until the hospital give us the outcome of their findings on the state of the injured man before you're likely to know what kind of claim he is going to make. I suggest you get on to your insurers immediately to warn them. Good luck, Mr Landor. I'll see you back at Langley Grove.'

As the traffic control cops allowed Landor and Swift an unobstructed exit, Derek noticed a distraught woman newly arrived at the scene shouting at one of the uniforms. He felt thankful that small mercies had spared him an introduction to Mrs Waterhouse.

TWO
The Paralysing Fear of Uncertainty

Thursday

'With your colouring, I recommend one of Shiseido's Advanced Performance range,' Victoria Donovan said earnestly, taking care to add the necessary sibilance to her voice. All women who worked on cosmetics and perfumery counters spoke with added sibilance and she saw no reason to break the trend. She squirted a 5p-sized amount of frosted pink lip colour from a silver tube on to the back of her hand and began to make small circles in it.

'You can layer the colour or mix it with gloss for that extra shine needed at parties,' she went on. Christ, she thought, it's so easy to sell this stuff if you make it sound like the most important thing in the world. She held her hand out gracefully to show the product to the woman in question, one of a small group gathered around for the closing stages of her first make-up demonstration of the day. 'For thirty pounds you get two tubes of lip colour plus the miracle lip-pen and special gift pack.'

She held up the black velvet-look gift pack. Clenched in her manicured grasp, the packaging looked irresistible to an audience which was already rooting about in Louis Vuitton handbags preparing to part with some of its disposable income. She reminded herself to put aside a box of freebies for her mum. Marie Donovan was from a generation and class of women who wore perfume only on Saturday nights and would never pay more than £2.99 for an eye pencil. Not like this lot; they wouldn't consider plastering anything on their faces which didn't run into double figures.

Vic bent down behind her demonstration stand and retrieved about ten of the special bags. After answering questions about colour choice and how long the offer was running for, she sold the pack to seven customers who, contented, walked off in the direction of an aromatherapy massage demonstration led by Vic's friend Lisa. Vic had spotted Lisa earlier that morning, already smoking her fifth Marlboro of the day and moaning about her hangover. Hardly holistic, but Vic was beginning to realise that the whole business of doing promotional work seemed to revolve around exercising the right to create an illusion. Didn't these people realise that one cleansing wash or foundation was as good as the next and it was only the styling and packaging which made the difference?

This kind of gig paid OK but not as well as the Motor Show, which she had been disappointed not to get for yet another year. She'd have to have a word with the agency. She was adequately qualified for high-profile work so why weren't they giving her any? The Kensington Cosmetics Fair didn't have the same kudos as the big exhibitions. For a start, the staff and clientele were almost exclusively female and bitchy, many of them taking their products far too seriously, and the potential bonus earnings of shifting a hundred miracle lip-pens was nothing compared to helping in the sale of a couple of TVRs – even if you did have to wear far less clothes and listen to a load of lecherous banter from the salesmen.

At least lecherous banter had a good streak of humour running through it, thought Vic. Humour was a rare commodity here, she noticed, as she watched a succession of over-made-up women with lizard-like skin file past her in earnest search of miraculous moisturisers. Also, the work hadn't proved to be much of a challenge. Vic knew she looked and sounded the part, affecting professional interest in her products as convincingly as if she'd trained as a beautician. It was important to be convincing in a role; that was what brought rewards. Qualifications were commonplace and experience could be faked. With her thick blonde hair, deep brown eyes, and a face which was the stuff of magazine covers, no one questioned her ability to represent their products. At the end of the day it was a clock-watching job, though, not a job of surprises. As she cleared the demon-stration area of used tissues and wiped the lids of tester-sized pots of differently toned foundation, she felt slightly piqued about her current state of employment. She'd much rather be acquainting herself with the new S-class Mercedes than the latest body contour firming gel.

Vic was not averse to spoiling herself occasionally with luxury cosmetics or body treatments but, in the big scheme of things, a load of eye-shadow and lip-gloss just wasn't important enough to form the basis of a career. She found the whole business of demonstrating make-up lacking in one essential ingredient: excitement. She wanted, craved, something she could get her teeth into. A commercial for a soft drink in June had brought her a couple of thousand pounds but since then there had been nothing coming through the agency other than demo work and modelling for the inevitable clothing catalogues.

It all added up to a year of odd jobs, near misses and few challenges. Apart from one job which she couldn't get out of her mind: the investigation work she'd fallen into as a result of temping at a legal firm – being in the right place at the right time – and a liberal amount of bluffing. It had set her thinking about a career change back in July and those thoughts hadn't gone away. As she looked around at the other promotions assistants busying about their stands or talking animatedly in a camp fashion, Vic realised she was finding less to be excited about with each passing job. It all amounted to a load of hype, she thought. The work wasn't feeling real enough any more.

One of the exhibition organisers came to tell her that she was entitled to a fifteen-minute coffee break and asked if she would like to go. She seized upon the opportunity. Sitting in the refreshment area, five minutes later, Vic twirled a plastic spoon in her cappuccino as she read the letter she had received that morning from her older brother, Kevin. The kids had finally settled down to life in Laindon again after their three-week holiday in Florida. Kevin had enclosed some photos. There were a couple of shots of the whole family in Disneyland: Kevin looked proud and healthy; the kids were in their element. Vic's sister-in-law, Nicola, was giving ballroom dancing classes in the local church hall to kids as well as adults this term. He was having to work twice as long to repay the loan they'd taken out to get to the States. Luckily, the work situation was looking up and he'd secured a contract painting job before they went away.

Mum had been down to visit last weekend and they'd taken her to the Harvester. Mum was okay, but Kevin knew that Tony was always on her mind. Had Vic heard anything from their younger sibling? No, Vic hadn't heard a word from him. Tony was a loose cannon, and thinking about him caused her to bristle slightly. No member of the Donovan family had heard from Tony since May. After getting out of Pentonville in April, there had been a family row and he'd gone to ground. Mum had lost two stone worrying about him. He was the only member of the extended Donovan family to have gained a criminal record. Why had he gone so off the rails? Vic had put in many hours consoling her mother about it but all her kind words couldn't change what he'd done.

At least he hadn't been directly involved in hurting the security guard. At the trial it came out that the guard had been fairly badly roughed up and subjected to racial abuse – all for a load of videos and hi-fi equipment which was recovered two weeks later. One of the gang had squealed and that's how Tony had been nabbed. The main mover in the gang had loads of previous and the Old Bill didn't have to put too many coppers on the case to turn up trumps.

The affair stank and Vic was still appalled at her brother's involvement. Despite this, she had to admit she'd found the trial interesting. It was so theatrical. She had been drawn into the wordplay between the defence council and the QC as if it were a TV courtroom drama. She'd somehow managed to distance herself from the fact it was her brother on trial and follow the proceedings as one would a play. It had seemed so staged, so unreal. Her mother's crying as he was sentenced had been real enough, though.

The rest of the letter asked after her. Was she doing anything exciting these days? Any more TV commercials lined up? What about that insurance business? That had sounded like an interesting line of work. Was there a boyfriend on the scene? Vic smiled. It was 'no' to all four questions. She liked getting Kevin's letters. He'd always write rather than call and Vic liked that. She would write back to him this weekend. She had nothing else lined up apart from a game of badminton with her mate Julian on Saturday and lunch on Sunday with her mum. She checked her watch. She'd taken slightly longer than fifteen minutes. The miracle lip-pen was waiting for her. It was time for her twelve o'clock demonstration. Big thrills.

Adrian Boxall pressed the button on the morphine booster rigged into his arm and groaned. Why me? he said to himself over and over. Why had fate dealt such a cruel blow? He was unable to move any part of his body, except for his arms, and even the smallest movement of his hands sent sickening waves of pain through his chest, where the muscles had been lacerated by the force of the airbag. He looked at the clock on the wall of his private room in Aylesbury General Hospital: it would soon be lunchtime but eating was the last thing he wanted to do. He wanted to slip back into unconsciousness but the injustice of his injuries prevented his mind from knowing such peace.

He would never forget the impact of the airbag smashing into his face and chest at 200 mph. It had been like sitting on top of an explosion. It was a sick irony that a device which was supposed to minimise injury had caused such devastating trauma. As the pain retreated for a blessed few minutes, Boxall wrestled with his thoughts. He knew he was right. The bag had gone off for no reason; the crash had come afterwards. He wasn't driving over the speed limit. He hadn't even had his foot on the brake. How could it have happened?

More than anything in the world he wished he had driven the car back to the garage after ten minutes in charge of the vehicle and not taken it that fateful couple of miles further. He remembered everything. The winking blue glare of police lights as he remained pulverised against the luxury upholstery; the nauseating sound of the fireman's cutter as they sawed through the steering column so near to his legs; the spotty, gawping faces of teenagers on their mountain bikes staring at him, and the girls screaming in disgust as he yelled in agony and vomited over the paramedics. And then the burgeoning fear of wondering whether he would ever walk or make love again. All of it played over in his thoughts like a sick video loop.

The last question remained unanswered. 'It's early days yet, Mr Boxall,' was all they had said when he had come round from three hours of surgery. An increasingly familiar wave of bilious fear took hold of his insides and gnawed at them. He wanted to vomit, and the shame of it made him want to die. He pressed another button on his console – the one which called for the nurse. He was taped up with reinforced bandages across his nose, chest and stomach. Both legs were immovable and had had metal pins drilled into them in the hope of joining the shattered bones together.

The most perfunctory bodily functions had become painful and embarrassing lengthy procedures. The odour of the congealed blood around his nostrils mixed with the cloying scent of the antiseptic dressing as he took deep breaths to try to abate the paralysing fear of uncertainty. It was too much. No one should suffer this agony or this indignity, he thought.

As he lay there, engulfed in the distress caused by his misery, rescue came in the form of a young female Chinese nurse holding a kidney-shaped steel bowl. She'd guessed that he wanted to vomit and immediately shoved the bowl under his chin, taking care to cradle the back of his head as one would a new-born baby. 'Some people have this reaction to the painkiller,' she said. Great. As if he didn't know. The only thing which provided some temporary relief had a side-effect. Was there no end to the unfairness of the situation? After several minutes of retching he managed to ask feebly, 'How long will it last? I can't stand the pain and I'm not able to sit up by myself.'

'The consultant is coming to see you after lunch,' she said in a sing-song voice. 'Your girlfriend left soon after you came round. She was waiting here a long time. Do you remember, Mr Boxall?'

He wasn't sure. He remembered everything that led up to him being carried into the ambulance but, since arriving at the hospital, he couldn't say what had been dream and what had been reality. At one point, he'd thought the family dog had been in the bed with him. He couldn't find the energy to reply. Throwing up had sapped him of all will to converse. All he could manage was to wag a finger in the direction of a mineral water bottle. His girlfriend must have brought it. Where were his belongings? He'd had a mobile phone and briefcase with him yesterday.

'The police are waiting to interview you, hopefully today. Shall I tell them to come at three o'clock? It's best to talk to them as soon as you can.'

For a second his thoughts focused. He did want to give his statement. Whoever was responsible for his injuries would pay dearly. Of that he was sure. The disorganisation of the situation was overwhelming. Thinking about all that needed doing threw his mind into chaos again and he collapsed exhausted back on to the pillow. The nurse gave him some alarmingly colourful but potent medication. 'Three o' clock will be fine, I hope,' he whispered. He would worry about everything later. Later . . .

At Langley Grove, the phones hadn't stopped ringing all morning. Nick Swift was doing his best to keep things running in a business-as-usual fashion but Derek Landor wasn't helping the situation one bit. He'd bumbled and stuttered his way through the first of the solicitors' calls and when Craig Johnstone had shown up for work in no fit state to do anything except shake and apologise, Landor hadn't even taken the sensible decision to send the lad home. Swift did that after taking one look at him. Johnstone had been up all night worrying he would get the sack and needed to know what his employers were saying about the situation. Nick had given him a pep talk in his office, made him a cup of tea and told him to take the day off. Landor should have done that instead of standing there like a stuffed shirt with his gob wide open staring at the kid. It wasn't Nick's job to play the paternal role.

Swift wondered how someone like Derek had come so far in business as he watched his boss nervously stutter his way through another phone call. He hadn't always been this incompetent in a crisis, had he? He didn't lose it this badly when the BMW had been nicked or when they'd had the break-in and the place had been trashed. OK, so someone had been hurt this time. Badly hurt. But it wasn't Landor Motors' fault. In a couple of weeks everything would be cushy again.

Swift cast a quick glance over the paperwork on his desk and reached into the silk lining of his inside breast pocket to retrieve a packet of Bensons. He had to get out of the miserable atmosphere in the showroom and on to the forecourt for a breather. He switched his answerphone on and walked out into the October air. He lit a cigarette. What a palaver. He wished the firm had a governor who had a bit of a clue. The silly sod didn't know the front end of a Mondeo from the back end of a Maserati. He may have been a sharp operator in the sixties and seventies but he was losing it these days.

He thought for a brief moment of the crash: Adrian Boxall howling in agony in the middle of a load of twisted metal. He pulled hard on the Benson. Nasty. This was something no one could have anticipated. Vehicles which had come new from the factory were already guaranteed safe. A top-drawer car like the Liguri 700 would have had a thousand and one tests run on it, surely. Either Boxall lost it at the wheel or some horrid design fault was to blame. Bound to be bad driving. No man likes to admit he can't handle a powerful machine. Too much ego damage. All that airbag stuff must be a load of bollocks. The bloke was probably confused or making it up.

He checked his watch and ran a finger around the inside of his collar; God forbid he should build up a tide mark on his new white M&S shirt. Swift stood between a couple of new Jaguar XK8s and watched the comings and goings on Langley Grove as he smoked his cigarette. There was nothing to interest him apart from a coachload of schoolgirls in sportsgear who were held at the traffic lights long enough for him to catch the eye of a pretty blonde of about sixteen. He smiled at her and she pulled a face back at him as her friends pointed at him and made obscene gestures. It wasn't difficult to work out the words they were mouthing at him: 'wanker, wanker.' What did those little sluts get up to in the showers after running around a field for two hours? he wondered, as his mind began to conjure up lewd scenarios with him involved in the action.

He felt a stirring down below and reminded himself of the sexual opportunities which may well present themselves to him at next week's Motor Show. The place always had a fair share of horny-looking women working on the stands. No dogs, either. Some of those promotion girls were classy enough to get top modelling work. And when they took their tops off or wore shorts cut right up between their legs, flashing everything at you, you knew you were on to a good thing.

Nick fancied his chances. He knew he looked smart – always nicely turned-out with a silk tie and decent cufflinks. He felt a little agitated that he hadn't been attracting the right sort of women this year. He had been too long without a good down-to-earth shag. All the women he'd been out with since breaking up with Mandy had been divorcees in their late thirties or early forties looking for their second or third marriage. What he needed were less romantically inclined women in his life. Maybe a young thing in her twenties who fancied a bit of cash spending on her but who didn't want to run him to the nearest registry office. That would do the trick. Some blonde piece without pretensions to running a company herself.

Swift had vowed never to get embroiled in business deals with a woman again. It had ruined his first marriage and he wasn't going to make a similar mistake a second time. Also, he couldn't relax with women about the workplace. You had to forever be on your guard that you weren't offending them or swearing. Things weren't simple any more now women were taking over in all fields of work. Some had even found their way into auto retail management. The one or two he'd seen were dragons, though, not *real* women.

Swift snapped himself back to reality to prevent an erection taking root in his pants. There was serious business to be done; no time for idle fantasies. Old man Landor would be wondering where he was. He crushed the Benson butt under his highly polished black shoe and kicked it under the Jag. He could see Derek gesturing to him as he took a casual stroll back to the showroom. What did he want now? Not another question about the accident, surely? He'd already told him everything he'd seen. He couldn't hold his hand through the whole thing. Shit happened and Landor was going to have to keep it together. He would have to deal with the legal side of things while Swift got on with closing the new sponsorship deal and planning an agenda for the Motor Show early next week. Buying and selling still had to be done.

Back inside the showroom, Derek was still having a tough time on the phone. Bob Waterhouse had been sounding off something chronic and his solicitor seemed to be of the opinion that Derek was personally responsible for the accident. He seemed to take pleasure in warning Derek that his client was entitled to claim not just for damages to property but also for loss of business from what should have been a thriving four-star restaurant opening that week. Horrible little man. He was determined to wring every last penny out of this unfortunate crisis.

With this conversation still ringing in his ears he took a

call from the Chalfont & Buckingham Building Society – Landor Motors' prospective local sponsors – and had to immediately effect a cheerful tone of voice. Of course they would have to be told the bad news but it wasn't necessarily the end of the deal. He couldn't face talking to them now, though. He would consult Nick's opinion before doing anything drastic. He finished the call and beckoned Nick over.

'You're due to meet the Chalfont lot today aren't you?' he asked, 'Well I've just had them on the line. They don't seem to have heard about the accident. Are we obliged to tell them?'

'I cancelled the meeting I was supposed to have with them yesterday afternoon. Didn't tell them why, though. If I get the contracts countersigned by this evening it will be difficult for them to back out. I'll get on to it right now.'

'Bob Waterhouse has said he's putting together a protest group of concerned parents to get test-drives banned in residential areas,' Derek moaned. 'That man is going to be a pain in the neck for us; I could tell that from the moment I saw him.'

'The whole situation's a pain in the neck, Derek,' said Swift. 'Less than a week before the Motor Show. Couldn't have come at a worse time, really, could it?' he asked, swaggering back to his own office not bothering to wait for a reply to his rhetorical question.

Derek was feeling increasingly put upon and unsure of what to do and who to call. His psoriasis had started up again and he was itching uncomfortably under his suit. So far, today was shaping up to be catastrophically awful. Yesterday, when he and Nick had given their statements to Sergeant Grant, the situation seemed surmountable; as if what had happened wasn't really so bad. Answering routine questions from an officer was a good deal different to being left to sort out the legal wrangles of the insurance claim yourself, or trying to explain to one of your oldest business associates why his star employee was in a critical condition in hospital.

Derek had asked Nick to phone Edwin Charlwood shortly

after the accident. At first his old friend had taken the news stoically. Later on, however, Derek had spoken to him from his own home and had suggested that the truth about what caused the accident would come out when Boxall was fit enough to give a statement. This suggestion Charlwood hadn't taken so stoically and there had been a frosty exchange of words between the two men. He hadn't meant to imply that Boxall was lying. He was beginning to doubt his ability to communicate what he was feeling. Thank God Deborah had been there. The woman was a brick. It was her un-swerving support and pragmatism that kept him going at times like this. How did unmarried men cope?

The phone rang again. This time it was Daniel Field of Field & Gaitskill Insurance. 'Hello Derek,' he said. 'Sorry I wasn't available yesterday when you rang. I hear there's some bad news.'

It was the call Derek had been dreading. The ensuing conversation was a long one and by the end of it Derek felt as if he'd been filleted. Field said that one of their men would be sent to visit the showroom first thing Monday. The damage to Waterhouse's property was likely to be the straightforward part of the claim; what would cripple them would be the personal injuries claim brought by the driver's solicitor. If Boxall stuck to his story, the manufacturers' report would be crucial to the outcome.

If the car had left the factory in a faulty condition, Landor Motors might be off the hook. There was always a chance that Adrian Boxall would admit liability when faced with the police, and put a sock on the whole airbag business. A good deal of investigation needed doing. Daniel Field had sounded reserved. Derek was aware that Field must be getting used to hearing bad news from Landor Motors. The two other claims this year had amounted to a fifty thousand pound payout.

Surely Boxall was mistaken about the accident, Derek thought. Airbags didn't go off by themselves. A young man such as he, a broker, would be honest in his statement, surely? He'd met Boxall at the Charlwood's banquet and he'd seemed a sincere sort of fellow. It was eleven thirty. He had yet to call the police for an update on Boxall's statement, arrange for the manufacturers of the car to pick the wreckage up, and meet with the company business manager to talk about the current stockholding levels. And all this before 2 p.m.

THREE
Fatneck

Friday

As on most mornings, Vic was trying to perform five different domestic duties at once. The kettle was on, there was some bread toasting under the grill, she was ironing a clean shirt with her hair wound on heated rollers and, with half an eye, watching breakfast TV. The morning light was filtering in through her living-room curtains, which were closed to prevent her being seen in her underwear, and the sound of next door's kids arguing and running around while they got ready for school was booming through the wall.

Vic glanced at the news. There was trouble in the Middle East again. There had been news reports of trouble in Northern Ireland and the Middle East since she had been old enough to recognise her own name. How come they never got bored of all that fighting? It seemed such a waste of energy. No point getting upset about things bigger than yourself or stuff you can't answer. What were most wars about, anyway? Religion? Old battles that should be consigned to history books? Abstract stuff, mostly.

She stood the iron upright and dashed to the grill. Just caught it. She burnt the toast at least two mornings out of seven. Now, what to put on it: peanut butter, apricot conserve or tahini and honey? Opting for the tahini and honey solution, she dug the knife into the oily consistency. She spread the grey goo over the toast and poured the boiling water into a pint-sized tea mug. Then, as she took the first bite of her breakfast, her mobile phone went off. She allowed it to ring three times before answering.

'Good morning, Miss Donovan. It's Daniel Field here. Are you well?' he asked.

Vic's full attention was now directed to her caller. 'Oh, I'm very well thanks, and you?' she replied, swallowing the remaining morsels of toast. Insurance people were always so polite – even when you got on the wrong side of them.

'Yes, fine. Are you working at the moment?' he asked. 'Only something's come up and it might be just the thing for you. We have our own man on the case but we want some private work carried out; something seems not quite right about this one. I thought that maybe you'd like to help out. You know how happy we were with your work on the Maynard investigation.'

Vic felt her heated rollers. They were no longer warm and she began unclipping them, allowing her blonde tresses to tumble over her shoulders as she thought fast. The Maynard investigation had been wrapped up nearly four months ago and she hadn't heard from Field & Gaitskill since then. She had resigned herself to thinking it had been a one-off: another odd job to add to a long list of odd jobs. She could do with some more hundred-pound-a-day work, that was for sure. The mortgage on her flat needed paying and her agent had been depressingly silent in recent weeks. 'I'm very interested,' she said, trying not to sound too desperate for the job. 'I'd like to know some more, Daniel.'

'The client is the managing director of a car showroom. One of the most prestigious showrooms in the Buckinghamshire area, in fact. They're about to put in a claim which could run to a million pounds. Maybe more. Thing is, it's their third claim in a year and we're beginning to suspect something strange is going on there.'

'Is it a robbery?' she asked.

'No. The last two claims were robberies. And they weren't straightforward, either. This is a big one. It involves an injured party and damage to private property; two third-party claimants are involved. Can you come and see me? We've someone else in mind if you don't want to take the job, but you're my first choice. Can you make it sometime today? What about this evening? At Chambers?'

Vic agreed immediately. The last job had earned her enough to refurnish her flat. Insurance fraud was usually clean, too. Nothing too dangerous. If someone was guilty, they usually went quietly. And it was a good deal more exciting than following up clients who'd booked facials and makeovers at the Kensington Cosmetic Fair. According to Daniel Field, most insurance fraud was hatched by people trying to cover up their own negligence or laziness. Vic had heard about builders trying to prove freak accidents had put them out of work, and teenage sons and daughters of wealthy families 'losing' expensive jewellery to fund burgeoning cocaine and heroin habits. These types of cases fascinated her. The story behind the fraud often proved to be interesting.

Vic checked the time. She should be leaving the house now to get to Kensington. 'OK, I'll call you about midday,' she said. 'Count me in. I just have to find some time to get away from the promotion work I'm doing. I should be able to meet you in Farringdon at eight, though.'

'I look forward to seeing you again, Victoria,' said Daniel.

'Me too,' she replied. Daniel was quite charming. Good-looking, too, she remembered. She felt a small frisson of excitement at seeing him again. This time she would try to investigate a few details of his private life without giving too much of hers away. Tricky, but not impossible. She signed off and finished her toast. There was just time to iron the sleeves of her shirt and drink her tea. As she stood in the kitchen and sipped from her mug, Vic felt genuinely excited. Unpleasant things like personal injury and property damage shouldn't be giving her such a rush of adrenaline but there was no doubt that her heartbeat had become more rapid over the past few minutes. It would certainly give her something to think about during another day of demonstrating the miracle lip-pen.

Daniel Field offering her another investigation job was a thrill – she had to admit it turned her on. She wouldn't want to be employed as a full-time loss adjuster – that would be too boring and she'd definitely need specialist qualifications – but being an investigator on a more regular basis would be rewarding and well paid. It felt kind of sexy to know that she was Daniel's first choice for the job.

A prestigious showroom in the M40 area, he'd said. That meant they needed someone who was able to mingle with the management: someone like home-counties Victoria rather than Walthamstow-born Vicky. Well that would be easy enough, she thought. Being 'Victoria' wasn't really fraudulent, she reminded herself; it was, after all, her real name, although none of her family used it apart from her mum. She knew she was able to look every inch the well-groomed young woman of good breeding and poise. Why should she spoil her chances by revealing her roots to the man who was helping her new career aspirations? There was a time and place for displays of working-class pride, thought Vic, but it wasn't to be in the wine bar around the corner from Field & Gaitskill Insurance Ltd. Of that she was certain.

Derek Landor sat at his desk feeling profoundly depressed. His hand rested on the telephone receiver. He felt impotent and weak and wanted to hide. The manufacturers of the car were based in Italy and it had taken a lot of phoning around to find where the UK representatives were located. Finally, he tracked down the approved workshop who had confirmed they were sending a recovery vehicle that morning.

The showroom was a quiet and lonely place without the activity of buying and selling to keep it busy. Since the accident, the only enquiries had come from the police, the press and Adrian Boxall's solicitors. Their client was conscious and 'as well as could be expected'. He'd now given his statement to the police and had been emphatic that the airbag had inflated for no reason. Derek's only hope that he would be cleared of blame lay with the manufacturers. And what if they denied responsibility? It was too awful to contemplate. The situation was a nightmare. Now that the initial shock of the accident had passed, he was left feeling empty and confused.

He kept going over the reason for the crash. He'd never heard of anything like this happening anywhere. No one had been with Boxall when the airbag allegedly inflated. Derek's solicitor had proposed they put a technical specialist on the case. He would charge about fifty pounds an hour.

Craig Johnstone – now back at work after a day off – entered Derek's office and approached him cautiously with a cup of coffee. 'Try not to let it get you down too much, Mister Landor,' he said solemnly. 'Accidents happen all the time.' Derek observed the young man and politely accepted the weak-looking coffee and the platitudes.

'I'm sure Adrian Boxall will recover,' Johnstone went on. 'He can afford the best medical treatment.'

'It's me that's going to foot the bill for it,' said Derek.

Johnstone looked imploringly at his employer. 'I feel terrible,' he said. 'If there's anything I can do –'

Landor braced himself and cut in, 'Look, just get on with your work, Craig. It must be business as usual. Nick will be relying on you to keep things ticking over while he's at the Motor Show. Still –' he threw Johnstone a glance '– it's good you were not in the car as well. There would have been little you could have done. I may have lost a salesman as well as a client.'

'He must have been driving like a maniac,' said Craig.

Derek returned to staring into space while Johnstone walked back to Swift's office. The young man's concern was touching. If he had looked him in the eye, he may well have started crying. He couldn't allow himself to let go; he had Deborah and the kids to think of. He must be strong.

A couple of hours later, a flatbed truck pulled on to the

garage forecourt. With the engine still running, the driver jumped out of his cab and strolled into the showroom. Derek stood up and watched through his office window as the ruggedly-built workman entered the reception area to find Nick Swift. The two men walked outside and Swift pointed out where the wreck of the Liguri was locked up in the garage. The driver got back in his cab and reversed alongside the building. Swift came back inside clutching a handful of paperwork. He walked into Derek's office and thrust the papers towards him. He was chewing gum – something Derek had always loathed in him.

'This one is for you to sign now,' he said. 'It's the release form, which hands the car back to the manufacturers. And this one is an accident report form. They want this filled in as soon as possible, of course.' He deposited the papers on Derek's leather-covered desk.

'That will take me the rest of the afternoon,' said Derek.

'That's the way it goes, I'm afraid,' Swift announced. 'Form filling's always a pain in the arse but it has to be done.'

'I've already explained everything to them on the phone,' he whined.

'Yeah, but you know these people need everything in triplicate. It's only to be expected with this kind of motor, really. They want a copy of the police report and Adrian Boxall's statement.'

Derek scribbled his name on the release form. He wished someone else would fill the other one in for him. There was the police statement, the insurers' claim form – and that was detailed enough – and now the manufacturers were hounding him. Worse still, he knew the accident would be in the local paper – the paper his mother had delivered every Friday. The thought made him feel sick. He could just about cope with the police and solicitors: they had a time limit to their jobs. His mother, however, had the rest of her life to pick over the details of the affair. He knew that whatever the cause for the accident, Gayle Landor would attribute it to negligence on someone's part. He knew who that someone would be.

He raised himself from behind his desk and went outside.

The autumn wind had a distinct chill to it and the sky promised rain. The driver of the truck was performing feats of strength with lengths of reinforced towrope and hydraulics as the twisted remains of the car were lifted on to his vehicle.

'Blimey,' he yelled out to Derek. 'Nasty one, this, eh guv? Few bob's worth of damage here. Puts you right off, doesn't it? Driving, I mean.'

Derek walked up to get a closer look at the mangled car being secured to the lorry. The fated airbag was still dribbling over the steering wheel like a gigantic piece of burst bubblegum. 'Yes, it does put you off,' he said sadly. 'It makes you think.' He beckoned Swift over. 'Look, Nick,' he said weakly, 'I'm going home to fill the papers in. I can't stand the thought of the local press or, God help us, Bob Waterhouse wanting to talk to me at the moment. I'll see you tomorrow, maybe.' He didn't wait for a reply, but set off for Little Chalfont. He wanted to shut himself away from a very cruel world.

Less than an hour later, Derek was at home. The manufacturers' papers stayed on the kitchen table where he had thrown them and he was sitting in his lounge armchair nursing a triple measure of single malt. To his disappointment, he did not have the house to himself. Veronica was talking to her college friend on the patio, and a series of electronic noises echoing from Richard's room meant that his youngest son was playing that damned sound mixing game again. He'd wired his computer into his stereo speakers and the result was an upsetting cacophony of techno noise. This, along with intermittent girlish laughter, robbed Derek of any peace. He knew they weren't laughing at him, but their whispering and giggling set him on edge.

A monosyllabic conversation with Veronica had given him the necessary information as to his wife's whereabouts: shopping, then to the hair salon with Margaret, her friend and 'lady who lunched'. He envied women – they always seemed so well-equipped to cope with misfortune. In a time of personal crisis, with all that had happened this week, Deborah had booked a hair appointment; Derek had barely remembered to shave.

He would ring his doctor and fix up an appointment of his own that afternoon. Maybe the doc could prescribe something to take the edge off his nervous tension. He didn't want another ulcer. It was only midday; too early to be drinking, but Derek needed a little something to calm him. Just a snifter and then some rest. Sleep had eluded him the previous night. Maybe he could catch a couple of hours while Deborah was out.

Having made this simple decision, but feeling right now that such small achievements were getting him through each hour, Derek propelled himself from his comfortable settle and dragged himself out of the lounge and across the hallway. The stairs to the upper floor were luxuriously carpeted. His Savile Row brogues ploughed through the thick pink covering as he heaved his bulk onward and upward to his sanctuary. He wanted the comfort it offered. Once in the bedroom he remembered he had to find the earlier insurance claim papers for his solicitor. It was an irksome task but best done before he surrendered his mind to unconsciousness.

He unlocked the desk in the far corner of the palatial room and reached for the file containing his insurance documents and verification of recent policy renewals and claims. Something fell out: a photograph. Derek turned it over and stared at it. He felt acutely weird. There was his son Alan at eight years old – blond and angelic-looking, a beautiful boy – standing in the garden. Next to him, smiling out of the picture, was Sally holding the infant Veronica. That was the summer she had become addicted to tranquillisers; the summer of her first attempted suicide. Cheerful family photographs could conceal so much heartache. The picture became indistinct as Derek's eyes filled with tears and his shoulders heaved with the pain of remembered loss. Was there nothing he could do to make things right, to repair the damage of the past and the present?

*

Alan Landor pulled himself out from underneath the ailing Ford Capri he'd been working on all afternoon and sighed heavily. A face full of oil and sixty-five quid was not his idea of a day well spent. Getting some skint bloke's motor through its MOT was the only legal job he'd been offered that week and he had to make some pretence of running a legitimate business. He walked over to the shelves which lined one wall of his small, chaotic garage and dipped his left hand in an open jar of Swarfega. The green slime oozed through his fingers and he caught himself becoming mesmerised by staring at the dirt lifting from his hands as he rubbed them together. He turned on the single tap which was hanging loosely from its fitting over the old enamel sink and allowed the cold water to run through his fingers, rinsing himself clean of the sticky substance.

He wiped his hands on his blue overalls, released his long blond hair from its pony tail, then tuned the radio to Girls FM. He'd been meaning to change the station for about an hour. There was only so much radio advertising he could stand. Smarmy voices selling pension policies and what was on offer at swanky restaurants didn't feature very highly on his agenda right now. He lit a cigarette and put the kettle on for his fifth cup of tea of the day, then leant against the Capri, smoking and looking at the place in the floor where Peter Bruton had stashed the pills.

He felt slightly cheered by knowing that he'd soon be seeing a return for his risky investment. There must be no fuck-ups on this one, he assured himself. At least the stuff was genuine; they hadn't been ripped off. He knew it had been a good idea to send Bruton to Amsterdam. No middle men this time. Once this deal was done and dusted he could get himself out of the shitty little garage he'd been running for the past year. Get something that wasn't falling to bits, something where people who wanted their cars fixed wouldn't turn their noses up when they saw the state of the premises.

He could also fund his creative projects: mixing computer graphics and knocking out visual installations at raves. The dance music scene in the UK was worth a billion quid and

Alan wanted some of the profits of that nocturnal economy. It paid good money for fiddling with a few knobs and making some pretty pictures. He wanted to prove that he could make a success of himself while his father watched his own business go down the drain. He pulled hard on the cigarette and felt his pulse race a little as he thought about the crash. Richard had told him about it when he'd phoned home on Wednesday evening. The rot had already set in. He smiled and stirred his tea.

The pumping mega-bass of Peter Bruton's car speakers from the other side of the wooden doors announced his arrival. Alan sipped at his tea as he heard him kill the engine and slam the car door. Looking through the crack between the garage doors he could see Bruton's large frame blocking out the sunlight. Alan strolled over and unlocked them. The sound of heavy traffic thundering along the Old Kent Road filtered in. He cast a glance down either direction of the narrow slip road before pulling open the right-hand door and allowing Bruton into the workshop.

'Fuckin' state of that now,' he moaned at Alan, pointing at the mud which had splashed the waxed black finish of his BMW. 'That car was spotless till I drove down here.' The driveway alongside the railway arches where Alan's garage was located was a chicanery of muddy potholes. 'Good thing I left the Air Jordans off today, isn't it?' Bruton blundered through the doors and flung his keys and mobile phone on to one of the work surfaces.

'If you want a cup of tea, the kettle's just boiled,' said Alan.

'No, you're all right. Got some lunch here,' Bruton replied, taking a can of chocolate Nourishment from his Daniel Poole jacket and giving it a good shake. He leant back against the wall and picked up the plastic milk carton which was covered in Landor's greasy prints. 'I thought I told you to always wear gloves on a job,' he joked. Alan didn't respond.

'Tomorrow should be a big one,' Bruton went on. 'Purity's become a regular Saturday night stint at Gaby's. Half of Aylesbury's going to be there. We've got Judge Jules and Pete Tong coming down; part of the Ministry tour. Gonna relieve you of some of that lot.' He indicated to where they'd hidden the pills. 'Bang out a couple of hundred little fellas. Prices are dropping though,' he said. 'Used to be fifteens and twenties. Now it's eights and tens. So much of it about, see.'

'Yeah but this stuff's the best we've had in ages,' Alan sneered. 'It's not dodgy gear. None of your special K shit.'

'I know,' Bruton said emphatically, sipping from his can of Nourishment. 'Who was it who brought it back? It's all right when you're over there in skunkhead central, but once you're on the ferry it's brown trousers time. It's me who's risking my neck, not you. I know it's good stuff but it'd be fourteen years if I got clobbered. You'd be eight grand out of pocket but I'd be dodging queers in the Scrubs and let me tell you I don't fancy that. Pretty boy like me.'

Alan managed a weak smile. If there was one thing Bruton wasn't it was pretty. His close crop of dark brown hair bristled from a solid-looking square-shaped head that sat on very chunky shoulders. A single earring and a couple of gold teeth were his only concessions to decoration and they flashed in the light as Bruton mouthed off about how many Es he reckoned he would sell that night; how the girls who came to his club were right up for it; how he had met a bloke who knew a bloke who could shift a thousand pills the following week. Bruton was always mouthing off.

Alan had come to realise that the bigger the job, the more risk involved, the louder Bruton announced it. He couldn't do a deal without letting the world know about it – as if he was worried that his partners would think he was slack if he didn't shout a regular bulletin. Thing was, he didn't seem to care where he did it. Alan had lost count of the number of times he'd had to tell him to keep his voice down in pubs and cafes. Bruton called him paranoid but Alan knew the benefits of keeping a low profile.

Still, he felt he'd got to know how Bruton worked much better during this Amsterdam job; it was the first time Alan had used him on something so big. It had been a great relief when he had turned up with the goods that Tuesday afternoon. Despite being a noisy bastard, he'd come through like the dependable fool he was. He'd driven to Amsterdam in his own car; he'd bought five thousand pills and hadn't switched the gear or tampered with it in any way – he'd even checked a few randomly at the drug-testing units they had over there – and he'd risked the chance of sniffer-dog searches at Folkestone. The whole thing had been wrapped up with remarkable ease considering the amount of money involved. Alan had half-expected Bruton to come back empty-handed.

'Shut the door, then. Let's sort it out,' said Alan, keen to get Bruton set up for the evening with a minimum of fuss. Bruton closed the heavy wooden doors together and secured the lock. Alan pulled back a pile of rubber slipmats and ancient linoleum to reveal a large polythene bag of pills nestling in a well-concealed hole underneath the workshop floor. 'They're broken down into smaller bags of fifties,' said Alan. 'I did it the other night when I was bored. I was thinking you might want to keep a few bags around the club; you never know when you might need 'em in a hurry.'

'No,' said Bruton, looking serious for a second. 'I'm not holding anything at the club. I thought we'd agreed that. I try to keep an eye on everyone, but the security who handle the money for the management are a bunch of wankers – totally straight. Not like the blokes on the door. If they found anything they'd be on the phone to the Old Bill like a shot. And I can't be watching it all the time. There's nowhere water-tight secure for this except the safe. Anyway, the deal was you'd hold them, I'd bang them out, remember? Nothing's changed. It all stays here, Alan.'

Bruton's face was only a few centimetres away from Alan's and he suddenly realised what a big head he had. It must be a twenty-pounder at least, Alan thought. No wonder he was known as 'fatneck' by his associates. 'Sure,' Alan replied in a placatory voice. Bruton wasn't absent-minded, then. Alan knew full well they'd agreed he would stash everything at the workshop and Bruton would travel light, not keeping any at his flat or at the club. Still, Alan felt just a little bit nervous with five thousand ecstasy pills ten feet away from where he worked day in, day out. It was worth a shot; Bruton

45

was the type who liked to be seen flashing fistloads of drugs and cash around.

'Give us ten bags,' said Bruton. 'I'll shift about two hundred at Purity. I can farm the rest out to the other boys. Andrew and Gary are doing security at some gig in Oxford. Do you know,' he continued, 'I always thought Oxford was a posh place: all upper-class students and punting and that. No way. A lot of the estates there are well rough as it goes. You'd never think it would you?'

Alan grunted at him. He had very little time for Peter Bruton's sociological comment and couldn't care less about what people were doing in Oxford – students or rough-necks. 'Is that what Andrew and Gary reckon, then?' Alan muttered.

'Yeah. They had a right load of trouble up there last summer. Inter-estate feuding. All white kids. Different sort of bother up that part of the country. Scary really. I mean, down here you know what's coming. If you set foot in some pub round Harlesden or Dalston and you realise you're the only white boy in the place you know you've taken a wrong turning. Up that way, you've no way of knowing whose manor it is. And you'd think they'd try and do over some of the privileged bastards at the university, wouldn't you?'

Again, Alan grunted at Bruton, not looking at him as he wrote down how many pills he was handing over.

'Well they don't. They just start on each other. Doesn't make sense really.'

Peter had a point. 'Same as the football used to be,' said Alan. 'Fifteen years ago it was the ICF and Millwall. Met some of that lot when I was doing the short sharp shock. All blokes from the same background. Just different territory. It's a feudal thing. They couldn't understand why I wasn't into football so I got beaten up for not having a firm. You can't win with geezers like that. You've just got to get what you can before some other bastard ruins your chances. Either that or keep your head down and out of their way. That's what it's all about.'

Bruton looked at Alan, then said, 'Well, I don't know. I

don't want my kid growing up thinking the world's full of bastards.'

'It is, though,' said Alan.

'Yeah, but right now, my son's eighteen months old and I'm enjoying him being an innocent little kid. I only hope his mother keeps it together. There's no way I'm going to let anything happen to him – social services care or anything.'

'I thought Sheryl was all right now,' said Alan, covering the pills up and replacing the mats.

'She's on and off. It's not her fault she's the way she is but her moods drove me round the fucking bend. You know that. Sean had only just arrived when your old man gave me the sack, remember? I couldn't give a toss but she went to pieces when I lost that job. She was still suffering from post-natal depression when it happened and it blew all her fantasies about us getting married. She expected us to get a house on the new estate down the way from your old man's gaff. She's better now she's on the Prozac but I can still only take her in small doses. If it wasn't for Sean, I wouldn't be seeing her. You don't think it, do you, when you're on the job, that one shag will change your whole life?'

'You've got to be careful, mate,' Alan smiled, dumping four bags of pills into Bruton's oversized paw. 'Careful in all things.'

'Just like your father,' Bruton laughed. 'Have you seen the *Gazette* this week?'

Alan knew he was referring to the crash but didn't let on. 'No, why would I have seen a local paper? I live in London now.'

'Right, well, I've got one in the car. Thought you might like a laugh.'

'Is my father in the paper? asked Alan, his face a picture of curiosity. 'What's he been doing? Opening a local supermarket?'

'No, mate. Getting stick from the local press. Some bloke took a Liguri 700 for a test-drive and trashed it into the Netcalfe Hotel. Mullered his legs. Now the hotel owner is saying test-drives should be strictly controlled and is setting up a campaign group to get the law changed and Landor

47

Motors to accept responsibility. Gave me a right giggle, fat old bastard. And this time I'm nothing to do with his misfortune.'

Alan felt a rush of adrenaline. 'Are there pictures?' he asked.

'Yeah, one of the wreckage. I'll get the paper.' Bruton stuffed the bags of pills in his bomber jacket pocket and walked to the doors of the garage. He turned and looked at the Capri. 'My old man used to have one of these,' he said. 'Right load of crap it was.' With a laugh he unlocked the doors and went to retrieve the *Aylesbury & District Gazette* from his car.

Alan stood at the back of his garage and smiled. It was good to know that his father had enemies. It was also good to have Bruton feeding him information. He'd have never guessed that Nick Swift had been embroiled in last year's test-drive theft if Bruton hadn't had such a big mouth. Keeping stuff confidential was anathema to him. Alan was glad to have information on Swift that might come in useful one day. The guy was a tosser. The BMW had never been recovered and the police hadn't shown much interest in the theft; after all, Landor Motors were insured, they'd said, and no one had been badly hurt in the incident. It was another robbery out of hundreds in the area that year, they informed him.

The car had been shipped over to the continent and had surfaced in Belgium with new plates, paint and engine number before the week was out. Nick Swift had got a back-hander and everyone had kept schtum. Except, of course, for Peter Bruton, who couldn't wait to tell Alan about Swift's involvement.

Alan hoped he was keeping quiet about who was funding their new line in imports. He winced as he imagined Bruton spouting off to some of his bouncer mates: 'Yeah, Derek Landor's son, Alan Landor, has put up the cash. You know, Landor Motors.' He hated Bruton using his real name. He always had to keep reminding him to use his alias – Drake Lewis.

Bruton came back into the garage, pushing the door open

and allowing a stream of late autumn sunlight into the dingy room. He threw the paper on the bonnet of the Capri. 'Keep it as a souvenir,' he said. 'Now, I'd better be off. Got to get ready for tonight. Some of the women coming in the club these days are worth it, mate, I tell you. Wearing these tiny little dresses right up here,' he said, slicing his hand across the top of his thigh. 'And once they're pilled up, they're all over you. Spend most of the evening with a right boner. I like taking them to the dressing room – give 'em a right seeing to.' Alan threw him a dubious look.

'Honest,' said Bruton. 'You want to get yourself down there. Get away from cars and computers for a bit. Meet some women.'

'Yeah, well don't slack on shifting those pills 'cos you're too busy chasing some pussy in a short dress,' Alan warned him, smiling. He thought he'd been too long without any sex himself and could appreciate Bruton's down-to-earth methodology. 'And remember – one shag can change your whole life.'

'What?' asked Bruton

'You said earlier, "One shag can change your whole life," ' Alan repeated.

'Well I'm more careful these days. One kid's enough, believe me,' Bruton muttered, zipping up his jacket as Alan picked up the paper and began leafing through it from the back.

'It's on the front page,' Bruton told him.

Alan turned the paper over and laid it in front of him. HIGH-SPEED CRASH FORCES RESIDENTS' ACTION OVER TEST-DRIVE STANDARDS read the headline, with a picture of the mangled car and hotel extension damage illustrating the article. Bruton went on to tell Landor the details – not sparing the gorier bits about Adrian Boxall's injuries even though he could read them for himself – and Alan listened patiently.

'I can just imagine your old man's face, can't you?' said Bruton. 'Neck all wobbling and eyes bloodshot, looking shifty. I tell you something, Alan,' he added. 'You obviously take after your mother, looks-wise. You're lucky, mate, 'cos I wouldn't want to look like him.'

Alan felt distinctly uncomfortable. It was fine that Bruton took the piss out of his father's business misfortune but he wished he'd put a lid on the personal stuff. Throwing his mother into the conversation was distinctly out of order. It had to stop. 'Yeah, that's enough, Peter,' he cut in. 'Don't mention my mother again, OK?'

'I was complimenting her. There's no need to give it the tiny one.'

'Yeah, well keep it to yourself, eh?' added Alan, beginning to bristle at Bruton's presence and the casual way he sounded off about his family.

'Oh, so it's all right for you to call him all the cunts under the sun, but I can't join in and have a moan about him, is that right? Even though the bastard sacked me on the spot when he knew I had a new-born kid to support?'

'Any other employer would have done the same, Peter. And keep your nose out of my family. It was your own fault you got sacked. I told you to leave off the thieving. Fancy getting caught nicking tools. I thought you'd have had more sense. It's hardly big time, is it?'

'Yeah, well it's all in the past now. I've moved on, mate. I couldn't give a fuck about your fat father and his poxy garage. I just think it's funny that all this has blown up,' he said, pointing at the paper. 'And I thought you'd find it a laugh, too. Christ, you're hardly what they call close, are you?'

Alan sighed noisily. He was annoyed now. He just wanted Bruton to shut up. He felt his face colouring with anger and frustration. 'Leave it, will you. Let's forget about what's going on with my old man and concentrate on the business at hand. I need twenty-five grand by Christmas or my garage is finished, right? You're making enough on it so let's not lose it, OK? Keep it together.'

'All right, all right. I'm keeping it together. Christ, I didn't realise you were so touchy about your parents.' Bruton looked hurt that his joke had fallen flat. He picked his keys and mobile from the shelf and walked to his car. 'I'll call you tomorrow. And I hope your sore head gets better.'

He almost slipped on a greasy patch of sump oil beside his car. 'This place is a shithole, Alan,' he shouted as his parting comment. With that he turned the ignition and roared the BMW and its music system into life. Then he was gone.

Fuck you, fatneck, thought Alan. And fuck your mad girlfriend and your ugly kid.

FOUR
Countdown to the Weekend

Friday evening

Vic swung her black Toyota Corolla on to St John's Street and motored down towards Chambers wine bar to look for a parking space. It was ten minutes to eight. The city streets became really quiet after six o'clock on a Friday evening but the upmarket bars made a good trade out of those who didn't have anyone to rush home to. Small pockets of convivial activity were sandwiched between deserted offices; young men in smartly tailored suits stood drinking continental beer out of bottles with collector's labels. They were complemented by a handful of young women with Pantene-glossy manes who kept the pace with exotic vodkas. It was designer drinking done by designer people in designer suits.

As she began looking for somewhere to park the car, she wrestled with the pangs of guilt which pulled at her conscience. The fact that she'd been economical with the truth had got her the investigation work in the first place. Earlier that year she'd been temping at a nearby firm of solicitors. One Friday evening, she'd been invited to a celebration drinks party at Chambers. In her coffee-coloured

Betty Barclay skirt and freshly-laundered silk blouse, Vic knew that she blended in with all the other legal secretaries. She'd got chatting to this attractive guy, found he was in insurance, and had concocted a couple of tall tales about her work experience.

She hadn't intended to lie: she'd had a couple of drinks and had wanted to introduce herself as something more interesting than a typist. Earlier that week, just for a laugh, she'd had personal cards designed and printed which were usefully ambiguous. All they said were: FOR ASSISTANCE – VICTORIA DONOVAN, and gave two telephone numbers. She'd never imagined the insurance guy would have followed up her offer of work – but he had.

Once she had convinced herself she was already involved in the investigation business, she'd had no problem convincing Daniel Field. She said she had been process serving for two years but was wanting to branch out into insurance work. The truth was she had been typing up injunctions which had then been handed over to people tough enough to carry them through. Now that she had one job under her belt it was unlikely they were going to demand work records. However, the thought was always in the back of her mind that Daniel Field would discover her embarrassing secret. Hopefully not tonight, though, when some more hundred-pound-a-day work was in the offing.

Vic parked her car and checked herself in the rear-view mirror. A day spent surrounded by some of the best cosmetics on the market had its bonuses: she had found time to cleanse her face of the heavy layers of foundation and eyeliner which was *de rigueur* for demonstration personnel, and apply a lighter tint over her flawless creamy skin. Her brown eyes were fringed by perfectly segregated eyelashes which had been curled and coated to maximum effect and her lips were full and smooth, covered by an application of Dior translucent lip colour.

She checked the batteries in her micro recorder and made sure her bag contained the necessary materials: pens, paper, diary and polythene sleeves to act as 'job bags', as Daniel would undoubtedly have paperwork to hand over. Vic liked to make sure everything was neatly filed, easily accessible, kept in order. Organised chaos was how many people seemed to work. Vic preferred to be just organised.

She locked her car and walked the few yards to Chambers. The bar was thankfully less raucous than the newer, more style-conscious places which had opened nearby in the early nineties. The place had an air of old money about it and one didn't have to be such an avidly conspicuous consumer of everything currently fashionable to gain acceptance into its clientele. Old-fashioned good manners and an impeccable wardrobe seemed to be the hallmark of its patrons. This was certainly true of Daniel, who was already seated on the upper level of the bar: the slightly more intimate area, away from the diners and groups of office workers. He was by himself, Vic was pleased to see. She had half-expected the senior partner – Ralph Gaitskill – to be present considering she had only undertaken one previous job. On the Maynard investigation, he had insisted on close supervision of Vic's MO.

Daniel was looking relaxed. He stood up as soon as Vic appeared in front of him. 'Victoria, you're looking spectacular,' he announced. 'Let me get you a drink. I recommend a glass of this,' he said, pointing to an opened bottle of white Rioja. Vic accepted and he grabbed another glass from a passing wine waiter. They both sat down. 'So glad you could make it,' he said. 'I just have a hunch about this one. It feels wrong. We need to send someone in who doesn't look conspicuous.'

Daniel Field paused, scanned his eyes rapidly over Vic's face and seemed to realise that what he meant to say had come out wrong. Vic was anything but inconspicuous. 'What I mean is,' he continued, 'someone the company won't be suspicious of. A sombre-faced man in a suit, such as the loss-adjuster, will have them guarding everything. Loss-adjusters tend to put claimants into a defensive role. I feel you would be the right sort of person in that you look –'

Vic cut in, 'I look like insurance fraud is the furthest thing from my mind?' she suggested in an ironic tone of voice, leaning forward slightly and smiling.

'Yes. Yes, I guess that's the important thing here. Whoever goes in to Landor Motors has to look as if they have no concept of corporate wheeling and dealing.'

Vic smiled. She could tell what Daniel was trying his best to avoid saying. The two 'B' words were hovering in the wings of their conversation but Daniel was far too polite and well educated to say what came to mind. It might also be a difficult admission from a man whose hair was almost the same colour as Vic's. In an era of clouded sexual politics, it wasn't inconceivable that some people may describe him as a 'blond bimbo'.

His thick fringe fell across his forehead. Unlike her, he had blue eyes and a very fair complexion. Vic's gaze couldn't help but wander just that bit lower to the top of his chest, where he had undone his collar to reveal a smooth, elegant neck, graced by a slender chain which was bound to be fashioned from the finest 24-carat gold. Everything about him was classy. His pen was a Mont Blanc, his shirt looked hand-made, and she would bet his shoes were crafted from the finest Italian leather. He smiled a lot and had a friendly, open face which Vic responded to. He put her at ease.

She felt a compulsive urge to slide her soft hand over his as it rested on the table. His hands looked as elegant as the rest of him; the way he held his wine glass was poised and yet relaxed. He didn't have to try to look impeccably civilised – it came naturally. Vic thought that some men looked uncomfortable drinking from anything other than pint glasses; as if their meaty paws would shatter a champagne flute or crush the handle of a bone-china tea-cup. Not Daniel Field.

Vic checked herself to stop her fantasies overtaking what was really happening. Now wasn't the time to flirt. She took her pen out from her bag to make notes and switched on her micro-recorder under the table as Daniel began to tell her about the case. Vic had learnt that even honest people didn't like being taped: they tended to hold back or get really animated if a recorder or camera was shoved under their noses. She'd learnt to be discreet.

'We've been insuring Landor Motors since the early

seventies,' he began. 'They've grown into a hugely successful top-drawer showroom specialising in prestigious cars and some high-performance vehicles. Anyone in the Aylesbury area wanting a BMW five series will go to Landor's. If a company want to lease something a bit flash, they go to Landor's. It's this kind of deal which has started the claim rolling.'

Daniel went on to tell Vic about Adrian Boxall's accident and his statement that faulty airbag technology was to blame. 'It may be purely coincidental,' he continued, 'but in the past year they've been very unlucky. There was a robbery at the showroom – computers stolen and plenty of damage – and this was followed by the theft of a BMW worth thirty-five thousand while on a test drive. They never traced the driver although an ex-employee, a Peter Bruton, was arrested on a charge of accessory to theft. In the end he was acquitted due to lack of evidence.

'It seemed blatantly obvious he was behind it but the guy who actually drove the car away was untraceable. Totally clean. And Bruton gave them nothing. The police took prints off the car and ran a check on the licence he'd given them but no luck. Of course, the licence was stolen. Licence number was from someone about the same age. Easily done, really, if you've a mind for such a career. Some go through the entire process of getting a provisional licence and then taking a test in a false name. If you pass, bingo, instant ID valid at post offices, banks and smaller rental companies who deal with cash-paying customers.'

Vic listened carefully. 'Do you have a transcript from the trial?' she asked. 'If Bruton's an ex-employee he may be worth checking out. Can't see that he's anything to do with a faulty airbag or someone's bad driving but it may turn something up.'

'I was sent along to assess the BMW case for payment, to determine if we thought Landor's had been negligent in security,' Field continued. 'Seems not and we paid out in the end. These are my notes from the trial. His address is in there, too.' He handed Vic a folder. 'A gang threatened the senior salesman with a baseball bat. He had no choice, being on his own with the driver. They pulled into a garage and the BMW was jumped by two other men waiting there. Driver had made some excuse about using the bathroom. They threw the salesman out of the car and made off with it after roughing him up. Bruton's not someone you would want to spend too much time with,' said Daniel, wrinkling his nose. 'Wouldn't want him turning up at your dinner party, put it that way. I can't for the life of me see why Landor's employed him. He was a mechanic there. I suppose most mechanics aren't known for their refined tastes but he was way off the sort of person you would expect them to go for.'

'What do you think is going on at Landor's, Daniel?' asked Vic. 'This is not the kind of claim which would be fraudulent. I can't think of any way they would be making money on it; the driver, Boxall, surely it's him that was at fault?'

'Not according to the statement he gave the police. I'm waiting for a copy of it; should be with us by Monday. There's no doubt the accident happened. It's not fraud we're looking at. In fact, I'm not sure what it is we're dealing with. The car is a write-off. The manufacturer's report won't be ready for at least another week. You could do worse by checking on Boxall, though. He's at Aylesbury General: compound fractures of both legs and a broken nose, as well as serious chest injuries from the force of the bag punching in to him. As I say, this may be a case of bad luck coming in threes but we can't lose anything by putting a private investigator on the case.'

Vic felt a warm glow of excitement. A private investigator. He meant her. From magic lip- and eye-pencil demonstrator to private investigator in one afternoon. Not bad. 'I'll check Boxall first thing Monday,' she said. 'I'll call them tomorrow and get a report on his condition. He can expect a visit from me.'

'His solicitor has a fierce reputation,' Daniel warned her. 'He's our fly in the ointment. If there's any loopholes in security, he'll find them out and take Landor's – that means us – to the cleaners. If the manufacturers come up with a clean slate, we have to try and prove reckless driving on

Boxall's part. It won't be easy. I've been speaking to Derek Landor, the owner and company director. His solicitor isn't as fierce but he's very thorough. Landor sounds worn out by the whole event.'

'I'm not surprised,' said Vic. 'This kind of thing will up his premium.'

'And some. I sense from the dealings we've had with him that he's a troubled man. Maybe there are financial or personal problems. Who knows? People's lives change and Derek Landor's seen more than his fair share of misery. He's been financially stable for most of his troubles though.'

'What do you mean, misery?' asked Vic.

'His first wife, Sally, committed suicide in 1979. She had a life insurance policy with another company but my predecessor found out about her dying when Derek renewed his business policy with us that year. He ticked his marital status as widowed. Gaitskill Senior heard more about the circumstances leading up to her death from an old friend of his who worked at Blackwell & Dewey. History of mental illness, apparently. There'd been lots of attempts before.'

'How did she do it?'

'Overdose. She'd become addicted to tranquillisers but it wasn't an accident. They found a note. It was really sad. Their eldest boy found her while she was still conscious. He was only eleven at the time, poor lad. Still, all that's a long while ago now,' said Daniel, appearing to make sure the conversation didn't take too sombre a course. 'There was a happy outcome for Derek. He remarried shortly after and he's still with his second wife, as far as we know.'

Vic found herself immediately drawn into the case. She was building herself a mental picture of Derek Landor, his company, his family and their adversaries. The break-in and the theft appeared to have no relevance to the accident they were currently investigating but Vic was aware that people's pasts had a way of catching up with them. She'd definitely check out Peter Bruton, unsavoury as he sounded. 'Give me two weeks starting Monday,' she said.

'We don't know if there'll be anything you can find out that the loss adjuster can't, but as I say, I've a feeling that if something odd is going on, you can get to the bottom of it. You saved us a lot of money on the Maynard job, Victoria. We never expected you to get so involved, and we wouldn't recommend it as a matter of course,' he added, a note of concern to his voice.

'I quite like getting involved,' she said, twirling her wine glass. 'Also, the money's good and I can be my own boss. I met plenty of shady characters when I was process serving,' she lied. 'They don't intimidate me.'

'You're quite an extraordinary young woman, Victoria,' he said. 'I'd like to know more about you. Maybe we could meet sometime when business isn't headlining the agenda.'

Vic felt her stomach tighten. That would mean questions about her private life and her background. So far she'd fudged the issue, muttering something about Surrey and boarding school. She couldn't face telling him she was brought up in Walthamstow and only had three A levels and a technical college education, could she? All the same, she was flattered and had to admit the prospect of seeing Daniel Field in a less formal position – and less clothes – intrigued her. She looked him straight in the eye and accepted. 'Yes, Daniel, I'd like that,' she said. 'For now, consider me under contract. Shall we say two weeks to begin with? If we say a hundred pounds per day plus expenses, plus one percent of whatever I save you, if there's a saving to be made, I'm sure that we can turn up the truth of what's going on, if anything.'

'Sounds fine. I'll draw up a contract first thing Monday. We'll go through the fine details then. Agreed?'

'Agreed,' said Vic. They shook hands.

Saturday day

Upper Street, Islington, was packed with cars and shoppers as Vic made her way on foot to the Angel tube station. On Saturdays it was quicker to get almost anywhere in London by leaving the car at home. She was due to meet Julian at the Barbican Fitness Centre at twelve o' clock. He was someone she'd remained in touch with since her time working on television. Vic loved their Saturday lunchtime initiatives, as Julian called them. An initiative could be a game of badminton, an extended brunch at the Dôme, an art exhibition or shopping in Covent Garden – when finances permitted. Today, it was to be badminton and then brunch.

She couldn't help thinking about Daniel Field. He'd been in her mind since she'd arrived home last night and was the first person she'd thought of on waking that morning. So, he was single, after all. He didn't look the type to ask someone out if he was spoken for. If Vic did a good job on this Landor case, he would be all the more impressed with her. It made her feel determined to come through with as much information as she could gather. There was nothing like a personal interest in someone to garner motivation for a task. Daniel was an attractive incentive.

She would have to stick to her home-counties upbringing story, though. Nothing would make Daniel lose interest faster than knowing she was the sister of a convicted criminal, even if Tony was only twenty-two. And she certainly couldn't imagine inviting him to Walthamstow to meet her mum and aunties. He would ask about her father and then she would have to say that he was dead. And that would be another lie because she couldn't face saying that he'd left home when she was seven years old and had never returned.

If only Vic could change her past – change who her father had been. She knew it wasn't her fault he'd left them but he never seemed to have time for her and Tony. He'd taught Kevin the rudiments of the building trade once his eldest boy was ten, but Vic's world of fairy princesses and Tony's bawling had played on his nerves. When he rowed with her mum, it was either about money or how noisy the kids were. The one thing she'd always remembered him saying was, 'Can't you get them to shut up?' Vic had been hurt beyond measure the first time she'd heard him say it. He was a man who should never have had children. Then again, she wouldn't be here if he hadn't.

Vic shook herself out of becoming too existential and forced herself to jump back to the present. Maybe an affair with Daniel would be too complicated to pursue. She'd ask Julian about it. She'd found out more about how men's minds worked from him than all her female friends.

As she approached the entrance to the fitness centre, she spotted Julian making his way along the concourse. He was already wearing his whites. They kissed each other on meeting. Both of them were punctual — a habit Vic had got into from her days on TV. Julian was always punctual because he liked everything to be perfect. He hated to be disorganised. His neat hair and spotless clothes were an example of that.

'Aren't you worried you would have got your whites dirty wearing them in the street, Jules?' said Vic, immediately launching into the good-natured deprecating banter they enjoyed at each other's expense.

'Yes, I know, but it was worth it to get cruised as I walked past the Bull and Pump just now.'

'I thought Sainsbury's was your favourite cruising ground,' joked Vic.

'It's hetero hell in there on a Saturday, darling! Let me tell you the nuclear family is alive and well despite what you read in the *Daily Mail*. And you're looking as lovely as ever,' he said, leaning back to observe Vic's outfit. 'Thank God you're not wearing pastels. Everywhere I go at the moment I see young women wearing a mass of pale secondary colours. Disgusting!'

'Not me, Jules. Beige, maybe, but never powder blue.'

'That's my girl,' said Julian, putting his arm around her as they walked into the foyer of the sports club. 'Now I'm going to give you such a thrashing!'

'Never!' said Vic, digging Julian in the ribs with her racket. 'Best of five and the loser buys lunch. Get your wallet ready.'

As usual, Vic won. She'd been playing tennis since she was very young and kept a regular routine of badminton in the winter and tennis in the summer. Julian was quick and agile but nowhere near as competitive as Vic. The kind of returns she would stretch herself to catch would have Julian pulling faces in disgust at his opponent's effrontery.

The Wimbledon season was Vic's favourite time of year.

It was a shame that rain had postponed so many games this June but Vic had enjoyed the matches she'd caught on TV. She also played whenever she got the time. Poor Julian didn't stand a chance but he made a delightful opponent.

They showered and changed and made their way back to the Angel. Julian liked the choice of cafés along Upper Street and Vic had needed little persuasion to lunch there as she too loved the European feel to the area in which she resided. It was about five miles from Walthamstow but could have been a different country. It was near enough to visit Marie but cosmopolitan enough to appeal to Vic's taste in food and designer accessories. The area had a vibrant, positive feel to it. The drawback was the cost of her monthly mortgage repayments.

'I'm so glad this work's come up, Julian,' she confided to her friend as they waited for their eggs Benedict in Upper Street's Dôme café.

'Being freelance anything is a nightmare these days,' he replied. 'It's the same in theatre, TV, wherever. Short-term contracts and long-term worry; that's the price you pay for not having the same old routine every day of the week. But I just can't believe what you're doing now, Vic,' he went on. 'When I met you you were mincing around in a pink lamé number on that terrible game show. It was so camp I thought I should have got the job but they made me stay in the dressing room, remember?'

Vic laughed. 'And do you remember the look on David's face when he caught us doing our rude version of the show?'

' "For every question guessed right the winner gets to take home a rent boy of his choice!" I still say he was as queer as Christmas but he'd never admit it.' They laughed and reminisced for a while about the time they'd worked together.

'I'm really winging it on this job, Jules,' said Vic, looking serious for a minute. 'The potential earnings are great and I like the excitement.'

'Aren't the potential dangers enough to put you off? Supposing someone has a go at you? A few self-defence classes wouldn't help you against an armed man or something.'

'Thanks for caring about me but I don't think there'll be too many armed men on this case. I can't talk about it in detail, of course, but it's really not that kind of investigation. It's a fraud thing at worst.'

Julian's eyes widened as he sipped his coffee. 'It's so exciting, Vic. It's like you're a policewoman but without the uniform and bad shoes.'

'Or having to answer to a superior every day. It's up to me to fact-find and assess what's going on in these cases. It's about getting people to trust you. I can be anyone I want to be. And as you know, I like that.'

'Your talents are wasted out there,' he said. 'I still maintain that you should go to more auditions.'

'No one wants to know when I tell them I don't have drama school credentials, Julian. Theatre workshops and a couple of A levels just aren't enough. And I have my bijou residence to pay for. I have to earn money.'

'Things are changing, though. Plenty of actors are breaking through without the RADA background.'

'I don't think I can take another rejection,' said Vic.

'It's a good thing we don't all think like that. I'm rejected about five times every Saturday night but I don't give up. Keep trying and you'll get there in the end.'

'I don't know what's worse,' she said. 'Sexual rejection or professional rejection. I guess I've not experienced too much of the former. I seem to have the physical qualities which are popular with most men.'

'I wish I could say the same,' Julian said sardonically. 'I keep falling in love with straight guys. That's a losing ticket, let me tell you, but it doesn't stop me dreaming about them all day. We've got one in the studio now and I know there's absolutely no chance he'll entertain the idea of going to bed with me but a tiny part of my imagination won't let go. It's all the what ifs and if onlys that keep us going, darling. The brave thing is to act on them. Try to make them real. And that's what you should do with your career.'

'In the meantime, I'm curious enough to give this PI

thing a stab,' said Vic. 'I've never told so many lies in my life, though!' She stared directly into Julian's eyes. It was good to offload some of the guilt by confessing to her friend. 'Already the insurance company I'm working for think I've been doing it years and the guy who's employed me is so charming I found myself going into Victoria mode in case he thought the real Vic was too wretchedly down-market for the job.'

'I remember her. Horrible Sloane!' Julian laughed, remembering how Vic had entertained him with her upper-class characters when they'd had time to kill backstage.

'Well, she might just pay my mortgage for the next year,' said Vic as the waitress arrived with their brunches.

Saturday evening

Peter Bruton's neck strained with exertion and the veins bulged out of his meaty arms as he pushed the 40-kilo weights towards the ceiling. Twenty at breakfast, twenty at lunch and twenty before going out of an evening. And that was just the bench presses. He'd work on his lateral pull-downs and abdominals for another half hour before calling it a day. Everything was coming on nicely, he thought. Alan wasn't to know that he'd got a better price on the consignment than he said he had. Prices had gone down. Five thousand pills had cost him ten grand – not the twelve he'd told Alan – and he felt a warm glow of clever pride knowing that Landor would never find out about his unexpected earner. After all, it was him who was taking all the risks – importing and distributing at the club. All Landor had done was put up two thirds of the money and stash the stuff.

Shifting it was a piece of piss. The management at Gaby's were a bunch of saps; too out of touch to know what was really going on in their club. They'd been in charge of the place since the mid-eighties and didn't even realise that seventy per cent of the punters at weekends were off their heads on gear supplied by their own security blokes. All the owners were interested in was the place making money, and to make money you had to give the kids what they wanted. The club seemed to have made the right noises about drugs to the Old Bill, though, and so far they'd been left alone. He occasionally read of an impromptu raid on an illegal party or a rookie cop busting someone's scam on a hunch – which was something Bruton could well do without – but the likelihood of that happening in a licensed gaff was slim. Gaby's was established, legal, protected. A different story from some of the hit-and-run raves Top Deck Security had done a couple of years ago, before Peter had joined the team.

The older boys had told him some stories about them having to sort out DJs who'd played at the wrong firm's gig. If you booked a name DJ – someone the punters want to hear at the decks – and he absconded to another party because they'd promised him a couple of hundred quid more, fair enough that the bloke should get a pasting. Having your fingers broken so you couldn't mix any tunes for a couple of months was rough justice if DJ-ing was your only source of income. Most of them knew better than to pull a fast one these days.

Bruton was well aware of how much money went into that safe on a Saturday night. He was biding his time. Selling a few pills kept the wolf from the door but one day soon Gaby's would be done over and he could come up trumps – with a little bit of help from Andrew and Gary. They were up for it. Always had been a pair of nutters. They'd come through like true gents on the BMW job. And they'd managed to keep Swift's mouth shut with a pay-off which, of course, they'd honoured as soon as they'd shifted the motor in Belgium.

Now the inside job. The three of them had been discussing it for months. It was time to strike soon. Gary had the shooter contact and neither of them were known faces at Gaby's. A weapon was a must on a job like that, otherwise the security were expected to sort it out. They might have muscle but they weren't expected to wrestle shooters from people. Alan could sort the motor. It was good to have a plan.

Peter had the radio tuned to the local pirate station. Every ten minutes they'd be giving big shout-outs to the

Buckinghamshire party people, telling them to get down to Gaby's for Purity. 'Respect to the Wycombe crew; hold tight the Aylesbury massive.' Trevor, his boss, must have had a word with the station co-ordinator again. His plan was to run things in the whole area, not just the legal clubs. The potential to clean up was there. It was an easy bribe to get the pirate stations to give you some free advertising on the promise of you lending them protection when they needed to relocate at short notice. The DJs would direct the punters to the clubs and parties where Top Deck controlled the security. And security meant more than keeping drunks in order. These days, security was about backhanders: sorting people out with what they wanted; lining your pockets with a little bonus cash. Not too much though. Bruton's main worry was that if Trevor got a sniff of his action, he would want a slice of the profits. Something Peter wasn't prepared to allow. He'd have to enlist someone else to push his Amsterdam souvenirs. Someone who'd be grateful for a little bit of cash and could keep his mouth shut.

As he plunged his key into the eighth notch on his multi-gym, he began mentally checking through a list of associates. Something would turn up; with so much ready cash to be made, he felt secure that he would earn his few grand before the month was out.

His TV was on but the sound was turned down. The blue light from the screen declaring the day's football results filled the room with a cold glow. He was happy to see that Tottenham had made a good start to the season. The evenings were drawing in. The clocks were due to go back in a couple of weeks; time to buy himself some new threads for the coming winter. He puffed his way through fifty lateral pull-downs then wiped his sweating face with a flannel. That was enough exercise for now. He was hungry and there was a steak in the fridge which demanded his immediate attention. He lifted his body off the machine and walked into his sparsely decorated kitchen to prepare some tea before getting ready to go to Gaby's.

It irked Peter that he had to waste time shopping and cooking. He knew he had to consume a load of calories to build up the muscle which earnt him his living, but the rigmarole of peeling potatoes and chopping mushrooms to go with his steak was a bloody nuisance. Until Sheryl lost it mentally she would do everything for him and he missed being waited on. He missed the company, too. He hated not having anyone special to sound off to. There was no one to tell about the new speakers he'd fitted into his BMW, for instance, or the row he'd had in the newsagents when he was shortchanged that afternoon. He wouldn't want her back, though — not how she was these days. But he wanted to find someone new to look after him. Soon.

He lifted the steak from its bloody wrapping and stuck it under the eye-level grill. He couldn't face peeling spuds so he reached into the freezer. He'd have microwaved chips again. He threw the packet on to the work surface then stood staring at the steak as it browned slowly. He thought about his son, Sean. He'd agreed to look after him for a couple of hours next Saturday. He looked forward to that. One day, when the kid was older, he'd buy him anything he wanted. He didn't want Sean to go without like he'd had to.

Alan Landor sat in his bedroom crushing a load of homeopathic tablets with an onyx ashtray he'd nicked from his father's place. Less scrupulous dealers used bicarb, anadins or even novocaine to cut coke but he'd found that boshing it with something less noxious paid off. These little pills were tasteless and didn't interfere with the numbing properties of the coke. No money had changed hands. Alan had gone to the flat in New Cross and had swapped three hundred pills for an ounce of the stuff from a tubby geezer in his late thirties he knew from around the garage. He had given him a reasonable nose up and the gear seemed fine, but the fact that the bloke was weighing up in front of his kids had been a bit of a shock. The two boys didn't seem to care, though. They just lay watching Pocahontas on the video while their dad prattled on about his estranged wife fleecing him for everything she could get.

Alan's curtains were drawn and a blue funk of skunkweed and tobacco smoke hung over the proceedings. As usual in

Alan's council flat, all visual appliances were in use: his computer was rendering some graphics and the TV was on churning out Saturday evening fare. His desk was littered with unopened official-looking letters and computer magazines. Alan had given up trying to sort out his council tax and he'd been getting grief from the housing benefit office since he'd come back from Germany. He'd been told it would be easy to sort out income support after his contract had expired but things had changed since he'd signed up for the work. Income support had become job seekers' allowance and his long hair and eyebrow piercing hadn't gone down too well at his restart interview at the Job Centre. Fuck them, he thought. What was the point chasing your own arse all day if they persisted in getting your claim wrong. He'd received nine letters from the council tax office in the past two weeks, all demanding different sums of money. They could stuff it. He had better things to do than work out their sums for them.

He tipped the crushed pills into the middle of the coke as if it were plaster being added to concrete. He liked this bit. He wished he had a small trowel to mix the two substances together. His hand, and the Stanley-knife blade he held, were lost in the small mountain of powder. Now he'd mixed it up, he needed to lose it – and fast. He knew to his financial detriment that he couldn't hold on to Charlie. One night out and he'd be banging it out to everyone in sight. Before he knew it, five grammes would be gone. He phoned one of Bruton's mates.

'Laurence, it's Drake, yeah.'

'All right, my man? What's up?'

'Remember a couple of weeks ago you asked about getting tickets but I was a bit tied up with something else? Well I got quite a few this week: twenty-five, mate.'

'Timing, guy. I'm doing the Motor Show in Birmingham. Start Tuesday. That's the day of all the press parties and stuff. Bound to shift it. Want to meet me there? I can get you a pass; nick one from the office. I'll post it to you, yeah?'

'Cool. I've just thought, my fucking old man'll be there. I can wind him up!' Alan laughed.

'Yeah, well you just come and check me when you get there. I've got to sort out rotas and all that first. We'll phone each other.'

'Brilliant, Laurence. I'll be there. You send that pass first class Monday, man. Don't forget.' Alan switched off his phone and giggled to himself. It was looking sweet. He'd be having a right laugh while his father was sure to be looking well pissed-off. He'd have to have a word with him. Express his commiserations about the crash and all that.

In a way it had all turned out better than if it had been Derek at the wheel. Shame a totally innocent bloke had had to suffer. Thing was, it would be his father who would pay for it; he had hit him in the pocket — where it hurt him most. Then his memory kicked in to his skunk-addled brain. He must remember to ditch from his hard drive that reconfiguring programme that he'd nicked from the factory in Germany. What with all the buying and selling, he'd forgotten to lose it. There was no hurry, though. Even the usual weed-induced paranoia hadn't made Alan think for one moment that he would ever come under suspicion for this.

Hardly anyone in the country knew it was possible to refigure the loom wiring from the cruise-control circuit to the airbag detonation control. His time in Germany had been more useful than he'd expected. Advances in sophisticated technology were gaining ground all the time and nowhere more so than over there. The fact he'd managed to get work in the computer-aided design department of the factory had been ideal. This meant that not only did he not have to get his hands dirty like the Turkish immigrant workers, but he could tinker with exciting programmes: things which were never likely to be fitted on to standard products because of their potential for malfunction.

Peter Bruton was so stupid to have held on to the keys to the Landor Motors annexe after he'd been sacked. Naturally, the locks had been changed to the main part of the showroom when they'd had the break-in earlier in the year. The burglars hadn't broken in to the annexe, though, and this had been overlooked when they'd had new locks fitted. It had only taken a few minutes for Alan to nip out and have one cut while Peter was fooling around fitting new speakers in his BMW. One day Fatneck would come unstuck big time.

FIVE
Nightfall Over Haver Dean

Monday

It was Monday morning and Vic felt privileged to have a lie-in until ten-thirty. The strong October sunlight streamed in through the white paper blinds and cast a yellowish hue around her immaculately tidy bedroom. She'd woken at eight and had prepared herself a croissant with apricot conserve and strong Italian coffee to kick start herself into action. Shortly after nine she telephoned Aylesbury General and enquired about Boxall. He was 'as comfortable as could be expected' they told her, and had managed to get some sleep last night, which was the usual line staff nurses gave out when someone had suffered multiple injuries. The main thing was that he was conscious and there had been no head injuries unless you counted the broken nose. It would be possible to visit later that evening. Visiting time finished at eight but given his condition they wanted to ensure that he had sufficient rest. Could she be away by seven? Yes, that would be fine. She was unable to get to visit sooner as there was a lot of work to be done while her boss was laid up due to this accident. There it was: first lie of the day. Vic knew there would be a few more like that before nightfall over Haver Dean.

Realising there was no need to be up so early, she had then gone back to bed to do some thinking. Mum had seemed a bit more cheerful yesterday. Tony had only been mentioned once: the usual question of whether Vic had heard anything from him. Marie had cooked a Sunday roast and mother and daughter had chatted philosophically about life, love and the state of the world.

Since Marie had stopped seeing Brian she'd let her lack of self-confidence creep back over her but she seemed to be getting over their break-up. Vic had expected they would marry. They'd been seeing each other for the past eight years but he'd never moved in. For the past three years he had kept Marie in a quandary as to whether they had a long-term future together. He was a widower and there seemed to be no sensible reason for his wanting to go on living on his own. In the end Marie couldn't stand the uncertainty and, in any case, she liked having someone to look after and wanted to be a man's wife again. Michael Donovan's Irish Catholicism had ingrained in Marie the belief that sex should only occur between husband and wife; it was a shame that he hadn't kept to his part of the marriage vows.

Brian was so independent that he hadn't really fulfilled Marie's needs in the domestic arena. Vic had thought him OK but a bit dull; he didn't seem to have much passion in him. He liked doing DIY and had a mild interest in model-building but there was little spark in the man. He was distant, like her father had been; like so many men of his generation who spent a lifetime hiding from the world from behind their newspapers.

What could she do for her mum to make her happier? she wondered as she sipped her coffee. Marie was fifty-four now and if she didn't do something soon to change the way things were going, she'd fall into the trap of thinking that all the good parts of her life were over or that she was too old to try new things. She needed a holiday. Somewhere foreign. What with the business with Tony getting out of jail in May, a summer holiday had been out of the question. It was high time Marie Donovan got out and enjoyed herself. If Vic did OK on this job she'd definitely treat her mum to a special trip somewhere. They could go together.

Although there was a generation between them, Vic found her mum easy company in most situations. It was only when Marie pronounced French or Spanish words with an unmistakably London accent that Vic had to hide her embarrassment. Vic was aware that her mother was in awe of her. She liked to visit Vic on Saturday afternoons and they would go shopping in Chapel Street market together before having tea at Vic's flat. The first time Marie had seen the place she had been struck speechless. 'Who would have thought that my daughter, my little Victoria, would be able to afford the likes of this?' she'd said.

Who indeed? Maybe the people she met who believed her story about the Surrey upbringing and her private school education. The flat was conveniently situated between Barnsbury and the Angel – an area which housed people from a multitude of backgrounds. Her taste for streamlined design and inventive interior décor influenced by the colours and styling of other cultures added to the appearance of middle-class taste. Each room had a particular theme. Her bedroom was based on Japanese minimalism – there was a predominance of white and her futon had only an expensive black lacquer table at its side. Her clothes were kept out of sight in a wardrobe with sliding doors and her dressing table was also black and flanked at either side by a matching pair of beautifully-carved alabaster statues of cats. She insisted they were Burmese but her friend Joe swore they looked Egyptian.

Vic's bathroom was her favourite room. The Alhambra in Granada had been the influence, and the tiles which ran around the bath and shower were based on traditional Arabic design and had cost her a fortune. Spiky ferns in brass pots complemented the deep blue paintwork – which was the only colour for a bathroom, according to Vic. Delicate opaque perfume bottles and the best hair-care products on the market graced the shelves and the bathroom cabinet was replete with sensuous oils and natural soaps. A small wooden shelf, filled with miniature books from the Penguin 60s series, was positioned above the bath. One could finish an entire book during a leisurely soak.

The kitchen and living room were more colourful and youthful than either the bedroom or bathroom. The African fabric thrown over the sofa was a contrast to the lava lamps and the framed Jean-Michel Basquiat poster. There was just enough room to erect a dining table for dinner parties but this was kept folded away for most of the time. Vic usually ate at her breakfast bar or sat on the sofa watching the TV. The kitchen wall was dominated by a large pin board of photographs of Vic and her friends at parties or from the theatre groups she'd joined plus clippings with relevant stories or surreal incidents that had made the newspapers.

A picture of Ruud Gullit looking particularly cheerful and dashing had been cut out from the sports pages and blu-tacked on to the fridge door with the words 'Is this the face of God?' taken from a serious article on theology. Vic loved her flat and intended to keep being able to afford it no matter what strange and difficult jobs she had to do. She'd cast a wide net and, for the time being, at least, her theatrical pretensions were to find an outlet sniffing around Landor Motors.

The M40 had been clear and Vic was able to push her Japanese rice-cooker – as Julian called it – to a hundred miles per hour for some of the way. It was naughty, and made more pertinent by the fact that she was on her way to visit a victim of a high-speed car crash, but she couldn't resist the temptation to go full throttle when she saw a clear road in front of her. Driving around London turned people into frustrated psychopaths and one needed the occasional antidote to stop-start traffic jams.

She'd rung Field & Gaitskill shortly after getting up and had liaised with the loss-adjuster, getting his itinerary for the day. His first call was Landor Motors, naturally, and later in the afternoon he was due to call on Bob Waterhouse to assess whether the damage to his property was roughly the same as that claimed for by his insurance company. She'd agreed to meet the loss-adjuster – Timothy Fuller – outside Haver Dean British Rail station at two o' clock and they'd proceed to the Netcalfe Hotel together. It was one-fifteen when Vic entered the town. The wide main drag was rather quaint: there was a proliferation of antique shops and tea houses bedecked with fairy lights. She stopped at a newsagents and bought a copy of the *Aylesbury & District Gazette*. There it was on the front page: an alarmist headline and a picture of the mangled car.

The story ran over three pages and another picture showed Bob and Eileen Waterhouse standing outside the wreck of their hotel extension looking mortified at the damage. The caption stated that the picture had been taken shortly after the crash. The *Gazette* said their 'reporter on the scene' had been there within minutes of the incident. Maxine Chesterton would be worth ringing, Vic thought. She knew how to write copy that made a drama out of a crisis for the local rag, but how much did she know about Landor Motors? The editorial voice was in favour of Bob Waterhouse's campaign for better road safety and an unflattering photograph of Derek Landor looking worried and guilty wouldn't do much to improve his defence of high-speed test-drives in the area – which formed the backbone of the story rather than the driver's injuries.

Vic wondered if Chesterton had been on the *Gazette*'s team when Landor's had the robbery earlier in the year. The files of local newspapers were frequent haunts of private investigators and Vic lost no time in making an appointment to see the reporter. Her second untruth of the day had been telling Chesterton she was from the Campaign for Better Road Safety and was writing a report on accidents caused by irresponsible driving. Saying she represented Landor's insurance company wouldn't have got her through the door. Chesterton seemed happy to meet with her. She could spare twenty minutes at four o'clock.

Timothy Fuller seemed less impressed by Vic's presence in

the town. She knew the moment she shook hands with him outside the station that he saw her as competition. He would have to do all the boring mathematics and she would take the credit – she knew that was what he was thinking. He looked almost frightened of her. He was shorter than Vic and this didn't help to alleviate the fear she suspected he felt in the company of any women over the age of twenty and under sixty. He was an unremarkable creature in his grey suit and straggly tie. His shoes were unpolished and worn and the trench coat slung over the arm with which he was holding his battered briefcase looked stained and grubby. What on earth could she talk about to this man apart from the Landor case?

He launched into practicalities. 'Where have you parked your car?'

'In the station car park, Mister Fuller,' said Vic, as cheerfully as she could. Maybe her happy disposition would be catching.

'Hmm. It would make more sense for me to drive us both to the Netcalfe Hotel, I suppose, as I have the address and I'm familiar with the town. I would then drive you back to your car later. Agreed?'

Vic agreed in a cheerful manner which Fuller probably thought overly casual. They walked to Fuller's Honda Accord. He volunteered no information about his visit to Landor Motors and Vic was getting impatient that he was being so tight. She realised she was going to have to drag it out of him. 'I like to concentrate on one thing at a time, Miss Donovan,' he said, releasing the central locking of a car which, Vic was amused to notice, was dark grey. 'We can discuss the showroom later. And I don't like to talk while I'm driving. It's not safe. Mr Waterhouse is expecting us in ten minutes,' he told her, before putting the car in gear. He even indicated his right turns while driving in the car park, where no other cars were moving. The guy was a scream. She'd have to tell Julian about him and they'd both have a laugh at some point mimicking his nasal twang and inventing the incredible adventures of Mister Fuller, loss adjuster.

★

Meeting the Waterhouses hadn't been Vic's idea of a dream afternoon but it was entertaining nevertheless to watch Timothy Fuller niggle the aggrieved couple as they played bat and ball with each other's opinions as to the value of the compensation. Fuller introduced Vic as his assistant – reluctantly, she noticed – and she made notes as they surveyed the damage to the restaurant's conservatory extension. There was no doubt that the entire front structure would need rebuilding, and the lawn had been churned up where the car had careered off the driveway. The main bulk of the new extension was sound, however, and Fuller let it be known that there wasn't a scratch to the interior walls and most of the furniture had been left intact.

The Waterhouses harangued him about loss of income, which looked most likely to be the sticking point in the claim as the amount of projected revenue was speculative. They'd put in a claim to their own insurers for the loss of two thousand five hundred pounds expected turnover on their opening night and a subsequent thousand for each night thereafter. Fuller had thought this astronomical for an out-of-town restaurant and had told them he would be looking into similar cases. Vic listened with amusement as a surreal debate about the opening night's menu and the impeccable credentials of the *chef de cuisine* ensued.

While Fuller and Eileen Waterhouse were speaking in clipped tones about who was responsible for the restaurant staff's loss of earnings, Vic managed to lure Bob Waterhouse into the driveway of the hotel, where she spoke in calm, even tones about his campaign to ban test-drives. A banner had been printed which read KILL SPEED, NOT PEDESTRIANS and now hung over the entrance to the hotel driveway.

Waterhouse went into the gory details of the accident and had said that Landor seemed to have taken his time getting to the hotel but his senior salesman, Nick Swift, was there within minutes. The police had done an 'adequate' job of crowd control although Waterhouse thought they should have been able to see the full effects of the crash. He portioned equal blame on Boxall and Landor Motors, saying they were all rich bastards who didn't give a damn about anyone but themselves – an odd comment from a man who seemed to be planning to milk maximum publicity and remuneration from his inconvenience, thought Vic.

He hadn't known any of the Landor Motors staff or owners before the incident. Fuller made some last minute notes about the decorators' invoice and told Bob and Eileen he would be in touch. It had been a less than cordial meeting and Vic wondered what effect dealing with defensive and angry people every day had on one's personality. Probably turned you into Timothy Fuller, she thought.

Back at the station, they sat in Fuller's Honda while he explained in a dull monotone that it was a very complex claim. Everything hinged on the manufacturer's report and, even then, the case could still go to trial if Boxall wanted to pursue his charge of gross negligence on the part of Landor Motors for not checking their vehicles thoroughly before allowing them to be driven by members of the public. The one useful piece of information he had to part with was that the company were going ahead with their appearance at the Motor Show in Birmingham, which opened to the press the next day. The general public didn't gain admittance until Friday. The senior salesman and Derek Landor were attending and they had spent the weekend arranging for the transportation of classic cars to the Exhibition Centre.

Fuller mentioned that both men had seemed exhausted. As Fuller had left at one o' clock, Landor and Swift were preparing to leave the showroom in the hands of the two junior salesmen. The ensuing week was expected to be a quiet one as the trade would be descending on Birmingham, rather than Haver Dean. Ideal for Vic. She would go to the Motor Show after all. She hadn't planned on being under-cover, but at least she'd be earning money while there. Her problem would be getting in as a member of the press. She checked her watch. It was getting on for four o' clock. She told Fuller that she would be hoping to work closely with him on the case, which left him looking somewhat startled, and made her way back to her own car.

The small offices of the *Aylesbury Gazette* were untidy and cramped but they had air-conditioning and some plants around the place to take the edge off the predominance of white and grey. Maxine Chesterton showed Vic into a cupboard-sized room which housed a broken photocopier and brought her a cup of coffee from the filter pot in their kitchen. An alert-looking woman in her early thirties, she was a touch overweight with blonde hair currently in the difficult stage of growing out of its perm. She wore a floral blouse with a neat rounded collar – which looked as if it had been run up on a home sewing machine – and a plain blue skirt and flat shoes.

Vic noticed she wore a gold cross around her neck and that her complexion – especially that of her hands – was pale and her skin almost too soft. Her fingers held a collection of jewellery which could have come from any high-street jeweller in any town in the country. She was married, and wore both wedding band and an emerald and diamond cluster ring on the same finger. 'I'm with Bob and Eileen Waterhouse all the way on this one,' was her opening gambit. 'It's amazing how you can find yourself thrown into a campaign like this and last week you wouldn't have thought twice about such a thing. It's a miracle no one was killed.'

'Absolutely,' said Vic, already disliking the woman's crusading tone of voice. 'I wonder if you could tell me what you saw at the accident,' she began. 'The article in the *Gazette* is comprehensive but is there anything you feel you weren't able to mention. For instance, is there likely to be a police investigation into the crash?'

'I'm disappointed so far with their response and so is Bob,' said Maxine. 'They say they're awaiting the results of the manufacturer's report on the sports car and we shouldn't allow emotions to get in the way of reason until all the facts are known. Can you believe it? I must say I didn't expect that kind of reaction from them. They have to deal with some worrying statistics on high-speed road death and I'd hoped for a more sympathetic voice. It would be helpful to our campaign if you were willing to structure your report around this specific case. I know Bob Waterhouse would be delighted to get something more official off the ground. The newspaper have helped out by paying for the banners and posters which are going up around town this week. How long has Campaign for Better Road Safety been going?'

Christ, think fast. Remember. No. Make it up. 'Since the mid-sixties. The pressure group initiated the old Green Cross Code for kids and advised on the design of pelican crossings to include sound for partially sighted and blind pedestrians.' Chesterton seemed satisfied with that.

'My feeling is that the pressure should be put on Landor Motors to make a statement of apology,' Chesterton stated.

'I was wondering if there had been any other cases in the Gazette concerning the Landor Motors company,' said Vic. 'It would add fuel to the campaign if there had been another case like this one or if there were any findings of dodgy dealings, perhaps.'

'There haven't been any test-drive crashes in the area before,' replied Chesterton. 'I already researched this for the article. Although since cars are being built with faster engines these days it can only be a matter of time before a tragedy occurs. With young men at the wheel, we all know where that leads. Racing each other, ram-raiding, car theft. Some of the culprits are as young as eleven. And with all these films coming out, glamorising violence and even car crashes, what can we expect next?'

Good old alarmism – always good for tabloid sales, national and regional, thought Vic. When you live in a place where nothing much happens, a moral panic always ups the circulation. 'The manufacturers are taking more responsibility these days, though,' Vic countered. 'A lot of them have in-built immobilisers to prevent this kind of crime.'

Chesterton seemed unimpressed by Vic's apparent defence of 'the enemy' and told her so. She got up from her chair and asked Vic to wait for a moment while she got a junior reporter to look up everything the *Gazette* had run on Landor Motors. Vic sat in the small room and sipped nervously at her coffee. It was a stroke of luck she'd not been asked for any ID. As a woman, she found less people mistrusted her intentions.

ID. There was a thought. Getting into the Motor Show the next day without it would be a pain. Within these offices there was enough material to fake something up. She looked around her at the scattered headed paper lying next to the photocopier. She folded a few pages into her bag. Chesterton came back and asked Vic to join them while they looked through the backnumbers file. Her assistant had done a few seconds' cross-referencing on his search engine and had come up with a couple of articles from earlier that year which featured Landor Motors. She would be allowed to buy back copies from the reception. He gave her the date of publication and the print numbers of the relevant editions. Vic told them how grateful she was to them for their help, wished Chesterton every success in her campaign, and told her she would forward a draft copy of the report as soon as it was written.

'You should pay a visit to Bob Waterhouse,' said Maxine. 'He really has the best interests of the community at heart.'

Yeah, sure, thought Vic. So why isn't he putting any of his own money into the campaign? And guess who will be top of the list for some free advertising when his restaurant reopens?

Adrian Boxall had just finished being fed when Vic found his room in Aylesbury General. She introduced herself to the staff nurse as a reporter investigating airbag accidents for a magazine. They told her she could have ten minutes unless the patient found it too distressing, in which case she would have to leave. Boxall was a grim sight, and reminded Vic that there was a point to speed limits after all. She could see that under his bandages he was probably an attractive man, but being regulated like an animal in a zoo had a wearing effect on someone who was used to a privileged independence most people dreamed of. He had the same colouring as Daniel Field and his bright blue eyes looked at her with a blank expression. 'I don't recognise you,' he said sadly.

'Don't worry, Mr Boxall. We don't know each other,' she replied. 'I want to talk to you about airbags. I'm currently writing an article which will attempt to highlight specific failings in their mechanisms. I know how much pain you're in – but I would really appreciate a few moments of your time to answer a couple of questions.'

Boxall nodded. 'You certainly can't be worse company than the police. I'm sure they thought I wasn't telling the truth. They kept asking me if I was using my phone or if my attention was diverted somehow. It's so unfair. And it's so boring in here. I've got nothing but the worry of the work I'm missing and daytime TV to occupy my mind. Believe me, I'm happy to sign my name to any article that says they shouldn't be fitted as standard.'

The exertion of his passionate statement had tweaked some stitching in his leg and his jaw locked for a moment, twisted in a rictus of pain. Then he began to tell his story – from the moment he'd entered the showroom to when the paramedics had lifted him into the ambulance. There was absolutely no doubt in Vic's mind that he was telling the truth about the accident. Poor guy. He was bewildered as to why this thing had happened to him. It was harrowing for her to see someone who was suffering so much pain while she was acutely aware of being there on false pretences. The whines and whinges of Bob Waterhouse and the unctuous bleatings of the holier-than-thou reporter on the Gazette seemed trifling in comparison to this man's plight. She felt angry on his behalf.

It would be so easy to wrap the case up if Boxall had been lying. But the statement he'd given to the police, and the way he told his experience to Vic, was the truth in her estimation; she knew a good actor when she saw one, and Boxall was in too much genuine pain to put on a front. She didn't tell him about Waterhouse's cynical road safety campaign, or the fact that Landor Motors were swanning off to the Motor Show, seemingly without a care for their client. She wanted to give Daniel a good result, save his company money, and earn herself a great commission in the process, but there was the factor of justice overriding the whole business. And that was the bottom line in anybody's book.

SIX

V8 Thrills for Married Suits

Tuesday

It was three o'clock when Vic arrived at the Exhibition Centre in Birmingham the next afternoon. She'd faked a press pass from the headed notepaper she'd snaffled and given to a local printing company whose skills at forging ID with a little help from a flat-bed scanner were unsurpassed in the Midlands area. A few quid in the right places worked wonders and saved so much time. She was now in possession of a smart laminated press card saying FEATURES EDITOR – AYLESBURY & DISTRICT GAZETTE. This, and a dazzling smile, had got her into the Motor Show. Bare-faced cheek and a low-cut top work wonders, she thought, as she blagged her way past the ageing commissionaires on the door.

She smoothed the creases of her pink Paul Smith skirt and checked the arms of her matching jacket for stray hairs before walking into the arena. She was looking her glossy, well-groomed-but-sexy best. Her skirt was short enough to ride up her thighs at a moment's request and her hair was teased into extra volume. She was wearing more make-up than any day she'd worked at the cosmetic fair. More lip gloss, more kohl pencil: more effort. She was even wearing high-heeled shoes. She needed to attract attention.

To get the information she needed, she knew she'd have to pander to male fantasies, manipulate their desires. It was no good coming here in casual clothes and trainers. This was the serious, thrusting world of the motor trade where car companies cashed in on male sexuality and all its neuroses and longings. A world where V8 engines and turbo-charged roadsters throbbing with power compensated for a balding pate or a three-inch dick. She'd driven back to London after visiting Boxall and had packed an overnight bag before jumping back in her car and high-tailing it to Birmingham. She'd left a message on her answerphone to call her mobile number if there was any urgency. The vastness of the place was overwhelming and corporate identity screamed at Vic from every direction. A glossy-looking woman – much like herself – handed her a guide to the exhibition, but only after three men had refused.

Everyone who could afford to exhibit was there. Smaller stands promoted car wax and spark plugs, and tobacco companies featured prominently. It was an eco-friendly person's nightmare. Most car companies had made concessions to the pollution problem by fitting catalytic converters as standard but one look around told her that the gas-guzzling Maseratis, Ferraris and McLaren superships were still the stars of the show. The place pandered to pure indulgence and unashamed decadence and Vic had to admit that she wasn't exempt from a bit of that fantasy herself.

She found a refreshment area nestled in the far corner of the upper level and sat down with her programme to consult the index. Landor Motors – stand 57. It was that easy. The difficult bit would be making contact and not blowing it. If they've been getting unwelcome attention from the local press, she thought, the last thing they want will be a journalist sniffing around. She needed another cover. And she needed to get a look at the stand before launching herself into the mouth of the lion. She took off her press badge and slipped it into her bag. Now she could be anyone. She'd wing it.

Ten minutes later, Vic was closely working her way

through a display which announced itself as COMMERCIAL VEHICLES FOR THE NEXT MILLENNIUM. It boasted some impressive hardware. They had rigged up a Royal Mail van to look like something from *Blade Runner*. The van was white and featured armoured shields and bulbous bullet-proof windows which were tinted a dark purple. It seemed the designers had a pretty pessimistic view of post delivery in the coming decade. From her vantage point, she could see a bunch of middle-aged men gathered on the Landor Motors stand. They were talking and posturing – doing serious 'men's work' which required suits and briefcases.

A banner which read 30 YEARS OF QUALITY formed a canopy over a gleaming row of immaculately preserved 1960s and 70s sports cars which was the defining feature of the stand. A Jaguar XK120 and an Aston Martin DB6 were flanked by three or four equally impressive classics. Compared to the manufacturers' part of the exhibition, the Landor Motors stand was a crowd pleaser with retro value. Vic waited until a visiting party of reps had moved on and then chose her moment. 'I've always wanted to drive one of these,' she said running a finger across the headlight of a crimson Jaguar E-type.

A tall, dark-haired representative of about forty spun round from rearranging a pile of brochures and smiled. She recognised him as Nick Swift from photographs she'd seen in the back numbers of the local paper. 'Set you back about twenty grand for one in that condition,' he replied walking over to her. His jacket was off and Vic noticed that he was wearing cufflinks. This seemingly unimportant factor encouraged her to form a catalogue of value judgements about his taste. He was certainly attractive, even if dress sense was lacking. Everything about him was neat, but it was also very out-dated. His face resembled the standard mug shots that old-fashioned barbers put in their shop windows: square head, square haircut, square jaw. He looked like a throwback to the kind of man they used to advertise cigarettes and Brylcreem in the 1960s. He was good-looking in a very masculine, conservative way, but it seemed that changes in fashion, music and lifestyles had passed him by. He probably looked the image of his father at a similar age. Curious, how men clung to convention. She continued talking. 'Is it for sale?' she asked.

'Why? You got twenty grand spare? If you have, you can take me for a drink.' He laughed.

She smiled wistfully. 'No. I'm only dreaming.'

'That's what I do all the time,' he went on, throwing his hands around in an animated manner. 'Dream about all sorts. Cars, women, winning the lottery.'

Oh God. Not the old lottery chestnut, thought Vic. She looked up at him. He was staring right at her with hungry eyes. She anticipated his next line before he said it, so she blurted out, 'I'm working for a PR company. Doing design. I put together packages for people who want to improve their image; overhaul their look, that sort of thing.' She tried not to laugh, considering how apposite her words were in the present circumstances.

'It's mostly computer-based these days. I'm just beginning to learn my way around web-site design. My side of things is creative rather than business oriented, though. I don't have anything to do with the money side of things.' She affected a slightly vacant look; a look which said, I don't really know about numbers — I like making pretty pictures. 'You still haven't told me if the E-type's for sale,' said Vic, smiling and giving her hair a quick flick.

'None of these are,' said the salesman. 'They're part of the Landor collection. The guvnor has a fleet of classic cars. It's been his hobby since he started the business. We do trade in quality collectors' motors, though. If someone's looking for something special, they can give us a bell and we try to track it down for them. We're known for that side of the business. Don't keep the classic stuff on the forecourt, though. Too high risk. Nowadays it's new stuff. Prestige motors. Anyway, what's your name? I'm Nick, by the way.' He extended an arm and clasped Vic's hand in a determined manner.

'Victoria,' she answered.

'Well, Victoria, you're the nicest person I've spoken to so far today,' said Nick, his eyes predictably roving to her chest as she undid the buttons of her jacket.

She needed to flirt some more. 'It's always so hot at these places,' she went on.

'If I didn't have to stay here, I'd offer to take you for a drink. There's a bar over there. I've got a pass to the VIP lounge.' He pulled it out of his breast pocket in a flurry of pride. 'We wouldn't have to drink at the exhibition bar with the riff-raff.'

God, he's keen, thought Vic. From the effort he was making to impress her, he looked as if he'd be susceptible to flattery. She noticed no wedding band on his finger. Given his penchant for flashy gold jewellery it seemed odd that his fingers were devoid of adornment. 'Maybe later,' she said. 'Or tomorrow. I'm here until Friday. It would be nice to have a friend to meet up with. I don't know anyone else here apart from the company I'm doing design for.'

'I've got a business engagement this evening, Victoria,' he said. 'Tomorrow would be fine for me, though. It's a trade day but I'm sure I can find a little time off.'

Vic walked slowly around the exhibits, bending over slightly to look inside and giving Nick a flash of her thighs. He followed her around the vehicles like an eager puppy as she continued to make small talk about her car-related fantasies. She had him hooked.

From behind a group of interactive display units Alan Landor watched Nick Swift posing and chatting to a very attractive woman. She was dressed to attract attention. Why was he talking to her for so long? Their conversation looked almost intimate. Who was she? And why was she looking around the stand and inside the vehicles? Maybe she was one of Swift's groupies. He'd heard from Peter Bruton how he liked them blonde and well-stacked. Well, she certainly fulfilled those criteria. The thought crossed Alan's mind that she may be from his father's insurance company, snooping around and making enquiries. No, she was too good-looking for that – but she needed checking out.

He watched as she flirted with Swift and he felt sickened by it. How could a beautiful woman like this want to go for a sad bastard like him? He was such a wanker. He didn't have a clue about music or clothes or anything except cars. Swift continued to flaunt himself in front of her, standing with one hand on his hip or running a hand through his hair. He should be looking pissed off after all that had happened last week.

It wasn't fair that the likes of Swift got off with women like her and he had no luck at all. It was about six months since he'd had sex and that fact was hard to come to terms with. Girls had told him he was nice-looking but they always went off with someone else at the end of an evening. Maybe he should take up Peter Bruton's offer to go clubbing a bit more. But he wanted to meet someone who had something going on in her brain. All he got at Bruton's place were eighteen-year-olds whose conversation revolved around hairdos and holidays. He had nothing to say to them. He was pissed off with Bruton, too. He should have off-loaded some cash at Alan's garage the previous day. When he'd phoned to chase him, all he could tell Alan was that he'd sent a wind-up letter to Derek Landor about the crash. He was such a child.

He carried on watching. This woman looked good. He imagined what she would be like in bed and this caused the first stirrings of arousal. She was bright, cute, and looked like she was up for something sexual. She looked fit, too. His desire was beginning to occupy his thoughts and his cock was hardening as he thought about rubbing it between her breasts. How sweet it would be to steal her from under Swift's nose. That would make his day. Blonde and up for it. Exactly what he fancied. He had to find out who she was and where she was working. He intended to get her talking about why she was chatting with Nick Swift. He would use his alias to get the information he needed, though. Couldn't risk her knowing he was connected to Landor Motors.

He had a couple of hours to kill before meeting Laurence. He wanted to get shot of the package that was nestling in his underpants as soon as he could. Laurence had called earlier saying he could probably shift the lot to a guy who regularly moved shed-loads of coke to Arabs. Until then, he'd spend some time chatting up this blonde woman and being Drake Lewis.

Just as Vic and Nick Swift were making arrangements to meet up the next day, a portly man in his early fifties walked on to the stand looking flushed and annoyed. He deposited a briefcase beside the desk and looked at Nick with a sense of urgency in his eyes. Nick looked back at him and signalled that he'd be finished in a second. Vic clocked immediately that this was Derek Landor. It was strange, and quite exciting, to know so much about these people and the events of the past week but for them to have no idea of her agenda. It was almost voyeuristic.

Part of her wondered what would happen if she casually mentioned that she'd visited Adrian Boxall yesterday. Of course there was no way she would do such a thing but the dramatic possibilities appealed to her. 'Well, I can see you're busy,' she said brightly. 'I may come and see you tomorrow.' Nick looked suddenly panicked at her non-committal attitude as Derek Landor walked over.

'Nick, I have to have a word,' he said nervously, 'the Chalfont rep is due in twenty minutes.' Then he looked at Vic, 'I'm sorry to interrupt, my dear.'

'That's all right,' she said, making moves to leave. 'I have to be going anyway.' God, but his voice was posh! Derek Landor sounded like someone pretending to be one of the landed gentry. His accent was laughable. She gave Nick a wave as she turned and walked away, leaving a worried-looking couple of men momentarily distracted from their problems by the sway of her bottom.

She had been looking at a Ferrari 355 for about five minutes, thinking of her next move, when a voice jolted her out of a reverie involving the Italian lakes and a suitcase full of Dolce and Gabbana.

'Sweet, isn't it?' said the voice. 'Yours for eighty thousand.'

This wasn't a car salesman, Vic ascertained in a flash. Dressed in a designer puffa jacket and Hilfiger trousers, he wasn't exactly management material. She'd yet to see a car salesman with an eyebrow piercing. Despite his designer labels, he was the scruffiest creature Victoria had seen that day. I suppose it would be just about possible with someone of that length hair to get a job in this business, she thought, but he'd have to tie it back, wash it every day and invest in some decent shaving equipment. Maybe he was a member of the press.

'You working here?' he asked, his eyes scanning her outfit and immaculate make-up. He seemed to show a lot of confidence for someone so casual.

'PR,' she replied, surprised that she found herself wanting to engage with this young man. He must be about my age, she guessed. His hair was as long as her own, and as blond. Underneath the wispy hair growth he had the face of an angel.

'Very swish,' he replied. 'PR for which firm?' he asked suddenly, catching her off-guard.

'Oh, I'm doing research for a PR company,' she said, nodding her head, hoping he'd change the subject or go away. She might as well stick to the same story with this character. 'I'm doing design work and looking at how companies with a slightly out-dated image can bring themselves into the new millennium and that kind of thing.'

'Are you using mostly PhotoShop or Xara for the design stuff?' he asked casually.

Oh dear. He knew about computers. It had been a stupid move to volunteer too much information. Unless she changed the subject she'd be out of her depth very soon. 'Oh, PhotoShop, mostly. It's amazing what you can do with a flatbed scanner and a bit of imagination.' Vic felt a bit peeved she'd been caught out like that.

She was just about to ask him a couple of questions when he offered her a cigarette. She declined. 'The Marlboro shop is giving them away,' he said. 'I know it's not good for your health but if I didn't smoke I'd probably have some other vice which would get me into trouble.' He smiled and pursed his lips in a sensual pout. There was something unusual and attractive about this creature: he looked as if he might be a male model gone rogue or someone cast to play a part in a film about piracy and lawlessness. 'Are you planning on getting one of these soon,' she asked, pointing to the 355.

'One day, maybe. Then again, by the time I've got eighty grand to spunk on a car, they'd have probably invented voice-control steering and head-up display which told you what colour knickers you had on.'

'So you'll be an old man by then?' she quipped.

'No. I'll be a rich man,' he replied, looking very smug for a second. 'I'm Drake – Drake Lewis. I'm not working here but I'm interested in people who are.'

He stood back a foot or so and didn't let the smile leave his face for a second. He certainly looked pleased about something. Well, it was a good enough way to pass the time. It made a change to talk to someone who didn't focus on her breasts throughout the conversation.

His mobile phone went off. He pulled it from the inside pocket of his voluminous jacket and turned away from her. It gave her a moment to think. What kind of business was this guy into? She was intrigued. She would launch into her 'sweet Victoria' persona, just for a laugh. Her Sloane airhead-cum-upwardly mobile career girl character always worked.

Like most mobile phone calls, it was over very quickly. 'It's quite a hoot being here actually,' she said. 'Some of us get to go to the press parties afterwards although, in Birmingham, I'm not holding out much hope.' She watched his pupils dilate as they made eye contact. 'David, that's my MD, well, he's having a little party on Friday but I'm keeping my antennae primed for rumours of things later on.'

'So you're the party animal?' he asked.

'Not an animal, Drake,' she said in a crisp and eloquent voice. 'More of a party person.' Victoria spotted a piece of tape which had attached itself to her shoe and she raised her leg to brush it away.

'You're quite tall, aren't you?' he said, flicking his long hair across his shoulders. Then he hit her with a direct invitation. 'If you haven't found a party by six, give me a call. I think I know where one's going to be on. Don't worry. It isn't beers and boozy reps. You'll like it. Your kind of thing. Champagne and glitz. I have to go now.'

He handed her a card and sauntered off. She watched him swagger off into the crowd. He was easily traceable with that ridiculous designer coat on. Its plastic reflective logo stood out in a sea of dull suits. Maybe her Sloaney talk had put him off. She didn't really care. She looked at the card and it reminded her of the ones she'd made on one of the machines you find at post offices. Just the basics – name and mobile number – appeared on Drake's card. There was no mention of any line of work. It looked shady, but not any more than Vic's own card.

Back at the Landor Motors stand Derek was suffering a renewed bout of depression. The public relations rep from the Chalfont & Buckingham Building Society had just paid a visit and he was still smarting. 'If only we'd done the deal earlier in the year,' he moaned, waving one of the now-redundant press packs at Nick. 'Telling us they're pulling out on the press day of the show is insult to injury. And the way he said it is what got me.' The labels which read QUALITY, EXCELLENCE, ACHIEVEMENT would not be appearing in the new Landor catalogue after all. 'We stand to lose about fifty thousand pounds' worth of advertising and the chances of finding a new sponsor are slim.'

Nick looked sympathetic but didn't seem to understand how bad things were. 'Surely you can't be that surprised, Derek,' he said. 'Isn't there any way we can nail them to the deal? They signed the contract, after all.'

'The rep says that the contract we signed last week amounts to nothing as they hadn't been told about the crash. I said we couldn't be blamed for a manufacturing fault but their solicitors are adamant they pull out. Apparently their chairman had thought it in bad form that we didn't tell them straight away. It's a goner. There's nothing we can do.'

As Derek had feared, the Friday paper had focused on the accident, which had brought the campaign for safer test-driving and greater speed restrictions to the attention of all the local do-gooders. The knock-on effect had been Chalfont's pulling out of the sponsorship. Suddenly Derek felt like the villain of the town; a criminal proved guilty by the very nature of his business: selling evil machines that hurt people.

'Apparently, they're now looking to sponsor a company "more aware of the needs of the local community".' Derek hadn't expected that kind of statement from the world of business investment. The man had sounded more like a social worker. What needs did the local community have? They lived in a prosperous area in the stockbroker belt, not the inner-city. He felt his integrity as a local businessman had plummeted. 'I feel like packing the whole thing in,' he complained to Nick.

'What we need is an image revamp,' said Swift. 'We don't need sponsorship to survive, Derek. There's enough money in the business to keep us going for years yet and people aren't going to stop buying cars. News in the *Aylesbury Gazette* doesn't stretch that far, you know. It's not national headlines – just a bit of a hiccup, that's all. It'll all blow over. We just have to find creative solutions. I'm having a beer with the lads this evening. I'll have a word; find out if anyone has any bright ideas. They're on our side, Derek,' he said.

Derek then looked up and spotted the last person he wanted to see making a direct line for the stand. Alan. What was he doing here?

'What do you want?' asked Nick, speaking for Derek the second Alan arrived in front of them.

'Thought I'd pop by, that's all,' Alan replied casually. 'What's your problem? I've come to see my father, not you. I've got a free pass for the whole week. Do you mind if we have a couple of minutes? Haven't you got a BMW to lose or something?' He laughed cruelly and Derek could see Nick was fuming.

'I'm going off to find Bob,' said Nick. 'See you later for dinner. We'll talk about things then, all right?' Derek felt a pat on his shoulder and Nick loped off. Now he was left alone with his wayward son when he should be closing the sponsorship deal over a bottle of champagne. It hurt. He didn't want to talk to Alan; he had nothing to say to him.

'I heard about what happened,' said Alan. 'Richard told me.'

Dammit, thought Derek. He'd told Deborah to tell the kids not to speak to anyone about the accident. 'Well it's terribly unfortunate. The driver's suing us for compensation, but I suppose you know about that as well,' he spat.

'No,' said Alan. 'I don't know the ins and outs of what happened. I just thought you could use some moral support.'

Derek was shocked. 'What do you know about morals? I can get all the moral support I need from Deborah,' he said coldly. Despite his current despondency, there was no way he was going to pour out his problems to Alan. He looked at him: a long cold appraisal. God, his son was a scruffy individual. He'd never been anything but trouble and it had been a mistake to let him back into the family again. Moral support, indeed! He was trying to soften him up so he could tap him for money. That rankled Derek and he went on the attack. 'You know, it wouldn't hurt you to have a shave once in a while and put some decent clothes on. You might be able to find some work then.'

'You don't know anything about fashion, do you?' Alan said cockily. 'This jacket cost two hundred and fifty pounds and the trousers are Hilfiger. In case you don't know, that means expensive. Don't tell me what to wear. Who d'you expect me to look like, Nick Swift, in his dodgy Marks and Sparks suits?'

'All I'm saying is that you'd have a better chance finding some work if you did something about your appearance. That tuppeny ha'penny garage of yours is no decent way to earn a living.'

'How do you know?' whined Alan. 'You've only been there once and you took off five minutes later. You're not interested in me. You only care about what your posh friends think.'

'That's not true, Alan,' he said wearily, desperately wanting this conversation to be over. 'I just want you to be able to look after yourself. You're talented. You could use your skills to make something of your life. Put the past behind you.'

'The past is what shapes the future, in case you've forgotten. I know you're ashamed of me but that's your problem. I'm still your son. Just because I don't put on all the airs and graces like Veronica does. If only you could look further than your own gut you would see she's a scheming little bitch. It makes me sick to see the way she sucks up to Deborah. And Deborah never had any time for me, did she? Not when I was a kid, not last year either, when I came back from Germany, skint.'

'That's not true, Alan. You're getting confused again. Deborah bent over backwards to make you welcome and you threw her hospitality back in her face.'

'Don't patronise me. Why should I be made to feel grateful for being allowed back into my own home?'

His voice was raised now and people were pausing, pretending to look at the cars, but Derek knew it was to overhear the argument. He felt even more uncomfortable. He didn't want a family therapy session here – not that they'd ever had such a thing. He had to retain some dignity. He thought he spotted an old business colleague and made moves to leave the stand. There was no way Derek was going to allow Alan to continue haranguing him in front of his peers. It had been a stupid move to criticise his appearance but he just couldn't help it. Alan had been right when he said Derek was ashamed of him. Every time he looked on that unkempt blond hair and those un-ironed jeans he felt appalled that he was his father. The pierced eyebrow had been the last straw.

'I came to say hello and all you can do is have a go at me,' said Alan. 'Well, that's the last time I bother to care what happens to you. You want to get personal? All right, then. I think you're fat and lazy and you're out of touch with what's going on in the world. You and that thick bastard of a salesman. I'll make something of myself without your help. I tell you something, though. I wouldn't want to be you, not for all your money and luxuries, 'cos you're sad.'

'Don't bother me again, Alan,' said Derek. 'I've got business to attend to and you're wasting my time.'

'Nothing's changed then,' muttered Alan. 'Same as it ever was. I've always wasted your time, haven't I? And Mum wasted your time, too, didn't she? How inconvenient it was of her to die like that, making you miss your nomination at the Institute of Directors.'

'Alan, don't you dare use Sally to score cheap points in an argument,' snapped Derek, feeling genuine hatred for his son. Before Derek could continue, Alan had worked himself up into such a froth that he stalked off with a petulant shake of his long hair. Derek watched him in the distance, trying to light a cigarette and then throwing the lighter to the ground in anger when it failed to strike. Derek wouldn't say that he felt actually scared in Alan's company but there was no doubt the boy was unpredictable.

He wasn't physically threatening – he was only about five feet six inches – but the fury he saw in those eyes was unnerving. He'd launch into a rage at the slightest criticism. It was impossible for the lad to hold a reasoned debate. Things would always turn into a full-scale row with Alan. Derek made a mental note to have a word with Gayle; there must be no way that she writes Alan back into her will. He would do everything to persuade her what a bad idea that would be. Twenty-five thousand pounds in his hands would be money wasted. A disaster. He'd probably spend it all on stupid designer clothes and hi-fi equipment. The boy would never use it wisely, that was a foregone conclusion.

He hoped he would stay away for the rest of the show. The thought of him turning up at the stand to badger him for the rest of the week filled him with gloom. Why couldn't he have stayed in Germany working in that car factory? Alan was a loose cannon and Derek didn't like things he couldn't control or feel sure of. In a week of unforeseen catastrophe, business failure and unending form-filling, Alan was the poisonous icing on a very unpalatable cake.

'So, Miss Donovan, if you want to arrive first thing tomorrow then we can run through things once more to check you've got the hang of the equipment and it'll be up to you to work to a commission basis,' said Jeff Halman, staring at Vic's bosom.

'That's fine by me, Mister Halman,' said Vic. Having spent the afternoon looking at cars she couldn't afford, Vic had found her way to TurboInteractive – a computer games company whose stand was currently being occupied by young media types reliving their childhood. Except in their childhood, computer games had been less exciting. PacMan and Space Invaders had come a long way.

'I'm glad we got talking,' said Jeff. 'I was panicking a bit when I found out that local schools are planning to bring parties of teenage boys to the Motor Show. We hadn't planned the staff numbers for that. It's great you're available for work.'

'I'm glad you were able to take me on at short notice,' she said. 'I work freelance all the time anyway so there'll be no problem with tax and National Insurance. I've always wanted to work at the Motor Show although I didn't expect it would be with car racing games.'

'You don't have to worry about scoring high points, Victoria. I want you here to attract the lads, to be honest. I'm not being funny or anything but Isobel,' he gestured to a shy-looking young woman in a floral dress, 'well, she's not what we call a bubbly personality. You're exactly the kind of assistant we're looking for. All you have to do is show them how to work the game and if any of the kids are with their parents, get their names and addresses. No, on second thoughts, get their names and addresses even if they're not with their parents. We're going into the direct mailing business next year and we're trying to build our database all the time. So, remember, smiles and names and addresses equal sales.'

Excellent, thought Vic. It's a simple job and I've got a legitimate entry to the show for the entire week. All I have to do is look the part and play a few games. I may even earn some more cash while I'm here. Vic checked her watch. It was nearly six and the press parties were beginning to get underway. The entire hall was buzzing with noise. Every stand seemed to have some kind of a gimmick or competitions and teasers to interest the media. Eyes were sparkling and champagne was being drunk by the magnum by people with deep tans and platinum credit cards who looked like they'd just flown in from Monte Carlo. She'd been invited by Jeff Halman to attend their party but hanging out with a group of computer designers having a geek-fest didn't really appeal to her. It was a shame that Nick was occupied elsewhere. She could go back to her hotel room or give herself an aching jaw by grinning at her new employers. There was another option, though, and Vic retrieved the card Drake Lewis had given her. He said to call about six. Well, she had nothing to lose by surprising him. She pulled out her mobile.

'Yeah,' crackled the answer.

'It's Victoria. We met earlier. Things are a bit slow where I am. I wondered if you were having better fun.'

'I'm working on it.'

'Where are you now?' she asked.

'Over on the Land Rover stand, I'm looking at a beautiful Range Rover Discovery, man.'

Vic hadn't been called 'man' before. 'Well, d'you want to meet up? I'm just finishing off business here with a computer company. They've been talking to me about developing their mail order package.'

'Great,' he drawled with no enthusiasm whatever. 'Meet me outside the Marlboro shop in ten minutes, yeah.'

'That's fine. See you, then.'

Vic put her phone back in her handbag and took stock of the situation. There was nothing more she could do today to prise information out of anyone at Landor Motors. Their showroom was closed now and the stand would be deserted. The loss adjuster was handling the assessment; if she didn't get anything out of their salesman tomorrow, she could always find out what she wanted from Peter Bruton. She consulted her programme to find the whereabouts of the Marlboro stand then made her way through the crowd. The ground was littered with discarded leaflets and the detritus from the fast food stands, and overhead monitors blasted out sales speak and loop tapes of high production car advertisements.

Ten minutes later she found herself making small talk with Drake. His attention seemed directed elsewhere and he spent more time looking over her head than at her. He led her through the crowd to the VIP lounge where the press party was getting underway. Vic was surprised that he walked past the doorman with nothing more than the raise of his eyebrows and a curt, 'all right?' The doorman wasn't an elderly commissionaire like those at the main entrance. This guy looked like he'd be more at home as a bouncer at a nightclub. He was huge and dressed entirely in black. A logo saying Top Deck Security ran across his bomber jacket. Vic felt she would have had trouble trying to wing it with her fake ID against him.

Once inside, Drake seemed to relax a little and procured drinks for them both. There was nowhere to sit but they found a corner away from the melee of press photographers and minor celebrities. Most people were decked out for a party and Drake seemed curiously unconcerned that his clothes were unsuitable for the occasion. He looked as if he couldn't care less what people thought of him. He was not the kind of date Vic would usually choose but he was very cute: kind of like the surfer boys she'd seen at Newquay a couple of years back when she'd gone on holiday with Kevin and his family. It had irked her then that she'd never got off with one. She liked that look: fit, long-haired, suntanned and rebellious with it. Drake wasn't suntanned but he had a lively look about him.

'What are you doing here?' she asked.

'That's the second time someone's asked me that today,' he said, smiling and showing her his amber eyes. 'I'm earning money, like most of us have to. See that bloke on the door?' Vic nodded. 'Well he's helping me out with a few contacts.'

'Sounds intriguing,' she said, careful to retain her well-spoken voice. 'Would they be contacts in the motor industry?' she asked as innocently as she could.

'Not exactly. It's about installing video walls and visual display stuff at parties.'

A bouncer? Involved in visuals? Sounded highly unlikely. Drake Lewis was here on dodgy business. She wasn't sure what it was yet but she had an inkling it was illegal. He finished four glasses of champagne to her one and then moved on to strong bottled lager. They chatted about school and cars. She told him the same yarn she'd spun to Daniel Field: boarding school in Surrey; father in the diplomatic service; loved horses and parties.

Drake didn't want to talk about his family. They were too boring, he said. He went on about music – techno and drum and bass – and seemed appalled when Vic told him she liked jazz and Paul Weller. He told her that he mixed his own tunes for fun and had a recording facility rigged up in his bedroom. Then he talked in depth about digital imaging and rendering rave graphics cut to ambient techno for parties and suchlike. Even when she said she knew nothing about it, he carried on. She was getting a little bored hearing about video monitors and was wondering where the evening was leading. Drake was good-looking but crashingly dull!

She began looking around the room at the other guests as Drake prattled on. It seemed that everyone was having a better time than she was. Forty something executives were laughing politely, trophy wives and girlfriends hanging on their arms. Young women like herself were being plied with refills of champagne and keen-eyed hacks were milling around with Dictaphones and notebooks. It was phoney, but the atmosphere was brisk and friendly. Then Vic heard herself being asked a very personal question. At first she thought she'd misheard and instinctively said, 'What?' rather vaguely. There it was again:

'When did you last have sex?'

She turned to see Drake Lewis staring her right in the eyes. His gaze bore through her in a way that was different from most men's lecherous advances. He was half-smiling and his lips were pursed into a kissable pout. It was strange, but he seemed to have the body language of a woman; there was little about him, except maybe his use of swear words, that one could say was obviously masculine. He was leaning forward to get closer to her and that smouldering look was reaching into the core of her psyche.

She felt something dart through her system like the aftershocks of intercourse. Her long-slumbering sexuality was beginning to wake up. She found herself moistening her lips with her champagne-coated tongue. 'I'm not answering that,' she said, then watched his face relax into disappointment before adding: 'that's for me to know and for you to find out.' She ran a hand down his arm, enjoying watching Drake's face as he looked longingly at her. She headed for the bathroom feeling slightly dizzy.

Alan seized his chance to make contact with Laurence. He lit a Marlboro Light and sauntered over to him. 'What's up?' he asked.

'How many Gs you holding, man, 'cos this lot are hoovering it. You should hear the sniffing that's going on in the toilets.'

'Got the half ounce on me.'

'My man over there wants a little taster before he pays out,' said Laurence, pointing at a smooth-looking white guy with a moustache and Mediterranean tan.

Christ, he looked a suave bastard. Probably never been stopped by the Old Bill in his life, thought Alan. He looked like he could sweet-talk his way out of anything. 'I've got a little wrap here,' he said, passing the folded paper parcel to Laurence. Alan spotted Victoria coming out from the loo and heading to the bar. 'Okay, Laz, see you in a minute.' He fought his way past the trendy press types to get to the bar at the same time.

'We've lost our corner now,' she said, grabbing two free bottles of lager from the counter. She turned around and leant on the bar, flashing a seductive glance at him. Alan felt happy. This was perfect: he'd shift the coke through Laurence then wait a bit for his money and take Victoria to the guest house where he'd already booked a room. Or maybe she would invite him back to her hotel. That would be a result. He could use a little luxury in his life. All he had to do was hold on to her, keep her out of the reach of the smooth-looking bastards.

He got the nod from Laurence. He told Victoria it was his turn to go to the loo. He entered a cubicle. The day will come when they start installing security cameras in toilets, he thought, given the amount of covert drug-related activity that went on in them. He retrieved the warm cellophane bag from under his testicles and held it up to the light and shook it gently. The bag had been heat-sealed with plastic. There were a few uncrushed rocks in there; that always went down well. Didn't want it to look too powdery, like he'd boshed it up too much. It wouldn't be as pokey as the stuff in the test wrap but once the guy had nosed his way through that, he'd never notice the difference.

He cut himself a line from another wrap of the original gear. Out with the sawn-off soft-drink straw and up the hooter. Nice. He wondered if Victoria indulged, being the Sloaney type. He didn't care. Probably wouldn't do any good letting her know his business. He wanted to shag her, not use her as a dealer. He flushed the loo and exited the cubicle.

Back in the party things were getting lively. Music was playing and camera flashes were going off. He found Laurence and pressed the bag into his hand.

'I'm gonna be wanting to shift this fast, man,' said his friend. 'I'll come back to you when I get the cash, yeah?'

'You'd better,' said Alan, looking over at Victoria. She was talking to a bearded bloke Alan didn't like the look of. 'Hey, Laz. I'm over with that blonde girl. If you can't spot me, just look for her. I ain't letting her out my sight, man. She's mine for the night.'

'Good luck, star,' laughed Laurence, showing his gold teeth.

'This is Jeff Halman,' said Victoria. 'I'm working for him.'

'That's nice,' said Alan. The guy looked like a right wanker: not only did he have a beard, he was wearing a novelty tie with cartoon characters on it. No excuse for that unless you're entertaining at a kids' party. 'What's your line? Pushing V8 thrills to married suits?'

'Sorry?' said Halman.

'You trading used motors or selling car wax?'

Victoria cut in, 'He's having a joke, Jeff. Drake's into multimedia installation, isn't that right?'

Alan felt a finger digging into his ribs. Against his temptation to be smart he swallowed his wisecracks. 'Yeah, multimedia,' he drawled, taking a swig of beer.

'Vic's into a bit of that, aren't you, love?' said Jeff. She looked embarrassed. 'We're going to have a great time working together,' the beard went on. 'This is a great party!'

Alan gave him a psychotic stare. It never failed to get rid

of bores and wanky-looking blokes who were trying to chat up the woman he had his eye on.

'Oh, look!' exclaimed Jeff. 'I think Jeremy Clarkson's just arrived. I'm determined to get TurboInteractive on a *Top Gear* feature, excuse me.' And off he went meandering through the party towards a tight gathering which was forming near the entrance.

'You should have given him your card,' said Victoria.

Alan ignored her advice. 'Can I call you Vicky? Victoria's such a mouthful,' he said, running a hand through his blond locks and moving closer to her. It was getting crowded and Alan was feeling horny. The coke had kicked in and he wanted some sex action. 'Where did you say your hotel was?' he asked, "cos I think we should go in a minute and I know you'd like me to come with you. You're right up for it, aren't you?' His cock was hard and he wanted to talk dirty to her. His inhibitions were melting. He usually felt uptight but now his nerves felt positively electric. He was truly turned on.

'At the Metropole,' she replied. 'I was lucky to get the last room. Someone had cancelled and I –'

Alan grabbed her hair and placed his lips on hers while his hand sneaked around her waist. She felt good and her perfume smelt fresh and lemony. He wanted her badly. So badly that he would be prepared to take her outside and fuck her right now if he didn't have to wait for his money. He pulled back from her and watched her lick her lips from their kiss. She'd entwined her legs around his. He desperately wanted to run his hand up her skirt, feel the silk of her knickers, dive right in there and feel her moisture. He was dying to ask her what she was talking to Nick Swift about but he couldn't find a way around explaining why he was interested.

He felt a tap on his shoulder. It was Laurence. 'A word, man,' he whispered. Alan made his excuses to Vic and walked over to the door with Laurence.

'He won't pay more than a grand for it,' said Laurence.

Alan's face fell. 'That works out at only ten quid more than I had to pay for it. I thought we'd agreed one one two five?'

'Yeah, but it's well boshed up, isn't it? And you can't expect me to be doing favours like this without a cut for myself. We agreed I'd get a ton for sorting it, right?' Alan nodded. 'Well I'm not going to stand and take a verbal from people like him 'cos he thinks it's sub-standard gear. D'you cut this up when you were stoned, or what?'

Alan did some mental calculations. A grand. When he took out a hundred to bung Laurence, he would be left with nine hundred quid: the equivalent retail value of the pills he'd exchanged for it. He was no better off, really. The other three grammes he'd taken out for testers and personal use were write-offs.

'You better take it and go,' said Laurence, passing him a roll of notes. 'Bad luck for you the man's got a keen nose.'

Alan looked to where he'd been standing with Vic. She wasn't there. He panicked and could feel an attack of rage coming on. The mixture of drink and class A drugs in his system suddenly didn't feel as good as when he'd been snogging Vicky. Now she was gone and he was on his own in a sea of wankers. Fuck it! he thought. The anger began to course around his system. He felt too hot in his thick jacket and the laughing faces of the jet-set party crowd made him want to puke.

'Did that hurt, that eyebrow piercing?' said a voice to his left.

'Fuck off,' he spat, catching a glimpse of a straight-looking girl with a poodle perm and pastel clothes. Her appearance was displeasing and he was in no mood for small-talk about his own.

'Apologise now. How dare you speak to my girlfriend like that,' said a guy who seemed to appear from nowhere. He was big and angry – looked like a rugby-playing type. 'What's the matter with you?' barked the brute.

'I'm out of me head,' said Alan, draining the last of the beer. 'And if you don't fuck off, both of you, I'm going to throw up over that ugly cow.' He started giggling. His mirth was short-lived, however, as he felt himself falling backwards over a table full of drinks. He heard the yelps of a couple of media types as he hit the deck. Luckily, his thick jacket prevented him from being cut by the flying glass. The metallic taste of his own blood welled up in his mouth. With sickening realisation, he felt that the punch had dislodged one of his teeth. He looked up to see Laurence extending a muscle-bound arm.

He was dragged to his feet, unsure of whether or not he was able to put one foot in front of the other. 'I'm gonna have to throw you out, man,' said Laurence in a low monotone.

'I didn't do anything,' Alan protested pathetically.

'You've done enough. By the way . . . that roll I gave you. I already took me hundred.'

Victoria had been queuing ages for the loo. Girls kept going in to the cubicles in twos and threes, taking longer than usual and sniffing a lot. Coke. She knew it. And she'd bet a month's wages that Drake Lewis was behind it. It didn't stop her fancying him, though. She hadn't had any close contact with people on cocaine – at least, not that she'd known about – and it would be interesting to find out what effect it had.

She returned to the party and looked around but there was no sign of Drake. She spotted the doorman and was about to ask him where his friend had gone when Jeff Halman grabbed her by the arm. 'There you are,' he said. 'Come and have a dance, Victoria. You just missed that friend of yours being helped out. Some guy punched him. I don't know what happened. Still, not to worry. We're here to enjoy ourselves aren't we?'

'Yeah, that's right,' said Vic, noticing his horrible tie. She felt a distinct pang of sympathy for Drake. She'd call him sometime. They had some unfinished business.

SEVEN
Two Boiled Heads and a Bad Idea

Wednesday

Nick Swift awoke with a boiled head. He'd been drinking for twenty-five years of his forty-four, and the hangovers had got worse since his early thirties, but he'd never learnt to spot when enough was enough. And a night out with Bobby Eames and the boys always did terrible things to his liver. He recalled the time they'd left him asleep in a hotel lobby after a notoriously heavy session with one shoe on and the other full of lager on top of the cistern in one of the men's cubicles. Buggers. He chuckled to himself. This brought on a fit of coughing which could only be remedied by a Benson and Hedges. He fumbled across the objects on the bedside table and found his cigarettes and lighter. He lit up and immediately noticed the no smoking warning stuck to hotel room door. Bastards. They'd probably have alarms going off if he didn't put it out immediately – and that would really be torture to his sensitive head.

He stubbed the cigarette out and attempted to stand up. Wobbly, as expected. He walked over to the window and pulled the curtain aside. It was pissing down but the light was still strong enough to cause his face to grimace in pain as if his brain was undergoing acupuncture. If he couldn't have a fag, he'd have a Solpadeine: best invention of the past five years. It was 8.00 a.m. He shuffled to the bathroom and set about his morning ablutions.

He guzzled the bitter fizzing liquid which would aid his recovery. A shave and a shower and he'd be perky within the half hour. Many people disliked spending extended periods of time in hotels but Nick was quite content at the prospect. He liked the order of hotel rooms – good ones, that is. He knew that he would come back from the day's graft and his bed would be made and clean towels in descending order of size would be piled on the bathroom shelf.

He'd just plastered his chin with shaving foam when a knock came at the door. Great. Room service with his breakfast. No. Derek Landor with a right gob on him. 'Good morning, Derek,' he said, trying to sound cheerful to see him but, in fact, dreading what he had to say. These days, Derek brought only bad news. He seemed oblivious to the undressed and half-shaven condition of his salesman and walked into his room without being asked. He sunk himself into the dressing room chair and stared into space. 'I – I just can't face another day,' he said in a small, broken voice.

'Look, Derek, I'll be with you in a tick, OK? Do you want to perhaps wait until after breakfast for this?' he asked, hoping his boss would take the hint. No. It didn't look like Derek was going to budge. 'Give me ten minutes. I haven't had a wash yet.'

'Oh, sorry, Nick,' said Derek, sounding vacant. 'Of course you must wash. I'm intruding.' The shaving foam was beginning to slide off Nick's face and this felt distinctly uncomfortable. There was another knock at the door. This time it was room service. Nick pointed to where he wanted the tray – as far from Derek as was polite – and hurried back into the bathroom. When he came out Derek had gone. He was moving about like a ghost these days.

Whatever happened, there was no way he was going to cancel his drinks date with Victoria that evening. He hoped she was going to come and see him today. He'd make sure he was nicely turned-out. It was hot under the lights at the show. He'd wear his favourite blue short-sleeved shirt and his chinos. That would be cooler than a tailored suit. He'd brought his old rugby club blazer and tie with him. He'd just had the blazer dry-cleaned and it looked good, he thought. Not a mark on it, even though it was getting a bit shiny. It was seven years since he'd picked up a rugby ball but she wasn't to know that. Women liked to know you were looking after yourself, keeping fit. He spread the clothes out on his bed and braced himself to face Derek.

Vic stretched her arms above her and sat up. Room service had brought her a continental breakfast. She'd slept well. She'd been tired after wearing high shoes all day yesterday and then dancing with various members of the press. Now she had to go to work. Even though the job was entirely phoney, she was looking forward to it. It would give her something to do before connecting with Nick Swift. It was just after eight. An hour to get to the show; this time she'd give her name at the door and a standholder's pass would be waiting for her.

This was all so much more exciting than going back to temping. She hadn't really known what she was going to do after finishing the cosmetic fair. This was working out quite nicely. The hotel was being paid for by Field & Gaitskill and the money she was expecting to earn with TurboInteractive would be a bonus. She was glad not to have to check out of the hotel. She must call Daniel today so they could give each other an update on how things were progressing. Adrian Boxall's condition would be interesting to follow.

Before showering, she brought her breakfast to bed with her and savoured the indulgence of eating warm croissants while watching breakfast TV. If one of her friends stayed over on the sofa Vic would always have them make her breakfast in bed. It was a fair swap, she thought. The kitchen was adjacent to her living room so it was easy for her guests to pay that small price. Shame that it was never a considerate lover bringing her tea and toast with fresh flowers adorning the tray, but that would again happen some day. Marcus had done stuff like that all the time but he always seemed to be trying too hard. By the end of their relationship she'd felt obliged to be grateful rather than being genuinely delighted about the things he did for her. She sometimes felt like calling him, letting him know her new address, but it seemed pointless. He was married now, and she'd heard he was a father.

This past couple of years she was beginning to realise that you couldn't keep in touch with everyone you'd been close to. From all her friends at school she barely knew two or three now and they – like nearly the rest of her class at senior school – had stayed in Walthamstow, content with going down the market on Saturday and then out to Stratford or Redbridge in the evening.

She'd left them all behind. It felt good to have escaped, she thought, as she sipped her English Breakfast tea and checked the teletext news. She was enjoying the seclusion of her hotel room. She was glad she hadn't accompanied Drake Lewis to God knows where. She'd have felt terrible the next morning. It could have turned disastrous. He might have turned nasty or done something odd. Who was to know how much coke he'd snorted? She bet he had a bad head this morning. She wondered if he'd be at the Motor Show today.

It was eight-fifteen. Time to shower and give herself the full make-up and hair treatment and select something showy yet comfortable. It was trade day today and she wanted to be prepared for all those lecherous sales reps. It was essential to make sure that she wasn't wearing something too low-cut, high-cut or hot. Her summer-weight cream business suit would do it. With a cropped black lace top underneath and black Chelsea boots for standing around in all day, Jeff Halman could stuff it if he didn't like the way she looked. She'd take along a pair of high-heels for later. The charming of Nick Swift had to be put into operation.

Nick was in Derek's room, helping his boss claw back his grip on reality. Derek Landor was a pathetic sight. He was hunched in a chair with his hands between his knees. His eyes were slightly glazed and he hadn't shaved yet.

'Nick, I've realised something,' he mumbled softly. 'The time that airbag went off was when I should have been driving the car. I should have had the car for the whole day, remember?'

Nick paced around Derek's sumptuous suite. The bloke had a point but it wouldn't do any good to feed his paranoia. Surely this was coincidence?

'When we sacked Peter Bruton he said I would be dead soon,' he went on. 'I think he must be behind what happened. Do you think I should call the police?'

Nick felt stumped. How could a thick bastard like Bruton plan anything like Boxall's crash? He didn't understand anything more sophisticated than using his fists. He hadn't been near the car. He hadn't been seen for months. That threat had come eighteen months ago, when he'd been given the sack.

There was no way Nick wanted to stir up a hornet's nest of trouble by having the police brought in. He was only too aware that Bruton knew things about him that could cost him his job and give him a criminal record. There was one very big secret that he could blow the lid off any time he wanted. It had been nerve-racking enough to sit through the BMW trial. It was like being shut in a room with a time bomb, not knowing whether anyone was going to set it off. He'd caught sight of Bruton's steely gaze in the court room and, as agreed, had denied that Bruton was involved. He was ashamed to admit that he had been too scared to do otherwise. The five grand he earnt from it had long since gone paying maintenance to Mandy.

God, how Nick wished he'd never got involved. Who would have thought Bruton would have turned up again – like the proverbial bad penny – to dog his relatively easy life. Nick was desperate for a fag. He must try to calm Derek down – take his mind away from Bruton.

'Last night I had a terrible dream that I'd been injected with a deadly virus and Peter Bruton was responsible. My flesh was rotting before my eyes! This morning I felt gripped by fear when I realised that what happened to Boxall could have – maybe should have – happened to me. I'm sorry I barged in on you the way I did. I feel scared. I feel like everything is conspiring against me.'

'Peter Bruton is history, Derek,' said Nick, hoping his words were true. 'He's too thick to organise anything other than his own breakfast. Get a grip,' he said, as gently as he could. 'You can rise above it. Something must have been wrong with that car. Maybe Boxall set it off somehow. There is no earthly way that Bruton could be anything to do with it.'

'I suppose you're right, Nick,' Derek said, seeming to wake up a little. 'It's stupid. I just had a bad dream, that's all. I suppose I should feel relieved that it wasn't me in the car rather than thinking it should have been me, eh? In any case, I think we've seen enough of the police for one week.'

Nick felt a weight lift from his shoulders. 'That's the ticket, Derek. Don't let the buggers get you down.'

Derek's chubby face seemed to brighten up a little. 'The BMW finance manager is due to meet us at eleven o' clock but I can't face any meetings today. I'm not sleeping well, as you know, and I could do with going back to bed,' he said. 'You don't mind, do you? I think I could sleep now if I laid down.'

Swift stopped short. Back to bed? Christ, the man was a lily-livered creature. Nick was beginning to realise that keeping the business ticking over was falling more heavily on his shoulders with each passing day. 'No Derek, I don't mind. You get some rest and sort yourself out. I'll hold the fort.' Anything for a quiet life. Nick knew there was no problem to meeting the BMW guy: it was a social call more than anything. If Derek couldn't face someone with whom they had a good relationship, how was he going to handle Boxall's solicitor?

Nick's headache had not completely gone away. Landor's hunch about the crash being meant for him had a sickening ring of truth to it. Who was after him? And how the fuck could they have organised such a thing as what happened to Adrian Boxall? It certainly would give him worrying food for thought for the rest of the day.

Alan first knew he was still alive when the cleaner charged into the room at 12 noon. The woman looked at his swollen face and, horrified, apologised profusely and closed the door behind her as she made a swift exit. Cleaning staff must have been faced with worse than this, he thought, as the residue of cocaine-fuelled logic cut into his thoughts. The radiator had been on all night and his brain felt like it had been steamed. He lifted his head over the covers and looked around the room. His clothes were strewn everywhere. His trousers were concertinaed in a rumpled shape, just as he'd left them, with his boxer shorts forming a rude lining as they remained sculpted in a collapsed form. At least he'd pulled the curtains.

He couldn't remember getting back to the guest house. He must have fallen into a cab. The house was on the outskirts of the city and run by a partially deaf Irish woman. He was amazed that he'd found the place. Then he remembered the name of the guest house was on the key. That's how he'd got home: he'd waved the key at the cab driver.

He stared at his trousers then remembered. The money! He dived out of bed too fast and, as he bent down to reach for his trousers, his head, and the gap which had once held his front tooth, throbbed keenly. His head possibly had the edge in the 'which hurts more?' competition and was spinning, whereas the bloody gap at the front of his mouth was numb and could probably be cleaned up with mouth-wash, saliva and a cotton bud. At least the arsehole who'd punched him hadn't got his nose. Could have put him right out of business.

He pulled the trousers towards him and rooted in the right-hand pocket. Nothing. Left-hand pocket. Still nothing. Back pockets, boxer shorts, socks (in desperation), all empty. Now he felt sick to his sphincter.

He got out of the bed, actually whimpering. His last hope lay over the dressing table chair. Oh please, God. Please let the roll be in there.

He ran his hand hurriedly through his hair and stood naked and shaking in front of the jacket as if a giant spider lurked under it. The apprehension, the nervous tension, was the worst sensation he'd felt so far that week. A dribble of moisture seeped from his penis and ran down his leg. He seized the voluminous article and shook it. Nothing fell out. Then he put it on. It felt cold and soft on his naked skin – like a sleeping bag. His mobile phone felt hard in the inside pocket. Maybe, just maybe, the cash was in there with it. No luck. One last place. He took a sharp breath and plunged both hands in the pockets then crumpled to the floor.

Either a Birmingham cab driver or one of the hotel staff was nine hundred pounds better off this morning. Reality was hideous. Sickening. After all the effort he'd made, why had fate put the finger on him in this way? No one would hand in a roll of money. It wasn't even in a wallet. The cruelty. Now everything throbbed. He collapsed back on to the bed and stared at the wall. The sugary pink wallpaper induced a bilious attack.

Wednesday afternoon

At TurboInteractive, Vic was improving her score with each game of Road Racer 2000 she played. By the end of the week, I'm going to be addicted to this, she thought. She wondered if she would be able to take one of the games home with her; it would be compensation for having to put up with Jeff Halman. He hadn't left her alone all day. Every time she tried to work on her own initiative he'd jump in and try to take over, worried that she was not saying the right thing or that she wasn't demonstrating a particular feature of the programme. And each time he interrupted her, he had the irritating habit of patting her shoulder and getting far too close for comfort. He talked to Vic as if she was a child, which made her fume with frustration.

There had been precious little for her to do today except persuade men in suits that playing Road Racer was the most fun you could have with your clothes on. A number of laddish car salesmen had noisily enjoyed competing against each other after a liquid lunch and she'd had to tolerate a few predictably lewd remarks about the way she handled the joystick. It was so crass it made her giggle. She hadn't got that sort of comment when demonstrating the miracle lip-pen.

There had been no sign of Drake but she'd found time to visit Nick Swift to firm up their meeting for tonight. He'd looked so chuffed when she'd turned up. They'd agreed to meet at his stand at seven o' clock which was only an hour away. An hour to plan how to approach a dinner date with someone who may or may not know what had been going on behind the scenes of Landor Motors for the past year.

She knew he was interested in her physically and she responded to that desire. Unlike Jeff's advances, which Vic felt were creepy, Nick Swift's attentions seemed to tap into some deep-rooted sexual fantasy she had about older men and which surfaced occasionally. It was something she'd tried to suppress, not understanding why she found the idea of being taken to bed by someone about twenty years older than her arousing. As the minutes ticked by, she realised she was actually looking forward to meeting Nick. The fact that she was intent on seducing him with a reason to gain information made the excitement even more potent. She felt like a spy. It was thrilling.

Alan was back in London and feeling ill. He'd gone into the garage but had barely done a thing all afternoon. Changing the oil on someone's van was the most challenging thing he could face. He'd rung Laurence and asked him if he'd seen any evidence of his money; anyone looking happier than they should be. He hadn't, which affirmed to Alan that the cab driver must have had it. Laurence had tried to make a joke about the fight but Alan felt insulted and had cut the call short. At 5 p.m. Peter Bruton called, sounding irritatingly cheerful. 'I've got someone you should meet,' he said. 'It's not what you're thinking but it could be worth your while getting out here to meet him.'

'I'm done in, to tell you the truth, Peter. Had a bit of bother last night. I'm not in a fit state to meet anyone,' said Alan.

'He doesn't care if you're not looking your usually beautiful self, Alan. All I'm saying is this could help sort you out a bit, financially like. I can't say more than that. It's only an hour's drive to Aylesbury at most. You'll kick yourself if you don't meet this bloke. I've primed him already. He'll go elsewhere if you don't show.'

Alan wished Bruton would get to the point but he was always cagey on the phone. Alan thought it was because he got a kick out of sounding shifty. He bet there was someone with him, listening to him showing off and sounding like the big man he wasn't. The annoying fact was that Bruton had made him curious. He wanted to get an early night but the offer of something financially beneficial was too tempting. And why hadn't Bruton volunteered himself for whatever it was? It was no good. He had to find out more. He told him he'd be there about nine. Before leaving the garage he called Vic's number. Her mobile was taking messages. He left one asking her to call him. There was a slim chance she'd want to see him again. In his experience, he found that women liked being chased.

Three hours later Alan was sitting with Bruton nursing a Guinness in the public bar of one of Aylesbury less salubrious drinking holes. Given the choice, he'd have slept through the rest of the day. Fatneck had teased him loudly about his swollen face and Alan was close to being at the end of his tether with him. Whatever this guy wanted, it had better be worth it, thought Alan. If this was another load of hot air designed to make Peter look like the big man, he'd be furious. Alan didn't want any unnecessary strife. They were due to meet the mystery man at half nine in the club.

'Boden's serious,' said Bruton. 'Andrew and Gary know him from when they were kids. Cut his teeth in Deptford, running errands for the Bradshaw mob. Don't mention anything to do with drugs, though. He's more your old-school hard man is Neil Boden; thinks drugs are dirty money. He's not averse to sticking a sawn-off in the stomach of a Securicor bloke but he wouldn't consider doing business with you if he thought you were shifting Class A.' Alan listened carefully.

'The eyebrow number might cause a stir, actually,' said Peter. 'So you just watch you don't lose that famous temper of yours. Still, the fact you can get hold of the kind of motor he wants should swing things your way.'

'I won't mention a word about the gear. And Boden will have to take me as he finds me. Just you make sure you call me Drake at all times, OK? I don't want anyone up this way using my real name.'

'Of course not,' said Bruton, looking unconvincing.

They drained their pints and left in their respective cars. Bruton's speakers kicked in as soon as he turned the ignition. Alan preferred a more modest profile and followed behind in his nondescript-looking Ford van. He was sure that Bruton would get pulled one day. Being white was probably the only reason that stopped him getting hassle from the cops. Laurence was always getting pulled over in his BMW.

He tuned the radio, trying to find some decent music. The news was on. There was still no trace of the gang who had kidnapped a wealthy American publisher's son. The money had been handed over but the kid had not yet turned up. The mother came on, distraught, to appeal for the return of her son. They were waiting for instructions as to his whereabouts, although the kidnappers had assured them he was alive and well. The police had reason to believe the gang had left the country and the kid was tied up somewhere. It was a race against time made all the more urgent as the kid had a heart condition from being unhealthily overweight.

As the woman's heartfelt plea faded into the rest of the news, Alan Landor was struck with a thought so clear, it charged through his system like a lightening bolt of inspiration. He decided with unflinching resolve that his family's history was about to take another turn: a development they'd be powerless to stop. He was going to up the stakes to gain compensation from the father and grandmother he despised so much.

They'd robbed him out of everything; every privilege had been denied him. To add insult to the emotional injury from the loss of his mother at a tender age, he'd lost the security of his childhood possessions, too: his room, his toys, his pets. While Veronica was horse riding and enjoying a childhood of luxury at Gayle Landor's estate, Alan was banged up in an approved school, taking the hard knocks that had pulverised him into adolescence. Kidnapping his father made sense and would be a piece of piss. The occasional visits to the family had provided opportunities to root about in bedrooms, take spare keys, find out from Richard what his dad was up to.

Alan had keys to everything his father owned, although no one knew this apart from him. Getting into the car showroom annexe had been a cinch once he'd copied Peter Bruton's key. None of the security cameras were positioned on that part of the building and Alan had been able to get in, disconnect the airbag sensor panel from the back seat, take it home and refigure the cruise control and break in again the next evening with the detonation timed for 1.00 p.m., Wednesday October 15th. Things hadn't gone to plan but he couldn't spend time worrying about that. The car crash was yesterday's news. Derek Landor would have bigger things to worry about soon enough.

The excitement at this brainwave of positive thinking cheered him beyond measure. All he had to do was choose the right people and stay out of sight himself. Bruton wouldn't be one of them, that was for sure. Too much mouth. He needed stealth and ruthlessness. There were a few blokes he knew who could pull it off on the muscle front but he was looking for someone special. And he wanted to move fast.

At Gaby's, the DJs were doing soundchecks and the lights were being checked over by their technical staff. Bruton was wearing his Top Deck bomber jacket and as soon as he walked through the door Alan noticed that he started throwing his weight around. He left the girl on the door strict instructions to call him as soon as Neil Boden arrived. He had a table reserved on the upper level of the club – away from the general punters – and was eager to make sure his guest was treated well.

Alan wasn't sure what Boden would make of the club if he was as 'old school' as Peter made out. They had an hour before the sounds kicked in and he didn't think the bloke would appreciate doing business to a techno soundtrack. Whatever the guy wanted, Alan wanted to be sure that he made the maximum amount of cash possible from it. Losing the nine hundred quid still made him feel sick. It was a serious dent in his profits. No more mistakes. He was going to stick to soft drinks tonight and try not to lose his temper.

The excitement of his new plan kept him on the edge of his seat. Knocking out a batch of E was pathetic money in comparison to what he was now thinking of. He sat on his own watching Bruton swagger about with huge bunches of keys and shouting orders to the bar staff. The DJs were just finishing their soundcheck when Bruton arrived at the table with a guy much older than Alan had expected. He looked as if he was made of iron. A steely expression and a closely-cropped head of thick grey hair were his defining features. He could see what Peter had meant about Boden being 'old school'.

He was roughly the same age as Alan's father although the difference in personality and appearance couldn't be more marked. This guy looked as if he wouldn't be fazed by a horde of rogue elephants. Derek was a coward and had always been so. The pictures he'd seen of his father at school were embarrassing. He looked like Billy Bunter: a fat kid wearing short trousers and specs. Derek was ashamed of Alan, and all the trouble he'd caused, but Alan was twice as ashamed of his father for being a whimpering fat coward.

Boden showed not a flicker of interest or friendliness towards Bruton or Alan. Peter almost fell over himself to get their guest whatever he wanted. Both Bruton and Alan registered a look of surprise when the hard man ordered a white wine and soda. It would have taken a fool or an armed man to laugh at that moment. Boden explained he liked to keep trim; too many of his mates had gone to seed propping up the bar every night in their local boozers. Made for loose talk, too, which had cost a number of his mates their freedom.

Peter and Alan nodded in agreement, and Bruton started talking about his daily fitness routine. Boden didn't even look at him but kept his gaze firmly on Alan, which was unnerving to say the least. He then cut in, 'You boys know what I want. I want to be sure I'm coming to the right man. The contact I was relying on has just been sent down for three years and all his associates have done a bunk. No one wants to touch things for a while. I need someone new; someone who has no connections with me or the firm.'

Alan wondered which firm but it seemed rude to ask. Around south London 'firm' was another word for family. Most outfits worked with their own family members: brothers, cousins, fathers-in-law. Less chance of someone turning you in if there was a blood connection.

'Drake's no one's man, are you?' chirped Bruton who suddenly found several reasons to sing Alan's praises.

Ten minutes later, Alan was quite relieved when the barman came over and took Bruton away from the table; the accolades were getting embarrassing. Apparently one of the basement locks was proving difficult and they needed Peter to sort it out. He also had to do his rounds checking the security cameras were recording. That would take about twenty minutes. 'I'm going to have to leave you to it for a while,' said Bruton. 'No mischief now.' Boden didn't respond to his joke.

'Anyone can get a set of plates made up,' he said to Alan, getting straight down to business as soon as Bruton had left their table. 'I want a motor that's legit. Something decent, no crap. I need someone to get me a car with diplomatic plates. Something with a bit of immunity. Know any boys in that game?' Alan nodded, racking his brains for mates he knew who would have the bottle to nick such a car. He was still in touch with one or two car ringers from his time working in a garage before he went to Germany.

They were mad bastards. They'd do anything.

'There's always a risk the driver will get pulled but he looks the part, and any right-thinking copper would know better than to start checking over diplomatic motors. Too much grief for 'em when they can do a few mini-cab firms down Peckham and get a result.'

Alan tried to imagine what kind of job he needed it for but thought that by not prying he would gain the man's respect. There was some information he did want from Boden though. 'When do you need it?'

'Not for a couple of months, son. I'm testing the water if you like. I need to know if you can deliver.'

'I can make enquiries. What sort of figure are you talking about here?' It was always tricky talking money with the professionals. Alan knew you couldn't haggle with them. The hard man's offer would be non-negotiable.

'Two grand. Nice earner for a kid,' said Boden.

'Sounds fair, Mister Boden,' said Alan, trying to build up the courage to ask him the million dollar question. The music started up and Boden winced. 'I'm going to disappear. I've got your number. I'll call you on Monday. I like to move fast once I've got a plan.'

'I've got a plan too,' said Alan, seizing what may be his only opportunity to work on his idea. 'Maybe some of your mates can help me out. There's someone I need sorting. He's loaded. There's a couple of million tied up in property and about a million in investment bonds. His mother's so rich she doesn't know how much she's got. I want him taken away for a while. A couple of calls to the mother and the wife. Get them to be generous. I'm looking for a professional firm to help me pull it off. It's worth at least half a million. I know they'll pay up, too. I need to use someone with the right amount of bottle. No fuck ups. Nothing traceable.' There it was. He couldn't believe he'd said it. If ever there was a sitting target, it was his father. He should have thought of it before.

Neil Boden leant across the table and fixed his grey eyes on Alan's. 'What are you saying, son? Kidnapping? What do you know about me?'

'I know you're someone who's serious about their work. Thought you might know some blokes who aren't afraid to take the challenge.' Of all the people Alan would want on the job, Boden would be number one choice.

'I'm not a hit man, Drake,' he whispered. 'I've never taken anyone out. Roughed them up a bit, maybe, but that's it. Clean jobs, only.'

'You wouldn't have to kill him,' said Alan. 'He'd be a pushover and so would his mother – the one who would be forking out.' The music was annoying Boden. Alan had to think fast. 'Say you'll meet me at my garage, Mister Boden. As soon as you can. This has to be done soon, too. Next week.'

Boden threw himself back from the table with a look of disbelief. 'You're joking, son,' he said. 'This kind of thing takes weeks of planning.'

'I can save you time,' said Alan. 'I've got keys to his house, his place of work and his car.'

'Who is this bloke?' he asked. 'You sound a bit desperate if you ask me.'

'Someone who owes me,' said Alan. 'And yes I am desperate. Desperate to see it done while it can be. Half a million quid, Mister Boden – and no security guards, no dogs, no risk. I don't know what your diplomatic job will be paying but you'll be able to retire on this. No alarms, no witnesses. Think about it, please. I wouldn't bother you if it was small-time stuff.'

Bruton was back at the bar, showing off to a bunch of girls and making an arse of himself. None of them were over twenty years old. Boden's gaze was fixed on Alan. 'One thing . . .' he said. 'Silly bollocks over there isn't in on this is he?'

Alan was never more emphatic in his life when he said, 'No. Absolutely not, and that's the way it's staying.'

Boden nodded. 'He mustn't get a sniff of this. I wouldn't work with him under any circumstances.'

Alan felt relieved. He had crossed a line – a line which put him in a different league. So Boden also thought Bruton was risky. That was good. The two men were thinking along the same lines. This was his big chance to take what he felt was rightfully his. There was no need for excessive violence. Nice and clean like Neil had said. Gayle Landor would pay up in hours of hearing her precious son was in danger. Alan would stay well away from the proceedings. The whole thing could be wrapped up within a fortnight if they moved fast. And guess who would be prime suspect? Silly bollocks who had been daft enough to threaten Derek with that stupid letter.

EIGHT
Someone So Inappropriate

Wednesday evening

Vic caught up with Nick Swift just after seven o' clock. She'd applied a new coat of make-up and put on a dressy pair of shoes. Her black lace top sat snugly over her breasts and its effect was not lost on her date for the evening. She was feeling confident that she looked as good as any woman he'd seen that day. She could smell that Swift had already had a couple of beers. He'd just returned from watching the Miss Auto Trader contest and said he was surprised that Vic hadn't been in it. 'You'd have won it, I reckon, if you'd have been entered,' he said. 'The girls were pretty but you're as lovely as any of them.'

She smiled to herself as he tried to explain – without sounding like a complete sexist – how much he'd enjoyed the show. Yes, I'm sure, thought Vic. And I bet you've still got a hard-on from it. She looked him over as they discussed where to go. He was trim under that shirt, she noticed, and was relieved to see he was at least wearing an OK pair of trousers. He wouldn't make an unpleasant escort for the evening. They agreed to start out in the VIP lounge. There was no need to take the wind out of his sails by telling him she'd already been there last night. She was acting as if it was all a big thrill. She knew this would prop up his feeling of self-importance and lull him into thinking that she was easily impressed.

Vic ordered a vodka and tonic and Nick stuck to lager. He lit a cigarette and began the routine which began with, 'So, tell me about yourself.' This was *carte blanche* for Vic to let rip with her character-acting skills. No boarding school and horse-riding credentials for Nick. She could tell he would be easier work if she brought herself down to a more realistic level. She didn't want to make him feel uneducated in comparison. It was definitely a 'Vicky' persona this time. Modelling. That always worked.

'Well, I did page three when I was twenty-two,' she said in a pretend shy voice. This wasn't too far from the truth. She had done some glamour work when she found out that it wasn't as sleazy as she'd expected. Lisa had got her the work and it had paid quite well, in fact. She hadn't done page three but she had taken her clothes off for the camera – once. It had helped her out of a tight spot at the time. She wasn't ashamed by it, but she didn't advertise the fact. She'd felt a lot less compromised by the modelling work than some of the TV stuff she'd done, such as having to bear the brunt of lame jokes on TV game shows. Still, it had earned her an Equity card, for what good that was these days.

'I'd like to see a copy of that!' said Nick and Vic smiled coyly. She carried on talking about herself. She suspected that Nick wasn't really listening. Most of the time he was staring at her chest or looking at her with his hungry expression. She told him she supported Chelsea – that was true. She'd been born the year they last won the FA Cup and for them to win it again at the end of last season meant this was going to be a special year for her. 'I think it means something,' she said.

'I'm a rugby man myself,' said Nick, pointing to the crest on his blazer. 'But I won't go on about that. I've never met a woman who's interested in rugby.'

Too right, thought Vic. A lot of grunting brutes fighting over a stupidly-shaped ball. 'I'd quite like to be in a scrum, that must be fun,' she said, squirming in her seat.

'Anytime you fancy it, you let me know,' said Nick. 'I'll show you a few holds.'

She pretended to look shocked, but was smiling at the same time. 'I think you'd better get me another drink, Nick,' she said. No sooner had she finished her sentence than he leapt to his feet. It was time. She sneaked her hand into her bag and found the sound recorder. She had enough spare tapes to last three hours, although she didn't expect to start recording just yet. To anyone's guess, it was a personal stereo. They weren't to know that the machine had a built-in highly tuned microphone. At the flick of a switch she could change from omni-directional to focused sound. As long as she concealed the tape heads moving round, she was fine.

Nick returned with the drinks. The bar was filling up with noisy reps greeting each other loudly. There was no sign of the black doorman tonight. There was a different guy on the door; a younger bloke who was less muscle-bound. So here she was again, in the VIP lounge telling some bloke an economical version of the truth. She made a play to get him talking about himself.

'I'm divorced,' said Nick. 'Married too young, really, that was my trouble. Got two grown-up daughters: one twenty-four, the other nineteen. The oldest one's in Australia, the other one lives with her mum. Love 'em to bits but you know what girls are like. Nothing but trouble.'

He smiled but looked a bit worried that he'd said too much. He'd given it away that he had a daughter only two years younger than Vic. And here he was trying to get into her knickers. Very naughty. Vic knew his type. Of course he'd brought his daughters up to be 'good' girls, not like the kind of girls he wanted to meet on nights like this – away from his home turf. 'What about work?' she asked. 'You seem to be very busy with your classic cars.'

'Oh, Vicky, love, if only you knew,' he said. 'It's enough to drive me to drink. I don't want to lumber my troubles on you. It's all boring anyway.'

A couple more drinks and he'll be ready to talk, she thought. She was wrong. She sat patiently as he asked her if she had a boyfriend; what she wanted out of life; what her flat was like, and if she would come to dinner with him tonight. There were some nice places not too far from the Exhibition Centre, he said, and they could take a cab. She agreed. Looking around at the other drinkers, she realised it would be a good plan to get him away from the masculine bonhomie so she could get his undivided attention. They'd already been interrupted once by one of the guys who'd been playing the racing game earlier that day.

They dined in a not-too-upmarket Italian restaurant. They ordered a bottle of white wine and, once more, Vic began gently probing him for information – sound recorder switched on. 'To be honest, I don't know where things are going with my job anymore,' he said, lighting a cigarette. 'The boss seems to be going through something of a mid-life crisis, although with his money I'd be happy as a lark. There's been a couple of mishaps this year, a break-in, and last week there was a bit of an accident.'

'Where?' asked Vic. 'In the car showroom?'

'No, on a test-drive. It's all a bit of a mess really. Some bloke crashed one of our high-performance vehicles. Thank God no one was killed, but it's all a bit complicated.'

'Oh dear. Why's that?'

'Well, he said that the airbag went off for no reason, and that caused him to spin out. I don't understand it, actually.'

'But none of this is your fault is it?' she said.

'It doesn't seem to be anyone's fault exactly, except possibly the manufacturers. I still can't believe the bloke's telling the truth about the crash. I reckoned he simply lost control of the wheel. Thing is, the guvnor seems to be in a right flap. Almost losing his marbles. It's not the money involved so much as there's been a local hoo-ha about it. Speeding cars near schools and pedestrians at risk, all that kind of thing.

We're suddenly the villains of the piece.'

Vic nodded sympathetically. She wanted to get him talking about Derek Landor. 'Don't you fancy taking over as the guvnor, then? Is your boss past it or something?'

'I might have to if he carries on the way he is at the moment!' Nick exclaimed. 'He's not retirement age yet. Fifty-three I think. A few years to go. It's a privately-owned business anyway so he can keep going as long as he likes. He set it up with money left to him when his father died in the 1960s. His mother's still going, though. Right tough old bird, she is. I think that's his trouble, really. He's a bit of a mummy's boy, you know.'

'What, gay?'

Nick looked shocked. 'No, he's married with three kids. He's just, well, he's not a man's man, if you know what I mean. Bit of a soft arse. Wouldn't fancy his chances in a scrum. You would do better than him!'

Vic smiled at Nick's joke. She was going to have to be patient. As yet, Nick hadn't really told her anything she didn't know already although he'd clarified Derek Landor's tendency to personal crises. 'I'm sure it'll all sort itself out,' she said, sipping her wine and not forgetting to look alluring.

'I hope so. It's been a cushy number for me. Nice salary, loads of perks. And I like the cars we sell. I've done enough time in some right dodgy outfits trying to push clapped out motors that wouldn't last six months. It was a delight to come to Landors. I had a proven track record at meeting the targets – that's why they employed me. I thought they'd want someone a bit more posh, you know, but I've been there fourteen years now and no one seems to mind the London accent.'

The waiter brought a *rigatoni carbonara* for Nick and Vic had *penne al forno*. Over the meal, Nick put the lid on work talk saying he didn't want to bore her with it. She protested but it was unlikely she'd get anything more from him this evening. More drinks were ordered and by the time they were ready for the bill Nick was grinning stupidly. He maintained his composure though. Vic was worried that he'd drink too much and start acting the lout. She was pleasantly surprised. She put it down to him being older. He'd had more time to learn how to hold his drink.

The way he'd leant back after they'd finished their meal and taken a long, appreciative look at her had sent her hormones into a spin. She tried to tell herself it was a job but she was feeling drawn to him. He was charming and had been sure to pay her compliments and make sure her wine glass was filled. He was after one thing but he was going about it in a successfully seductive way.

'Please don't go back to the Metropole, Vicky,' he said. 'You know that I find you incredibly attractive, don't you?' She nodded. Then he leant forward and caressed her leg under the table. 'I want to make love to you, Vicky,' he said with a totally serious expression.

She tried not to giggle. She wondered what Nick Swift's version of making love would entail. Running his hands over her arse as soon as they were in his room? Unzipping his flies the moment she sat on the bed? Grabbing hold of her hair and making her suck his cock? Yes, she could tolerate some of that. She looked into his blue eyes and gave her consent. The hunger was still there. She could read the thoughts going through his mind. How he'd get the blonde over the bed, tell all his mates about it tomorrow, watch them go puce with envy as he went into details. Well she wouldn't disappoint him. She'd been too long without physical contact herself. It was welcome, guilt-free sex.

The kissing began as soon as they'd got into the cab. He'd grasped her breasts in both hands and rubbed them until her nipples poked through the lace top. By the time they'd reached his hotel, she'd felt the outline of his erection through the fabric of his beige chinos. It was impressively hard and promising in size. In the lift, and all the way along the corridor to his room, he'd tried to release her breasts from her bra. It was a privilege to worship them, he'd said. Vic was enjoying the fact that she didn't have to do very much to make this man happy. He seemed overjoyed to be about to take his pleasure from a girl young enough to be his daughter and she was about to live out a long-held fantasy but not be shamed into admitting that turned her on. What was it all about, anyway? Something dark and long-buried. Something she didn't want to disturb now.

They went into his room and Nick offered her a drink from the mini-bar. She declined. She'd had enough to drink. Her desire for sex was over-riding other needs. She couldn't wait for him to start. She had one thing to do first: flick that switch and start taping, just in case he started talking Landor Motors. She wanted to be prepared. She placed her bag on the bedside table and dimmed the light. While Nick went to the bathroom she positioned the microphone next to the small square of black gauze on the side of her bag. It was perfectly camouflaged – looking like part of the bag's design.

She slipped out of her cream-coloured business suit and allowed her long legs to stretch out on his bed. She was wearing black hold-up stockings and an expensive brassiere she'd bought at Harrod's lingerie department. It was beautifully made with small purple silk bows on the straps and in the front. It encouraged a generous cleavage from her already firm breasts. She didn't want to look too passive, though. Maybe lying down was a bad idea. She needed to be occupied with something. Maybe she would have a drink after all. She walked over to the mini bar and fixed herself a vodka and tonic mixer. As she was stirring the drink with a glass cocktail stick, Nick emerged from the bathroom and threw a streak of light into the room.

'Come here,' he said. 'I can't see you properly over there.'

'Come and get me, then,' she teased, twirling her stick and sucking on it provocatively. Nick Swift needed no further encouragement. He'd left his clothes on, Vic was pleased to see. This is what she wanted. To get her older man while he was fully dressed. She wanted to strip down to the barest essentials and have the feel of his shirt and trousers chafing her skin. That was part of her fantasy. He kissed her, gently at first, then more passionately as she dug her nails into his shirt.

'You're a wild one, aren't you? You like it, don't you?'

'It's been quite a while since I've been this rude with anyone,' said Vic.

'Aren't I the lucky one?' he joked, easing her to the bed. Once horizontal, he dived on her. Kissing her ravenously and rubbing his groin into her, it was obvious that he didn't want to delay the proceedings. There were to be no preliminary chats or gentle stroking but Vic didn't mind that. She was enjoying the total attention of having this man on top of her. He was going to enjoy her whatever she did.

She ran her hands down the front of his shirt, lightly scratching him, which he seemed to like. Her blonde hair was spread out fan-like around her head and her breasts rose and fell with the deep breaths she was taking. She was enjoying this much more than she thought she would. It was a surprise to be in such an intimate situation with someone so unlikely. It wasn't a relaxed love-making session. This was pure lust, but its energy was refreshing and highly-charged.

'I wish I could wait longer, Vicky,' he apologised, already undoing his belt, 'but you've got me so hard, I have to have you now. You don't mind do you? Are you ready for me?' He reached between her legs and felt her moisture. She was hot. She was ready.

Usually she would be disappointed by this lack of foreplay. Any guys her own age who behaved so inconsiderately would get a severe upbraiding. But the drink had loosened both their inhibitions and she wasn't in the mood to educate Nick Swift in how to pleasure a woman with his fingers. She would do that while he was fucking her. Seeing as he hadn't prepared himself for the event, Vic reached over to her bag and produced a condom. 'I insist,' she said.

'Very wise,' said Nick. 'I guess I was in too much of a hurry just then to sort things out. I'll back off for a minute.' He was panting. 'I would love you to suck me before I wear that, though.'

Vic knelt up on the bed and flicked her hair away from her mouth before leaning in to him. She unzipped him and drew out his hardened penis. He smelt clean and masculine.

She tentatively swirled the tip of her tongue around the top of his cock. He groaned in pleasure. Then she moistened her hand and rubbed him up and down before taking the length of him into her mouth. Her lipstick was rubbing on to his shaft and leaving a shimmer of silvery pink colour along it. After a minute he pulled away from her. 'I'm going to come too soon if you keep doing that. Please stop,' he pleaded.

'But I thought that's what you wanted,' said Vic, coyly.

'I didn't expect you to be that good at it!' he exclaimed.

'I like to pleasure a man in that way,' she said. 'But I have selfish reasons. It makes me almost come by doing it.'

'Let me watch you,' he said, grabbing hold of himself and masturbating.

This was unexpected escapism for Vic. She would feel far too shy to do it in front of someone she'd just met if they were her equal. Somehow, the imbalance of ages and education became a liberating feeling for her. She gave in to the lewd pleasure of performing in front of this man. She didn't have to worry that he might think she was sluttish. She was happy to be that. She watched him as he pulled on himself, his head leant back and his eyes closed. 'Watch me!' she ordered. 'I want you to see how I do it.'

She circled her finger over her clitoris. It was heaven. But she wanted it all. 'Now put the condom on, Nick,' she breathed. 'I want you now.' She lay back and heard the tearing of the wrapper and waited a few seconds before opening her eyes. Then Nick slipped into her with a sigh of relief. The feel and smell of him was adding to her pleasure. He'd tried to take his shirt off but she stopped him. She was glad he didn't mind although he'd said that she was a bit kinky.

Now he was noisy. Maybe the noisiest she'd ever been with. With every lunge inside her he gasped and grunted. It was bestial and rough. She could feel herself slipping into her fantasy. That was it: he was unable to control himself. He'd seen her and had to take her – this older man she hardly knew. The more she surrendered her fantasy self to him, the closer her climax became. And her arousal was bringing Nick to his explosion, too. He pulled back to look at her, resting his weight on his arms.

'Vicky, you're making me come,' he sighed. This was enough to send her to the point of no return. She looked at him; his face was frozen in concentration. For a second he opened his eyes and the hungry look was burning into her. That was it. She felt truly possessed and totally wanton. Her fingers barely had to touch her swollen clitoris. She came in loud spasms, sucking on his cock with her internal muscles as they flexed and relaxed in rapid succession. It was madness but this was the first mutual orgasm she'd experienced. It was so good she wanted it to last an hour.

Unfortunately, she wasn't even able to enjoy five minutes' relaxation. A knock came on the door and a voice calling for Nick. He shot up from his recumbent position and let forth a groan — this time one of exasperation. 'Who is it?' whispered Vic, in a state of half-sleep.

'Don't worry. It's only the boss. He's probably got a touch of the night-time jitters.' Nick got up from the bed and made himself decent. While he was zipping up his flies, Vic moved her bag nearer to the door before disappearing rapidly into the en-suite bathroom.

From the secrecy of the bright, tiled room she could hear Nick trying to get rid of Derek Landor. She looked in the mirror. Her make-up had worn off and she reeked of sex. What the hell was she doing? Daniel Field would never have expected her to go so far! She threw herself into the shower and washed the smell of Nick Swift from her body. It had been great, but she wanted to consign it to experience. As the water drenched her, the muted sound of the two men's voices became even more indistinct.

She soaped her body with shower gel and a thick sponge, scrubbing at her arms and thighs. How could she have allowed herself to get so carried away after a couple of drinks? Still, there had been a result. She felt smug that the recorder was picking up whatever was being said. Landor was in the room with Nick now. She was bursting to know what it was they were discussing. She must return to her own hotel to listen to the tapes.

After finishing her shower and brushing her teeth with

her finger – she didn't want to use Nick's toothbrush – Vic listened carefully at the door with a towel wrapped around her. After a couple of minutes the door was closed and she gingerly stepped back into the bedroom. 'I could've done without that,' said Nick, collapsing back on to the bed. He was holding something in his hand but quickly folded it and put it in his pocket as Vic joined him. 'Trouble?' she asked.

'Nothing to worry yourself about, love,' he answered. That answer came as no surprise. At least he didn't say 'pretty little head'. Nick rolled over and grabbed a scotch from the mini-bar. He was spent and sated. Vic began dressing, and popping back and forth to the bathroom. By the time she was finished, he'd slipped into unconsciousness and was snoring gently. She slipped out of the door, turning the bathroom light off as she went.

She clutched the precious contents of her bag close to her chest as she made for the lift. She looked composed but felt weird – as if what had happened had been in a bubble. Not only had she just had sex with a man old enough to be her father – that was a first – she'd experienced orgasm at the same time as him. She'd never done that with any of her boyfriends. Why had something so beautiful happened with someone so inappropriate? Her release had been surprisingly powerful. What did it say about the nature of sex? Maybe her body had allowed it to happen because she was not trying too hard. Maybe this meant that she could only climax so easily with someone older or someone who treated her roughly. Her head was reeling.

She hailed a cab and ordered the driver to take her to the Metropole. She'd forgotten to check her messages all evening. Damn! She fished out her mobile phone. There was one from her mother. Did Vic want to come down the market on Saturday? There was one from Daniel Field, returning her call, and one from Drake Lewis saying he wanted to see her again. There seemed little point, in Vic's mind, to seeing that strange creature again but it would be one way to exorcise the demon older man from her memory. He was young and cute and he had certainly given her the right signals. Her passion had been awakened by this night – albeit in a strangely perverse way – and she could sense that a previously hidden facet of her sexuality was beginning to demand exploration.

NINE
A Monster in the Imagination

Thursday

The next morning Vic was at work demonstrating Halman's products to a group of school-uniformed teenage boys, but her mind was elsewhere – she was trying to process the information she'd gleaned from the previous night's investigation. Listening to the tapes had thrown up some surprises. The first twenty minutes consisted of X-rated chat between herself and Nick Swift. She couldn't resist replaying the sound of their mutual orgasms over and over in shocked fascination. The sound of Nick's climactic grunting had actually made her blush as she listened, hidden under the bedclothes in her hotel room. A curious souvenir – but a potent reminder of the unexpected pleasure she'd gained as a by-product of their meeting.

The end of the tape, however, revealed a possible clue as to why Derek Landor was falling apart. Listening to the conversation between Derek and Nick, she had realised that something far more serious than fraud could be at stake – something as serious as attempted murder. This was real PI work, not process serving or following people who were fiddling their claims for lost jewellery. She tried to concentrate on demonstrating the game. The boys were watching her with eager adolescent excitement. Their bright eyes and sweaty hands betrayed their interest in Vic's body. They stared at the hardened nipples under her tight scoop-necked top, at her compact, rounded bottom covered by a short tartan skirt, and her long legs clad in dark opaque tights and knee-high suede boots.

Most of the lads were gawky and uncomfortable but one or two had developed into attractive young men. One dark-haired lad with noticeably long eyelashes was chewing gum and had draped himself over the machines in a nonchalant manner. Every few seconds he'd flick his eyes at Vic and look her up and down. When it was his group's turn to watch the demonstration, he seized the opportunity to get in as close to her as he could. The touch of his young body close up against her was unnerving. After what had happened last night she felt vulnerable to desire. She'd slept too deeply and had awoken late. She felt tired. It was not helping her control of the game.

She fluffed a couple of starts. The lad took control of the joystick from her and immediately sent the score rocketing. He swerved his lithe body this way and that to add extra display to his prowess. Little show-off, thought Vic. Jeff Halman whispered in her ear, 'See. I knew you'd be a hit with the lads.'

At the end of the demonstration, Vic got two-thirds of their names and addresses before making an excuse to find the bathroom. Away from the stand she phoned Daniel. Hearing his voice put everything into perspective: the Motor Show experience; the evening with Swift; the unpredictable quality of the work. It was a curious experience being thrown into the lives of strangers. Talking to Daniel gave her a much-needed anchor, especially after the odd experience she'd had with Swift.

'Daniel, I've got something which must be relevant,' she said, trying to keep her voice relaxed. 'Landor's had death threats. He received a letter a couple of days ago which has sent him into an apoplectic state. His senior salesman, Nick

Swift, has been holding his hand all week from what I gather. The pressure on him from local protest groups and the press has put him in the spotlight. And I don't think he likes being in that position.'

'Have you got the letter?' asked Daniel.

'No. But I've taped a conversation between Landor and Swift where Derek reads out the words of the letter. It was a home-made collage of words cut out from a magazine. Very brief and almost illiterate, apparently. Whoever sent it couldn't spell or punctuate. I'll make a copy of the recording and send you it today. It's strange how Swift seems to brush the whole thing off as a joke but the boss is cack– is really scared by it. I want to find out whether it's a local nutcase who's upset about the crash or someone he knows.' She'd just managed to stop herself from lapsing into the vernacular.

'I heard about Bob Waterhouse's safety campaign from Timothy Fuller,' said Daniel. 'There's still no word from the manufacturers of the car. If they're at fault then perhaps Derek Landor will be left alone to get on with his life.'

'I've still to check out the Bruton connection. I need to get closer to the source of things. Stuck up here, it's a bit difficult to find anything out.'

'Are you calling from the Motor Show now?' he asked.

'Yes. It's open access day. The place is heaving with wannabe Jeremy Clarksons and spotty youths with sweaty hands.'

Daniel laughed. 'I've always been more of a Quentin Willson man myself,' he said.

'Oh, me too,' said Vic. 'I find his voice quite sexy.' She wondered what Daniel would make of that. She continued: 'If Landor has enemies his salesman will know who they are. I've tried to get him talking about work but he says he doesn't want to bore me. Before this show's over I'll get it out of him, though. I'll be in touch as soon as I know anything else.'

As she made her way back to the TurboInteractive stand, her mind was reeling with how to handle the investigation now it had taken such a dramatic turn. She wrestled with the information she'd gleaned so far. Someone really seems to have it in for Landor Motors, she thought. And if, as

Derek Landor suspects, Peter Bruton is the man behind all the crimes perpetrated on them so far, what kind of a person am I likely to be coming up against?

She was surprised to find Nick Swift at the stand. She could tell from his body language that he wasn't at ease. He was quizzing Halman, who looked uncomfortable. Maybe something had happened to Derek? That notion was quickly dispatched as she saw the look on Swift's face was one of anger, rather than concern. As he caught Vic's eye, she knew it was her he was annoyed with.

'What do you mean by sauntering off like that?' he shouted, walking towards her. 'No woman does that to me. I thought we were going to spend the night together but you fucked off as soon as you'd got what you wanted.' Vic looked around her. Her audience of teenaged boys were nudging each other and giggling while Jeff Halman was blinking and looking ineffectual in a loud shirt.

'Do you get a kick out of acting like a tart? Imagine if it had been me that walked out on you after we'd just fucked each other senseless. You wouldn't like it, would you?' He had raised his voice and was panting and cross. Vic wanted to be annoyed with him but she found his over-reaction quite amusing. The schoolboys were laughing and making lewd noises, the long-eyelashed one taking great delight in the scenario. Jeff was trying to distract them with other computer games but they were far more interested in the real-life drama that was going on in front of them.

Vic knew she would do better to keep calm and look unruffled than launch into a slanging match and conform to stereotype. 'I thought I'd rather listen to some late-night jazz back at my own hotel than tiptoe around a snoring man,' she said quietly. 'I don't call that behaving like a tart.'

'Well you are one,' said Nick. 'You look all suave in your designer clothes but you're a right little tramp.' They stood looking at each other in silence. Even though what he was saying was crass and out of order, there was an undeniably sexual thread to the argument. The atmosphere between them was electric and Vic found the situation curiously exciting and made more so by the fact of having an audience;

it was worth the insults to see Jeff Halman flapping about pretending everything was business as usual.

Swift looked as if he was about to devour her, partly in rage and partly out of raw lust. She knew it was dangerous, but she stepped nearer to him and whispered in his ear: 'I want to suck your cock again. It makes me horny thinking about it.'

This inappropriate reaction left Swift in a bewildered state. Vic knew she was supposed to be upset – to take offence or cry. She knew he'd be astounded by this move but she liked to be one step ahead of everyone's expectations of her. Close up, he smelt musky and raw and Vic felt herself becoming aroused by their highly-charged public display of emotion.

'You bitch,' said Swift, a smile creeping over his face as he realised how stupid he'd been. 'You little tart. You'll get me right into trouble, you know that?'

He was right. Jeff Halman and a male colleague stepped in and asked Nick to leave the stand as he was causing a scene. Halman got an earful from Nick as he reluctantly strolled away, his eyes fixed on Vic. He pointed a finger at her. She knew this wasn't the end of their strange alliance. Halman then turned to Vic and asked her to take her problems elsewhere. The Mister Nice Guy charm was no longer in evidence. Vic knew all along that Halman was only interested in profit but she wasn't prepared for the ensuing diatribe. He was going to have to 'let her go' he said, especially as children had witnessed her 'boyfriend's' foul language.

It was obvious that sexual jealousy was at work. Halman hadn't stopped looking at her breasts since the first day of the show and it seemed to Vic as if it was taking all his control to prevent himself from reaching out and grabbing at them. The guy didn't know how to make himself popular. Both Nick and Drake had insulted him. That reminded her: she owed Drake a call.

Being undercover, she didn't have to care one iota about what was happening. In silence, she casually picked up her jacket from a chair and put it on. She slung her bag over her shoulder and issued a goodbye wave of her fingers at him as he was still talking about staff conduct and the good name of the company. She walked over to the console where the boys were beginning to find renewed interest in their game. She couldn't resist it: she tapped the dark-haired one on the shoulder. As he turned to face her, she planted a huge kiss on his lips to the uproarious cheers of his mates.

Her time at the Motor Show was over. She needed to get back to her hotel and decide her next move, which she knew would involve the hunt for Peter Bruton. Maybe the investigation needed to be approached from another angle. First, she needed to see Nick once more. See if she could get him talking. The bastard owed her an apology. As she turned the corner to where the Landor Motors stand was positioned she almost walked into him.

'I'm so sorry,' he said, in hushed tones, grabbing hold of her arms. 'I don't know what came over me back then. I was going to catch you at lunchtime and apologise properly. I've been under so much stress recently. You were the first good thing that's happened to me in ages and I guess I lost my temper. I'm sorry, Vicky. Say you'll forget it. I didn't mean those things I said about you.'

'You made me lose my job, Nick,' she said, looking mournful. Here was a chance to play up to his guilty feelings. She expected another offer of dinner or a drink as compensation. This was her last chance to prise some information out of this volatile man. She wasn't prepared for what he said next.

Before she could elaborate he launched in, 'I want to make up for it by offering you some work for a couple of weeks. We need an image overhaul. We've just lost a promotion deal and I have to come up with some new ideas before the boss tops himself. There's some money in the advertising budget and anyway I thought it would do the place good to have a pretty face around. We want someone with creative ideas to help us organise some good PR – let the local press know that we're not prepared to see our profits suffer because of one accident. Maybe you could set up one of those web page things.'

Vic knew she'd have to accept his offer: this was too good to turn down, although how the hell she was going to bluff her way through revamping a car showroom's image or designing a web page was beyond her. She'd have to ring around her friends in the business; farm some work out to her mate Mike in Chalk Farm. He did computer graphics and stuff like that. That was next week's problem. She needed to sound calm; in a state of being persuaded. 'I suppose driving in from London won't be too bad,' she said nonchalantly. 'What about your boss, though? Won't he want to interview me? Check me out for references or something?'

'He leaves all that kind of thing to me and anyway he's not going to be there. His doctor told him to take a couple of weeks rest. He's already gone home. Left me to look after this lot for the weekend. Swift gestured around him. 'Mind you, he's so depressed, it's better not having him around.'

Vic looked Nick straight in his eyes and widened her own in faked remembrance. 'Last night. Of course! He knocked on your door, just as we'd er —'

'Yeah, that's right,' Nick cut in and smiled. 'The bastard's timing was appalling.'

'What's the matter with him, then?' she asked. 'I thought it was a bit off, you having to rush off to see to him as if he was a child.'

'You might as well know, seeing as you'll be around next week,' Nick explained. 'Someone sent him a stupid letter in the post. It arrived at the showroom yesterday and they forwarded it to the hotel. It said he was being watched and that he'd be dead soon.'

'And he's taking two weeks off to recover!' she joked. 'I'll remember that one when I get a particularly nasty phone bill. Who would send your boss something like that and why?'

Nick wasn't being pushed. He shrugged his shoulders and said, 'Some nutter,' and nothing more.

Vic had heard Bruton's name mentioned on the tape recording. A visit was overdue. The only address she had for him was in Aylesbury. He may well have moved since the stolen BMW trial several months ago. Vic wondered why

Swift was reluctant to mention Bruton. Did he think she would tell someone? Maybe Bruton had threatened Nick, too, and he didn't want to seem soft. She remembered from the trial notes, and had seen pictures in the back issues of the *Aylesbury Gazette*, that Nick had suffered a pasting in the BMW incident.

For the first time in Vic's short career as an investigator she felt slightly unnerved. She was beginning to think that some very unsavoury characters may be lurking in the wings. And now they were after Derek Landor. No wonder he was scared. 'Have you informed the police?' she asked casually.

Nick looked suddenly alarmed. 'What can they do? They couldn't give a toss,' he said. 'Anyway, Derek doesn't want to cause a fuss. He's had enough bother with the police for the past couple of weeks.'

She decided to ease up on the questions – although it was blatantly clear that Nick Swift knew more than he was letting on. There would be plenty of time next week for probing into these people's lives. It would be strange working with Swift. She looked at him and flashed a smile. She had to keep him trusting her, wanting her. Would he sneak her into his office after everyone had gone home? Maybe take her for a drive in some powerful machine before stopping to fuck her in some secluded lay-by? Why was this thought so exciting? There was a brutal sexuality to his expression. They recognised something similar in each other.

It was his turn to whisper in her ear: 'You can stay with me at my place if you like. No need to drive from London every day. I'll give you the time of your life. You're making me hard just looking at you. Call me over the weekend.' He handed her his card with his home number written on the back.

'I'll do that, Nick,' she said, looking forward to getting back to her flat and thinking things through.

An opportunity was being handed to her on a plate. She would have two weeks to get to the bottom of life at Landor's – as long as she could bullshit her way through being a PR expert. She must call Timothy Fuller to warn him she would be undercover at the showroom. Daniel will be impressed, she thought, although he must never know about her sexual liaison with Swift. Those tapes needed editing! She couldn't imagine what he would think if he knew what she was up to. She could barely believe it herself.

Alan Landor was sitting at home working out the profit margins on his dealing endeavour. There was little to be excited about. A steady trickle of pills had been going out but everyone he knew who could shift them in numbers worth his while wanted their cut. Instead of making a fiver on each pill, it was turning out to be more like two pounds. Not a king's ransom. And not enough to get him out of the financial mess he was in. Bruton had been slack. He'd passed over some cash but it had been hard getting money out of him. He was too slippery, too busy larging it up. All Alan's hopes were pinned on Neil Boden. He'd called him earlier in the day and the man had sounded interested. They would meet on Saturday to talk seriously. It was time for retribution.

Alan's phone rang. It was his young half-brother, Richard, asking if he would come over at the weekend. He wanted help with installing some new Internet software. He said that he'd asked his mum and she said that he was welcome to come for Sunday lunch. Alan could just imagine Deborah's face as she reluctantly agreed to allow her son to see his older brother. Yes, Alan would definitely make an appearance in Little Chalfont that Sunday. A nice family get-together before an unfortunate family upheaval.

Despite Richard having the comforts Alan had never known, he didn't resent the kid. He had talent and a sense of humour and no trace of the angst Alan had inherited from his mother. Richard was connected to the world through technology; he was happy in his world of shoot-em-up games and alternative universes. Alan's half-brother knew so little of what had happened to Alan and his mother. She'd died three years before he was born and Alan was in a reform school by then. Richard was Alan's link to the Landor household. He was good at getting Richard to talk to him in a brotherly man-to-man fashion. The kid was useful at chatting away happily about what was going on there; it was his world. When you're that age, school and home are everything.

Richard always knew what car Derek was driving. And he talked regularly to his nan, too. She had told Richard the time and date his dad would be driving the Liguri. Alan had hidden his panic when he found out that Derek hadn't been near the car that day. He remembered how sick he had felt when Richard told him that he'd hurried home from school in his lunch hour to see the vehicle before his dad drove it to his nan's and had been disappointed to see no sign of it. It was a shame Richard hadn't known that Boxall had booked a test-drive for October 15th. Still, couldn't blame the kid for that.

'Who was that you were talking to, Richard?' asked Derek Landor as he walked into the kitchen.

'It was Alan,' his son replied guiltily without looking up at his father. He opened the biscuit tin and began delving about. 'He's coming over on Sunday to help me install my new Internet software.'

Derek winced and then launched into an ill-timed patriarchal laying down of the law. 'I've told you I don't want you spending too much time with your brother. He's a bad influence. Anything you want help with you can ask your Uncle Robert.'

'Uncle Robert isn't interested and Alan knows more about computers,' Richard complained, munching on a Jaffa Cake. 'Mum says it's all right.' The boy looked out of the patio windows for a sign of Deborah and made clicking noises at their African Grey parrot. It whistled back loudly in reply. Derek cursed his son's quick logic. It was true: Deborah's brother, Robert, was no technician and he bored the kid senseless. But this was just another niggling incident that had joined the pile of unpleasant things which were fighting for supremacy in Derek's tired brain.

Just at that moment, his wife walked in from the garden carrying plastic plant pots and china tea mugs. She was wearing gardening gloves and her busy look. 'Is this true?' asked Derek. 'Have you invited Alan for Sunday lunch?'

'What's the problem?' she asked casually, seeming not to notice Derek's concern as she tipped the pots into the sink. 'He's helping Richard with some computer thing and I thought it would be a chance to let him know he's welcome to visit. I was speaking to Gayle last week and she even expressed an interest in seeing him. You can't hide from Alan forever, Derek.'

But Derek did want to hide. From Alan, from Nick, from his finance manager, from all his troubles. Now his wife was being blind to his concerns. It hurt that she couldn't see his point of view. 'You didn't have to listen to him shouting at you in front of your colleagues,' he protested. 'The boy's a disaster. He's only trying to soften you up to get money from you.'

'Well he won't,' she said in a pragmatic voice. 'It's only a Sunday lunch, darling. He's not moving in.' She began washing cups and putting things away in cupboards.

'Thank God for small mercies!' sighed Derek.

'That's all you're ever worried about,' piped in Richard. 'Money. That's more important to you than us, isn't it?' The boy jumped back on to one of the kitchen work surfaces and began kicking his heels against the doors underneath. This was a shocking statement from his son. Even Deborah reprimanded him. 'Richard, your father's under a lot of pressure at the moment. And don't kick that door, please. I'll not have showing off.'

Derek had taken his afternoon tranquilliser but it seemed to be having little effect. Even his youngest son was cheeking him. The indignity. Where was Veronica, sweet Veronica? She knew what Alan was like. She wouldn't be pleased that he was turning up on Sunday. At least Derek would have one ally. Richard threw himself off his perch and stomped off to his bedroom leaving Derek and Deborah alone in the kitchen.

'What's got into you?' she asked. Now their child was out of the room, she allowed herself to show some concern.

'I just want everything to be right,' said Derek realising, even to himself, that he was sounding a little pathetic. 'Since Alan's come back from Germany, we've had nothing but bad luck. He's a curse, that boy. A mistake. I wish he'd leave us alone.'

Deborah looked genuinely concerned. 'Look, darling, Richard likes him and he helps the child out with things we don't know anything about. We can't deny Alan access to his brother. There's nothing to suggest that Alan's after money, either. He's not mentioned it the past couple of times he's been over. You're just suffering stress because of the crash. Don't let tiny things upset you. You know what the doctor said: "try to live in the moment and not project into the future." '

'A businessman has to live in the future. He can't rest on his laurels.'

'Even businessmen have to know when to give themselves a break from their problems,' said Deborah. She rubbed his arm comfortingly. 'Don't worry about Alan. He'll have some lunch and then disappear into Richard's room. He's not expecting you to entertain him and he's not coming here for a showdown. You let that lad get to you too much. He's probably as apprehensive of you as you are of him. Don't allow Alan to become a monster in the imagination.'

'It's the disappearing into Richard's room that worries me,' said Derek. 'Who knows what he's telling the lad. He's at an impressionable age.' Derek was feeling helpless, but looking at his wife's lovely face and her soft brown hair and kind eyes made him feel better. She did understand after all – she just had a different view of the situation.

'We're all at an impressionable age, Derek,' she said. 'However old or young we are. You mustn't let him push your buttons. You have the choice of reacting to a situation in a number of ways; you are in control at all times. It's your decision how you react.'

Those self-help books which Deborah consumed by the lorry-load made easy targets for ridicule, with their Californian jargon and impenetrable syntax, but right now he was glad she was his wife – psychobabble notwithstanding. She never lost her sense of justice. She was more than he could have hoped for in a partner although he was aware that she was probably better than he deserved. These days, he awoke each morning with the fear that she would leave him for a better-looking, emotionally stronger man. He hated himself for showing his weaknesses to her yet, curiously, he was unable to prevent himself from doing so. She just seemed to have a knack of getting Derek to reveal his insecurities by talking about them. People would unload their problems to her and she would never allow her own ego to impinge on a conversation. How did she find the patience?

One thing she hadn't squeezed out of Derek, though, was the existence of the hate mail. He didn't want her knowing every last thing that happened to him; he had to keep some things secret. Nick Swift had taken the letter from him the second night they were in the Birmingham hotel and he hadn't given it back. That had made Derek feel even more impotent: it reminded him of having notes confiscated by a teacher. Swift had told Derek he was keeping it out of sight for his own good as having it around would cause him to worry. Looking back at this incident, Derek wasn't so sure about Swift's logic. At the time he had gone along with Swift's advice as he'd been so frozen with fear and indecision that he hadn't found the energy to take control of the situation.

Despite his initial agreement to not ring the police, he'd chewed the idea over and over in his head and had come to the conclusion that in fact this would be a good idea. Surely they would be sympathetic? He could ask for Sergeant Grant who had been in attendance at the crash and had taken his statement at the showroom afterwards. He seemed like a decent man: mature, late forties, well educated. The letter had arrived a couple of days ago but his reluctance to ring earlier would show a degree of calm. He wasn't panicking.

Yes, thought Derek, tomorrow would be the right time to phone. He knew it was Bruton who was trying to intimidate him. It was true that no one had reported seeing him for months but the bad spelling in the note and the words used convinced Derek that Bruton was responsible. Who else would it be? The local road safety activists were quite militant but they were middle-class liberals. They wouldn't write a letter using that kind of language, would they?

Inside he was scared. He always had been scared of Bruton. He was a fool to have taken the lad on. Why hadn't he trusted his instincts instead of being swayed by the man's mechanical competence? He didn't like his type of character. A bit too much of a wide-boy. A bit too much like the thugs who had given Derek a hard time at school. He wondered if he and Alan were still in touch. The two seemed to have made friends with each other during his employment with Landor Motors. He knew they had gone out drinking together a couple of times before Alan had gone to work in Germany. Surely Alan wasn't involved in the letter? This thought made him feel weak and sick. He stood in the kitchen, his arms around Deborah, feeling as if the life force had been drained out of him.

'Why don't you rest in the living room, darling?' Deborah said, jolting Derek back to the present. 'Or do something which will take your mind off things. What about the HydroMet project?'

Somehow, everything but a conversation with Sergeant Grant seemed pointless at the moment. Derek felt a sense of impending doom about everything. He was unable to concentrate on outside interests – mainly because he didn't want to go outside. He didn't know who might be waiting for him. HydroMet – an American sports and leisure company – and the Local Business Investments Group were scheduled to hold a crisis meeting that weekend and Derek's attendance was central to their agenda. Planning permission had been granted by the local council to build a multi-million pound recreation complex on the outskirts of the town. The problem was that environmental protestors had got wind of it and were planning disruption before building even commenced. It was crucial that the project stayed in Buckinghamshire. Shares in HydroMet were very healthy right now and Derek had made a substantial investment in the project on the advice of Edwin Charlwood. Unfortunately for Derek, it was Adrian Boxall who was supposed to be handling his money.

As yet, the protestors were unaware of Derek's involvement with HydroMet but it was bound to be only a matter of time before some over-zealous journalist got wind of it. This was also to be the meeting where everyone present would expect a statement from Derek about the crash. To not turn up would be tantamount to admitting liability. He had to make an appearance – if only to convince the directors of HydroMet that their UK-based finance manager's top broker wasn't in hospital because *he'd* let him drive faulty machinery.

TEN
The You-Know-What

Friday

Vic was back at home and feeling dazed from her Birmingham experience. She'd spent the latter part of Thursday getting some rest in the hotel and spending some time alone. On arriving back at her flat by lunchtime the next day she threw herself into her bathtub and allowed herself the luxury of a long soak. Her body felt good but her thinking was troubled. She sat in her bedroom rubbing Issy Miyake body lotion into her legs. If she wanted to, she could pack the whole thing in and report her findings as inconclusive. She'd still be paid for this past week. All she'd found out was that Derek Landor was unpopular and his salesman was highly-strung and liked sex with young blondes. Not a triumph of detection.

She felt apprehensive about the PR work she'd been offered. How long before they found out she was an impostor? The worst part about it all was that she had no one with whom she could discuss the case apart from Daniel Field – and then she couldn't tell him about the sex – and that had bothered her the most.

Vic felt alone and strange. There was no law saying she had to see Nick Swift again. She didn't have to go to Haver Dean. But the mortgage needed paying and there were no other jobs lined up. The financial incentive had to be seized. Daniel Field had promised her one per cent of everything saved if she turned up with proof there was something untoward going down at Landor Motors. It was a challenge too meaty to resist. She wouldn't be able to face herself if she didn't go for it. At least turn up for work on Monday, she thought. You never know; you may enjoy it.

The offer of staying with Nick Swift was something she'd have to think about. That would be just too weird. Maybe she would book into a guest house, pretend she was commuting each day. That way she'd be nearer to the source of whatever the hell was going wrong and be able to keep tabs on these characters' movements. For the rest of the day, however, she wanted to be herself again: see her friends, talk to her mum, do normal stuff.

First she had to make the copy of the Swift tape for Daniel. She walked into the living room and slotted the original recording into the tape-to-tape facility. She put the headphones on. There it was again: the unmistakable sound of her own sexual release. She hugged herself in embarrassment. When the sound of Derek knocking on Nick's hotel room door came through, she rewound the tape a couple of seconds then hit the record button. This wasn't a bad bit of surveillance, she reassured herself. The voices were so much more distinct listening to them on her sound system than through the tinny little earphones on the recorder. She listened to Derek's plummy voice reading aloud the words from the note: 'Shame about what happened to your car. I'm watching you and you'll be dead soon.' There was some comment from Derek about bad spelling and punctuation and an emphatic statement that he knew it was Peter Bruton.

At first when she'd heard the recordings she thought Nick had sounded quite casual about the whole thing. Hearing it again, though, she was sure there was the hint of a patronising tone to his voice. He was talking to Derek as if he were a child. Why had he kept the note? She wondered if it had been thrown away or if he'd hidden it somewhere. Maybe he had given it back to Derek. Maybe Derek had informed the police?

It would be very helpful if Vic could track down Peter Bruton before starting work on Monday. She would begin by paying a visit to his most recent address. A mini stake-out in her Toyota. The thought made her smile. She sealed the tape in a small jiffy bag and marked it for Daniel Field's personal attention. Then she decided it would be easier to hand deliver it. It would be nice to see him again. Let him know she was keen to keep up the investigation and keep herself in his employ. There must be no copping out, now, she told herself.

It was a short drive from the Angel to Farringdon; barely worth taking the car but Vic wanted the security of her own space. She'd wound her hair into a loose knot and had applied a light covering of foundation and eye make-up. She was looking casual but well groomed. Daniel Field would see a calm Victoria, despite the fact that she was secretly feeling quite frazzled. As she walked into the offices, she spotted Timothy Fuller crouched over some notes and scribbling. He chose to ignore her, which was no surprise to Vic, but she had to be sure that he wouldn't do anything to put her investigation in jeopardy. 'What news, Mr Fuller?' she asked brightly, forcing herself to smile. 'Have you heard anything from the manufacturers yet?'

'Inconclusive, so far,' he said, observing her with piggy eyes. 'They're running some more tests now and we're expecting a report some time next week.' This meant she'd be at the scene when the call from the manufacturers came through to Nick. That would be something worth watching. She told him about getting into Landor Motors as a PR person and he was not to give her cover away. 'Don't worry, Miss Donovan,' he said. 'It's unlikely I'd be expected to converse with a temporary employee, anyway.'

At that moment, Daniel appeared and greeted her. She followed him into his office. She'd brought her tape recorder with her and proceeded to play the information to him right away. He sat and listened, his clear blue eyes fixed on some point in the distance. 'How did you get this?' he asked.

'By being sneaky,' she said and smiled. 'I suppose it's possible that Bruton could be conducting some form of extortion on Landor. I've no proof he sent this note, though. Without handing it over to the police we can't say whether his prints are on it. As far as I know, the letter is in Nick Swift's possession. This is what I intend to find out. I'm working at Landor Motors next week. By this time next week I'll have a better idea of what's going on although Derek Landor himself is off work for a fortnight. Doctor's orders.'

'A worried man, I'd say,' commented Daniel. He congratulated her on getting the work at the showroom. 'It must feel strange to pretend to be something you're not,' he said. 'I admire your strategy. It must take a lot of courage.'

'I just want to find out what's going on,' she replied. 'My next move is to track down Bruton. I'm going to drive to his address in Aylesbury tomorrow.'

Daniel looked worried. 'Please be careful, Victoria. Bruton has a criminal record. He hid it from Landor while he was employed there. This information came out at the BMW trial. He's no stranger to violence.'

Vic assured Daniel she'd be very cautious. It was nice to know he was concerned about her, though. 'The tape is a copy for you to hold on to,' she said. 'I hope to be in the showroom when the manufacturers' report comes through. This is what everyone's waiting for, I guess. I still can't see how Bruton is involved in airbag malfunction. At the moment, it's all a bit of a puzzle.'

'That's why we've got you on the case, Victoria,' said Daniel. 'You're proving to be invaluable.' They held each other's gaze for a moment before Vic said goodbye. There was no denying she desired him. Was something similar happening in Daniel's mind too?

As she drove home, churning everything over in her mind, she got a call from Drake Lewis. With all that had been happening, she'd forgotten to return his call. 'What are you doing tonight?' he asked. 'I'd like to hook up with you again.

I'm back in London. Thought we could go for a drink somewhere.'

She had no other plans as yet. Why not see Drake again? She could have a night off from work; let herself go a bit. 'I'm back in London too,' she said. 'OK, Drake. Where do you want to meet?'

'I'm south London based,' he said. 'Do you know Brixton?'

'I've been to the Ritzy cinema a couple of times.'

'I've got some business down here at the moment. A couple of gigs. Could meet up by the tube station and take it from there. I've got free passes to the Fridge tonight.'

Vic knew it was gay night: Love Muscle. Seemed a strange place for him to invite her to. Still, the music was always danccable. 'OK, Drake. I'll meet you at nine,' she decided. 'I've got your number if anything comes up and I can't make it.'

'I hope you can make it,' he said, his voice breaking up slightly.

'See you there.' She signed off.

Vic wanted to enjoy herself tonight. She knew it was curiosity rather than desire which had made her agree to a date with Drake but at least it was a night away from her usual manor and he was a good-looking boy. She'd be back on the hate mail case by tomorrow lunchtime. The weekend was going to be busy.

Peter Bruton was checking tickets on the door of Gaby's nightclub. He'd offloaded a thousand more pills to one of his helpers and was feeling smug. A heavy shower earlier had left an aroma of dampness in the air. It mingled with the fruity scent of perfume worn by the teenage girls in the queue. Blokes were chewing gum and eyeing up the competition. The knowledge that none of them would dare to give him trouble made Peter feel good. He knew he was seen as something of a hard man in the area. He didn't get any trouble at these nights anyway. The most bother you got was someone skinning up in the club. He'd never had a serious run-in at Gaby's. The job was sweet.

He'd caught up with Andrew and Gary earlier in the

afternoon. They'd met at Gary's house in Gerrards Cross and worked out the basics of their planned robbery on the nightclub. He was pleased to find they were still up for it. Andrew was skint these days and badly needed the money. Gary wasn't quite so badly off but he liked the thrill of doing a job. It was them who had introduced Peter to Neil Boden. He wondered how Alan Landor was getting on trying to sort that motor for him. He hadn't called Alan for a while. Every time he got on the blower he'd get an earache from the miserable git. Peter had decided against roping Alan in on this job. He was already in enough debt to him. They could get a car through one of Gary's contacts instead. All much cleaner.

They'd had a laugh when they'd talked about how they would pretend to do Peter over. They'd strike after the club had turned out. Minimise the risk of getting punters involved. Punters were witnesses and the fewer of those, the better. The money from both Friday and Saturday nights stayed in the safe over the weekend. The decision they had to make was whether to strike last thing Saturday night or 9 a.m. Monday morning just before the takings went to the bank. Bruton and Gary preferred the Saturday night choice, opting to do things in the dark. It was easier both to move about and to make a clean getaway at night. Andrew had a fancy for first thing – break into the club and take the security by surprise before they'd had their breakfast. Bruton wouldn't be about then, though, and he wanted to make sure that he could have the best alibi there was: staring down the barrel of a sawn-off shotgun and cacking his pants.

The following weekend would be an ideal time to strike. There was a big event happening on the Friday, and Saturdays were always packed. This seemed a bit soon, but Bruton would have the advantage of working this weekend to check the security procedure one last time. Now it was really happening, he felt important and full of bravado. It had been a long time since he'd made any decent money. And he'd be taking it off people who had quite enough of the stuff. No one would be hurt. Just a bit of swagger and verbal and the pickings would be ripe.

★

As Vic ascended the escalator at Brixton underground station the smell of overstrength lager and damp trainers assaulted her nostrils. She sidestepped a couple of drunks in the ticket area selling travelcards and bounded up the stairs into the street. Outside the entrance assorted groups of people on a mission were selling everything from incense to Jihad. A couple of derelict youngsters were arguing over a bottle of amyl nitrate while their skinny dog took a crap on the pavement. As usual in Brixton on a Friday evening there was a buzz in the air. A big gig was going on at the Academy and pockets of student types and kids in baggy skate clothes filed past. It was just after nine.

A few minutes later a black BMW pulled over at the traffic lights and Drake got out before the car sped away. Vic was immediately pleased that she'd agreed to meet him again. He was a stunning-looking creature. It was a shame that his communication skills didn't complement his beauty. His method of greeting her was to flick his long hair over one shoulder and drawl, 'All right?' in a slack-jawed manner. His face was recently shaven. His brown eyes looked a touch heavy-lidded and his lips were full and dry. His seeming lack of enthusiasm gave Vic the impression that he felt obliged to meet her rather than him being the one who'd suggested it.

'It's strange meeting you here,' said Vic, keen to puncture the silence with some chitchat. It was no lie. She asked herself for what reason, other than sex, either of them had turned up. They had nothing in common with each other apart from their age and their hair and eye colour.

'Let's go for a drink,' said Drake. 'No point going to the Fridge until pub closing.' They walked to a bar on the corner of Coldharbour Lane. Drake bought them both a beer and proceeded to tell Vic he was stoned. So that was why he looked so unenthused. She felt insulted that he would turn up to meet her in such a soporific state.

'Couldn't resist banging on some of my mate's wicked charas,' he said. Vic didn't know what charas was but, from listening to Drake's semi-incoherent drawl, was sure it didn't enhance one's social skills.

Vic did most of the talking for the first twenty minutes. She told him she got the sack from her job at the Motor Show. He seemed to find this amusing. She said it was because she couldn't stand another day of working for Jeff Halman.

Drake remained guarded about his own line of work. Although he spoke a lot, he said very little that was noteworthy. He told her about getting punched at the party and insisted he'd done nothing to deserve it, although Vic remained sceptical. Mostly he went on about the joys of computers and vision mixing at various rave nights he'd been to. It was difficult for Vic to keep up her privileged persona while talking to someone who was obviously from a working-class background. Drake's slurred Thames Estuary accent and drug-related slang was the by-product of an urban upbringing. She didn't want to sound as if she was lording it over him. He looked the type who would offend easily.

She talked about theatre and acting and her time working on game shows. When she began describing the outfits she used to wear on the shows, he seemed to brighten up a little. As she talked about the tight dresses and the stockings and high heels the show's producers made her prance around in, she had his undivided attention. He seemed to be getting a thrill from hearing about this stuff and Vic, being something of an exhibitionist, found herself enjoying talking about it. Drake said she seemed like a 'naughty girl' and that he liked naughty girls.

At this, Vic found herself wanting to show him how naughty she could be, which was a far more interesting prospect than hearing about his technical skills as a vision mixer. He seemed to lighten up now there was some spark of sexuality between them. He wasn't volunteering any information about his background but Vic didn't imagine it was particularly interesting. She didn't want a relationship with Drake Lewis; she had to admit her interest in him was purely physical.

Unexpectedly, he began to talk about his fantasies and his sex life. He'd had numerous partners, none of them lasting longer than six months, and most of his bedroom activities seemed to have been fuelled by illegal drugs. The only woman he'd felt strongly about had been Turkish and her family hadn't approved of his looks and nationality and had stopped their daughter from seeing him. Vic found his personal information more easy to digest than the techno-babble. This was real stuff: relationships, desires, affairs of the heart.

By the time they were leaving the pub, Vic was eager to kiss him deeply. She desperately wanted to feel his body. She hoped that was where the evening was leading. They went to the Fridge and Drake got her in on his guest list. Inside, a parade of oiled and muscled male flesh – all of it off-limits to women – writhed and pumped its stuff on the dance floor. She stood at the bar drinking beer through a straw while Drake went off to check what time the following day the DJ who had hired his equipment was bringing his mixing desk back to his flat.

The place was filling up and the atmosphere was sexual and predatory. It was interesting to watch how men operated when trying to pick up a member of their own sex. There was an openness about such cruising which rarely happened between heterosexual strangers. Uncomplicated sex. Was there such a thing? Vic wondered. If it did exist, it was more likely to exist between gay men, she thought. Just as she was mulling over gender difference and sexual attraction, Julian appeared in front of her.

'Hello, gorgeous!' he announced loudly. 'How are you? This is Patrick.' A callow-looking young man pouted and muttered a greeting to Vic in a heavy French accent. He was one of the 'precious darlings' Julian went out with from time to time for their aesthetic value. They were both wearing white T-shirts and immaculately clean Levis. They were perspiring and their hair was damp from the exertion of dancing.

'Why on earth are you here?' Julian asked. 'Bit of a waste of time from your point of view, isn't it?' At that moment Drake reappeared and Julian's jaw dropped in astonishment. Vic knew Julian would be impressed. She introduced Drake, who grunted something inaudible and flung his hair about in his usual manner.

'We met at the Motor Show,' she said. 'Drake hires out vision mixing equipment to clubs. This one included. We're not staying here long.'

'How's it all going, Vic?' asked Julian. 'How's the you-know-what?'

Drake looked keen to find out what he was referring to and the French boy stood silent, looking fashionably bored. 'Still going on, Jules. Can't say much about it but I'm in Haver Dean next week starting a job at a car showroom. I'm doing PR of all things; helping them revamp their image, get a web site, that kind of thing.'

Vic noticed that Julian was staring at Drake – but that Drake was staring at her. 'You just stay in touch, Vic, OK?' said Jules. 'How are you fixed for badminton next Saturday? Can't make it tomorrow as Patrick's in town but I'm up for a game next week.'

'I'll have to see how it goes,' she replied, then Patrick pulled Julian away back to the dance floor leaving Vic to the task of seducing Drake.

'What's this job then?' he asked. 'And what's the "you know what"?'

Vic had no intention of talking about her PI work to anyone. 'A car showroom in Haver Dean are looking for an image overhaul. They've just lost a sponsorship deal and I'm being brought in to brainstorm.'

'What's the company called?' he asked. 'I knew someone who worked in Haver Dean for a while.'

'Landor Motors. Anyway, I don't want to talk about work: it's too boring,' she said, smiling to herself as she realised she was echoing Nick Swift's words. 'What shall we do after this?' she asked, then bravely ran her hand through Drake's hair. He swigged from his beer bottle for a few seconds looking moody. He was a sulky individual. He didn't look as if he laughed or joked around a lot. She'd barely seen him smile apart from when they'd first met by the Ferrari stand.

'How about going back to your place?' he said casually.

'I'd love that, Drake,' she whispered, snaking her arm around his waist. God, he felt nice. 'That's why you called me, isn't it?' she asked. 'To finish off what we began at the press party on Tuesday? It's your chance to find out how much of a naughty girl I am.'

This seemed to jolt him out of whatever daydream he'd become immersed in. He took hold of her hair and began to snog her. She could feel his cock twitching as it hardened in his pants. She lifted his shirt out and ran her hand over his naked flesh; it was warm and soft. Vic adored the moment she felt the first touch of a lover.

Within an hour they were back at Vic's flat. She made some coffee, put some music on and persuaded Drake to dance with her, holding her close so she could writhe against him. He was very responsive to her caresses but not at all aggressive in the way he touched and kissed her. He was quite passive and seemed to want Vic to take the lead. She took him by the hand and led him into her own bedroom. He told her the flat was beautiful; that one day he would live somewhere as nice as this. He looked a little sad when he said this – as if there was some reason beyond his control why home comforts had eluded him. Vic dimmed the lights and began to remove her clothes. Underneath she wore matching black and white lace bra, panties and suspender belt, and lace-topped, champagne-coloured stockings.

Drake's pupils dilated as he looked at her and for a moment there was a mutual admiration for each other's good looks. Vic knelt on her futon and asked Drake to join her. He removed his footwear and sweatshirt and sidled on to the mattress. They faced each other for a few moments. Vic was struck by how similar they looked. Their hair was almost identical, as if they were from the same tribe. She reached down and felt his groin. His cock was stiff in his jeans and she rubbed her hand against it. 'I like what you're wearing,' he said. 'Do you have anything else like it?'

'Oh, I've loads of stuff like this: I've a weakness for fine lingerie,' she said, running her hands around his buttocks and waist.

He unbuttoned his jeans to reveal cotton boxer shorts and an enormous erection. Vic seized upon it immediately. It was not only long but also as thick as her wrist. It weighed heavily in her grasp. Drake leant back against a big cushion, forming a lewd tableau as he took himself in hand. He began to pump his cock slowly, his lips pursing in a rude pout.

'Come on, then, naughty girl, tell me what you like. I want you to tell me what turns you on.'

She couldn't tell him about her penchant for suave insurance brokers or older car salesmen so she told him a fantasy about being ravished by the TV repair man in the middle of the afternoon. Vic made herself excited by her own story and by watching the spectacle of such a gorgeous, angelic-looking guy perform such a private act on her bed. She was more than ready to plunge his meaty wand into her moist canal but he wouldn't let her – not yet.

He tugged at her knickers and flicked his fingers between her legs, but tantalisingly avoided the core of her pleasure. Vic was wet and craving for him to stop teasing. Then Drake pulled her knickers right off but, instead of casting them aside, he put them on himself. Vic had always told herself to expect the unexpected but this was a first. However, she was so given over to her own needs, she didn't really mind. She watched as he began caressing himself, rubbing his stiff cock through the feminine material. He was writhing around like a porn star – a female porn star.

She joked, 'Do you want the stockings as well?' to which he nodded his head. This was all getting a bit strange, but if a guy had to have a fetish then wearing women's underwear was one of the more attractive kinks, she told herself. She unclipped the suspender belt and fastened it around Drake's slender curving waist. She couldn't resist grabbing hold of his penis and squeezing it.

'When I've got those on,' he gestured at the stockings, 'I'm going to fuck you so hard. Then we can be naughty girls together.'

Vic began giggling out of embarrassment. This was certainly one to tell Julian about. She rolled the stockings from her own legs and unravelled them on his. By the time she snapped the studs of the belt into the sheer nylon, he was ecstatic. She had to admit there was something appealing about the feel of his masculine hardness encased in satin and lace. She lay on top of him and ran her hands under his buttocks. This was the first time Vic had felt stockings and suspenders on another person. It felt good. Weird, but good.

He pushed his cock against her and whispered lewd things in her ear. She sat up, positioning her legs astride him. Her sex was aching; needing to be filled. Drake lay back and allowed her to prise his penis from its lacy covering. She played with it for a while.

'I've got a rubber in my jeans' pocket,' he said. Vic reached over and found it. He made no effort to put it on himself so Vic took charge. Now the moment had arrived. The joy; the release of being united with the male of the species. And what a fine specimen he was – even if he was more than a little strange. He thrust deeply and slowly and Vic was propelled into a state of ecstasy. She threw her head back and gasped with each lunge of his cock. It reached her G-spot with every nudge. He kept his eyes open throughout and he was vocal, too. Not in the way Nick Swift had been, with his grunting and groaning. Drake was articulate, talking to her, encouraging her to talk back. He rolled her over and assumed the on top position. His hair swayed with the movements of his body like a heavy curtain. He'd broken into a sweat and was thrusting with the relentless motion of an engine.

Forty minutes later, Vic was exhausted. They'd done it every way possible and still he hadn't come. Vic thought her own orgasm would have been enough to trigger Drake's release but his balls refused to give up their contents. When she told him she didn't expect a display of endurance he confessed that he'd taken half a pill while they were in the Fridge and that he could probably keep going for another hour. Vic groaned and looked at the clock. Drake certainly seemed to have a problem enjoying himself without drugs. She would have been happy with a half hour of great sex and a good night's sleep. She was staking out Bruton tomorrow and a sleepless night hadn't been in her plan. It was no good telling Drake to get some sleep. He would be awake for a good while yet. With MDMA and whatever else charging around his system, repetitive movement was all he was interested in.

He stopped thrusting for a few minutes while she worked out a compromise. It was already half past two and her eyes were feeling heavy. It was nice to be held and stroked but it was a disappointment to Vic to find his affection was drug-induced. She would never have known he was pilled up if he hadn't told her. At least he seemed happier than at the beginning of the evening. However, she could imagine it would be a very morose creature which crawled out of her flat the following morning. That delight was yet to come.

On waking, Vic had a hazy memory of Drake finally reaching his orgasm. He'd put on and pulled off a further two condoms and eventually found his own release by masturbating. At around 5.00 a.m. she'd been allowed some peace. It had been enough sex to last her a month. She awoke at nine but Drake was comatose, still in the stockings and suspenders – a curious but strangely attractive sight to wake up to. In sleep his face looked even more angelic. Rousing him, however, was not something she was looking forward to. It had been an interesting and draining experience having sex with Drake. No wonder his relationships hadn't lasted very long. The poor women were probably worn out!

Vic threw herself into a hot bath and allowed the aches and pains of the night's gymnastics to dissolve into the aromatic water. Sex with Drake had been different, challenging and a little bit scary. She'd seen plenty of men in drag but he was probably the first transvestite she'd met. This didn't seem to fit with his druggy antics, the computer chat and the designer casuals he wore. What a strange bloke he is, she thought, gazing at the colour of the frosted bottle of bath oil as the morning light filtered through it. So many contradictions and anxieties. He was certainly not someone she wanted to develop a regular relationship with. If he was more at ease with himself he would make a good lover; he was a great performer but he needed to lighten up a little. Learn how to enjoy himself without relying on illegal substances. What if he wanted to see her again? He knew her address. She hoped she'd done the right thing by letting him into her flat. Vic resolved to remain casual and friendly. But she wanted him out of her house very soon. She was preparing herself to spend the day following a potentially dangerous man and she wanted her wits about her.

After dressing in her bedroom, which failed to wake the sleeping lover, Vic made fresh coffee which she hoped was as strong as amphetamine. It seemed, however, that Drake Lewis needed a grenade to go off next to him before he began interacting with the day. She shook him, prodded him and talked loudly to him. His face was flushed and squashed on the pillow and he had sprawled his body over the entire bed. He failed to respond. She bit his toes. That did it. He yelped angrily and pushed himself half off the mattress. He looked at Vic with an expression partly of confusion and partly of the embarrassing realisation that he was still sporting her underwear. Vic tried not to laugh. She already knew enough about Drake to realise that jokes at his own expense would not be appreciated or taken in jest.

'I have to leave the house within half an hour,' she said, as gently as she could. 'There's coffee here. How's your head?'

'It's fine,' he replied, blinking his bloodshot eyes. 'Can I stay here until you get back?'

Vic was amazed by this question. He seemed not to think for a second that such a thing would be inappropriate; that she wouldn't dream of it. She didn't show her disapproval but simply said, 'No. Sorry Drake, that isn't possible. There's only one set of keys and I need to double-lock the door from the outside.'

He groaned and then reached out his arm to caress her leg. He had a nice touch, this chancy, kinky, moody, blond reprobate. Part of her wished she could dive back under the covers with him. The pale light on his face illuminated the faint downy hairs which covered his cheeks. He was beautiful. And his thoughts looked so far away. There was a sadness in his eyes which Vic had not seen in anyone before. She made light of her observation by saying, 'Hey – it's not that bad is it? I can see you're not used to getting up before lunchtime.'

Drake hauled himself up and stumbled to the bathroom. Five minutes later he returned naked to Vic's bedroom. She couldn't take her eyes from the sight of his pendulous member swaying heavily between his legs. Even when not erect it looked heavy and substantial. She made to put her arms around him but he seemed to shy away from this. Showing affection was not something which came easily to him. He refused the offer of both breakfast and a shower and shrugged himself into his clothes, which looked crumpled and reeked of smoke.

In the living room, as he laced up his trainers, he muttered that he'd like to see her again. When asked what he was doing for the rest of the day he started wittering on about computers again and Vic cut the conversation short by changing the subject. Listening to people prattle on about things she didn't understand was very tiring. There was a slightly awkward moment when she made to kiss him at the door as she saw him out. It was a simple, friendly gesture but Drake looked quite horrified by it. He said he would call her.

Vic was relieved when she heard the downstairs door close. She walked back into her bedroom to tidy up. As expected, Drake hadn't made any effort to tidy the bed. Always a sign of laziness, she thought. Unmade beds were horrible things. She pulled the cover and sheet off and rolled them into a ball along with her discarded underwear, which she found lying on the bathroom floor. As she bundled them into the washing machine, Drake's watch fell out. It was a genuine Tag Heuer. Had he left it there on purpose or was he so drug-addled he'd forgotten to put it back on? She'd have to return it to him but he could wait until next week. There were more important things for her to do before then.

ELEVEN
A Right No-Brainer

Saturday

Derek stood in the kitchen staring out of the window. Deborah was out shopping and Richard was watching Saturday morning television in his room. Derek had barely exchanged two sentences with his son since he had snapped at him the other day. The HydroMet meeting had gone OK but Derek's mind hadn't been on the business at hand. He knew that he'd made a lame presentation to the group. Maybe it was the tranquillisers making him sluggish. A younger, more dynamic speaker had taken the meeting over and Derek had found his concentration drifting at moments where he was expected to participate. He couldn't wait until the end and had left early, claiming illness. His associates had appeared sympathetic but there was little room in that world for taking time out. Business needed to forge ahead. Investments had to be made which couldn't wait for Derek's mental health to improve.

At times like this he wanted to run back to his mother's estate and leave it all behind. That may have been possible if she hadn't known about the crash. Curse the local paper.

There was no privacy these days. Of course, Gayle Landor had been on the phone as soon as she'd read the headlines. Now the Motor Show was over, he knew he was going to be summoned to a meeting with her. Far from escaping his problems by visiting her, he was going to have go through every detail as she grilled him. It wasn't his fault. The whole situation was so unfair. He was being treated as guilty until proven innocent. His gut pained him and his head ached. There was so much anxiety racing through his veins he felt both dizzy and tired. The thought of Alan showing up the next day was the final straw; he honestly didn't think he could face it.

He heard a key in the front door. A minute later, his daughter Veronica came into the kitchen to make a cup of tea. She asked Derek how he was feeling and he stuttered in clipped tones, trying not to choke on his words. It was no good. He couldn't lie to Veronica; he couldn't tell her that everything was fine when it so clearly wasn't. But she didn't know anything about the world of business. She was wrapped up in her studies and the lives of her friends. How could she understand the worries Derek was going through?

He'd explained to her some of what had been happening but she couldn't grasp why her father was so troubled by something for which he wasn't to blame. He couldn't tell her about the note. He hadn't been able to tell any of his family. It was taking all his strength to prevent himself from blurting out how scared he was. He wanted to cry; to ask his wife and daughter to protect him from Bruton.

'You know that Alan's coming round for Sunday lunch tomorrow, don't you?' he asked.

'Yeah, worst luck. It's mum: she could stop Richard from having him round if she wanted, but you know what she's like these days since she's been doing that counselling and therapy course. She thinks she's able to turn him around; make him into a well-adjusted person. I've told her not to waste her time.'

Derek watched his daughter as she made herself a sandwich. He wished his appetite would return. The tranquillisers seemed to have suppressed his hunger.

'I'm not going to speak to him,' said Veronica. 'I never invited him round. If he starts winding me up I think I'll hit him. Remember the row we had about calling Deborah mum?' Derek certainly did. That was the time he'd stormed out and broken the glass in the front door. Derek had thought he'd have to have the boy sectioned again.

'I know that was a while back but I still don't trust him. You never know when he's going to throw a fit of anger,' she went on.

Derek wondered if his son's anger would ever end. There was an animosity between the siblings which had been apparent from their early childhood. Veronica had always been well behaved while Alan had to be locked in his room for the sake of the family's sanity. A succession of nannies had walked out of the job of looking after him. He'd bitten one of them hard enough to draw blood – and that was when he was only five. By the time Veronica had been born, his rages had become a daily feature and the attention focused on his sister only served to increase his infant wrath.

Sally hadn't handled it. Already suffering post-natal depression, she was, by then, doing strange things like walking out of supermarkets without the children or forgetting to take them to school. Veronica had been seven years old when Sally died. Gayle had looked after her while Derek had mourned his wife but was – like most people – unable to handle Alan and the boy had by this time gone from bad to worse. No one expected a sixty-year-old woman to put up with a violent child.

Within a year he was in a private boarding school for difficult children while Veronica had recovered from the shock with amazing strength and had blossomed into a bright child. Now she was a bright twenty-three year old and Derek was proud of her. He hoped she would look after herself on the long trip she was planning for next summer. He looked at her. Her hair was brown and thick and cut into a sleek bob and she radiated physical vitality and health. She was a credit to the family. He hoped Richard would follow her example. He was at a difficult age and Derek had noticed some tensions between him and his half-sister. He hoped

Alan hadn't been filling the boy's head with lies and stories about the bad times.

'Deborah will keep everything in order,' said Derek. 'We must try to act relaxed. We both know that Alan thrives on creating discord in this family. We have to all be strong to make sure he doesn't start his old games.' Derek couldn't let on to Veronica how apprehensive he was feeling. He was sure that if he allowed himself to reveal the smallest anxiety he would break down in tears. Strong. He had to be strong.

At the Motor Show Nick was playing the part of the enthusiastic salesman but most of the real business had been done over the past four days. Now it was punters' weekend: Britain's great unwashed and its wives and kids had descended on the show in bulk. Every five minutes some greasy-fingered brat was poking around the cars, smearing the windscreens or trying to climb in the E-type. Thank Christ Johnstone was working the weekend with him; Nick wasn't in the mood for humouring the kiddies. He'd just had a call from Derek which he had to act on fast. Derek hadn't taken Nick's advice. He'd gone right ahead and phoned Sergeant Grant and bleated like a stuck pig about the note. This was something Nick hadn't expected.

He left Johnstone holding the fort while he went to make a call. It wasn't something he was looking forward to, but it had to be done – for the sake of his own skin. He found a rank of phones by one of the bars.

'Is that Peter?' he asked.

'Who's this?' came the reply. 'Yeah, it's Peter.'

'It's Nick. Swifty. What you playing at? I've got old man Landor shitting himself.'

Bruton laughed. 'Get my little note, did he?'

Nick was furious that he found this so funny. 'I thought you might like to know that I took it off him. It must have had your prints all over it. I just want to tell you that if the Old Bill come knocking on your door, it's nothing to do with me, OK? I tried to stop him going to the law but it's too late. He's off work for two weeks under doctor's orders. You've caused him no end of worry. He wants the note back from me first thing Monday so he can hand it over at Haver Dean Old Bill station. You silly sod. What d'you send a thing like that for?'

'I dunno. Spur of the moment. I was bored. I thought it was really funny that his car got trashed by some fuckin' yuppie ponce, that's all.'

'You were nothing to do with that, though. It was an accident, right?'

'Course I was nothing to do with it. Why d'you think I could have been involved? I was at home at the time. Kipping probably.'

'Well, Landor's taking it seriously. He thinks you're trying to kill him. If you get brought in, you're still going to be schtum, aren't you? I mean, this is nothing to do with me.'

'Well, the note's just going to have to disappear, isn't it? Easy.'

Swift groaned. Even though this was nothing to do with him he was being made to commit an offence – withholding evidence – again! Swift knew the bloke was a hardnut, but Nick had been around, too. He wasn't physically intimidated by Bruton; he was just apprehensive of his wagging tongue if he was brought in for questioning.

'What am I going to tell Landor?' asked Nick.

'That's your problem, mate,' replied Bruton. 'Look, I'm too busy to listen to your complaints. No need to cack your pants. Just lose it. I know you'll do it. You'll keep your old chum Peter out of the nick like you did last time.'

'That was supposed to be it,' said Swift. 'A one-off which is done and dusted. The case was thrown out of court and we all got a little bit of dough for it. Why couldn't you let things lie, eh?'

'I said it was a spur of the moment thing. I saw the crash in the paper and Landor's ugly mug staring out of the picture. I couldn't resist it. It was a wind-up. Nothing more.'

'Just leave me out of anything else you're planning, all right?' Nick said. 'Stop acting like a loose cannon. There's other people involved here, too.'

'Little Nick worried about his job is he? Don't worry. I wouldn't plan anything else with you in mind. You ain't got a clue, mate. You're just the boss's yes man.'

And with that, Bruton hung up the phone, cutting Swift off and leaving him to stew. It was easy enough to lie about losing the note, though. One scrap of paper in the melee of the Motor Show could easily go missing. Maybe it would all blow over if the police had nothing to go on.

Vic drove to Aylesbury and parked her car within sight of Bruton's address. Council estates in the suburbs had a more menacing feel to them than those in the inner city; a different kind of anger. Young white blokes with too much time to spare and not enough money to fill it populated places like this. The problem was that people were segregated in the suburbs – kept away from culture. In the city, everyone was thrown in together and had to learn to get on with each other and you were usually a bus ride away from something vibrant. Here, the unemployed and the undesirable were parcelled off to the outskirts of the town where not a lot went on after dark except family rows. The feel–good factor was absent from this estate. In fact, there was little sign of life at all.

A couple of women with push chairs and bags of shopping walked past slowly, smoking. Litter was scattered around the grass area and the neighbourhood shopping precinct had only the most basic of amenities: a launderette, a newsagents, a Happy Shopper mini–market and a fish and chip shop. This was British suburban architecture at its most bleak.

She sat and waited. She was dressed in tracksuit bottoms and a bomber jacket, with her blonde hair tied up under a dark and wavy real hair wig. In her bag was a change of clothes and a box full of cosmetics, just in case. Vic remembered how she'd been required to change appearance at short notice on her previous job. That had been nearly all surveillance. She'd bought a cheap single–lens–reflex camera and a long lens after that. This would be her first chance to use it but no one had come out of or gone into the address in the two hours she'd been there.

This was the dull part of the work. The only thing to keep her occupied was the radio. She knew that it would be sod's law that if she went to the shop or stretched her legs something would happen, so she'd also brought a packed lunch with her. She only hoped that someone would appear before she needed to pee. She'd brought an emergency Tupperware container with her, just in case, but hoped that she didn't have to resort to such a demeaning procedure.

The garden of Bruton's house was unkempt and the fence was broken. The paintwork on the front door was cracked and peeling and the windows looked as if they could use a wash. Vic just wanted to ring the doorbell and take her chances. She'd racked her brains for excuses. Surveys were always good. Most people had an opinion about local facilities. She'd kept her copy of the *Gazette* and had leafed through it before leaving London, looking for offers which wouldn't be of any interest to Bruton. She considered using the God option but realised that would get the door slammed in her face too quickly. If she said she was lost, she had no reason to know his name. She'd hit upon a last resort ploy and had armed herself with clipboard and printed out a list of street names from a local map in case he got nosy.

She couldn't stand hanging around much longer. The guy could be out for the whole day. If he was in the house she wanted to meet him. With the wig and the dull questions she was about to ask him, he'd never recognise her later on. The Liverpool accent would complete the disguise.

She rang the bell and heard movement. Her heart was racing but she had the advantage. A skinny, dark-haired young woman opened the door with a child in her arms. She looked numb from watching too much bland TV and having sleepless nights. 'Yeah?' she sneered, suspiciously.

'All right, love?' Vic began. 'I'm working for the local council, checking the names on the electoral register. Are you Mrs Bruton?'

'I fuckin' should've been,' she replied. 'You've got your records all wrong. The name here now is Taylor. I registered at the beginning of the year, before the general election. Bloody council. Can't get anything right.'

The child started grizzling. His hands were grubby and his clothes looked too small. From what Vic could see of the hallway, the place needed money throwing at it. Money this woman obviously didn't have.

'Does Peter Bruton live here?' Vic found the courage to ask. By now she was convinced that he'd left the address. 'Only I've got him down as being registered here,' she continued.

'No. He left a year ago. Don't live here no more. He's over at Millfields now. I shouldn't think he's too bothered about voting, mind. He's this one's father,' she said. 'Only useful thing he ever done.'

Vic made some friendly noises to the child.

'He's supposed to be picking him up for the day but he's late, as usual. Probably sleeping off a sore head again.'

The woman looked as if she wanted a good old bitching session about the no-good bloke her ex-boyfriend was. I bet she knows everything about Bruton, thought Vic. If only I could get her talking. 'So, your name is Taylor . . .'

'Sheryl,' she chipped in. 'And this is Sean, although he's a bit young for voting yet,' she giggled.

'Don't worry, love. I'm sure his dad will turn up,' said Vic, not wanting to appear too nosy. 'Thanks for helping me with these records. It's a bit of a boring job but you've got to pay the rent somehow.'

'I wish I could work,' said Sheryl. 'I used to work as a barmaid in the centre of town. That's where I met his father. It ain't worth it now, though. I'd be working just to be able to pay the childminder.'

'My mum has the same problem back home,' said Vic. She didn't need to fill the conversation with more lies. Sheryl was only too keen to keep talking.

'Of course, I've asked him to look after him Friday and Saturday nights so I can go back to the pub but he wouldn't even if he could. That one likes clubbing it so much he's working at the fucking place now.'

'I didn't know there were any clubs round here,' said Vic, hoping that Sheryl would take the bait.

'You must know Gaby's,' she said. 'Where you been living?'

'I'm not really the clubbing type,' Vic went on, almost light-headed with how easy it had been to get her talking.

'Better get on, love. I've got the whole estate to do.'

'You watch out for Dagmar House. They're a bit rough in there,' Sheryl shouted as Vic walked off as if to knock next door. She waited on the next doorstep until she was convinced Sheryl was back inside her own house and then scooted back to the car. Gaby's. Sooner or later he'd turn up there. If what Sheryl said was true, he was bound to be there this evening. It was Saturday night after all. She'd wait just a bit longer, though.

Despite a shaky start to the day, Alan had focused on what needed to be done to put his plan into effect as soon as he'd left Vicky's place. Boden was due at the garage at three. Alan had gone home, shaved, showered and changed into something clean and was now a bundle of energy as he went over his strategy. He wanted the hit to happen next week and there was no reason why it shouldn't as long as there was a secure place to keep Derek. There was a disused aircraft hangar just outside Basingstoke he'd done a few raves in with Bruton on security, but who knew who owned it these days? He needed somewhere that was guaranteed secure; preferably a gaff that had no connection to himself or any of his drug mates.

He wanted to keep everything clean for Boden. It had to be far enough from Little Chalfont to take the heat off family members as suspects, yet near enough to the house to be manageable. Boden wouldn't want to be driving around for too long with sixteen stone of whimpering evidence in the back of the motor. There was little, other than the location, to sort out. Derek's movements were regular as clockwork. After tomorrow's Sunday lunch, Alan would know everything about his coming week.

As Alan opened the garage door to Boden he pictured himself in his father's forthcoming position. He'd be shitting himself; there was no doubt of it. Boden had turned up with two assistants, both half his age and twice as fierce-looking. Silent and huge, the three men entered the garage.

'This is Dave and Clem – not their real names of course,' said Boden. 'I don't expect that anyone here will be using anything other than aliases. Dave, Clem, meet Drake. He's getting us the diplo car later on. But something's come up, hasn't it, lad? And this is where you two come in.' He turned to Alan. 'I've filled 'em in on what's what.'

The two younger men looked at Alan with blank expressions. Boden was taking over the show. He was providing the muscle and the experience. All Alan had to sort was the car and Derek's movements for the following week. Taking a look at Boden's friends was enough to make sure he'd do the most accurate job he could. Pissing these guys off wasn't worth thinking about. Alan and Boden talked for about forty minutes while the other two listened. Boden had a mate who leased out shipping containers on the outskirts of Tilbury. It was a long way from Haver Dean but the place would be tight as a gnat's chuff. Nothing legit went in there and no one renting space had anything but moody gear to shift. The containers were all individually sealed and no one else had keys. The mate wouldn't ask questions. He'd run with Boden back in the sixties and knew the benefits of keeping his mouth shut.

Alan was happy with his choice. No one he knew could do it better. 'In and out. Swift and hard,' was the man's advice on the job and Alan wasn't going to argue. The only problem would be getting Derek from Haver Dean to Tilbury. That would mean the M25 to Thurrock then a short drive to the site. The long way round, but going through London would be a kamikaze mission. Too many traffic lights; too many cops; too many chances for something to go wrong. On the motorway they could bomb it but they reckoned it would still take about two and a half hours. Clem said the solution was simple. 'Knock him out. Only way.'

Alan looked worried.

'Not over the head. Out. You know. Give him a dose of sleeping pills. Always keep 'em for this kind of job. The kidnapper's friend.' Clem laughed and Dave snorted in agreement.

'You can see these boys are professionals, son,' said Neil. 'Wouldn't use anything but. They'll see you're all right. We'll clean up.'

They agreed they'd ask for half a million. That gave some room for manoeuvre. If they came out with a quarter of a million everyone would be happy. A hundred thousand and things were getting tight. Neil grilled Alan over and over about the money being available. Alan told them he knew from working for Derek Landor how loaded his mother was and how she followed her son's every move and doted on him.

Dave and Clem seemed ready to go just for the excitement value. They wanted to get a look at their target before strike day, though. Alan said he would know by tomorrow when and where he'd be all week and to stand by for calls. For proof he handed Derek's home and work address to the men. He also gave them all his telephone numbers. Alan needed to prove he was serious. 'Go on. Ring him up. Give him a fright,' he challenged them.

Dave blocked a trace on his mobile number and dialled Landor's land line. His face stayed calm as he asked to speak to Derek. Then he cut the phone dead. 'Girl answered. He's there, fair enough.' Clem and Neil nodded their heads in acknowledgement. Alan had intermittent pangs of doubt about the seriousness of the operation but his desperation for money and justice was overriding the apprehension. They had decided Wednesday was going to be the day of action. They had three days to watch their target.

Vic drove past Gaby's a number of times before parking the car. She'd changed into clubwear and put on a load of make-up in the town centre's public loos. A calf-length raincoat covered her legs but once she took it off she was guaranteed to attract attention. She'd got a look at Bruton as he finally turned up at Sheryl's house around four o'clock. It was nine now and Gaby's had a hefty queue lining up outside it. She paid her ten pounds and found a spot near the bar from which to observe the movements of the security guys.

Sure enough, Bruton was there. His fat neck rubbed on the collar of his bomber jacket and he swaggered around as if he owned the place. He was quite an ugly sight but that didn't seem to prevent a gaggle of local girls flirting with him and getting him to show them tricks. Whatever it was that attracted them to him, he seemed to have enough of it to satisfy his admirers. She noted the Top Deck logo on his jacket: the same one as worn by the guys who'd patrolled the party at the Motor Show. This was an interesting connection! She wondered what rackets he had going in this place. It crossed her mind that he might know Drake Lewis. Maybe Lewis supplied Bruton with drugs as well. She would have to tread carefully.

Vic stood sipping from a glass of coke and waiting for her moment. The place was huge and as yet not even half full. The DJ was playing a tepid mixture of swing and lo-fi happy house which seemed to keep the punters happy before the serious dancing began. There were a number of empty seats around and Vic nestled herself in a corner after walking past Bruton and catching his eye. One look at his face was enough to realise that she'd made her mark. His expression was an open book; a look that said 'I can pull you and you'll want me.' She was prepared to let him do most of the talking. It was going to be painful but Vic resigned herself to the fact that intellectual conversation had to go out of the window for the evening.

Vic acted like a magnet to Bruton, who was sitting next to her within minutes. 'You're not here on your own, surely,' was his opening line. Vic played at being aloof. 'Where's your boyfriend tonight?' he continued as his eyes roved over her body. 'I can keep you company for a while. I'm Peter. What's your name?'

He was persistent and his eyes were out on stalks as he ogled her breasts. He sidled up next to her. He seemed to regard any woman without a man in tow as fair game. Evolution hadn't made any quantum leap when it came to Bruton's method of attracting the female of the species. Vic was half expecting him to start leaping around and beating his chest. He was a lunkhead el supremo. He began sounding off about the club – how he thought it was better than the Ministry of Sound; that he went on holiday to Ibiza last year and had a 'mad one'; that he was thinking of setting up his own club. He dominated the conversation because he obviously didn't think that any woman would have much of interest to talk about.

This was fine by Vic. She was about to surprise him. 'I'm Julie,' she announced in her best Thames Estuary accent. 'I was expecting to meet someone here tonight. Someone told me you Top Deck boys have got a few sidelines.'

Bruton's expression changed; darkened. He looked worried for a second. 'What d'you mean, sidelines?' he asked quietly. 'Is it 'cos you want to sort something out? Y'know – some business or something?' He was looking around him to check no management were about before he mentioned the business by name. 'Who told you about it? D'you know Andrew and Gary?'

Vic smiled. Surely he was too thick to pull a bluff. Those names were as good as any. 'Yeah, Andrew, I think his name was. We're in the same line of work, if you know what I mean. We discussed a few things which might be mutually beneficial. They said I should pop down here.'

Bruton was almost frothing with curiosity. 'How many d'you want? What you looking at? Hundreds? Thousands?'

'No, you got me wrong. I'm not buying, I'm selling.' It was a risk. If Bruton had turned straight he could call the cops on her or throw her out. Thing was she had nothing on her that was illegal. It was bluff all the way.

'Sorry, Julie, but we're already sorted for more pills round here than we can lose. No disrespect but I think you've been given a bum steer.' He was in deep already. His eyes were flickering over her, sizing her up. She could see his brain was trying to process the information. He probably hadn't come across a female dealer before.

'You're not Old Bill are you?' he asked, a sudden moment of panic seizing him. He grabbed her bag and began rooting through it. She'd locked her camera and ID in her car. All she had with her was make-up, a mobile phone, keys and money.

She snatched it back from him. 'Do me a favour!' she exclaimed. 'No, I'm not Old Bill. And I'm not selling pills, either. I heard you might be able to shift some Charlie.'

'Terry Farley!' Bruton laughed.

Vic didn't recognise the name but went along with it anyway. 'Yeah. Terry Farley.'

Bruton looked over his shoulder again. He was trying to keep an eye on the club as well as talk to Vic. 'Not much demand for it round here. Most of the kids can't afford it. It ain't economical, is it? A pill's gonna sort someone for a whole night and they'd still have change out of a tenner. The other gear's too much fuckin' hassle, to be honest. You get some older, rich types in here occasionally but they're usually sorted already. They wouldn't dream of buying coke in a club. You're better off shifting it in London, really. I'd still like to buy you a drink, though. You can tell me a little bit more about yourself. I like intelligent women.'

Oh well, it had been worth a try, Vic thought. At least she hadn't been thrown out. Her mission was to get more information out of Bruton without finding herself in the awkward position of being his food for the night. The thought of that big square head rubbing itself anywhere near her face – or worse! – filled her with horror. He told her he had to do the rounds, make a few checks around the club, then he'd be back to chat some more. Great. The evening was shaping up to be a right no-brainer.

About twenty minutes later Bruton returned with a well-built older guy in tow. He was wearing a Hard Rock Café brown-leather jacket and a baseball cap. He looked about thirty-five.

'Julie. This is Johnny,' said Bruton. 'He does the sound and lighting here. I had a word with him about your offer. Johnny's interested aren't you, Johnny?'

Vic had to think on her feet again. 'Yeah, hi Johnny. How much are you after?'

'Five Gs. Got a few gigs coming up next week. It'd be well handy as it goes. Always like a bit of the old pearl barley.' He laughed and Vic joined in.

She was keen to keep in with Bruton's cohorts. The guy seemed pleasant enough. He was a member of that tribe of technicians who liked to strut around with carabinas hanging off their jeans and do endless soundchecks. Strictly FM guys who raked in the cash and liked the champagne lifestyle. He was no crook.

'Thing is. I'm not holding tonight,' said Vic. 'I was just testing the water in here. Had to make sure I wasn't going to be searched, you understand. I know some of these places have female security.' Johnny looked disappointed.

'Tell you what I'll do. I can meet you here on Tuesday with it. Can you wait until then?'

'Well, I don't know anyone else useful in that way at the moment,' he said.

'You're here on Tuesday I hope,' said Vic. Johnny shook hands with her and went on his way. 'Don't worry,' said Bruton. He'll be here. If not, we'll sort something out. Now. How about that drink. Anything you like. On the house.'

TWELVE
The Stultifying Sound of Suburbia

Sunday

Unknown to Alan Landor, Clem and Dave cruised a safe distance behind him as he left his council block at the Elephant and Castle at one. They'd been following him since he left his garage the previous night. It was drizzling but the two men were patient. A security precaution, they'd agreed. Wouldn't do them any favours to go into a job like this blind.

'He looks a bit rough, what do you reckon?' asked Clem as he pressed the pre-programmed radio channel to something more upbeat than GLR's Sunday morning fare.

'Rough and bricking it,' said Dave. 'There's one thing for sure. We control the cash. He ain't going nowhere without us divvying up the result, okay?'

'He's on his own, mate,' laughed Clem. 'He's a walking advertisement for trouble. You can't go around looking like that without attracting attention.'

'For sure.'

They drove most of the way in silence, then conversed minimally with each other as they became increasingly sure of his destination. They followed him up the B4442, passing a succession of properties – each looking more valuable, with a driveway longer and wider, than the last.

'Size of these gaffs. Ever done a job indoors?' asked Clem. 'Gets the adrenaline going like nothing else. The best is when you separate the bloke from his wife, take her away and get him sweating. Then you tell him you're going to take his missus every which way. Never fails to trigger the memory for the combination to the safe.'

'That was the Highgate job, wasn't it? What did you clear on that, forty grand?'

'Fifty, all told, once the bits and pieces were flogged off. Not bad for an evening's work. And we did the wife.'

Dave laughed crudely and hit the breaks as Alan swung his car into the driveway of the Landor property. They got a good look at the house. It was magnificent. 'How come a bloke like that can turn up here on a Sunday lunchtime?' asked Clem.

'I dunno. Maybe he's picking up his P45.' They laughed, and parked at a suitable vantage point to survey the scene.

The grandfather clock in the hall chimed two as Derek peered drowsily over the top of his *Sunday Times* business section. He'd taken a second tranquilliser an hour before which was fusing quite nicely with a relaxing quantity of vintage wine. Deborah was in the kitchen roasting a joint of beef and potatoes. Richard was in his room and Veronica was in the garden helping out with some autumnal leaf raking. All was peaceful.

Derek had felt a little better since informing Grant about his poison letter. At least he'd been able to get it off his chest to someone other than Nick. The sergeant had sounded sympathetic but wanted to wait until the police were in possession of the thing before they jumped to conclusions. It could be an embittered anti-car fanatic, they'd said. Everything was in a state of limbo. The manufacturers' report was due within a couple of days, and that was playing on Derek's nerves as well as Alan's imminent arrival. With all the added stress, Derek had justified the use of the extra tranquilliser.

He hoped Alan's visits wouldn't become a regular event. Now Richard was getting older, he wanted male company around. Derek made a note to himself to encourage his son to invite schoolfriends home. He heard some noise in the kitchen. Veronica was getting on her high horse again about the rest of the family having beef for lunch. When the BSE crisis had hit the headlines, Veronica had become almost intolerably sanctimonious and had achieved a state of beatification among her vegetarian friends for refusing to dine at the same table as her parents.

Then, Derek heard the sickening sound of Alan's car draw up outside and didn't know whether to run upstairs or sit firmly and try to pretend everything was OK. He walked into the kitchen – to where the women were busying themselves with preparing the lunch – and stood there feeling helpless. They didn't seem to be sharing his distress.

'Get the wine would you, darling,' said Deborah giving Derek an excuse to disappear downstairs into the cellar for a few minutes.

As he perused the wine racks, he heard the doorbell ring, then footsteps going upstairs. The rude bastard must have walked straight up to Richard's room without stopping even to ask Veronica and Deborah how they were. The ignorance of the boy made Derek angry. As angry as he could be with more than the recommended daily dose of Diazepam coursing through his system.

When Derek cautiously entered the dining-room, the table was beautifully prepared. He opened the wine and left it to breathe on the table. 'Is he upstairs then?' he asked quietly.

'Yes,' replied Veronica. 'It's here. As communicative as ever.'

'Please try to be pleasant, Veronica, even if Alan isn't,' said Deborah. 'If you operate on his level the two of you will cancel each other out. To be friendly is to be strong. I'll tell them dinner will be five minutes. Derek, take the joint out of the oven and let it cool before you carve. We're going to have a traditional Sunday meal. There's no need to worry about anything. Any of you. I could knock all your heads together sometimes.'

Despite her attempts at pragmatism in the face of animosity, it was Deborah who started the shouting. She made the mistake of entering Richard's room too soon after knocking and had stumbled on her thirteen-year-old son swigging from a can of lager supplied, of course, by Alan. Derek watched open-mouthed at the bottom of the stairs as she bounded down, apron flapping, with the offending can in her hand.

'Drink,' she announced to Derek and Veronica. 'No wonder Richard's so keen to have his older brother around. I can't believe he's being so irresponsible. Derek, tell him. He's your son.'

Derek made a lame attempt at calling Alan and Richard down with everything from threatening to ground Richard to reporting Alan to the police. Neither of them stirred and Derek felt more impotent with each burst of laughter from behind the closed door. Veronica stormed up the stairs and charged into the room then slammed the door. All went quiet and both parents left them to it. Derek sunk into his chair with the exertion of shouting up the stairs and Deborah walked into the garden to still her mind.

Ten minutes later, Veronica returned. 'I've thought a couple of times recently he's been drinking but I wasn't sure. But now I know it's Alan that's bought the stuff for him. Richard's been drinking that alcoholic lemonade.'

Derek sat with his head in his hands. He couldn't face any more problems in his family. 'I'll get Deborah to talk to him later,' he said. 'Let us have our lunch now.' Veronica prepared her own lunch while Deborah silently dished out the potatoes and greens. The meat sat uncarved waiting for Derek. Alan and Richard bounded into the dining room giggling and looking mischievous. The sight of their parents' distress only seemed to increase their mirth. Deborah watched anxiously as if she was witnessing the first signs of Richard's decline into adolescent petulance. It was like history repeating itself.

Vic sat in her living room holding her mobile phone in one hand and chewing at her finger with the other. She'd just left a message on Drake Lewis's mobile to call her about some business. Bruton had exhausted her the previous night with his tiring tales of bravado and martial arts skills. She'd said all the right things and laughed in the right places but was left reeling with the certainty that he was not the kind of company she would choose to spend another Saturday night with. She'd only just managed to escape his advances. Again, it felt lonely to be living a schizophrenic life. Dipping in and out of other people's lives was simultaneously educational and alienating.

She had a feeling that Bruton, Nick Swift and Drake Lewis were all connected with each other in some unholy alliance. But Swift was in no way part of the club and drug scene that Top Deck security seemed to have an angle on. She read through the transcripts of the BMW trial over and over. She looked at the photographs of the bruised and beaten face and body of Swift that Daniel Field had handed over at their meeting at Chambers. She'd held back from telling Bruton that she was starting work for Swift on Monday morning. It would have been too risky and too soon. It had unnerved her the way he'd grabbed her bag thinking she might be plain-clothes.

Bruton was like a domesticated Doberman: dangerous and unpredictable but easy to tempt with tasty titbits – money, drugs, or a cut of whatever was going on under his nose. She knew the only way to gain his respect was by turning up with the goods for his friend, Johnny. She was reluctant to do it, but she knew the only person who could help her ease in to that world was Drake.

She'd packed a bag with enough clothes to last a week. She was going to have to move around in a number of environments. Hopefully, they would cover her for any occasion from a board meeting to an assault course. She had to psyche herself up for an unknown situation. Bluffing and smiling would hopefully enable her to get to the truth of why everyone she'd met connected to Landor Motors seemed to be hiding something.

Paul Weller's *Stanley Road* CD was filtering through the speakers. 'Walk on gilded splinters. Walk on gilded splinters.'

She still felt a little unnerved that Drake Lewis knew where she lived. She'd made a report on microcassette of everything she'd ascertained so far and sealed it in an envelope addressed to Daniel Field. She knew he wouldn't be calling her while she was at the showroom but it felt good to process the information and pass it on. At times like these, Vic wished she smoked cigarettes. Her nerves were jangling. So much to remember; so many people to be. She'd thrown a Marks and Spencer's chicken dinner in the oven but didn't fancy it now it was ready. She hadn't made it to Mum's for lunch today, and she'd lied to her about where she was working. Right now, she didn't feel like eating or explaining.

Vic had been asleep for an hour when the phone rang. It was Drake.

'Can I come round?' he asked. He sounded wide awake. Vic sat up in bed and flicked the light switch on her bedside lamp. She held her head as he garbled his thanks for letting him stay the other night. She told him she'd had fun, too, but she had an early start the next day.

'I'm only forty minutes' drive away,' he said.

She steeled herself and threw the question at him. 'I need something for a party. I wondered if you could sort me out something suitable. For the nose rather than the throat.'

'Not for tonight,' he replied, sounding put off that she hadn't responded to his sexual invitation. 'But I can definitely sort something out for tomorrow. Can I meet you somewhere? You've got my watch, too, right?'

'Yeah,' she said. 'I've got your watch. And I'll meet you somewhere tomorrow.' She resigned herself to the fact that she was going to be doing a lot of driving in the next couple of days. 'How about Earl's Court? I'll meet you at the tube station at eight. We can take it from there.'

'I'd like to take you from there,' he said. 'I want to go home with you again. I might be going away for a while this week. I'd like to see you before then. See you dressed up again.'

Vic was trying to be practical but Drake seemed to have only one thing on his mind. She was surprised at the flippant way he seemed to react to her request for class A drugs. Was it really that easy? 'I'll be dressed up,' she promised, hoping to God that she could get away before he embroiled her in another marathon sex session. 'I'll call tomorrow to make sure you're still on for it.'

'I'll be up for a couple of hours yet if you change your mind,' he said.

'Save it for tomorrow, Drake,' she said, trying to muster some enthusiasm. She needed to conserve energy, not burn it all night in curious drug-induced transvestite shenanigans. When this job was over, she'd treat herself to a long, luxury holiday where she could be herself. The idea felt blissful. She checked the alarm clock one more time and drifted back to sleep.

Landor Motors' long-standing secretary gave Vic a suspicious look as she was shown around the offices the next morning by an effusive Nick Swift. Vic wanted to reassure the woman that she wasn't after her job. She realised it must be threatening to have someone like herself turn up – unannounced, she discovered – and start working on hi-tech projects which paid well and often resulted in redundancy. She made an effort to be as friendly as possible to the older woman, who was a sensible-looking forty-something part-timer. She looked as if she'd seen a few indiscretions in her time. A chat with her may prove to be enlightening, Vic noted.

Craig Johnstone had nearly fallen over himself to make Vic comfortable and bring her tea, coffee and anything else she wanted. Now she was settled in a makeshift office. A computer had been installed and she had a phone line away from the business area of the showroom. This was very useful as she had to begin the task of trying to bluff her way around web-site design. She'd primed her mate Mike to expect a few panicky calls and talk her through the basics. It would all go down on expenses to Field & Gaitskills.

She hadn't found a guest house. She'd accepted Nick's offer of staying at his place. Foolish, maybe, she thought, but she'd justified her decision as being useful for observing anything which sounded suspicious. If things were too uncomfortable she could always leave the next day. The underlying reason was that the dynamic passing between them was tangibly sexual. Although she'd promised herself she wouldn't be swayed by the chemistry, Vic had to admit to herself that the kind of sex Nick Swift offered was irresistible. And far less hard work than Drake Lewis!

At noon a chauffeur-driven car pulled on to the forecourt and a fragile old woman dressed like the Queen Mother was helped out by the uniformed driver. It looked like something from a TV series. She watched from the interior of the showroom as Nick Swift hurried outside to greet whoever it was.

'Oh Gawd, that's all we need,' said the secretary, whose name was Janice. 'Must be one of the old girl's royal visits.'

The 'old girl', Vic discovered, was Gayle Landor, who made a habit of arriving at the showroom without warning. Her 'royal visits' were either to praise her son's achievements in business, while everyone else showed grovelling respect that he'd employed them or, if she was in one of her stern moods, to harangue Derek in his office while he ran around in circles to make things right. Judging by the expression on her rumpled face, today's visit wouldn't include a free lunch at the Ritz for all the staff.

'You mustn't say anything to upset her,' Janice warned. 'You'll be out the door if she doesn't like you. I wouldn't have wanted to be in Derek's shoes when she found out about the crash. Do you know about that?'

Vic went on to explain why she'd been brought in to the showroom and that she did know about the crash. But as she was speaking to Janice she had her eyes firmly fixed on Gayle Landor, a woman who looked as if she didn't miss a trick, even if she was seventy-six years old. Nick ushered her into Derek's office and came striding up to Vic and Janice rubbing his hands nervously. 'Get her some coffee, will you, love,' he said to Janice, who complied reluctantly. 'Vicky, love,' said Nick. 'That's Derek's mother. She's come down here to grill Craig, poor kid. Wants to know everything, of course. She has to be kept sweet at all costs. She part owns the gaff. She's already asked who you are. It'll look

189

good if you tell her a bit about all the design and PR stuff you do. Don't you go saying anything about us, though,' he warned. 'That's our little secret, OK?'

Of course she'd keep their liaison secret. As if she'd be stupid enough to tell Gayle Landor she was sleeping with Nick Swift! How many secrets can one have in a lifetime? she wondered. What about Derek Landor and his mother, or Janice, or me? We all live life pretending to be something we're not to get a head start. Vic was very aware that lies and secrets had got her this job. Where would we be without them? she thought. She'd grown up being told that she didn't live in a society that rewarded honesty and things didn't seem to be changing. Now was not the time to get analytical, however. The old girl was waiting to be introduced.

Vic did a good job with Gayle Landor. She turned on the charm as soon as the door was closed, introducing herself as Victoria and talking about her father's property in Dorset. 'Near the Blandford Estate,' she'd said. Once she'd heard her background, Gayle seemed comfortable with her. Vic showed interest in the woman and listened with dewy-eyed fascination as she spoke of the summer balls she'd attended as a young girl in the thirties. They chatted about clothes and cars and horses, which was fine by Vic as she held a genuine interest in all three subjects. Now she'd buttered the old lady up, maybe Johnstone wouldn't get such a quizzing.

Before Vic finished her coffee, Gayle Landor beckoned her over to her side. She grasped Vic's soft hand with her arthritic claw and held it firmly to her knee so Vic had to bend down. 'What are you doing this Wednesday?' she asked.

'Working here, Mrs Landor.'

'Well, you tell Nick Swift that you're leaving early that day to visit me at the stables. You can come and see the horses. Come and ride if you like. My granddaughter's always putting it off. I'll have Ballard pick you up from here at four. How does that sound?'

That sounded great. That sounded better than she could have anticipated. She emerged from the office with a smile on her face and Nick was beside himself to know why. 'It's nothing,' said Vic. 'Just a feeling that Mrs Landor's not such a bad old stick after all.' Silly, upper-class old tyrant. Vic knew that she wouldn't have been given the time of day if she'd betrayed her genuine background.

After speaking to Johnstone for about half an hour and instructing Nick to inform her as soon as they had news from the manufacturers, Gayle Landor was helped into her Bentley and driven back to her estate.

'You did well, lad,' Swift said to Johnstone as the young man put the kettle on. 'She could have us all fired tomorrow if she wanted. Well done for not letting her wind you up. Vicky made a good impression, didn't you?' he said, calling her over to the kitchen area. 'How about me and you taking a lunch break now?' he asked. 'I think I need to get out of the office for a while after all that.' He ushered her into his room.

'You can bring your stuff round to my place,' he said quietly. 'It's not far. I'll show you your room and everything.'

Once at Swift's place, Vic began to feel nervous about putting herself in the position of being his guest. She explained that she wanted her own key and must be free to come and go as she pleased. Swift looked horrified, although Vic suspected he was more alarmed by her bold declaration of independence than any suggestion he would try to monitor her movements. His fifth-floor flat was situated at the top of a private block of apartments in a leafy street just outside Coleshill. The flat was as tidy as his office, and just as soulless. A large, predominantly white living room backed on to the kitchen-dining area. About thirty per cent of the brickwork had been left unplastered and the large chrome-legged, glass-topped coffee table and framed prints of classic cars rendered the room unmistakably male and distinctly eighties in design.

The bedrooms were bright and spotlessly clean, with fitted wardrobe units and colourful duvet covers. Vic was aware that, alone with Nick in his apartment, and with half an hour to kill, eating was only one of the things on the agenda for that lunchtime. She had dumped her bag in the smaller bedroom and was standing in the kitchen watching Nick prepare a couple of cheese salad sandwiches. He chatted about his mortgage, his ex-wife and her business aspirations that bled him dry; about his favourite cars and about what a good idea it had been to get Vic working on revamping their image. After eating their sandwiches, Nick invited her through into the lounge and they stood looking out over the parkland surrounding the flats.

The room was silent and there was a privacy to the apartment that Vic never felt in her own place at the Angel. There was no noise outside the window except the sound of an occasional car passing or dog barking. This kind of seclusion would drive Vic insane, she thought. She liked a little more activity around her than this – the stultifying serenity of suburbia.

When Nick laid a hand on the curve of Vic's waist she knew instantly how the rest of the lunchtime would pan out. The feel of him, hard and strong standing behind her, set her mind reeling with possibilities. He had her in his lair and he was going to make the most of it. He ran his hands over her buttocks and kissed her neck. She did nothing to prevent him reaching round and taking her breasts in both hands as he pressed his groin against her. It was the sense of urgency in his movements which turned her on. Again, she knew she wouldn't have to do very much to bring him pleasure beyond his fantasies. She didn't turn around to face him but allowed him to quietly explore her most intimate anatomy. He had loosened her skirt and wriggled his fingers into her knickers and between her legs. At the first touch of her hot, silky moisture he'd groaned a sound of lustful surprise at just how wet she was.

Vic felt embarrassed by her body's betrayal of her arousal in such prosaic circumstances but the forthright and methodical way he was inspecting her only served to increase her sense of sexual abandon. It was all right to let him do this, she reasoned. She didn't have to tell him it was what she wanted. She was prepared to let him take his pleasure from her without having to admit his direct approach was having an effect on her which contradicted all the things she believed she wanted in a sexual relationship. There was no slow build-up; no extended kissing and tender exchange of emotions. It was raw and unsophisticated and yet so powerfully erotic that her insides ached with the desire to be plundered by his iron-hard penis.

She found herself writhing against him as he muttered lewd things to her. She didn't care that she had nothing in common with this uncultured car salesman, even if he was attractive for his age. All she cared about was the powerful feeling the situation was creating in her. She knew she could come so easily. All she had to do was gently guide his hand to the rhythm she knew worked for her. The feel of his cock pressing into her buttocks as she braced herself against the window frame, and the sense that what she was doing was so unethical, brought about the first twinges deep in her sex. Before she could reach the moment of release, however, Nick Swift stopped his caresses and turned her to face him. She flushed with shame now she was forced to look him in the eyes. He pulled her over to the sofa where she reclined and waited for him to finish what he had started.

He produced a condom from his shirt pocket and eased it over his tumescent shaft. When Vic tried to take her clothes off he stopped her from doing so. 'We'll have to get dressed again immediately. There's no point wasting time,' he said. The only concession he'd made to the event was to slip off his shoes before climbing on top of her and finding his way to where he wanted to be. He pushed her skirt up around her thighs and plunged into her in one quick, fluid movement. It was heaven for both of them. As Vic had anticipated, he began to issue a series of bestial groans in time with his thrusting. His head was buried in the hollow of her shoulder as she sensed his impending crisis would not be long in coming. Her own orgasm was upon her, but as it took hold of her body with a violence that shook her to the root of her being she noticed a piece of paper had inched its way out of Nick's right-hand trouser pocket. As the afterglow of her orgasm spread through her body, she deftly folded the paper into her palm and secreted it about her person.

During the drive back to the showroom Vic was feeling she'd done the wrong thing by allowing herself to be so easily coerced into such a private act. After their rough coupling, she'd insisted on being allowed to shower and had taken one of Nick's towels out of sequence from the bathroom cupboard and sent the others in the pile tumbling to the floor. This had sent him flying into an irrational display of annoyance which hadn't abated. It had also annoyed him that they hadn't left enough time to wash their plates and cups from lunch. In fact, he'd thrown himself into a sulk and was changing gear in an unnecessarily violent manner and driving too fast for comfort. She had apologised for her carelessness and he'd muttered that it was nothing and that he was fine, but this display of moody behaviour gave Vic cause for concern. It reaffirmed her decision to not give in to his sexual impulses so rashly another time.

Vic realised she'd mistaken Nick Swift for an easy-going rogue. He was actually beginning to display signs of being an aggressive man with a hair-trigger temper. She vowed to tread very carefully around Nick Swift in future. As she suspected, the piece of paper was the hate mail which Derek had handed to Nick the night they were at the Metropole. Why was Swift holding on to it? she wondered. She had gathered from the conversation Nick had with Derek that it was supposed to be handed over to the police.

But then she remembered Nick had previously said that Derek was tired of police investigation. Was Swift holding on to the note for the purposes of blackmailing Bruton? Now it was in her possession, she was in charge of some powerful bargaining power. It would be interesting to watch how Swift would deal with its real absence. She was faced with a moral dilemma: return the note to Derek Landor, hand it over to the police, send it to Daniel Field or directly challenge Nick Swift?

Before the end of the working day Vic firmed up her meeting with Drake Lewis. It was unfortunate that he called her on her mobile phone just before she and Nick had arrived back at the showroom. Nick had wanted to know who it was and why she was meeting someone in London that evening. Vic had been put out by his questions and had told him it was to do with designing the web site. Bloody cheek! It was none of his business who she met and for what reason. The truth would have been a smack in the eye, though, she laughed to herself. She imagined the conversation:

'I'm off to buy some cocaine from a transvestite drug-fiend.'

'Oh, all right, then. I'll keep your dinner in the oven for you.'

Before the close of the working day she'd written some copy for a press release about the company and phoned around a few supermarkets trying to elicit their involvement in possible cross-promotional initiatives. It had been enough to convince the other staff that she was genuine although she'd have to get to work very soon designing the web site. If she didn't get any more investigation work, at least she'd find something out about new media.

THIRTEEN
A Chasm of Unknown Dangers

Monday Evening

If that little tart thinks she's going to pull one over on me, she can think again, Nick Swift told himself as he sat in an Earl's Court café watching the pub where Vicky had arranged to meet her mystery friend. He had nothing better to do that evening now that she'd thrown over his idea of a romantic meal in the Haver Dean Steak House. It had hurt him. He had wanted to show her off to his pal who worked as the bar manager there but Vic had turned him down saying she had to chase some computer software from a friend in London. He knew she was lying but he couldn't put his finger on what she was up to. He was in a sore mood. After Derek had given him an earache about the letter he searched high and low for it and couldn't for the life of him remember where he'd last seen it. It had vanished from his sight. It didn't seem to be anywhere at the showroom. He'd have a thorough search of his flat before going to bed that evening.

It was raining, and outside the café window, groups of Antipodean tourists and sleazy-looking foreigners shuffled past in search of cheap hotels. Nick was glad he didn't live in London any more. He'd had enough of the big city. It wasn't as good as it had been in the seventies. The discos had been great fun in those days: Saturday Night Fever, the Hustle, running around all over the West End with the boys. Where had his life led? he asked himself. He was sorted for cash, he had a nice gaff and two lovely daughters who were doing their own thing, but he wanted some sparkle put back into his routine. He wanted Vicky to be that sparkle. If only he could communicate more successfully with her. She seemed like a real cracker at first: ex page-three girl – she was exactly his type. Now she was working for him she seemed distant and aloof. He didn't want her to slip away from his grasp. She was too good. The best he'd had in years.

He stirred his coffee and continued staring at the pub. Then he spotted Alan Landor swaggering along the road with his usual arrogant gait and almost retched in horror. When he saw the bastard go into the pub he knew the likelihood he was meeting Vicky was too strong to be coincidence.

He sat fuming over his third cup of unpalatable brew. If he'd have been drunk he'd have stormed into the pub without a second thought and confronted the scruffy git. Sobriety prevented such rash action, though, and he pulled hard on another cigarette as he planned his move. If they left together he would follow them. In the dark and the rain, he could keep a low profile. They wouldn't be expecting to be followed; they would probably be wrapped up in a lovers' clinch. The thought made him feel rabid with anger. What the fuck was Landor doing meeting his bird?

Nick had to suffer a further forty minutes of sick suspense. When they emerged and went their separate ways he was suddenly at a loss as to which one of them he'd follow. Vic would be heading back to Coleshill, surely, but where was that bastard Landor off to? He had to make a snap decision. With the rage that was coursing through his veins he knew that venting his frustration on Vicky would not be wise. She'd run a mile from him if she saw him lose his temper. He'd tag that waster of a bloke who had brought Bruton to Landor Motors.

Alan Landor got back to his flat feeling sorry for himself that Vicky had not been up for coming back with him. He'd thought they could have done a few lines, gone to bed and phoned for a pizza or something. She'd brought him his watch but she'd also brought him the bad news that she didn't want to get sexually involved with him. Weird chick. She'd seemed right into the idea before. She had turned out to be a right spoilt little bitch. All she was interested in was getting the coke and leaving as soon as possible. Alan was through with dealing now. That would be the last time he would risk getting arrested to do favours for anyone – even tall blonde models who had posh parties to go to in Dorset.

She hadn't even invited him to the party. Not that he could go, of course, given the impending job in hand, but it would have been nice to have been asked. It was weird to have slept with someone who was working for his father. He wanted to stay in touch with her not least because she was a good source of information. When she'd mentioned she had been invited to Gayle Landor's place to ride the horses, Alan had almost given in and told her his real name. The situation was unnerving. When he'd first seen her at the Motor Show she'd been hustling for a job but it was strange that she didn't seem to know what she was talking about when he'd asked her about the web-site design. She hadn't even known what HTML stood for. She'd probably got the job because of her looks. Women. Nothing but trouble.

He rolled himself a spliff, threw some techno into his sound system and sat back to relax for a while before meeting Clem and Dave at ten o'clock. There was a quiet boozer off the Blackfriars Road they wanted him to turn up at for a 'preliminary chat' before the job, they'd said. When these guys gave orders, Alan knew he had to jump. He wished he could set them on to Fatneck; shake him down for some of the cash the bastard still owed him. He would have been in deep financial shit if he'd only had Bruton to rely on. He was glad he had the hit to look forward to.

One more day and then it would be time for action.

Alan had found out on Sunday that Derek had an appointment with his doctor at 11.00 a.m. He'd prepared a map for Clem and Dave. It couldn't be easier. As he emerged from the doctor's surgery they would bundle him into the motor and whisk him away to his temporary accommodation.

Alan wished he could be there to see the two hardmen standing no nonsense. He'd told them that Derek was a coward. Dave had remarked that they'd have some fun with that and the sinister laugh from Clem had temporarily worried Alan. He wanted justice and the money but he didn't want them to be unnecessarily violent. Boden had promised a clean job. Alan just had to trust the older man's word that his boys were not going to turn psycho on him. In this line of business you couldn't ask for references.

Swift pounded his steering wheel in a fury. He'd lost Landor at the lights at the end of Earl's Court Road and, despite doing fifty through to the King's Road, had not been able to catch up with him. It had been a nice idea – kicking Landor's door in and slapping him around a bit. Still, there was always the chance it would have got back to Derek and then there would have been hell to pay. Although Nick knew there was no love lost between father and son, it didn't pay to meddle with someone's family. Families had a curious habit of uniting against outsiders despite the differences they had keeping their own internal squabbles under control. It was getting late. He motored out to the Westway and on to the M40. He'd find out the truth from Vicky when he got back.

Vic had closed the bedroom door and was hoping that Nick would leave her alone. She'd managed to give Drake Lewis the big swerve and couldn't face a night of macho bravado from Swift. She missed Julian and her theatre friends. She was in the house of a man who aspired to mediocrity and whose idea of a good night out was a trip to the local steak house. It was culturally grim but she had to hang on for just a few more days. By then she would have visited Gayle Landor's estate and maybe got to see Derek. You're in a play, she kept telling herself. Act your heart out, girl.

She'd paid Drake Lewis three hundred pounds and had received five individual wraps of the expensive white powder that was so treasured by the clubbing fraternity. She unwrapped one. Sixty quid a go. What a waste of money! That would buy five CDs, two pairs of trousers, a pair of good leather shoes or a brilliant night out. For some people, though, a brilliant night out wasn't possible without it. She dabbed her finger cautiously into the powder and rubbed it around her gums. It felt strange to be in possession of the stuff. It was so risky carrying it. She wanted to be shot of it as soon as possible. By this time tomorrow she would have got her money back and hopefully extracted some juicier information out of Peter Bruton. She had to find out if it really was him who had sent the poison letter to Derek Landor. She felt within a whisker of uncovering something useful. She felt as though a whole bunch of dodgy stuff was going on around her but she couldn't quite put the finger on what it was.

She heard a door slam and almost jumped out of her skin in shock. She hurriedly wrapped the cocaine and slid all five grammes into the zip compartment of her handbag. She'd been sorting out her clothes and they lay strewn around the room. The tape recorder was within easy reach. She set it to record and put this, too, into her handbag which she placed under the bed, microphone facing the door.

Nick's voice came booming up the stairs, 'Vicky. Vicky I want to talk to you.'

She heard him going to the fridge. He sounded in another bad mood. Surely he didn't expect her to stay around with him in the evenings? It didn't seem like he was going to come upstairs so her recording opportunity had been futile.

She entered the kitchen determined not to be browbeaten by Nick Swift's grumbling. He was leaning against the sink and sipping from a bottle of lager. 'Do you want to tell me where you've been this evening?' he asked. 'Because I think you're taking the piss.'

'I went to London to see someone about the web site. And I'll remind you that you can't talk to me like I'm one of your daughters. Who do you think you are? We've had sex twice. I'm doing some work for you. I'm not your girlfriend or anything like it, OK?' Vic was furious. He was overreacting as badly as anything she'd ever seen.

'And what exactly did you find out about the web site?' he asked. 'Come on. Tell me. I'm waiting.'

Vic was stuck but she threw some technobabble at him as he looked at her through disbelieving eyes. She was going to have to try harder.

'And what's your friend's name?' Nick asked. 'Come on, spit it out, what's your game?'

'It's none of your business who I meet. Why do you want to know his name? And I don't have a game as you call it. I drove to Earl's Court, I met my friend, Drake, and I drove back. I'd promised to meet up with him a few days ago. Sorry I hadn't planned in advance that I'd be expected to hang out with your old cronies in nowheresville.' She was marching around the kitchen with her arms folded across her chest. 'Can I have a beer, too, please? Do you think you can stretch to that?' She went to open the fridge door but Swift slammed it shut. For a second she felt scared of him.

'You can have a beer when you've told me why you went to meet Derek Landor's son tonight in a pub in West London. I don't know who you think this character Drake is, but I saw you leave the King's Head with Alan Landor. Explain that, Miss Donovan.'

Vic couldn't have been more shocked if Nick Swift had admitted he was gay and had been cruising Earl's Court before adjourning to the Colherne. The fact he'd followed her disgusted her. She didn't like being put on the spot and given the Spanish inquisition. But she was at a loss to come up with a reply to his revelation that her curious drug-dealing transvestite acquaintance was the son of Derek Landor. Now she knew the truth, a number of things fell into place, all of them unnerving.

The news hit her like a thunderbolt; the possibility that Alan Landor was hiding behind an alias for nefarious reasons could be the key to the entire investigation. She thought back to the circumstances in which they'd met. It was Alan

Landor who had picked her up at the Ferrari stand. He must have been watching her talking to Nick Swift just moments before. His approach had been so casual, too. Damn! Vic felt confused and discomfited. First Nick, and now the man she had known as Drake Lewis, had been watching her; spying on her, for reasons she couldn't figure out. Why had he been so keen to chat her up? Who did he think she was? She racked her brains to try to recall everything she'd told him about herself.

He knew her address, he knew she was working at Landor Motors, he thought she was a cocaine user with posh friends, and he'd found out a little about her sexuality. Who was to say that he wasn't watching her now; sitting outside the apartment block, staking her out? Shit! She'd effectively told him there was little chance they'd see each other again. She'd broken contact with him too early. Vic was annoyed that she'd let her guard down and been followed so easily. She should be moving about with greater stealth. She should be the spy, not the person being spied upon.

'Nick,' she said, 'let's talk about this in a rational manner. Now, please can I have that beer?' He released his hand from the door and she cracked open a bottle. Despite the shock, Vic mustered all her skills of artifice and strength of character to appear nonplussed by the revelation. She turned the situation around by quizzing Nick on the ethics of following her. She began to interrogate the interrogator and Swift was forced into admitting he had been jealous that she could have wanted to turn down his surprise invitation to a swanky dinner in favour of meeting someone else.

She allowed him a few concessions to the truth: that she'd met Landor at the Motor Show; that he'd seemed a bit of a technical whizz kid and knew about computers; that he was useful for gaining access to cheap software packages.

In the end, Vic managed to persuade Swift there was nothing sexual between her and Alan and that the reason they knew each other was coincidental. It was also the truth when she told him that she had no idea why he used a false name. She agreed not to see him again if he promised to lighten up and put an end to the bad moods and following her.

She needed some time alone to work out what was going on. She was going to have to be very careful that Swift didn't tail her to Gaby's the next evening. She felt that time was running out. She hadn't accounted for Swift's jealousy. She realised she was going to have to come up with a result to this investigation before the thin ice she was skating on gave way to a chasm of unknown dangers.

The contretemps with Nick Swift had been worthwhile to the investigation – cathartic, even. As she maintained a casual attitude to the 'coincidence' of knowing Alan Landor, Nick Swift went into a long account of what a bad lot he was and how he had developed from a difficult child into an uncontrollable adolescent and then an unpredictable adult. Nick regaled her with stories of him turning up at the showroom out of his head on strong lager as a sixteen year old and trying to pick fights with his father which Nick had to physically stop by throwing him out.

'I was at the peak of my fitness then,' he told her. 'That was 1986 or thereabouts. It was a nightmare for the old man when Alan got out of boarding school, or special school as my family would have called it. It was a glorified borstal, really. They kept him locked up for hours. Of course, when he was sixteen he was let out into society again. First place he headed for was home but they couldn't handle him. The lad was out of control. He soon found his way into a detention centre.

'I saw and heard most of what went on then. At first I felt sorry for him, what with his mother committing suicide and that, but he was so unpredictable. He could turn on you at any time. He was nicking things left right and centre. I tried to help the kid at one point by letting him stay at our place but I learnt my lesson there all right.'

'What happened?' asked Vic, cursing herself that her tape recorder was picking up silence under the bed upstairs.

'I came home and found him snogging my half-naked wife in the kitchen. Five minutes later he would have been

203

shagging her over the table, the dirty little sod.'

Vic couldn't prevent herself from laughing for which she immediately apologised. 'What did you do?'

'Knocked seven colours of shite out of him and sent him packing. He couldn't keep it in his pants back then. I doubt he's changed.'

Vic thought back to the night she'd spent with him. Nick was right; he hadn't changed, except whose pants he wore was a matter of contention.

'Didn't Derek do anything to help him get better. Surely he could have helped him financially?'

'His mother, the old girl, wouldn't allow it. She has such a hold over Derek. If he farts she wants to know about it. You saw how she is earlier today. The younger sister told the old girl that Alan tried to have sex with her when they were kids and that did it. She's Gayle's favourite. Once she heard that she wanted to punish him. Maybe the girl was making it up. They fought like cat and dog from what I know. Kids tell lies; I know from having two girls of my own. Who knows what the truth is. Anyway, the upshot is that he moved to London and disappeared for years, but for the past year or so he's been back in the manor, sporadically like. I even heard that he's been visiting the family house so maybe they've sorted their differences. Who knows? I want to stay well clear of him, though. And I'd advise you to do the same.'

Tuesday

The atmosphere between Vic and Nick Swift had evened itself out after their long chat. She agreed to have a meal with him later in the week and he seemed satisfied that she wasn't about to jump into bed with the boss's son. She felt confident that her visit to Gaby's would be free of interference by Nick. She kept going through the conversations she'd had with Alan Landor. Why did he use an alias? She had certainly been wrong about that working class, Thames

Estuary accent. He must have acquired that in the detention centre. Why hadn't he responded when she told him where she was working? A lot of what Nick had told her fitted in with his sullen moods and sad expression. Maybe he was trying to build a new life for himself and didn't want to retain any vestige of his family. Conversely, he could just as easily be a scheming, manipulative bastard who could turn violent at any time.

There were questions she suspected could be answered by Peter Bruton. The Top Deck Security connection could hold a key. Bruton would have some tales about his time at Landor Motors, that was for sure. She had to find out if Alan was around at the same time as Bruton was working there. Maybe they were both involved in the BMW theft. What if they had plotted some minor-level extortion? If Derek Landor had refused to pay up, maybe the theft and the break-in were their way of getting back at him. But the recent crash was an unfortunate accident, wasn't it? It was surely too far-fetched to think it was an act of sabotage

Dave, Clem and Neil Boden were at Alan's garage running through the procedure for the next day. They'd agreed that all three of them would seize Derek Landor. Neil would drive. He wasn't going to get his hands dirty before they got to Tilbury, he said. Alan had got hold of an executive motor for the job and it was decided they'd look like a bunch of businessmen: 'suited and booted' as Boden put it, except with the tools of a different trade. He remarked that it was a good job Drake wasn't coming along as he'd stick out like the proverbial sore one. Everyone laughed except Alan. He had arranged to meet up with them later but to stay concealed. Derek was to be kept blindfolded for most of the time but Alan didn't want to take any risks.

They all had mobile phones, Dave had the shooter, and Clem was providing the knock-out drops. The car had been checked, filled up and provided with the plates of an identical model that had gone for scrap. All was excited anticipation. After the money drop was made it was decided they'd rendezvous at an address in New Cross. Boden didn't dwell too long on what they'd do if the family didn't come through – although the result would incur extreme discomfort for their guest, he said.

They would demand twenty-four hours from picking up the money to depositing their charge at a location to be decided. There were numerous desolate places along the Thames Estuary. They could take their pick. Boden knew them all. Whoever went to collect the money would get a bigger share and wear the flak jacket. There was always the chance some trigger-happy cop would get it into his head to play marksman of the year.

They all needed to sort out alibis during the time they'd be in the lock-up. With Landor out for the count for most of the time, they could take turns being seen in their usual manors. Clem, Dave and Neil all fancied themselves as being a bit cheeky. Dave planned on getting home Thursday night to shag his girlfriend and Neil said it was good form to be seen in one's local boozer. Boden had already stocked the lock-up with food, drink and tools for any occasion. He'd even installed the picnic table with its floral umbrella and the chairs he used on his caravaning holidays so the men could sit comfortably and play cards while they waited to get rich.

Alan couldn't believe how blasé they were being. It was like they were planning a weekend at the seaside. They'd take turns sleeping and watching out for each other, Neil said. If Landor was half the big Jessie they'd been led to believe, the job would be a breeze.

Peter Bruton had had a good day so far. Andrew and Gary were primed for their Saturday night special, as they'd named their forthcoming job, and everything was in place. It would be weird staying on in the job after they'd robbed the place but it had to be done. He would just have to be careful not to flash his new-found wealth around. He was spruced up and sporting some new clothes. As he stood at the bar in Gaby's after doing his early evening rounds, he spotted Vic walking in. She was in a different class to the silly girls he usually took home for the night or, if he could get away with it, up to the office for a quick one while they were pilled up. This one walked with confidence and looked high-class. She had poise and style. He thought of the state Sheryl had been in on Saturday when he'd gone to visit Sean. She looked well rough: pale and drawn and her hair was dull and needed attention. He wanted to be seen around town with a bird with some panache. The fact she was a coke dealer might mean there was some tasty black geezer in the background, though. He didn't want to tread on anyone's toes.

Vic spotted Peter leaning on the bar. 'All right, Julie, how's it going?' he asked.

'Your mate Johnny should be pleased,' said Vic, eager to lose the criminal contents of her handbag. 'I can sort him out right now.'

'Oh yeah, Johnny. He's not in tonight. He's off sick. Still, I dare say you can shift it elsewhere,' Bruton said casually. Vic felt hollow with disappointment but made sure she didn't show it. Shit! All that effort for no payback. She wouldn't be able to wangle this on expenses and Bruton didn't look as if he was about to offer to take it off her hands. No result there, then. Getting her money back wasn't as important as pumping Bruton, though. Given her current persona, as a clubbing chick into class A drugs, it would be impossible to start talking about any possible connections Bruton had with Landor Motors. The link was too tenuous. She decided not to throw a spanner in the works by mentioning Swift's name.

She strongly suspected that Alan Landor was supplying Bruton with drugs, but if there was anything else going on she needed to find out as fast as possible what it was. Since Nick had dropped the bombshell of information on her the previous night, Vic realised that she had to find out where Alan Landor lived. She knew that mentioning his name or alias would start the ball rolling, but in what direction she was unsure. She steeled herself for an unknown reaction.

'You know Drake Lewis don't you?' she asked and watched as Bruton's face darkened in shock.

'Don't tell me that's who you're buying the Charlie from!'

he exclaimed. 'He's a right moody bastard. How do you know him?'

'We met at the Motor Show. He said this place was sweet for dealers. It's near to where a friend of mine lives. When I said I was coming up here he told me to check in at this place. I'm kind of new at this game. I've been doing low-paid jobs for ages and I wanted to make some money. We got talking and he let me have these few grammes at a good price.'

'Oh he did, did he?' Bruton said sarcastically. 'That's nice of him.' Vic could see he was beginning to bristle. 'Where's your friend live, then?' he asked, looking at Vic suspiciously.

'Near Haver Dean Garden Centre,' she replied, this being the first landmark which sprung to mind.

'That's right near Alan's old man's gaff,' he said as if he was thinking aloud.

So. It seemed that Alan Landor's alias wasn't widely used in his home town. 'Alan?' she queried.

'Sorry, Drake. His real name's Alan but he doesn't use it any more. Yeah, I met him in 1991. We were kind of in the same business back then. Motors. I'm just your average grease monkey but he's always been a right whizz kid. Went off to Germany for a while working in a car factory. The computer programming end of things.'

'Well, he doesn't seem to have anything much to do with motors these days,' said Vic, becoming more and more puzzled by Alan Landor's multiple identities. They were as confusing as her own.

'You said you met him at the Motor Show?' Bruton said, sounding slightly puzzled.

'Yeah, I did. But he wasn't there for the cars, Peter. He was hanging around in the press parties, selling a few grammes.'

'You don't know his garage, then?' he said. 'It's round the corner from where he lives. It's on Maybury Street, just off the Old Kent Road.'

Vic saw this as an opportunity to get the vital information: his address. 'No I don't know the garage. I've been to where he lives once.' Please, she thought. Please bite the bait.

'It's a right dump, isn't it?' said Bruton.

'The Old Kent Road isn't the prettiest part of London,' she answered.

'Alan's always moaning about his lot. He can't cope with the fact that he's living in a council block in the Elephant and Castle while his family are lording it about round this neck of the woods. If you've never had money you don't miss it, I guess, but Alan was born with a silver spoon in his mouth and should've been set up for life.'

'He told me about his mother and all that,' Vic casually threw in.

'Yeah. Right old nasty business. He's the black sheep all right. His father's such a tight git. I used to work for him until the bastard gave me the sack.'

'What did you do?' Vic asked, worrying that the moment to prime the exact address out of Bruton was passing.

'It's a long boring story, Julie. Put it this way: I'm no angel. I like the good things in life and I want money. I didn't earn enough at his tight-arsed father's poncy showroom to make ends meet. I helped myself out, so to speak.'

By getting some of your mates to organise a robbery and the theft of a shiny new Beamer, Vic thought. 'That's not such a bad thing,' she said in a flirtatious voice. 'Everyone has to have a little something on the go to keep the devil away.' She could tell from the way Bruton was looking at her that his hormones were dominating his behaviour. He wasn't concentrating on what he was saying; he was focused on her body. His pupils had dilated, he was breathing heavily through his nose and his stocky frame was filling the space between them. He looked as if he was about to pounce on her. His gaze kept flickering to her legs. She expected he might grab her bottom or her breasts at any moment. He was bull-like and impatient. He looked as if every cubic centimetre of his being was packed with testosterone.

It was now or never. The million dollar question. 'I feel a bit silly,' she began, 'but I wonder if you could help me out with something?' She forced herself not to flinch from being in such close proximity to this oafish creature who was looking more predatory with every movement.

'What's that?' he asked, puffing out his chest and leering at her.

'Well, I'm going to get really out of it tonight and I have to make it to Drake, sorry, Alan's place tomorrow to pick up some more gear but I can't remember the directions from the Elephant and Castle roundabout. Do you think you could draw me a map so I don't get lost. I've mislaid my A to Z.'

'No problem, darling,' Bruton said, reaching behind the bar to get a pen.

Vic pulled some paper from her bag and Peter made a commentary of the directions to Landor's flat while he drew an untidy scrawl. 'There you go,' he said. 'Anyway, I don't want to talk about misery guts Landor all night,' Bruton said. 'I want to know whether you fancy coming out with me some time. What are you doing Friday? We've got a big one here that night. It'll be bangin'. Right hardcore fuckin' uproar.'

Vic wished to God these lunkhead men would stop having designs on her. She hadn't promised anything to Nick Swift and he was already proving to be a pain in the arse, getting jealous and following her around. She didn't want to incur the wrath of the Neanderthal Bruton who made Swift seem like a Renaissance man. He would have to be nipped in the bud right now, before she found herself in an uncomfortable situation.

'I'm not looking for that right now, Peter. I have a boyfriend in London at the moment.'

For some reason, this rejection made him fly into an instant rage and he hissed at her through gritted teeth: 'So you're just down here trying to sell a few grammes of Charlie? Pull the other one, love. What's your fucking game? Is Landor your boyfriend? Has he sent his bird along to shake me down for the cash I owe him? What were you going to do? Roll me?'

Christ, he was really getting into a strop. Vic tried to backtrack and make light of it all. 'If you owe him money it's nothing to do with me,' she said, trying to back away, looking around her for witnesses or someone to come to her aid. 'I couldn't care less about Landor's money and he's not my boyfriend.'

Suddenly, she felt her arm being gripped painfully by Bruton's meaty paw. He pulled her through the club, across the dance floor and over to the flight of stairs marked STAFF ONLY. As one of the bartenders asked what was going on Bruton told her he'd caught her trying to deal drugs in the club and was taking her upstairs to call the police. She felt weak with fear.

He pushed her up the stairs and into the office, then slammed the door. 'Right, you little bitch,' he spat. 'You might look classy but who the fuck are you and what are you after? If you don't tell me it'll take one phone call to have the Old Bill down here like a shot. They'll love you. Sloaney London coke pusher who dresses like a whore. So you better own up.'

Vic was mortified. A whore! Fucking cheek. She had to think fast. Whatever she said was destined to anger Bruton. 'It's as I've said. I know about you from Drake. I mean Alan. He told me loads of the blokes working for Top Deck were into dealing and stuff. He wanted me to try and find out what you were up to. He hasn't heard from you in ages and he wants his money.' Vic didn't have a clue how much money was at stake or for what he owed it to him but Bruton looked as if he understood.

'You can tell him he'll have to wait. What do you know about Andrew and Gary?' he snarled.

'Nothing. I've never heard of them. Honest. Please let me go.' Vic was thinking as fast as she could.

'You said you knew them,' he barked.

'I was lying. I only know Drake, Alan, whatever you want to call him. I've never met anyone called Andrew or Gary.'

'How do I know you're not lying now?' he asked, the veins on his forehead bulging angrily.

'You just have to take my word for it,' she said in desperation. Bruton had forced her up against the wall and was staring into her face from close range. He looked like he was about to go into a roid rage.

'Your word for it?' he sneered. 'You're lucky I don't take

something else for it, you fucking little prick tease.'

'I haven't come here to cause trouble,' she pleaded. 'I'm only trying to make a living. I'm sorry if you thought I was looking to be asked out. It's not that I don't like you, but I'm spoken for at the moment.'

'Tell the truth. Is it Alan?' he asked 'Cos it's about time he found himself a woman.'

Vic nodded her head. He seemed to relax slightly although it was clear he was still quite annoyed. 'Look. Alan and me go back a long way but he's a pain in the arse sometimes. We did some business together recently and things have gone a bit pear-shaped money-wise. But you just tell him to get off my fucking case, all right? If he thinks he can send his bird down here to spy on me he's really losing it. That's real last resort tactics. I'll pay him when I'm good and ready.'

Bruton unlocked the door. He seemed to have convinced himself Vic wasn't worth losing his temper for, for which she was very much relieved.

'I don't want to see you around here again, is that clear?'

Vic nodded her head again.

Bruton grabbed her by the arm once more and frog-marched her down the stairs to the emergency exit. He pushed the door open and shoved her outside into the yard. 'Now beat it, you fucking little tart. If I see you around here again there'll be serious trouble,' he said, leaving Vic shaking but relieved in the damp Tuesday night air. Things hadn't gone all that badly, really. She still had her bag, five grammes of Class A and, most importantly, Alan Landor's address.

After getting home from being unceremoniously thrown out of Gaby's Vic had skulked off to her room and locked the door. It had been her first brush with violence since she'd been in the business of investigating. This brought home to her the reality of how rough it could be. She rubbed her arm where Bruton had pressed his fleshy fingers into her tender skin. She hadn't banked on the case being so complex and populated by so many touchy blokes. She could imagine Bruton, Landor and Swift all capable of stuff which would land them behind bars for twenty years. There was a desperation to all of these men which bordered on psycho-pathology. Whatever they did, it seemed the risk of doing time was a minor consideration. It was as if their lives were so damaged, they couldn't see beyond the red mist of revenge.

She was annoyed at herself for not getting more information out of Bruton but she hadn't expected him to fly off the handle so suddenly. A personality type like Bruton would never take a woman seriously, Vic told herself. He's a bloke who thinks with his dick. Consequently, he would have been unlikely to open up to her. Sometimes she wished she worked with a partner: a guy who was as convincing a character actor as she. Another bloke may have had the advantage with Bruton. Never mind. There was no point dwelling on the failures. And the mission hadn't been a complete disaster. She now knew where Alan lived and worked.

Tomorrow she would make a photocopy of the letter and send it to Daniel. The original was burning a hole in her bag. She decided to post it to her home address. Get it as far away from Nick as she could. For the meantime, it would live folded up inside a box of Tampax at the bottom of her bag.

FOURTEEN
Big Trouble in Little Chalfont

Wednesday

The only topic of conversation between Landor Motors' showroom staff the next morning was the call from the manufacturers' representative. Their initial theory – that a mobile phone call had set the bag off – had been ruled out. Boxall's solicitor had obtained a print-out from his client's phone company which had disproved their speculations. After painstaking reassembly of the car's mangled electrical system, a wire had been found connecting the car's cruise control sensor to the device which triggered the airbag detonator. They promised there would be a recall of all Liguri 700s from the same batch to check that they too did not carry the deadly fault. A random test of five vehicles should enable them to say whether sabotage was likely. The initial safety check had passed without a hitch. If the car had been tampered with in any way while stored at Landor Motors the responsibility would rest, once more, with them and a police investigation would follow.

While Nick was caught up on the phone with his office door closed and Janice was away from her desk, Vic collared

Craig Johnstone making some tea in the kitchen area. She smiled at him and they started chatting about the news.

'That's the trouble with a car as advanced as this one,' he said. 'When something goes wrong with a sophisticated mechanism, it goes *really* wrong. Needs a computer expert rather than a mechanic to sort it out.'

'Has anyone told Derek Landor yet?' asked Vic.

'Nick's been trying to get through to him all morning. His mobile's taking messages and his home phone's been engaged for some time. I guess he doesn't know about the results yet. He'll probably need another month off or something to get over the shock,' Craig said sarcastically. He took the opportunity to have a dig at his employer for being a lazy hypochondriac.

'He gets two weeks off for depression and shock and I get one day. It was me who was driving the thing minutes before the airbag went off. He should have been grateful that he wasn't driving.'

Vic froze for a moment. The intonation in Johnstone's voice implied that Derek, and not Johnstone or Boxall, should have been at the wheel.

'You mean, Derek should have been driving the car?'

'Oh, didn't you know?' Craig said casually as he poured the boiling water into the waiting mugs. 'Derek was supposed to be driving it to the old girl's place that day. Boxall booked in for the test-drive at the last minute and Derek didn't get to even sit in the thing. He was pissed off about it at the time but look how lucky he was in the long run.'

More lucky than he could imagine, thought Vic. 'Who else knew that Derek was supposed to be driving the Liguri that day?' she asked, dizzy and dry-mouthed, trying her best to sound like a nosy person and not a detective.

'Nick and me, of course, and his mother and his son, Richard. The kid had been pestering Derek to take him for a drive in it.'

'Does Richard have long blond hair?' she enquired.

Craig pulled a confused expression. 'Richard. No way. He's only thirteen. They wouldn't allow that at his school. I think he's got brown hair, actually.'

215

'Oh, sorry,' she said. 'I didn't know Derek had a young son,' she replied as Craig carried the teas through to Nick's office. There was no time to lose. She had to get on her mobile to Daniel Field immediately. She still had to tell him about Derek's son's dual identity. She had a lot of information to unload and discuss. As she was leaving the showroom, Nick emerged from his office, car keys in hand.

'I'm going to drive round to see Derek,' he said. 'Their phone's been engaged for half an hour. Must be one of the kids gassing with their mates, it being half-term and all. It'll only take about twenty minutes for me to get to his place. I'll see you later. You're off to the old girl's gaff this afternoon, aren't you?' he asked. Vic nodded. 'Well . . . I'll be back before then, I hope, but you never know how long things will take with Derek involved. I'll probably have to hold his hand through it all.'

Vic watched Swift stride out and start up his car. She needed to think carefully and act fast. She realised she would be better off spending the afternoon tracking down Alan Landor than taking tea with his grandma. The undercover employment at the showroom was now an inconvenience. She would soon have to come clean as to why she was there. She didn't need to wait for the manufacturers to run tests on recalled cars. She knew they would be wasting their time. Only one car had been faulty, and Vic would bet her season ticket at Chelsea that it had been made so by a computer expert with a grudge against his father. She'd found out all she needed to start building a case against Alan Landor. The thought that he was watching her was a nagging fear in the back of her mind. She would have to make sure she was on her guard at all times.

Derek Landor was struggling to remain conscious as two grammes of Librium took hold of his senses. Even though he was in an achingly uncomfortable position, crumpled up with a blanket over his entire body, handcuffs around his wrists, a gag in his mouth and his eyes covered with a blindfold, he could feel himself drifting into unconsciousness. Sleeping had never been this easy. The man sitting next to him in the car was still holding the gun which had been rammed into his back then held at his temple while Derek was forced to swallow the pills. He knew this because the man kept leaning his arm across the blanket and poking him with the metal barrel.

He hadn't got a good look at the driver but he knew that none of the men were Peter Bruton. He'd gone over to help them with directions and then everything had happened so fast he hadn't been able to call for help. Not that anyone was around in the quiet street where his doctor's surgery was situated. It was sickeningly ironic that he'd walked out of the surgery with a prescription for tranquillisers.

His kidnappers' conversation had been sparse. They'd answered none of Derek's questions and had threatened to kill him if he continued moaning. The man with the gun seemed to enjoy making these threats.

'We're taking you away from it all for a while,' was all he'd been told. The strange thing for Derek was that now his worst nightmare was actually happening it was easy for him to surrender all responsibility to his captors. He didn't have to think; he only had to do what they told him and keep quiet. He wasn't about to try and make a dash for freedom. The almost silent motion of the luxury saloon was carrying him to oblivion. Maybe when he woke up things would have all been sorted out. He didn't care much about anything right now.

Alan threw handfuls of cold water over his face and groaned. He'd just thrown up for the third time that morning and was seemingly unable to prevent his stomach from churning with the realisation there was no going back. His body shouldn't be acting in this way. Everything was under control, he kept telling himself. All was going to plan. There had been no hitches. Dave had phoned to say their passenger was aboard and out for the count but the bile kept rising to Alan's throat and his eyes were watering from the violent retching he was powerless to stop. Like a condemned man, he was aware of every passing second, every noise, every physical sensation. He felt as alive as he ever had but the adrenaline hit was disorientating. He had to calm down, keep his thinking clear, be patient, wait for instructions.

Nick Swift politely refused a third cup of tea from Deborah Landor. He was seated in the overstuffed chintz armchair in their lounge and feeling very incongruous. He felt uncomfortable in the old man's gaff with his missus fussing around him and making small talk. Smoking was banned in the Landor house and lack of nicotine was driving Nick round the bend. Derek should have been back from the doctor half an hour ago. As the grandfather clock struck half past twelve he knew he wouldn't be able to stomach waiting around with no news for a moment longer. He asked Deborah to call the doctor. It transpired that Derek had left the surgery an hour ago.

'Maybe he's gone for one of his walks,' Deborah said as she placed the receiver back on the kitchen wall. 'I've been encouraging him to take some exercise to help clear his mind of all that worry,' she told him. 'Although,' she added, with the first hint of concern in her voice, 'he always tells me where he's going and he said he'd be back for lunch, which is now.'

Nick told Deborah to get Derek to call him as soon as he returned. The last thing he wanted was the old man going AWOL. He had a horrible feeling that the whole showroom business was about to fall apart. No one had been at the helm for a couple of weeks and custom had been dropping off. He'd made a fool of himself over Vicky and hadn't been concentrating on his orders. Added to this was the worry of Bruton's hate mail and now the findings that didn't rule out foul play as a reason for the airbag explosion. Bruton had denied he was anything to do with it. If he was lying there was no way Nick could go along with protecting the bastard.

If someone was trying to kill Derek, he couldn't stand back and say nothing. Maybe he should have handed the note over to the police. A couple of backhanders were one thing, but murder? That was too much. He felt it was only a matter of time before questions were being asked and his involvement in the car theft would cost him his job, his lifestyle and his freedom. Who would employ a forty-something ex-con? Christ. Maybe he should own up to his part in the crime before Bruton opened his big gob and landed him right in it. If there was a case of attempted murder to be investigated, Bruton was prime candidate for being the first one brought in for questioning. There was still a chance that the second round of tests on the recalled cars would throw up a design fault. It was a slight chance, but it would buy Nick a couple of weeks' extra time while he worked out what he was going to do.

He knew the afternoon was poised to bring a barrage of calls from the various legal eagles who Derek usually handled. These blokes always sounded like they were speaking with a mouthful of plums. Nick hated dealing with them – smarmy bunch of public-school tossers. He was going to be very pissed off if Derek expected him to handle things in that department.

Where was the bugger? Nick wouldn't put it past him to do a disappearing act and join the thousands of names on missing persons files. He was an ideal candidate for that kind of move. Nick thought he noticed a definite sense of unease in the way Deborah looked at him as she saw him to the door. Was this his imagination? Why was everything feeling so ominous? So out of his control?

Vic spent forty minutes speaking on the phone with Daniel Field. Timothy Fuller had been on to the manufacturers who had faxed the insurance company the results of their investigation. Although the manufacturers didn't think it was technically possible, their findings pointed to the airbag having been programmed to go off at a specific time rather than being primed to release on impact. They were at a loss to understand how this could have happened without detaching the car's computer circuit and reprogramming the airbag trigger via the clock so the device became live at 1 p.m. on Wednesday October 15th. The original factory tests had passed the car and its airbag in perfect working order. However, the computer system had been mangled in the crash and it would be impossible to retrieve information.

Vic told Daniel of her suspicions that Alan Landor was at the bottom of the incident. He was a known computer expert with a history of working on cars. The coincidence was too strong to be spurious. Add to this the brooding resentment he held for his father and you had a volatile mixture.

Daniel reminded Vic it was up to the police to put together enough evidence to bring Landor in on a charge of attempted murder. They wouldn't take the claim seriously until at least another two cars had been tested for faulty wiring. She'd done enough and should pull out now, Daniel told her. She had recovered the threatening letter, revealed the true identity of Drake Lewis and discovered that Nick Swift had been lying to Derek. Her evidence would be valuable if the case went to trial. Vic didn't want to wait that long. She wanted to track down Alan Landor and follow his movements for a few days.

Daniel thought it odd that Derek hadn't been on the line. He'd rung his home address but his wife hadn't seen him since 10.45 a.m. when he'd left the house for a doctor's appointment. It was now 1.30 p.m. and he was late for lunch. She'd checked his diary and he had no other meetings scheduled for that day. Vic suggested he might be paying his mother a visit. She was due at the Landor estate herself in a couple of hours. The chauffeur was picking her up from the showroom at four. As a parting shot before pulling out of Haver Dean, Vic would keep her appointment with Gayle Landor. She decided to kill the next two hours by calling at Derek's house. Some pieces of the puzzle were still missing. Maybe the final clues would turn up in Little Chalfont. First, she had to drive to Swift's place and retrieve her belongings. She had the feeling she wouldn't be spending another night there.

Vic hadn't prepared herself for the opulence of the Landor household. It was a world away from Walthamstow, but wealth seemed to have caused more problems than comforts for this family. Vic looked forward to getting back to her London life. A night out in Upper Street with her mates sounded like heaven to her right now, stuck as she was in the nightmare of affluent suburbia. She motored up the long driveway and was greeted at the entrance to the house by an elegantly-dressed woman in her forties.

'Oh,' said the woman. 'I thought you were my husband. Who are you? Are you here to see him? You're not from the HydroMet project are you? Only I don't know what arrangements he made for today.'

She sounded nervous. Vic recognised the tone in her voice was one of emotion and worry. It was the same tone her mother had when she talked about Tony. Worried mothers, worried wives. Why were women's lives so often filled with worry? Vic stood by her Corolla and suddenly felt she'd had enough of skulking around, pretending to be a graphic designer, a drug dealer, an ex-model. She wasn't prepared to lie to Deborah Landor, whose life must be something of a personal hell right now.

'Mrs Landor. My name's Victoria Donovan. I've been working at Landor Motors since Monday on a marketing project. But that's not the only reason I'm there. Nick Swift has been here earlier, yes?' The woman nodded silently. 'Did he tell you the manufacturer's report came through? You know – the report about the cause of the car crash?'

'No. He wouldn't talk to me about that kind of thing and to be honest I didn't think to ask him. Derek should have come back an hour and a half ago. He never said anything about a new member of staff.'

'He probably doesn't know. Your husband has had other things on his mind recently, am I right?' The two women looked each other in the eyes. Deborah Landor looked horrified and nodded silently once more. 'Mrs Landor,' said Vic. 'I'm a private investigator. I think I know something of what's been going on in your husband's life recently. May I come in?'

'Whatever do you mean?' she asked, her voice betraying the shock. 'Who's hired you? Are you saying my husband's having an affair?' She was sounding desperately unhappy. Vic immediately reassured her that marital infidelity was not the issue. 'We must talk,' she said. 'If you'd rather sit in the car, Mrs Landor . . .'

'No, dear. No. Of course you may come in. I'm sorry to have appeared rude just then. I'm just worried, you see. Derek has become more and more withdrawn recently. We have some family problems and things are going through a rough patch right now.' She showed Vic into the hallway and through to the lounge and then perched on the edge of the sofa as she hung on to Vic's every word.

'Are you aware just how rough, Mrs Landor? Do you know about the note, for instance?'

'Note. What note?'

'The hate mail your husband received during the time of the Motor Show.' Vic produced the photocopy from her bag and handed it to Deborah Landor.

Her face turned ashen and she grasped at her throat and began toying with the gold chain which rested around her neck. 'Oh, poor Derek. I had no idea. Oh why didn't he tell me?'

'Is his son Alan a regular visitor here?' Vic asked, moving swiftly on. 'How does he get on with other members of the family?' There was stony silence. Deborah was still trying to process the information about the hate mail.

'Mrs Landor. You don't have to tell me anything. I'll leave now if you want me to but I think I may know more about Alan than you suspect. I know about his mother's suicide, his troubled childhood, his time in reform school and detention centres.' Vic launched in with the crux of the matter. 'Look . . . I think that your husband is in some kind of trouble. I may be able to help. I'm currently building a case which involves his son Alan. Was he here recently?'

'Yes. On Sunday. He was here for lunch. There was a row. He'd been smuggling bottles of alcoholic lemonade to my son, Richard. But what do you mean, a case?'

'Richard's thirteen years old, yes?'

It was a bizarre kind of power to have: being a stranger who knew so much. Deborah Landor's face was a picture of distress.

'Yes, he's thirteen. What's this case, Victoria? Please. You must tell me. Do you think Alan's been sending my husband hate mail?'

'Maybe,' said Vic. It wouldn't do any good to tell Deborah the findings of the crash report; certainly not before Derek Landor turned up.

'Oh, poor Derek. I'd have never allowed Alan here if I'd have known. Veronica was right. Oh I've been so unfair to Derek.'

'Mrs Landor. If you didn't know about the note, you wouldn't have thought there was anything wrong in inviting Alan to the house. Alan is only one suspect in this business. Who's Veronica?'

'That's Derek's daughter. She's marvellous. Completely different from her brother.'

'Where do you think Derek is now, Mrs Landor?' she asked.

Deborah looked sadly into Vic's eyes. 'I don't know,' she said in a small, scared voice. 'I don't know.'

'Fuckin' hell, Neil, you've done us proud here, mate!' shouted Dave as he and Clem bundled the semi-conscious captive into the metal shipping container. 'All the comforts of a Holiday Inn. You've even got the picnic tables out. Bit different from what you're used to, I'll bet?' he shouted at Derek who couldn't see anyway because of the blindfold. 'Once we've got you settled in we'll let you have a look round your hotel room.'

Clem laughed and the three men dragged Derek over to one corner where he was thrown into a cage and manacled to the thick, upright metal bars. There was a tatty mattress in there and the blanket from the car was thrown in as minimal comfort.

'Used to be a lion's cage,' Neil said. 'Got it from the Isle of Sheppey when the circus closed down. Always knew it would come in useful.'

'Brilliant. Did you bring any straw?' he joked.

'That's a point,' said Neil. 'He'll want a bucket in there, won't he?'

'Christ, I didn't think about that. He's gonna stink the

223

place out. Just as well he's in the far corner.'

'You've got to keep the noise down, boys,' said Neil. 'All the nearby containers are empty but there are one or two further along the unit which are in use. Barry's got to make a living, so be careful. We should be pretty safe at night but daytime activity should be kept to a minimum.'

'Where's pretty boy, then?' asked Clem. 'He should be here by now. He wants to be around when the call goes through to Landor's wife.'

'You sure he was OK about the directions?'

'Yeah, no problem. I'm thirsty. How about cracking those beers open, Neil?'

'Go easy. It's only three o' clock. I don't want anyone here getting pissed up thinking he's in the Baader Meinhof gang or something.'

'Who the fuck are they?' asked Clem.

'Some German kidnappers, I think,' Dave answered.

'What happened to them?'

'They either got whacked in jail or topped themselves. They were a bunch of fucking hippies anyway.'

'No. That was Charles Manson's lot,' Clem said. 'Helter Skelter. Death to the pigs.'

'You what?'

'They'd get out of it all day and listen to the Beatles' Helter Skelter. Then they tried to blame the murders on a bunch of niggers.'

'Fair enough, I guess. Can't see why you would go to all that trouble if there was no money in a job, though.'

'Some fuckers are just plain mad,' said Clem.

'Look,' said Boden. 'While you're discussing Charlie bloody Manson, old fat boy over there's coming round. One of you sort him out, will you. Keep your mind on the job, eh.'

Alan pulled his van into the flat, desolate landscape of East Tilbury. He consulted his directions. There should be a left turn coming up at any moment. There were no security guards and the place looked like a waste ground. He'd just passed a couple of landfill sites which stank as bad as anything he'd ever smelt. It nearly brought on another attack of heaving, but there was nothing left for him to bring up. As he rattled along the muddy path, he could see the metal containers shimmering in the distance. The place looked like the ends of the earth. He hadn't passed another car for miles, which was a good sign. Boden had picked an ideal spot. He'd noticed a couple of lorries making journeys to and from the dumping grounds at the landfill sites but there were no private cars around at all.

His heart leapt as a flock of birds suddenly flapped into the air yards from his van. The terrain was marshy and wild, although a proliferation of old tyres, milk crates and unidentifiable man-made matter prevented the area from being anything near to picturesque. He cruised to a stop beside the tall containers, which seemed to come in a choice of silver or rust red. As he killed the engine and got out of the van, he was struck by the silence of the place. It was God's forgotten part of England. He began walking around, looking for the luxury saloon; it was nowhere in sight.

Then he heard a metallic creaking sound and Boden emerged from a container about 30 yards to his right. Alan hurried towards him.

'Where's the Audi?' he asked.

'Safely locked away in another of Barry's hidey holes,' he replied. 'It'll be getting a paint job as we speak. One of his boys is taking care of the respray and the plates.'

Alan was stunned. That hadn't been part of the deal. He had that motor lined up for someone else. But he could hardly protest. It seemed like Boden had pulled a fast one on him. Any area left uncovered was ripe pickings for the likes of this lot. Alan felt acutely naïve.

'Just in case, lad,' Bruton continued. 'Can't be too careful. We'll use your motor until Clem brings his down from London. If some good citizen happened to spot anything untoward on our journey down here, they would have taken the number, you can bank on that. Law-abiding punters have been doing that since *Police 5*.'

'How's Derek doing?' Alan asked. 'Can I see him? Has he got his blindfold on?'

'I'll just check. He came round about half an hour ago.

We let him take a piss and drink some water before giving him another dose of knock-out drops. He's well secure in there. He's got the basic comforts.'

Boden's steely-grey hair was caught for a moment by the watery sunlight. His expression was calm; cheerful even. The journey had been trouble-free and Boden almost seemed to be enjoying himself.

'In a minute, we'll talk about making that call,' Boden said, then slipped back inside the metal box. A few seconds later he popped his head out and motioned Alan to step in. If Alan had thought Boden was taking the business calmly in his stride, the sight of Clem and Dave drinking beers and playing cards was one of the more unexpected things he'd witnessed in his life. He wasn't sure what he thought they should have been doing but sitting as they were, feet up on chairs, fags on the go, and cards in hand, didn't seem like the sort of behaviour he expected from hard-core kidnappers.

They threw him a token. 'All right?'

'Is he OK?' Alan whispered to Clem, who didn't bother looking up.

'If you mean is he alive, then yeah,' he said gruffly, staring at his cards. 'I dare say he's had better days but he's not here to enjoy himself.'

'Shouldn't you be keeping an eye on him?' Alan asked.

'What? You think he's going to break out of his cage?' he snorted. 'We'll get enough chance to "keep an eye on him" when things start to liven up a bit.'

Clem was in his element being the hard man. Alan could see the difference between himself and his accomplices: there was no spark of humanity to either of these two younger men. Boden was an old-school charmer. He'd sell your mother to a Russian-mafia pimp for a tenner but at least he'd put his arm round you and smile while he did it. Neither Clem nor Dave were interested in displaying even the most basic common courtesies. In their circles, blokes were measured by how hard they were, and Alan knew he had almost no respect from these two because of his looks and his size. In their world he was a soft cunt and not one of the hard boys.

226

Alan crept over to where his father was lying on the mattress. He was turned towards the wall and his substantial bulk looked inanimate and untidy. He was still wearing the suit he'd put on that morning and it was now really crumpled. Alan had never seen his father looking so untidy before. He stared and stared, transfixed with fascination and horror at what he had put in motion. Derek's arms were stretched above his head and his hands were manacled to the cage. His chubby face was pressed against his upper arm, the eyes covered with a black blindfold, and his mouth formed into the shape of an open purse which was letting forth a variety of snuffling and snoring noises. He was in a deep sleep. His right leg was flung over his left and the suit trousers had ridden up to expose a few inches of pale, hairy leg. His shoes were missing, Alan noticed. Maybe Boden had taken them off to prevent his feet from swelling.

Boden came up behind him. He towered over Alan. 'This is the easy part of the job. The difficult bit is keeping occupied, not letting yourself get bored. That's why I encouraged these two to play cards, dominoes, Gameboys, whatever. I've seen too many jobs where blokes have too much time to kill. That's when the arguments start, right boys?'

'Right, Neil,' grunted Dave and Clem.

'So, Drake,' said Neil, laying a hand on Alan's shoulder. 'Isn't it about time we told Delboy's missus he won't be home for tea?'

Vic had spent longer with Deborah Landor than expected. The woman was helpful, polite and genuine. As the time had ticked by, Deborah had opened up about herself and Vic had heard what it was like to marry into the Landor family. She admitted she had turned to therapy as a way of coping with Gayle Landor's hold over Derek and the old woman's attempts to involve herself in everything Deborah tried to organise. She told Vic that Gayle would get to hear about everything the family were up to, including the local charity events Deborah initiated. She insisted on vetting the causes her daughter-in-law was putting the Landor name to. Compared to Gayle Landor, Marie Donovan seemed like the ideal mum.

At three o'clock Vic persuaded Deborah to call Gayle. Ballard answered the phone, as was customary. There was no need to disturb the napping old lady, he said; Derek hadn't been there today and Ballard hadn't been given any notice of his arrival. He had, however, been instructed to wake Mrs Landor at 3.30 p.m. so she could prepare for a visiting guest – a young lady.

Deborah looked frightened as she slowly racked the phone. Vic knew it was time for action. She phoned Ballard immediately and told him the 'young lady' wasn't able to make it this time. She phoned the showroom and, luckily, Janice answered. Derek hadn't been there either. Vic told Janice she was with Derek's wife and to tell Nick Swift she wasn't coming back that afternoon. 'Tell him I'm visiting Gayle Landor,' she said. She trusted Janice to keep her whereabouts secret. She and Nick Swift were not the best of friends in any case.

'I'm going to phone the police,' said Deborah, consumed by worry and unable to sit down or stand still now that they'd exhausted the obvious places where Derek could be. She'd rushed out of the front door a few times to look for any sign of her husband's car and was becoming more tearful with each fruitless search. On Vic's recommendation she rang Haver Dean police station, rather than emergency services, to report her husband's disappearance. They wanted her to come to the station to fill out a missing persons form – which Deborah was reluctant to do. She wanted action, answers, results – and sooner rather than later.

Vic said she would accompany her. It might be a chance to find out what they knew about the note. Vic had heard Swift mention the name of a police officer to Derek one time he'd been called on the car phone and been asked to give it back to him. What was it? She racked her brain. Grey, Grierson, something like that. Vic wanted to drive back to London as soon as possible. Hopefully, one of Deborah's children would be home soon and Vic wouldn't have to feel guilty about leaving the woman to worry alone. A visit to

Alan Landor's place might tie up a few ends. If something serious was going down, either Peter Bruton or Derek's son was behind it, of that she was certain.

On the way to the station, Vic suggested that Deborah drive via Derek's doctor's place. When she spotted his MGF still parked outside the surgery, Deborah was at first relieved. 'At least he's not been in an accident,' she said. But then came a barrage of rhetorical questions Vic didn't want to reply to. She had her own answers, but each one of them would be sure to throw Mrs Landor further into a spin of worry. Vic tried to take her mind off the situation by getting the woman to talk about her children. She thought of Veronica as her own. When she married Derek his daughter was only six and took to Deborah like a long-lost parent. She talked about her garden, her therapy and her friends, and by the time they pulled up outside Haver Dean police station she was in a calm enough state to face the missing persons form.

Vic placed a strong hand on the woman's shoulder. She was glad to be there with her, to be able to comfort her and tell her not to worry. Vic had to keep reminding herself this was a job and that it would all be over at some point. To think it was only a couple of weeks ago that she'd thought her work wasn't real enough. This was hyper-real. It was a long way from the cosmetics counters of Kensington. Daniel had wanted her to pull out now, return to London and type up her report in anticipation of a police investigation. Vic couldn't help thinking that things would get a bit more frantic before that could happen.

FIFTEEN
Hairy

Wednesday Evening

'It's a bloody answerphone. You can't leave a ransom demand on an answerphone,' Dave shouted. 'I thought you said she'd definitely be in at four.'

'Well as far as I know she usually is,' Alan replied. 'She doesn't do fuck-all all day. Maybe she's in the garden. Why don't you call her mobile number? Both him and his wife have one. I've given you the number.'

Dave reached for his paper with all the numbers and addresses on. 'Oh yeah. I suppose she uses it in the supermarket. Rings her old man up and asks him what he wants for dinner. "Steak or pheasant, darling?"' Dave threw on a high-pitched voice.

'Pheasant would be absolutely super,' Clem answered, then laughed – a little too loudly, maybe, Alan thought, watching his father move around in his drug-induced slumber.

'It's getting dark in here,' said Dave. 'I can barely see the numbers. Where's that camping lamp, Neil?'

'Don't worry. I've got it – and the gas canisters. We'll clip it to the ceiling so we get the maximum light, OK?'

The men grunted.

'Go on. Ring her on the mobile,' Alan hissed, agitated that contact should be made with Deborah as soon as possible.

Alan was feeling significantly less at home than the others appeared to be. He certainly wasn't about to join in with their stupid jokes. Boden ribbed him about being a 'first-timer' and told him to relax, put his feet up and have a beer. Alan didn't want a beer; he wanted a spliff. It would be the only way he could relax.

As soon as he reached into his pocket he remembered he'd left it in the kitchen. If only he could keep track of all his stuff. He was always losing things. There was no way he was going to be able to survive the night without a puff. It would be the only thing that would keep him from going mad and stressing out about the whole situation. There was no point telling the others. Boden was anti-drugs and Clem and Dave would take the piss mercilessly. He was only about forty minutes from London. He could be back by eight if they really wanted him there. He was hoping they'd let him take first turn for a night off. Night time was the most vulnerable time for being recognised. Once the call was made, he'd drive off. It would be good to get an alibi, too.

Vic and Deborah were in Haver Dean police station. Deborah had tried calling home a number of times on her mobile but still no one was there. Vic had remembered the name of the relevant officer and, although he wasn't on duty that day, another sergeant had found the file and brought it to the desk. They asked Vic her relationship to the missing person and she came clean about her work. She hadn't expected to be laughed at. The bloke made her look a fool in front of Deborah, and Vic was not pleased.

He went through the file in a methodical manner, looking for a long time at the statements about the crash. Vic bit her tongue to prevent herself from blurting out the results of the car manufacturers' report too soon. You'll find out soon enough, she thought. Then you'll take me seriously when you need my evidence to make a conviction.

'Yes. Mr Landor came here just last Friday,' said the

sergeant, closely reading the report. 'He said he was going to hand over the note but he never turned up with it. Nine out of ten times these things turn out to be hoaxes. Anyone could have got hold of the address of the showroom, Mrs Landor. You know the fuss the local paper kicked up about the crash. It was probably one of those anti-car nutcases.'

'I've got the note right here,' Vic said casually, pulling it from her bag. 'His senior salesman at the showroom, Nick Swift, was holding on to it for a while but I think it burnt a hole in his pocket, so to speak. It's all yours now.'

Vic was watching his reaction to this when Deborah Landor's mobile went off. She soon realised the call wasn't from one of the woman's children. Deborah grabbed the desk sergeant by his tie and put the phone between their ears. Vic was fuming that she couldn't hear what the caller was saying. Who was it? Derek? Some other policeman with bad news?

'Half a million pounds. It's not possible!' Deborah cried. 'No! Don't hurt him. We'll do something. Please. Who is this? How did you get my number? Please don't hurt my husband.'

As she crumpled over the desk in tears, the gaunt-looking and astonished desk sergeant suddenly leapt into action. Vic wasn't that surprised at the call. It was inappropriate, but she actually felt like laughing: both at the change in expression of the desk sergeant – who had just been so supercilious – and for the fact that the kidnappers had called Deborah Landor while she was in a police station. It was like choosing to have a heart attack in a hospital. Now maybe things could get moving.

'Clem knows where Drake lives, Neil,' said Dave. 'Even if he loses him on the motorway he'll catch up with him at his flat. Drake wouldn't for a minute suspect he was being followed. Not by anyone on a motorbike, anyway. Smart move, that, getting one of Barry's boys to bring the bike down here. Clem can drive it back to his son's place in

Deptford, then pick up his own motor and return in that. Very handy.'

Neil lit a cigarette and sat down to face Dave. 'I just don't trust the bugger. I want tabs kept on him at all times. There's something not quite right, you know what I mean? He doesn't have a clue. It's like taking a kid along with you. Sooner we get this done and get out the better. If it starts dragging on, I'm going to get cold feet. He could be undercover for all we know. I mean, he's just not like anyone we've dealt with before.'

'I don't think he's Old Bill. Look at him, for a start. He couldn't fight his way out of a paper bag. He's right about this one, though,' said Dave, nodding in the direction of their captive. 'Everything he's said about this Landor character seems to be bang on. The bastard's definitely loaded.'

'I hope you're right, Dave. I've been in this game a long time and this one's got a weird smell to it. When it comes to wages time, we'll give Drake Lewis what we reckon he deserves. He'll get out what he's put in, agreed?'

'Yeah, sure. All he's given us is a few phone numbers. He couldn't have done this without us. No four-way evens, Neil. What's he going to do if we shortchange him? If he had a hard crew we'd have seen evidence by now. We could walk it. Just stroll out of here with whatever the fuck we like.'

'Lewis is a bit of a lone wolf, I reckon. There's no firm, no mates – not unless you count Peter Bruton – fuckin' foghorn almighty. Christ! If he knows about it, you can be fuckin' sure that half of Aylesbury are in on it. What's the time?'

'Six o'clock,' Dave replied. 'It's time for the next instalment. This is where we put the frighteners on. Do you want to do it, or shall I?'

'I'll do it, son,' said Boden. 'I haven't done a good wind-up like this for a long time.'

'For Christ's sake move over,' Vic shouted at the car in front of her as she thrashed her Corolla down the M40 back towards Paddington. She wanted an open road and a faster car. She was in the outside lane and using her lights to flash everyone who was holding her up. She'd received a few blasts from the horns of pissed-off BMW drivers but she didn't care. It was times like this that she wanted a blue flashing light and a siren, although she didn't want to be a cop.

Of course the phone call had been untraceable. Deborah Landor had thrown herself into the trustworthy care of the police and had been ushered into a private room with a WPC to make a statement about the phone call and Derek's movements over the past couple of weeks. At the point where a car had been sent to chase Bruton's whereabouts, Vic had walked out of the station, frustrated that they'd not made the call to Southwark police station she'd requested. Someone had to get round to Alan Landor's – but it looked like it was going to have to be her. She threw his address at them and told them she was going there. They still weren't taking her seriously. Their way of doing things seemed far too slow considering the information she held. The moment she'd mentioned she was a PI they'd become derisory – hostile, even. If she stuck around she knew she'd lose her temper. She left, taking Deborah's mobile number with her. She promised to ring the woman for regular bulletins.

With the gas pedal flat down to the floor and her mobile pressed to her ear she had a conversation with Daniel Field. She told him his client was now at a location and in a condition unknown. Once again he tried to advise her to pull out, but she wouldn't hear of it. 'I don't want to pull out, Daniel. You can stop paying me as from now but I've got to follow my instincts on this. I must find out what's going on. I can't just go home and turn on the TV and have a quiet night in – not after everything that's happened and what's going on right now.'

'Victoria, you're crazy. Be careful. Why are you doing this?'

'One day I'll tell you, Daniel,' she replied. 'When I've figured it out for myself.' She didn't say any more, but smiled and ended the call after telling Daniel where she was heading. Now both he and Haver Dean police knew where she would be if anything went wrong. If poor old Derek was locked up in Alan Landor's garage, Vic wanted to be first on the scene.

6.30 p.m.

Finally I get to see where Alan Landor lives, thought Vic as she waited in the car park on his council estate. He'd certainly come down in the world from Little Chalfont. The place was noisy and run-down and huge silver bins overflowed with the rubbish from a hundred and fifty low-income households. An overflow pipe at the top of the building was dribbling water down the brickwork and patches of dark-green slime had formed in places.

Vic was in her disguise: dark wig and scruffy tracksuit. She wasn't sure what she was going to do when she spotted Alan Landor, other than follow him. Supposing he recognised her and turned violent? She reckoned she was probably stronger than him; she was certainly taller, but would she be able to hold her own? If Bruton was with him then things would turn very hairy. The only protection she had was a red pepper spray she'd smuggled back from America. She felt it in her pocket. She'd often looked at the red release button on the little tube and felt tempted to flick it off. She hoped she wouldn't have to use it.

All she needed was a sign that Derek was in the area. He was bound to be at the flat or the garage. Maybe it was all a misunderstanding or a cruel prank. Alan hated his father and Deborah – that much was fairly common knowledge – but was he up to the job of kidnapping someone? He must be stupid to pull a stunt like this, thought Vic. Surely all the evidence pointed at him even though the police were following the Bruton connection. She was still keen to know what Bruton's involvement in all this had been. She wondered how the police were getting on with their visit.

The smells of ethnic cooking wafted into the car re-minding Vic she was hungry. A warm can of coke was the only refreshment she had. She wished she'd grabbed something on the way. She hadn't eaten at all that day. Sitting in the car just watching and waiting was driving her mad. So far, there had been no movement to or from Landor's flat. How much longer am I going to be here? she thought. Then, just as she was cleaning out the glove compartment of her car to stay occupied, a white Ford Escort van came into the estate and backed up near the stairwell leading to Landor's flat. It was him! She'd recognise that blond hair anywhere. From where she was parked, on the other side of the quadrangle, Vic was confident he wouldn't spot her.

He didn't appear to be in a hurry and he was alone. She wrote down the registration number of the vehicle. He got out of the van and went up the stairs. If only she could chance looking into the van. Should she? Dammit, she had to do something. She couldn't stand not knowing what was going on. She got out of the Corolla and skirted her way around the perimeter of the quadrangle until she was at the bottom of the stairwell. There was no sign of him. She could risk a little peek through the back windows. No bodies inside, just a crumpled blanket and a tool box. Curious. Maybe Landor wasn't involved at all. Maybe it was Bruton all the time and the police had been right. She nipped round to the driver's side and, again, couldn't see anything suspicious. The ashtray was overflowing and there were empty cans on the floor.

There was a map poking out from under the passenger seat, though. There were only a couple of inches of map visible, but it was enough to make out the curve of the north Kent coastline. The only towns she could make out in the brief seconds she had were Maidstone and Gillingham. Of course, this could have nothing to do with Derek's kidnap but right now anything was a clue. She walked back to her car the way she'd came. Less chance of being spotted. Surely it was only a matter of time before the police would arrive on the scene? Waiting and waiting.

At 7.20 p.m. he finally emerged. He'd changed his jacket. Vic watched him get back into his van and drive out of the estate. She couldn't do it. She couldn't follow him. She'd heard how difficult it was to track a moving car further than a couple of streets. Supposing he spotted her? She imagined herself getting into an unholy mess. The better plan was to get into the flat. Derek could be there. If she had no joy in the flat she'd take the short drive to the garage.

She found herself outside the door. She'd rung the bell three times and peered through the letterbox. No sign or sound of movement. The hallway was strewn with unopened letters and the place looked desolate and not lived-in. The kitchenette window was easy to pull open from the outside and, while no one was about, Vic shimmied through, propping her hands on the sink unit for support. She checked each room, expecting to see a trussed-up Derek Landor, but there were only bare floorboards, some tins of paint and furniture which looked as if it had been claimed from a skip. Everything needed hoovering and cleaning. Alan certainly didn't live in style.

In Alan's bedroom a computer was switched on and there was a reasonable amount of hi-tech equipment piled up in one corner. She dialled 1471 to check the number of the last person who had called him. She didn't recognise the number but she made a note of it. It didn't belong to Bruton, Deborah or Landor Motors. She began looking for anything that might indicate what was going on in this person's life. There were official letters and bills scattered on his table, but nothing of a personal nature.

She sat down at the computer. What did he have on that hard drive? A load of graphics packages, a few games, Internet software. She browsed around for a few minutes. She was tempted to play a game of Quake but thought better of it. As she scanned the C drive, a curiously-named folder caught her eye. Was this a new game? She double-clicked the readme file marked 'auto'. An icon of an airbag opening and deflating was enough to slot another piece of the puzzle into place.

Vic was just about to ring Deborah Landor when she heard a noise coming from what sounded like just outside the door. She nearly jumped out of her skin; she'd been so engrossed that she'd forgotten there was a world carrying on its normal life out there.

For a few moments she didn't move. Then she tiptoed to the doorway, listening. There was no conversation. Gingerly, she put her head round the corner and looked down the hallway, straight into a pair of eyes looking through the letterbox. Whose eyes were they? They weren't Alan's. Oh my God!

'Open the door!' the man shouted. 'Is Lewis in there?'

Vic was scared. She dashed back into Landor's bedroom. She couldn't phone Haver Dean nick; they'd do her for breaking and entering. She could phone Deborah, but she'd be no help. She could call 999 but that would be admitting defeat. Maybe the guy at the door was nothing to do with the kidnap. Keep calm, she told herself. He could be here to buy drugs, get his motor fixed – any number of reasons. She called no one, turned her phone off and slipped it back into her bag.

He pounded on the door. 'Open up. Police.'

Thank God! They must have contacted Southwark after all. She ran and opened the front door, had time to take one look at the thug standing in front of her, and then realised her stupid mistake.

'What have we got here then?' he asked. 'You Lewis's bird? Popped out has he? What's the matter? Aren't you going to invite me in for a cup of tea?'

Vic backed away. What could she say? Whoever this guy was, he was twice as fierce-looking as Peter Bruton and about five inches taller. Christ! How was she going to talk her way out of this one? He looked as if he'd use the pepper spray as seasoning on his hot dog. Trying to scare him off with it would be a pathetic stab in the dark which Vic didn't want to risk – not just yet anyway.

He grabbed her by the wrist and pulled her into one room after another until he was satisfied Landor wasn't there. Vic kept quiet. She wasn't about to put him to rights about Alan's real name. She'd had to find out the hard way – so could he.

'Come on, babe. Me and you are going to go for a little drive. I'll tell you my life story and then you can decide whether you're going to tell me where Lewis is, all right?'

Oh my God, thought Vic. Why didn't I listen to Daniel? I've really got myself in the shit this time.

Peter Bruton sat grim-faced in the interview room of Haver Dean police station. He kept telling them – he didn't know why Derek Landor was missing. He hadn't done anything! Yeah, he'd sent the note, but it was a wind-up. A wind-up and nothing more.

Some bastard had grassed him up and now they were trying to pin something big on him. They wouldn't say what, but Bruton cursed himself for sending the note in the first place. There was only one shithead it could have been. Nick bloody Swift. There was no way he was going to stay quiet for his benefit anymore. Swift had been so close to blabbing after the BMW job that Peter, Andrew and Gary had thought they were going to have to seriously do him over. Not just a broken nose, either.

He wished he'd never given Swift any money. It was all fucked up and now they'd found the shooter at his place in Millfields. With his previous record, there was no doubt he would go down for possession of an illegal firearm. He knew it. Bastards. Now the Saturday Night Special had disintegrated into dust. Sheryl would go mad; her mother would have the final say; when would he see Sean again? Fuck it all. This was terrible.

'Do you know who you're fucking dealing with, you bitch!' Clem screamed, frustrated at Vic's silence. They'd been to Alan Landor's garage and there was no sign of him. The big man had hammered on Landor's doors and asked other mechanics working late nearby if they'd seen him that day. No sign. Now he was getting impatient that the trail had run cold and he was looking increasingly narked.

He wouldn't let Vic go and she wouldn't tell him anything. He hadn't even let her return to her car to get her jacket before they'd left the esatate. Vic was feeling shabby, hungry and increasingly desperate. Even the warm can of coke would be nectar right now, she thought. Her environment had become all grubby railway arches and greasy motors. She thought hard about her flat. Why wasn't she there, relaxing in her bathtub or reading in her bedroom? Mister X was frightening company. She'd never complain about being bored by anyone again. Being bored would be heaven.

They motored down past New Cross, out to Deptford and through Blackheath. She'd pleaded to be allowed to get out of the car. 'I won't tell Lewis you're looking for him,' she said. 'He owes me a load of money and I owe him nothing.'

This fell on deaf ears. 'You're staying right by my side,' he said, ignoring her suggestion. 'You might turn out to be useful.'

The way he looked at her as he said this sent waves of horror coursing through her body. If he tried to lay a hand on her then she'd fight to the death if need be. The veins in his neck bulged with tension and he kept clenching his teeth. He was definitely a steroid freak. No one's face naturally looked that mean. He was wearing a leather jacket and dark jeans. His hair was almost black and his eyebrows were thick and met over his nose. His legs were huge – long and thick – and his hands were the size of small plates. He was a brutal-looking, cretinous, mad-dog son of a bitch – and she was trapped in his car with him. To think some woman has willingly lain down for him, she thought. How does someone deal with that? Then she thought about her own weaknesses: Swift and Alan Landor in one week. She cringed inside.

She'd grudgingly admitted to being 'Lewis's bird', which seemed to shut the thug up. He was the third fatnecked bully to assume she was Landor's girlfriend. Then he produced the gun. It was small, silver and loaded. She knew because he showed her the clip.

'I know his real name isn't Lewis, so you better tell me it, darling,' he said. 'Come on. You must know it. Being his bird and all.' He waved the gun around.

She didn't usually like being called 'darling' but this time she let it pass. She had no need to cover Landor. This guy was thick, though. If he hadn't been in such a hurry he could have just picked up one of the letters in Landor's hallway to find out his quarry's real name.

'It's Landor,' she said. 'Alan Landor.'

On hearing this, he nearly ran into the car in front. Then it was full steam ahead for an unknown destination with thug-features grimacing and grinding his teeth and his foot flat on the accelerator. He'd shut up, which was a bit of a relief, as interacting with a homicidal maniac was hard work.

As soon as he was able, he stopped the car somewhere secluded. He got out and made a call on his mobile. Vic was locked in the car and couldn't catch all of what he was saying but what she did hear sounded grisly. He was giving instructions to someone to put the boot in. Maybe they were giving Derek a pasting. The poor bloke. Being on the receiving end of this guy – and whoever his partners were – was an awful thought. He wasn't keeping a good enough eye on Vic. He kept turning his back to the car and it was easy for her to pull her own mobile out of her bag, bring it to her left ear and lean on it, as if she was tired and depressed, while she made a call.

'Deborah. Listen. It's Victoria,' she said in a small, scared voice. 'Write this down. I've been abducted from Alan's flat. I'm on the A2 in a maroon Sierra with a nutcase. We've just gone past the Dartford turnoff.' She gave the registration number. She'd always had a photographic memory for car number plates. 'I can't be certain but I think that I'm going to be seeing Derek very soon. If the police can find me, they've found Derek. That's it. Help me, please. Help me.'

Twenty minutes later, Vic was dragged out of the car at gunpoint and dragged through the marshland. She felt like crying with fear. Deborah was her only hope. She didn't even know if the woman could hear what she'd said. It was almost dark now and she'd never felt so vulnerable. As she stumbled over the boggy grassland the thug grabbed at her. He twisted her arm, felt her arse, pulled her hair, pushed her over and laughed. She lay in the mud, the wig beside her, her hair fanned out around her.

'Oh, so you're a natural blonde!' he mocked. 'If we weren't

in such a hurry, I'd like to spend some quality time with you.' He laughed and the sick sound rang out into the deserted landscape. Then, an unexpected noise. A ship's horn. They were near the docks. The noise startled both of them. Vic jumped up and began running. The ground was a blur beneath her feet but she didn't care. She just had to run.

'Stop, you slag,' he shouted and fired into the night air. She dived to the ground. Her hands were cut and her knees stung.

'You stay right there, you fuckin' tart. We're going to have some fun now. I've got to teach you a lesson. You don't run away from Uncle Clem.'

He dragged her to her feet and wound her long hair around his left hand until her neck was jerked back and she could feel his thumb pressing into the base of her skull. In his other hand he held the gun and began rubbing her breasts with it, poking at them with the end of the barrel as he pulled her head back and forth.

'Does your mummy know where you are?' he said, prodding the pistol into her body and twisting her hair. 'Does mummy know where her little daughter is? She's not going to make it home tonight,' he continued in a sickly sweet voice as if he were talking to a child. 'She's going to be showing everything she's got to the boys. Isn't that right? Isn't that fucking right!' he screamed.

'Please, don't shoot me. I don't know anything. Please let me go,' she pleaded.

'You're a right fucking laugh, darling,' he said. 'You think I'm going to let you go? How sweet.'

'What the fuck is going on?' said another voice – a voice of reason.

Vic saw a torchlight and the figure of a taller man, an older man, walking over to them. Thank God.

'What do you think you're doing?' he spat.

The thug let go of Vic's hair and she felt her head fall back into its normal position. She rubbed her neck. It hurt.

'It's Lewis's bird.' he said. 'Or should I say Landor Junior's bird. He'll be happy to see her, I'm sure.'

'Get back in here now,' the older man said, looking at Vic

242

in surprise. 'D'you want all of Tilbury in on the party?'

Vic looked up to see a row of shipping containers. There was a light coming from one of them. She was marched over to them with the feel of the loaded pistol in the back of her neck. Was she going to join 'the boys' now? This was hell. This was the lowest, darkest place she'd ever been. Please let Deborah Landor be on the case, she thought. Please God help me.

'Throw her in there with the other two,' said Boden. A man called Dave opened the padlock and pushed Vic into a dark cage. A number of empty bottles were lying around the container and there was a strong smell of drink. Derek Landor was slumped against the wall, handcuffed to the bars and dazed, but looking intact. Next to him, to Vic's utter amazement, was Alan Landor, also sitting on the floor, but his nose was a pulverised mess, his hair was matted with blood and his face was wet with tears. What the hell was going on here? If he'd organised her kidnapping, and the kidnapping of his father, why was he now locked up?

'Lovely,' said Dave, looking at the three prisoners. 'All girls together. One thing, though. We'll have that bag off you.' He pulled Vic's small leather handbag from her shoulders and stuffed it under his arm before locking the cage. He carried it over to where he'd been sitting, turned the bag upside down and watched the contents spill out. Vic winced as she heard her mobile phone crash loudly on to the metal floor. A small packet also fell out. Vic had forgotten about the cocaine.

'Is this what I think it is?' asked Dave, carefully opening the paper wrapper. 'Naughty naughty.'

'Come on, lads, Clem. Keep it together,' said Boden. 'You know I don't like drugs around the place. Give me that shit; I'll dump it outside.'

'Christ, we've got to have a laugh, Neil,' steroid features butted in. 'It'll help us stay awake. Anyway, I don't give a fuck what you think. It's expensive gear and it's free.'

Vic realised he was obviously still annoyed that the man called Neil had broken up his sport. Whoever these three

243

men were, there was a marked sign of tension between them. Clem took the packet off Dave, retrieved a penknife from his pocket and began chopping up the white powder on the plastic table. He rolled up a ten pound note and snorted the huge line up his nose.

Another reason for Vic to be mortified. She'd paid for that stuff with money out of her own pocket and now the bastard who had roughed her up was enjoying himself at her expense. She wanted to throw the lot in his face. He was already a fearless and over-muscled barbarian. What would the effect of a huge line of quality cocaine do for his confidence and his sex drive? The horror. The trail of investigating Landor Motors had taken a strange and frightening turn. There was no point in going through the what-ifs and if-onlys. She was deep in the soup and there seemed to be no way out. Even if Deborah had the police on the case, how would they ever find out where she'd been taken? The trail would dry up by the Dartford turn-off.

She could just make out the shape of her mobile phone lying on the cold floor. If only she could get to it; trick one of the men into letting her out of the cage. She turned her attention to Alan Landor. He was a sorry sight but she had no sympathy for him. He had obviously brought together this ugly bunch of fuckwits who were making their lives hell. Vic had narrowly escaped God-knows-what sexual molestation – for the time being at least – Alan had had his nose smashed, and his father was looking decidedly ill. She feared for him the most. He was a large man but he was in bad shape. He was sweating, despite the fact it was cold in the container.

'Do you think you can get us some water, please?' she begged Neil.

'You can have a beer if you like,' he said.

'No. We need water. This man looks ill. It's for your own good to keep him well.'

'He's worth half a million quid, you know,' shouted Dave. 'We're going to trade him in. Then again, we might get bored and just kill him. *And* you,' he added, pointing at

Alan. Both men laughed. Vic couldn't argue with that one. She wanted to kill Alan, too.

'What the fuck are you doing here?' Alan asked Vic.

'Oh, like you don't know?' she answered sarcastically, her arms crossed defensively in front of her. She was the only one in the cage standing up. The other two didn't look as if they had any fight in them.

'No, I don't know,' he answered, holding his nose. 'The last time I saw you was in a pub in Earl's Court,' he whined. 'What's going on?'

'We picked her up at your place,' Clem shouted. Alan looked confused.

'I think you're reaping the rewards of your recent endeavours, Alan Landor,' said Vic. 'Don't tell me you're innocent. You've tried to kill your own father. Then you sent that animal –' she pointed at Clem '– to kidnap me, you bastard. And I don't know what you did to get your nose broken, but I'll bet you deserved it.'

'I didn't,' he said, his voice already sounding like he had an appalling congestive problem. 'And I don't know what you're talking about. You were working at the showroom, right? Working with Nick Swift. And I didn't try to kill my father. It's this lot. They kidnapped him and then came for me.'

Vic threw Alan a look of pure hatred. He was leaving a trail of chaos and lies everywhere. Even now he couldn't admit to what he'd done. He had painted himself into a corner.

Neil handed Vic a bottle of water. 'Stay awake, Derek. Stay awake,' said Vic, concentrating on trying to pour sips of it into his mouth. 'Do you know where you are?'

'Sally?'

'No, not Sally. Victoria. The Motor Show. Do you remember the Motor Show?' she asked. 'I was talking with Nick Swift.'

'I thought Sally was here, I think . . .' His voice trailed off and his eyelids were flickering. He was well out of it.

'Stay awake!' Vic shouted.

'Shut up!' yelled Dave. 'You lot are giving me fucking

earache, moaning like a load of old women.'

'It's more fun with three of them in there than just dozing fatboy, though,' answered Clem.

The dim light of the camping lamp threw a shadow across Clem's craggy face, adding to his already sinister expression. Vic was keeping it together but she was genuinely scared of thug-face. 'Fun' he'd said. Vic could barely imagine what his idea of fun entailed. Boden, who had been pacing up and down the room and taking looks outside the container, stood still for a moment, then called Dave over. The two men went outside leaving the three caged prisoners to the mercy of Clem.

'This is getting out of hand, Dave. The whole thing's falling apart. We had a tight situation here and now there's drugs involved, there's a woman in the place, and Clem's losing it. What's got into him? We've got the night to get through. Whose side are you on?' asked Boden.

'Don't worry about Clem. He's only having a laugh,' Dave replied. 'He won't do anything stupid.'

'He already has. He's taken cocaine *and* I caught him roughing up that woman. She's not Alan Landor's girlfriend. She said she worked at the showroom.'

'Forget Clem for a minute, Neil. Alan Landor's fucking lied to us all along the way. No wonder he was at Derek's plush house last Sunday. He's his fucking son. You took the job on. You should've checked him out properly.'

'I don't really care he's Landor's son,' Neil said. 'I'm more concerned they might be in it together. Set the whole thing up. What else might he have lied about? I don't like it there's a woman involved, either. She's nothing to do with any of it but we can't let her go 'cos she'll go straight to the police. Fuck this, Dave. It's a mess.'

'Are you suggesting we pull out?' he asked.

'I'm suggesting we find out more about this woman. If anyone's following her, for any reason, we're stuffed. Let's go back in. Just make sure you keep Clem under control, that's all.'

★   ★   ★

Back in the container, Derek Landor was coming out of his stupor and Clem was leaning on the outside bars of the cage watching the captives with a sick smile on his face. He'd put the radio on. Vic didn't recognise the opening bars but when the vocals kicked in she realised it was Suede's 'Trash'.

'What are you doing here?' asked Derek of his son. 'Tell me you're nothing to do with this.'

'They came for me, too,' said Alan. 'I don't know what they want. I —'

'Don't lie, you bastard,' Vic shouted at Alan. 'Tell him the truth. I know the truth, these bastards know the truth. You can't deny it any more. You're the reason for this mess.'

Alan Landor looked stunned for a moment, then let rip. 'No,' he said, pointing at his father, 'he's the reason for this mess. He's always hated me. He never wanted me. He has so much and I've got nothing.' His voice was laden with emotion and his nose began bleeding again. 'He's the reason my mother died so young. He didn't care about her either.'

'You're wrong, Alan,' Derek said. 'I loved your mother. I know I was wrong to leave her alone for so long but I was trying to build a business. I was a young man. I wanted my family to have everything. Time ran out for me before I could put things right. Please believe me, things weren't easy.'

'Touches your heart, doesn't it?' said Clem.

Vic, Derek and Alan all glared at him. He shrugged his shoulders and strolled back to the radio.

Derek was shaking. He looked pale and ill and wracked with nerves.

'Alan,' he said, 'I've never hated you. You're my first-born son. I wanted the best for you. We all make mistakes. Why have you done this? Why?' He sounded pitiful.

Vic watched as the tears began to roll down Alan Landor's bruised face. He then screamed at his father in a hurt voice, 'Why the fuck didn't you ever help me?' This was a family therapy session that was long overdue. And what a time for it to happen. What a mess.

'Turn that radio down,' yelled Boden. 'And you lot, shut up. Someone's phone's ringing.'

'It's the woman's,' said Dave, picking it up. 'Hello.'

He listened for a couple of seconds. 'Victoria Donovan. Yeah, she might be. Who's calling?' He walked over to the cage and handed her the mobile through the bars. 'Not one word about where you are, OK?' he said, menacingly and quietly. 'Everything's just fine.'

Vic put the phone to her ear. Never had a voice sounded so welcome.

'Vic, it's Daniel Field. Listen. We know where you are. I've been in touch with Deborah Landor. The police are surrounding the area. I'm not going to explain how they know right now. Just pretend it's a social call.'

'Oh, hi Daniel. Look. I can't make it tonight. Sorry, I should have phoned earlier,' she said, as casually as was possible. In front of her, Alan and Derek were deeply engrossed in their emotional battle and seemingly oblivious to everyone else's presence.

'Just hold on, Vic. You're not hurt or anything are you?'

'No, Daniel. I'm fine, just a bit tired, that's all.'

'You're in Tilbury Docks. In the container park. Just say yes or no.'

'Yes.'

Before she could say any more, Dave snatched the phone from her and turned it off. 'That's enough of that. No more calls from the boyfriend.'

'Call it off,' said Alan, rushing to the sides of the cage. 'Neil, please. Call the whole thing off. We can't go through with it.'

'We? Who's we? You're a fucking disgrace, Alan Landor,' Clem said, producing a gun from inside his jacket and pointing it at him. 'You're all staying exactly where you are. Nothing changes. We're going to get our whack out of this. Right now your family are sorting out half a million and his bank manager's working overtime for us. I'd up the ransom demand, only I don't think I would get much for you.' He waved the gun at Alan and then screamed at them. 'I'll take out the pair of you if I have to.' Clem laughed.

Derek made an effort to stand up but he toppled to one side and sank down on to the floor, too weak to support his own weight. Alan knelt beside him saying, 'Oh, Christ,' over and over, blood, tears and mucus oozing down his face. Vic stood motionless, her insides in knots, her arms folded, chewing the side of her face as she watched the desperate behaviour of the men around her.

There was no point having a go at Alan Landor even though she wanted to smack him. Another person shouting would do nothing to improve the situation. Instead, she stood back and watched father and son immerse themselves in self-pity and apologies.

Neil Boden began kicking various objects in frustration. He'd become increasingly aggressive. So, there were at least two armed men in the place. Vic thought back to her friend Julian's warning about having to deal with such things. It seemed like a lifetime ago. When would she see him again?

Boden walked over to the table and grabbed the wrapper containing the coke. 'This shit goes right out the door now!' he said. He pulled the door open, allowing a beam of light to escape into the night. Just then, a glaring light streamed into the container and the distinct sound of a helicopter came hovering overhead. It was deafening but very welcome.

'Neil Boden,' came an amplified voice of authority. 'This is the police. Boden, drop your weapon. The place is surrounded. Release the hostages and come out with your hands above your heads.'

Boden slammed the door shut. 'You fucking idiot, Clem,' he yelled. 'This woman's a fucking cop. Why do you think she was at Landor's place? She's fucking tricked you, you thick bastard!'

Then, all was panic. Clem snatched the keys from Dave and threw open the door to the cage, grabbed Vic by the arm and twisted it behind her back.

'Keep those two in there,' he yelled at Boden, expecting him to relock the cage. Instead, Boden then ran to a dark corner of the building and began kicking at the side of the container. A pre-cut escape hatch fell out.

Clem shouted, 'I'm going out,' and Vic felt herself once more in the clutches of the brute. He pulled the door open and Vic felt the cold blast of chill air on her face. Now she was outside, at least she had a chance. But she was frozen with fear and the gun was at her temple. There was no way either of the Landors were going to be have-a-go heroes. She was on her own. Her fate was in the hands of the cops. Gently does it, she thought.

'Let her go,' said the voice. 'Police marksmen have you surrounded. You can't escape. Let the woman go.'

The beam of the searchlight was swinging over the area and the turbulence caused by the rotating helicopter blades was blowing rubbish around the containers. There was a sound of banging from inside and Alan Landor suddenly dashed out, waving his arms frantically. 'He's gone unconscious,' he cried at Vic. 'I think he's having a heart attack.'

'Lie down on the ground,' the police shouted. 'Stop right there.'

Vic felt the pressure tighten on her arm as her assailant began swearing at Alan. She felt numb, worrying that Clem's finger would squeeze the trigger of the gun at any second.

'Get an ambulance,' yelled Alan.

'Alan Landor – this is your last chance,' came the megaphone. 'Lie down on the ground now.'

But Alan ignored the voice of the police. He wasn't even looking at what was going on around him. He was in a state of panic and concerned only for his father. He looked into Vic's eyes and she remembered the intimate moments she'd shared with him.

'I can't help you. Do what the police say, Alan,' she cried, watching as he started acting frantically. She knew the police could not hear a word any of them were saying. She watched as Alan reached into his jacket.

'I have to phone for an ambulance,' he shouted. 'My phone won't work inside the container.'

Vic shouted 'No!' realising his fatal error, but her voice was drowned by the sickening sound which rang out. It wasn't a hail of bullets: just a meaty blast from the barrel of a police rifle. In front of her, Alan's body twisted into a spastic shape as his hand relaxed and the mobile phone fell to the ground. It was all over for Alan Landor, Drake Lewis, whatever his name was. She felt Clem's grip on her relax –

whether in fear of his own skin or with shock, she didn't care. She still had one hand in her pocket. The pepper spray was there. It was time.

She flicked the red lever – the one she'd wanted to pull so often – and pressed down hard on the button as she spun round and the gas blasted into the man's face at point-blank range. It worked. He covered his eyes and staggered around at the same time as a small army of police appeared from every corner of the area. They were all dressed for combat; not a recognisable uniform among them. Her captor was thrown to the ground, disarmed and cuffed. Vic stood shivering as a blanket was thrown around her. She felt sick.

'He wasn't armed,' she cried, throwing the blanket off in anger. 'Alan Landor. He wasn't armed.'

'You're safe now,' said a voice, ignoring her comment. 'It's all over.'

'Get the medics in here now,' shouted one of the men from the container. Military procedure quickly replaced chaos. Vic watched as Derek was attended to in the cage. Then she saw the body of Alan Landor being covered and carried into the ambulance. Another helicopter was flying overhead, its searchlight scanning the jetty of the docks for the two escapees.

'Come on,' said another unfamiliar voice. An arm grabbed her and ushered her to a waiting car. Vic felt drained as she collapsed into the seat of the police vehicle. She didn't feel triumphant or even relieved as the car pulled away from the desolate landscape. She'd been through a disaster zone. There was never going to be another day like this. There would be questions. Lots of questions.

Epilogue

Two weeks later, Vic sat in the Dôme in Upper Street telling Julian about her ordeal.

'You know, the worst thing about it all was just before the police arrived on the scene, there was a reconciliation going on between father and son. To think I slept with a man who's now dead. It's tragic.'

'It's happened to a few of us,' said Julian, looking wistful for a moment. 'How did they find you, though?' he asked.

'Peter Bruton,' she replied. 'Once he was in the police interview room, he told them the names of all his associates and those of Alan Landor. He even told them about a girl called Julie who was Landor's girlfriend. When he gave my description, even the police could put two and two together.

'Neil Boden was a known villain. He'd been caught loading dodgy gear at Tilbury a year earlier. They knew once I'd given Deborah my whereabouts that Boden would be somewhere near his old hideout. They picked him up in the river, trying to climb aboard a Greek ship. A warrant's out for the other guy's arrest. Who knows where he is.' She picked at her food then pushed it aside.

'What happened to the family? Did Derek Landor survive his heart attack?'

'He's convalescing,' said Vic. 'His wife insisted they go on holiday – just the two of them – to recover. She drove them to their house in France after Alan's funeral on Wednesday. It's a tragic irony that the only people to attend were members of his family. I think it'll take a longer time to get over the fact the police killed his son than it will the heart attack. I don't think the family are calling for an investigation into the police, though. Sad as it may be, a big problem has been removed from their lives. Although, who can tell what would have happened if he was still alive? Stupid bastard; I tried to stop him but he just didn't realise how it looked from the marksman's point of view. He was oblivious to everything except his father's suffering. All a bit late for that, really.' Vic sighed. The experience had knocked her for six. She'd still felt a little empty and sad about the whole event. She'd seen the futility of resentment and the mess it brings.

'What about more work like this, Vic. Surely you've had enough now?'

'I think Daniel Field's reluctant to offer me anything but petty fraud and process serving from now on,' she said with a smile. 'But I've saved him a huge payout and we do have a date next week. Also, the driver of the crashed car, Adrian Boxall, has a present for me. I was the only one who thought he was telling the truth about the airbag. When the evidence was found sitting on Alan Landor's hard drive, no one could dispute his claim.'

'So, what about this date with insurance man?' said Julian, keen to return the conversation to a personal level. 'Are you going to be Vicky or Victoria?' he asked.

'I think I'll just be me,' she laughed. 'Right now, I'm a little tired of being other people. Victoria would understand.' As the waiter passed by, she grabbed him. 'Another bottle of white Rioja, please,' she said.

'It's only lunchtime,' Julian remarked.

'What the hell,' she said. 'It's Friday. And that's a good enough reason to celebrate.'

Julian grabbed her hand and gave it a squeeze. 'It's great to have you back,' he said.

Vic smiled warmly at him and looked around her. Even though it was late October the sun was shining. It certainly felt good to be back.

CRIME & PASSION

DEADLY AFFAIRS
by
Juliet Hastings

ISBN: 0 7535 0029 9
Publication date: 17 April 1997

Eddie Drax is a playboy businessman with a short fuse and a
taste for blondes. A lot of people don't like him: ex-girlfriends,
business rivals, even his colleagues. He's not an easy man to
like. When Eddie is found asphyxiated at the wheel of his car,
DCI John Anderson delves beneath the golf-clubbing, tree-
lined respectability of suburban Surrey and uncovers the
secret – and often complex – sex-lives of Drax's colleagues
and associates.

He soon finds that Drax was murdered – and there are more
killings to come. In the course of his investigations, Anderson
becomes personally involved in Drax's circle of passionate
women, jealous husbands and people who can't be trusted. He
also has plenty of opportunities to find out more about his
own sexual nature.

This is the first in the series of John Anderson mysteries.

CRIME & PASSION

A MOMENT OF MADNESS
by
Pan Pantziarka
ISBN: 0 7535 0024 8
Publication date: 17 April 1997

Tom Ryder is the charismatic head of the Ryder Forum – an organisation teaching slick management techniques to business people. Sarah Fairfax is investigating current management theories for a television programme called *Insight* and is attending a course at the Ryder Hall. All the women on the course think Ryder is dynamic, powerful and extremely attractive. Sarah agrees, but this doesn't mean that she's won over by his evangelical spiel; in fact, she's rather cynical about the whole thing.

When one of the course attendees – a high-ranking civil servant – is found dead in his room from a drugs overdose, Detective Chief Inspector Anthony Vallance is called in to investigate. Everyone has something to hide, except for Sarah Fairfax who is also keen to find out the truth about this suspicious death. As the mystery deepens and another death occurs, Fairfax and Vallance compete to unearth the truth. They discover dark, erotic secrets, lethal dangers and, to their mutual irritation, each other.

This is the first in a series of Fairfax and Vallance mysteries.

CRIME & PASSION

INTIMATE ENEMIES
by
Juliet Hastings
ISBN: 0 7535 0034 5
Publication date: 15 May 1997

Francesca Lyons is found dead in her art gallery. The cause of death isn't obvious but her bound hands suggest foul play. The previous evening she had an argument with her husband, she had sex with someone, and two men left messages on the gallery's answering machine. Detective Chief Inspector Anderson has plenty of suspects but can't find anyone with a motive.

When Stephanie Pinkney, an art researcher, is found dead in similar circumstances, Anderson's colleagues are sure the culprit is a serial killer. But Anderson is convinced that the murders are connected with something else entirely. Unravelling the threads leads him to Andrea Maguire, a vulnerable, sensuous art dealer with a quick-tempered husband and unsatisfied desires. Anderson can prove Andrea isn't the killer and finds himself strongly attracted to her. Is he making an untypical and dangerous mistake?

Intimate Enemies is the second in the series
of John Anderson mysteries.

CRIME & PASSION

A TANGLED WEB
by
Pan Pantziarka
ISBN: 0 7535 0155 4
Publication date: 19 June 1997

Michael Cunliffe was ordinary. He was an accountant for a small charity. He had a pretty wife and an executive home in a leafy estate. Now he's been found dead: shot in the back of the head at close range. The murder bears the hallmark of a gangland execution.

DCI Vallance soon discovers Cunliffe wasn't ordinary at all. The police investigation lifts the veneer of suburban respectability to reveal blackmail, extortion, embezzlement, and a network of sexual intrigue. One of Cunliffe's businesses has been the subject of an investigation by the television programme, *Insight*, which means that Vallance has an excuse to get in touch again with Sarah Fairfax. Soon they're getting on each other's nerves and in each other's way, but they cannot help working well together.

A Tangled Web is the second in the series
of Fairfax and Vallance mysteries.

CRIME & PASSION

A WAITING GAME

by
Juliet Hastings
ISBN: 0 7535 0109 0
Publication date: 21 August 1997

A child is abducted and held to ransom. As the boy's mother is a prospective MP and his father is a friend of the Chief Constable, Detective Chief Inspector Anderson is required to wrap up the case cleanly and efficiently.

But the kidnappers, although cunning and well-organised, make up a triangle of lust and jealousy. Somehow Anderson's tactics are being betrayed to the kidnappers and, after a series of mishaps and errors, and a violent death, Anderson's latest sexual conquest and his ex-wife become involved in the conspiracy. Anderson's legendary patience and willpower are stretched to the limit as he risks his own life trying to save others.

This is the third in the series of John Anderson mysteries.

CRIME & PASSION

TO DIE FOR
by
Peter Birch
ISBN: 0 7535 0034 5
Publication date: 18 September 1997

The cool and efficient Detective Chief Inspector is keen to re-establish his reputation as a skilled investigator. The body of Charles Draper has been found in the mud flats of a Devon estuary. The murdered man was a law-abiding citizen and there appears to be no motive for the killing. There are also very few clues.

When Anderson is sent to assist the Devon and Cornwall constabulary, he's led towards dubious evidence and suspects whose alibis are watertight. The investigation also brings him in contact with forensics assistant Anna Ferreira whose intellect and physical attractiveness makes her irresistible.

The only suspect is then found murdered. Local antiques dealer Nathan Cutts fits the murderer's profile but Anderson feels he's not the man they're looking for. Against the backdrop of windswept Dartmoor, the chase to catch a killer is on.

This is the fourth in the series of John Anderson mysteries.

CRIME & PASSION

TIME TO KILL
by
Margaret Bingley
ISBN: 0 7535 0164 3
Publication date: 16 October 1997

Lisa Allan's body is found in the corner of her kitchen by her husband, Ralph. Everyone knows Lisa was ill, suffering from a complicated heart condition, but no one expected her to die – least of all her doctor. DCI Anderson met Lisa socially only two days before her death. He found her desirable but disliked her husband on sight.

Two autopsy reports pose more questions than answers and as Anderson struggles to untangle the relationships of the dysfunctional Allan family, he becomes involved with Pippa Wright, Ralph's attractive PA and ex-mistress. When a second murder occurs, Anderson realises that getting to know Pippa was not one of his better ideas. Against a background of sexual intrigue and hidden secrets, he needs to harness all his skills and intuition if he is to ensure that justice is done.

This is the fifth in the series of John Anderson mysteries.

CRIME & PASSION

DAMAGED GOODS
by
Georgina Franks
ISBN: 0 7535 0124 4
Publication date: 20 November 1997

A high-performance car has spun out of control on a test drive. The driver has suffered multiple injuries and is suing Landor Motors for negligence. He says the airbag inflated for no reason, causing him to lose control of the car.

This is the third and most serious claim Landor Motors have had to make this year. The insurance company aren't happy, and they bring in Victoria Donovan to assist in their investigations.

Landor Motors is a high-profile car showroom situated in the stockbroker belt. But the Landor family have a history of untimely deaths and brooding resentments. Soon, Vic is up to her neck in a complex web of drug-dealing, sexual jealousy and deception involving Derek Landor's wayward and very attractive son. When Derek Landor is kidnapped, only Vic knows what's going on. Will anyone take her seriously before time runs out for Derek Landor?

This is the first Victoria Donovan mystery.

CRIME & PASSION

GAMES OF DECEIT
by
Pan Pantziarka
ISBN: 0 7535 0119 8
Publication date: 4 December 1997

Detective Chief Inspector Anthony Vallance and television journalist Sarah Fairfax team up once more when an old friend of Sarah's is caught up in the strange goings-on at the science park where she's working. Carol Davis says someone there is trying to kill her but the squeaky clean credentials of her colleagues don't tally with the dangerous and violent nature of the attacks.

When Vallance becomes sexually involved with Carol Davis, he begins to realise that she has a dark side to her nature: she's manipulative, kinky and possibly unstable. As Fairfax and Vallance peel away the layers of respectability to reveal a background of corporate coercion, deceit and neo-Nazism, they discover that Carol has not been telling the truth about the people she's working for. But who is going to reveal what's really going on when Carol winds up dead?

This is the third in the series of Fairfax and Vallance novels.

CRIME & PASSION

ANGEL OF DEATH
by
Richard Shaw
ISBN: 0 7535 0255 0
Publication date: 15 January 1998

Victoria Donovan is called in to investigate the theft of valuable marble statues from Blythwood Cemetery. This should be a straightforward piece of detection. However, it soon transpires that the lives of the cemetery staff are as tangled as the undergrowth which surrounds them. Vic's plan is to nail the thieves and stay out of harm's way but a lot of surveillance takes place at night – a time when the cemetery becomes dangerous. One of the management team is having perverse liaisons by moonlight with a Blythwood security guard; a recently released mentally ill patient is on the loose, looking for the 'daughter of darkness', and the rest of the ground staff are lining their pockets.

When a body is found which shouldn't be in the ground yet, accusations start flying and Vic suddenly finds herself involved in a murder investigation. Unfortunately, the police are less than co-operative and when one of the grave diggers is arrested and charged with murder, Vic strongly suspects they've got the wrong man. To add to all this, her current lover is getting friendly with the manipulative Chloe, the cemetery's assistant manageress, and her family is giving her problems. How can she find the time to see that justice is done?

**This is the second in the series of
Victoria Donovan mysteries.**